Bedford Cultural

CHARLOTTE PERKINS GILMAN

The Yellow Wallpaper

Bedford Cultural Editions

CHARLOTTE PERKINS GILMAN
The Yellow Wallpaper

EDITED BY

Dale M. Bauer
University of Wisconsin—Madison

BEDFORD/ST. MARTIN'S   BOSTON ♦ NEW YORK

For Bedford/St. Martin's
President and Publisher: Charles H. Christensen
General Manager and Associate Publisher: Joan E. Feinberg
Managing Editor: Elizabeth M. Schaaf
Developmental Editor: Katherine A. Retan
Editorial Assistant: Aron Keesbury
Production Editors: Lisa A. Wehrle, Stasia Zomkowski
Copyeditor: Maureen Murray
Cover Design: Susan Pace
Cover Art: Josephine H. Hatfield, illustration, reprinted from "The Yellow Wallpaper" by Charlotte Perkins Stetson, *New England Magazine: An Illustrated Monthly,* n.s., vol. 5, o.s., vol. II, September 1891–February 1892.
Composition: Pine Tree Composition, Inc.
Printing and binding: Haddon Craftsmen, Inc.

Library of Congress Catalog Card Number: 97-74959

Manufactured in the United States of America.
2   1   0   9
f   e   d   c   b

For information, write: Bedford/St. Martin's, 75 Arlington Street, Boston, MA 02116 (617-399-4000)

ISBN: 0-312-13292-1 (paperback)
ISBN: 0-312-21066-3 (hardcover)

Published and distributed outside North America by:
MACMILLAN PRESS, LTD.
Houndmills, Basingstoke, Hampshire RG21 2XS and London
Companies and representatives throughout the world.
ISBN: 0-333-73075-5

Acknowledgments

About the Series

The need to "historicize" literary texts — and even more to analyze the historical and cultural issues all texts embody — is now embraced by almost all teachers, scholars, critics, and theoreticians. But the question of how to teach such issues in the undergraduate classroom is still a difficult one. Teachers do not always have the historical information they need for a given text, and contextual documents and sources are not always readily available in the library — even if the teacher has the expertise (and students have the energy) to ferret them out. The Bedford Cultural Editions represent an effort to make available for the classroom the kinds of facts and documents that will enable teachers to use the latest historical approaches to textual analysis and cultural criticism. The best scholarly and theoretical work has for many years gone well beyond the "new critical" practices of formalist analysis and close reading, and we offer here a practical classroom model of the ways that many different kinds of issues can be engaged when texts are not thought of as islands unto themselves.

The impetus for the recent cultural and historical emphasis has come from many directions: the so-called new historicism of the late 1980s, the dominant historical versions of both feminism and Marxism, the cultural studies movement, and a sharply changed focus in older movements such as reader response, structuralism, deconstruction, and psychoanalytic theory. Emphases differ, of course, among schools and individuals, but what these movements and approaches have in common is a commitment to explore — and to have students in the classroom study interactively — texts in their full historical and cultural dimensions. The aim is to discover how older texts (and those from other traditions) differ from our own assumptions and expectations, and thus the focus in teaching falls on cultural and historical difference rather than on similarity or continuity.

The most striking feature of the Bedford Cultural Editions — and the one most likely to promote creative classroom discussion — is the inclusion of a generous selection of historical documents that contextualize the main text in a variety of ways. Each volume contains works (or passages from works) that are contemporary with the main text: legal and social documents, journalistic and autobiographical accounts, histories, sections from conduct books, travel books, poems, novels, and other historical sources. These materials have several uses. Often they provide information beyond what the main text offers. They provide, too, different perspectives on a particular theme, issue, or event central to the text, suggesting the range of opinions contemporary readers would have brought to their reading and allowing students to experience for themselves the details of cultural disagreement and debate. The documents are organized in thematic units — each with an introduction by the volume editor that historicizes a particular issue and suggests the ways in which individual selections work to contextualize the main text.

Each volume also contains a general introduction that provides students with information concerning the political, social, and intellectual contexts for the work as well as information concerning the material aspects of the text's creation, production, and distribution. There are also relevant illustrations, a chronology of important events, and, when helpful, an account of the reception history of the text. Finally, both the main work and its accompanying documents are carefully annotated in order to enable students to grasp the significance of historical references, literary allusions, and unfamiliar terms. Everywhere we have tried to keep the special needs of the modern student — especially the culturally conscious student of the turn of the millennium — in mind.

For each title, the volume editor has chosen the best teaching text of the main work and explained his or her choice. Old spellings and capitalizations have been preserved (except that the long "s" has been regularized to the modern "s") — the overwhelming preference of the two hundred teacher-scholars we surveyed in preparing the series.

Original habits of punctuation have also been kept, except for occasional places where the unusual usage would obscure the syntax for modern readers. Whenever possible, the supplementary texts and documents are reprinted from the first edition or the one most relevant to the issue at hand. We have thus meant to preserve — rather than counter — for modern students the sense of "strangeness" in older texts, expecting that the oddness will help students to see where older texts are *not* like modern ones, and expecting too that today's historically informed teachers will find their own creative ways to make something of such historical and cultural differences.

In developing this series, our goal has been to foreground the kinds of issues that typically engage teachers and students of literature and history now. We have not tried to move readers toward a particular ideological, political, or social position or to be exhaustive in our choice of contextual materials. Rather, our aim has been to be provocative — to enable teachers and students of literature to raise the most pressing political, economic, social, religious, intellectual, and artistic issues on a larger field than any single text can offer.

> J. Paul Hunter, University of Chicago
> William E. Cain, Wellesley College
> Series Editors

About This Volume

Charlotte Perkins Gilman is best known today for her 1892 short story "The Yellow Wallpaper," which, since its republication by The Feminist Press in 1973, has entered the canon of American literature and generated extensive critical commentary. To her contemporaries, however, Gilman was known more as a social critic than as a writer of fiction. Her reputation was established with the publication of *Women and Economics* in 1898, which was immediately translated into several foreign languages. Her journalism, like her stories, ran in popular magazines and newspapers, and from 1909 through 1916 she single-handedly wrote and edited the magazine the *Forerunner*, which she used as an organ for social reform. Gilman was an accomplished public speaker who preferred to test her ideas in the lecture hall, women's clubs, or meetings of Nationalist organizations and Women's Congresses before putting them in print. The lecture hall was still, at the end of the nineteenth century, the primary venue for the circulation of opinions on national and international issues. As Gilman writes in her autobiography, *The Living of Charlotte Perkins Gilman* (1935), she lectured from New Orleans to Oregon "and everywhere between. . . . To have traversed one's country from side to side, top to bottom and corner to corner, for thirty-six years, gives one a fair working knowledge of it" (294).

This edition of "The Yellow Wallpaper" includes a generous selection of cultural and historical documents that illuminate how

Gilman's classic feminist tale can be read as a springboard for her subsequent career as a cultural critic. "The Yellow Wallpaper" calls into question the attitudes of Gilman's contemporaries toward such subjects as self-help books and conduct manuals, consumer culture, female sexuality, and the increasing regulation and "medicalization" of motherhood at the turn of the century. And as the documents included in this volume demonstrate, the social discourses of the 1890s often seem as full of internal contradictions and as potentially threatening as the wallpaper in Gilman's story.

The documents accompanying this edition have been selected to help readers situate "The Yellow Wallpaper" in relation to Gilman's time period and wide range of interests. Included are nineteenth-century advice manuals for young women and mothers; medical texts discussing the nature of women's sexuality; social reform literature concerning women's rights, the working classes, and immigration; and excerpts from periodicals, diaries, and writers' notebooks that give readers a sense of the changing literary scene into which Gilman entered. Both Gilman's story and her subsequent career as a social critic are illuminated when we see her as a writer about and a citizen of her time.

ACKNOWLEDGMENTS

My debts in creating this volume are many since I drew on a number of friends and colleagues for their helpful counsel and, at times, good humor.

My work on Gilman began with an essay I co-authored with Mary Marchand; her insights into American women's salon and social reform cultures have influenced me immensely in establishing Gilman's purposes. Susan Bernstein, Jeanne Boydston, Elana Crane, Maria Lepowsky, Lisa Long, Tacey Rosolowski, and Sarah Zimmerman — my Wisconsin community — gave advice, talked through Gilman lore, or read drafts of my work; I thank them for their responsiveness and patience, their intelligence and wit. Diane Price Herndl provided a way of thinking about Gilman that has spurred my own. Ann Ardis and Priscilla Wald gave invaluable and necessary support throughout the project; they are the best critics and friends a scholar could have. From the beginning of this project in 1995, Jean Lutes was both researcher and friend; when I could no longer walk up Bascom Hill during my pregnancy, she literally did the leg work. The project itself would not have been half so rich or rewarding had she not been willing to contribute so thoughtfully in every phase.

Thanks to the reviewers — the late Elaine Hedges, Ann Lane, Tom Lutz, Dana Nelson, Joel Pfister, and Bill Veeder — whose critical suggestions and comments were exemplary. Joel Pfister is an intellectual model; a more generous and enthusiastic reader I couldn't hope for. Dana Nelson's and Bill Veeder's spirited responses — in both readings — fueled my own energy for Gilman. Dana's exuberance is remarkable; her insight, equally so. Bill's brilliant essay on "The Yellow Wallpaper" is both an influence and a paradigm of scholarship, and it has shaped my work and a generation of others since 1990 when it appeared in *Arizona Quarterly*. Bill Cain, the series editor for American titles, has been a mentor as well as a friend; I thank him again for including me in his plans for this series.

Four research assistants — Kathryne Auerback, Elizabeth Evans, Rita Soenksen, and Sarah Zelazoski — helped me through the last details with grace and humor. I also want to thank the many librarians with whom I worked, most important of whom were Phyllis Kauffman and Nancy Spitzer, University of Wisconsin Health Sciences Library; Yvonne Schofer and Robin Rider, Memorial Library at the University of Wisconsin — Madison; and Jeffrey Anderson at the Library of the College of Physicians in Philadelphia. The College of Letters and Science at the University of Wisconsin — Madison granted me a sabbatical in 1996–1997, and the University of Wisconsin — Madison Graduate School, along with the Women's Studies Program, released me from teaching for a semester.

The remarkable people at Bedford Books — as everyone who has ever worked with them can attest — made this edition worth doing: Chuck Christensen and Joan Feinberg shared their acumen and good sense through many years of conversation. Kathy Retan, the editor for this book, is an author's editor, the kind of critic we all yearn for, especially for her tact and her persistence. Aron Keesbury handled the numerous tasks associated with preparing the volume before production, while copyeditor Maureen Murray and production editors Lisa Wehrle and Stasia Zomkowski gently and expertly shepherded this work through production. Their attention to every detail is evident in these pages.

Finally, and most important, I dedicate this book to Gordon Hutner, my husband and best advisor. I began writing the introductions while pregnant with our twin boys and revised the project during their first — and second — years. Gordon now knows more about "puerperal mania" than he could ever have imagined. Danny and Jacob Hutner have inspired me in so many ways, as has their tireless father. To them, I owe everything.

Dale M. Bauer
University of Wisconsin — Madison

Contents

Illustrations

Bedford Cultural Editions

CHARLOTTE PERKINS GILMAN

The Yellow Wallpaper

Part One

The Yellow Wallpaper
The Complete Text

Charlotte Perkins Gilman in 1896. Reproduced by permission of the Schlesinger Library, Radcliffe College.

Introduction:
Cultural and
Historical Background

"I'm getting really fond of the room in spite of the wallpaper. Perhaps *because* of the wallpaper," the narrator of "The Yellow Wallpaper" declares. "It dwells in my mind so!" (see p. 48). Charlotte Perkins Gilman's short story charts the narrator's progressive deterioration from sanity to madness after she is ordered to bed following childbirth. The narrator watches and interprets the wallpaper in the bedroom where she is confined, eventually discovering another woman hidden in the pattern, trying to escape. The wallpaper obsesses the heroine of Gilman's most famous short story, and the story's meaning has intrigued Gilman's audience since the story was first printed in 1892, reprinted in 1920 in William Dean Howells's collection of the "best" American short stories, and in the story's many reprints since then. For Gilman's contemporaries, her story raised issues concerning woman's proper place in modern American society, particularly in relation to the growing international and industrial culture of the day. The Gilded Age of the 1880s had challenged conventional ideas about women's roles, even as it affirmed many traditional nineteenth-century notions about gender identity. The growing confusion about women's roles encompassed a host of other disorientations concerning immigration and citizenship; sexuality and definitions of masculinity and femininity; illness and health; and high culture and popular pastimes.

"The Yellow Wallpaper" first appeared in the *New England Magazine* in January 1892 and has since become the focus of feminist controversy, as well as celebration, concerning the heroine's confrontation with patriarchy and social duties. Gilman hoped to instruct her audience through her depiction of a woman who wants to write, who wants to do anything to avoid the boredom of isolation and the tedium of mothering. In her autobiography, Gilman claims to have written the story to influence "Dr. S. Weir Mitchell, and [to] convince him of the error of his ways" (*Living* 121). Mitchell, who was known as one of the greatest nerve specialists of his day, had treated Gilman during her "breakdown" after the birth of her daughter, Katharine, in 1885. He applied to Gilman the "rest cure" he had first invented to treat shell-shock victims of the Civil War and then used for the "nervous prostration" of "the business man exhausted from too much work, and the society woman exhausted from too much play" (*Living* 95). Although Gilman knew she fit neither category of Mitchell's conventional patients, she wanted to get well and return to productive work so badly that she underwent a month of the "cure" in 1887:

> I was put to bed and kept there. I was fed, bathed, rubbed, and responded with the vigorous body of twenty-six. As far as he [Dr. Mitchell] could see there was nothing the matter with me, so after a month of this agreeable treatment he sent me home, with this prescription:
>   "Live as domestic a life as possible. Have your child with you all the time." (Be it remarked that if I did but dress the baby it left me shaking and crying — certainly far from a healthy companionship for her, to say nothing of the effect on me.) "Lie down an hour after each meal. Have but two hours' intellectual life a day. And never touch pen, brush or pencil as long as you live." (*Living* 96)

Gilman did not object to the treatment at the time, but in retrospect she came to see that Mitchell's cure led to her "progressive insanity" (*Living* 119), what we might characterize today as manic-depressive illness.

According to Gilman, Mitchell attributed her illness in part to her relation to the Beechers, her famous, reform-minded ancestors. Charlotte Perkins Gilman, grandniece of Harriet Beecher Stowe and Catharine Beecher, was the younger of two children born to Mary Westcott and Frederick Beecher Perkins. Gilman's father abandoned the family soon after her birth on July 3, 1860, although she did stay in touch with him for most of his life. According to Gilman, her heredity included "the Beecher urge to social service, the Beecher wit and gift of words and such small sense of art as I have" (*Living* 6). Yet it was an unstable childhood. Over four years Gilman's mother sent her to school in seven different institutions, and Gilman's education ended at her fifteenth year according to her autobiography (*Living* 18). Mary, Charlotte, and Charlotte's older brother, Thomas, were forced to move again and again, sometimes from relative to relative.

Not wanting her life to be like her mother's — spent waiting for her husband's return — Gilman began early to train herself to be self-supporting by painting, teaching, and serving a short stint as a governess. She was always ambivalent about marriage, but her determination to avoid it failed when she met the painter Walter Stetson in January 1882. At the end of two years of indecision, she accepted Walter's proposal after he had suffered "a keen personal disappointment" (*Living* 83). Her feelings regarding marriage had their source in her idea that "[o]n the one hand I knew it was normal and right in general, and held that a woman should be able to have marriage and motherhood, and do her work in the world also. On the other, I felt strongly that for me it was not right, that the nature of the life before me forbade it, that I ought to forego the more intimate personal happiness for complete devotion to my work" (*Living* 83). She had been plagued by depression three years before meeting Walter, and her nervous prostration left her devastated for most of her life. Her regrets about what she *would* have accomplished had she not been subject to manic-depressive bouts recur in her autobiography: "Twenty-seven adult years, in which, with my original strength of mind, the output of work could have been almost trebled. . . . It was always a time of extreme distress, shame, discouragement, misery" (*Living* 103).

Gilman came of age in a time of transition: when New Women frequently had careers of their own and did not depend on their husbands for economic security, as in the age of "true womanhood." The True Woman, according to mid-nineteenth-century middle-class cultural ideals, maintained the virtues of piety, domesticity, and industriousness. In contrast, the New Woman of the 1880s through the 1920s agitated for social change and greater freedom, seeking independence, careers, suffrage, and often birth control. Gilman lamented the increasing "sex-development" that resulted from consumer culture's tendency to force women to compete with each other for men and for financial security. Gilman contended that this perverse "sex-development," or the privileging of sexual characteristics in lieu of *human* qualities, drove women to display themselves in competition for the wealthiest, most socially prominent mates, rather than those with the best genes, who were most likely to improve the race.

Until the end of her first marriage, we might be tempted to classify Charlotte Perkins Gilman with many of the other young women of her day, who were forced to make uneasy compromises between their ambitions and the traditions of marriage and motherhood. Gilman's divorce from Walter Stetson, filed in 1892 and granted in 1894, did not shock the public as much as her decision to relinquish custody of her daughter, Katharine, to her husband and his new wife, the former Grace Ellery Channing (who was Gilman's best friend). Charlotte married Houghton Gilman in 1900, a relationship founded on the reform principles she advocated. Despite her continuing depression, she kept up an incredible range and volume of publishing and public speaking. In her autobiography, Gilman sums up her theory of literature as writing "with a purpose" (*Living* 121). Her early lectures led to her best-known book, *Women and Economics* (1898), the first draft of which she proudly claimed to have written in seventeen days. In this work, Gilman states that the source of most social ills is women's "industrial position [as] that of a house-servant," an economic arrangement that suffrage alone could not rectify (*Living* 235).

Gilman's work for social change — along with her challenges to traditional gender roles — led to her fame as a dynamic rhetorician, creative writer, and reformer. Exerting her will to the end, Charlotte Perkins Gilman took her own life on August 17, 1935, preferring "chloroform to cancer" and advocating euthanasia (*Living* 333–34). She wanted her death to serve as an argument for human progress, as her life had served what she imagined to be collective ends.

MOTHERHOOD MANUALS AND CONDUCT LITERATURE

"Of course it is only nervousness. It does weigh on me so not to do my duty in any way!

"I meant to be such a help to John, such a real rest and comfort, and here I am a comparative burden already!" (see p. 44). So claims the narrator at the beginning of "The Yellow Wallpaper," already aware of her deviance from wifely duty. Any nineteenth-century middle-class woman well understood society's expectations for young wives and mothers. A wealth of conduct literature and advice manuals designed to provide American culture with the proper etiquette for genteel living was available in the popular press.

English conduct manuals, one of the most famous of which was Mrs. Sarah Stickney Ellis's *The Women of England* (1839), were widely read in the United States throughout the 1840s. Sarah Josepha Hale, editor of the influential *Godey's Lady's Book* from 1837 until 1877, also offered U.S. women advice on the proper government of middle-class life. While early American conduct books couched their advice in religious terms, often borrowing from the Bible various injunctions for women to be virtuous, nineteenth-century conduct books recast that advice in more secular terms, as directives to women to be chaste, pious, and industrious — what historian Linda Kerber calls "the Republican mother." Emphasizing woman's domestic "influence" upon the family as a necessary antidote to the competition associated with the marketplace, such manuals placed woman's mission within the home. A woman's "sphere of influence" thus could only be defended by her utmost sincerity and morality; Ellis and Hale, among others, argued against worldliness (such as reading novels or writing) and overreaching ambition or extravagance. "The Yellow Wallpaper" can be read as a reaction against such prescriptions for feminine behavior and the ever-constricted notion of women's prospects and duties they helped to foster.

Conduct literature became a staple of British and American middle-class readers in the nineteenth century, when bourgeois status depended in part on mastering the rules of politeness or entry into genteel society. These etiquette books were addressed especially to the wives of upwardly mobile or professional men, middle-class women whose beauty and accomplishments became a sign of the leisure time and money they could afford to devote to maintaining themselves as symbols of their husbands' prestige (see Veblen in Part Two, Chapter 4). As Gilman would explain in *Women and Economics* (see Part Two, Chapter 4), women were chained to an economic system which positioned them as consumers rather than producers of goods, ignoring their contribution to the economy as providers of important services, such as childrearing and housekeeping. Conduct literature and advice manuals, Gilman posited, were the handbooks of indoctrination into a competitive and exaggerated world of sex differentiation.

Many of Gilman's contemporaries would have taken her heroine's commitment to writing as a distortion of cultural prescriptions about women's primary duties. Repeated injunctions against *reading* novels, let alone *writing* novels, filled advice books, as we can see in the chapter on novel reading from Frances Willard's *How to Win: A*

Book for Girls (see Part Two, Chapter 1). Even as late as 1888, women were still being cautioned against the dangers of fiction, in particular its propensity to excite them and distract them from their maternal obligations. In *Womanhood: Lectures on Woman's Work in the World* (1881), Richard Heber Newton argues that only a few women can produce such masterpieces as Elizabeth Barrett Browning's "Aurora Leigh" or George Eliot's *Daniel Deronda;* because too few women have this writing talent, he maintains, they should instead commit themselves to their instinctual skills, especially nurturing the young. Dr. John Harvey Kellogg seconds this advice by claiming that novels produce intoxicating, even addictive effects: "sentimental literature, whether impure in its subject matter or not, has a direct tendency in the direction of impurity. The stimulation of the emotional nature, the instilling of sentimental ideas into the minds of young girls, has a tendency to develop the passions prematurely, and to turn the thoughts into a channel which leads in the direction of the formation of vicious habits" (*Ladies' Guide* 158). While Gilman's heroine was writing in her diary, perhaps in an attempt to effect her own cure through intellectual activity, the dominant advice of her time was to preserve mental energy and channel it into reproduction and consumer culture.

Among the advice offered in conduct manuals, such as when to use a handkerchief and when not to examine its contents, was a proliferation of medical and social injunctions for mothers and children. While the narrator of "The Yellow Wallpaper" fails in her duties as "angelic mother," her husband's sister, Jennie, accomplishes all that the maternal advice literature suggests she should: managing the domestic arrangements, orchestrating John's life so that he need not consider the household, and negating her own desire for the sake of his marriage. As the narrator observes, "She is a perfect and enthusiastic housekeeper, and hopes for no better profession. I verily believe she thinks it is the writing which made me sick!" (see p. 47). Nineteenth-century mothers were instructed to feminize the home as a haven for men retreating from the capitalist world (see Sangster in Part Two, Chapter 1), and Jennie steps in to fill the void that the heroine's mental absence or distraction creates. John willingly acquiesces so that his time is free for his practice and for his frequent appointments in town.

The mid-nineteenth century also saw the production of a substantial literature on "boy culture" and male conduct. Boys were schooled in the proper ways of exerting their masculinity. They were enjoined to become models of Christian gentlemen while retaining

[handwritten margin notes: "yeah they do"; "quotes taken from the story but I'm not really sure what they mean."]

some of their boyish aggressiveness for the marketplace. Mothers taught their sons how to behave in the domestic sphere, but sons, unlike daughters, were allowed a space outside of this domesticated culture and educated to take their place in the public sphere of politics and economics. Gilman herself resented the fact that her brother was given this sort of freedom. The birth of the son in "The Yellow Wallpaper" would have occasioned advice about the proper ways for the mother to raise the son in the home while the culture reinforced a division between domestic and business life. Immediately after birth, a son was caught up in his culture's ambivalence about the mother's world, a haven that every capitalist male had to leave in order to stave off the enervation and effeminization associated with woman's sphere. The qualities that women were expected to foster in the domestic realm — "interdependence, spirituality, self-restraint, kindness, cooperation, and affection" — were antithetical to those required for success in the newly industrialized capitalist world and the professional realm represented in "The Yellow Wallpaper" by the narrator's doctor-husband (Rotundo 34).

Gilman's speeches and writings signal a crucial transition from nineteenth-century models of the domestic ideal to twentieth-century paradigms of the new family. While nineteenth-century conduct literature heralded the individual mother's self-sacrifice for her family, Gilman celebrated a whole new model of universal motherhood. Her autobiography recounts her affections for three women — Martha Luther, Grace Ellery Channing, and Adeline ("Dora") Knapp — and her attachment extended to those she called her "adopted mothers," a group of women who provided her with a "female world of love and ritual" (Smith-Rosenberg 53). Gilman responded to the three cultural transitions that Carroll Smith-Rosenberg describes as occurring from the mid-nineteenth century to the 1930s: the Jacksonian era of close female ties in response to socially enforced gender restrictions; the rise of urban, bourgeois culture; and the post–World War I years of bohemianism (53).

The seemingly "obsolete" status of the narrator of "The Yellow Wallpaper" after giving birth reflects Gilman's concern that women needed to have a more purposeful — and intellectual — connection to the public sphere. The industrial revolution that began in the late eighteenth century had resulted in a restriction of the middle-class woman's sphere of activity. While her husband or brother could participate in the public sphere associated with work and self-interest, the middle-class woman was limited in her activities outside the home

to reform work, social visits, and shopping. However, by the end of the nineteenth century, educational reform and growing opportunities for work outside the home were opening up new possibilities for women. In the 1890s, when Gilman wrote "The Yellow Wallpaper," Susan B. Anthony was fighting for women's suffrage, Jane Addams was establishing her settlement houses in Chicago, and newspaperwomen such as Nellie Bly were challenging the boundaries of women's proper sphere. No longer would women be restricted to their previous roles as wives, mothers, and consumers. New times required new advice and new models of womanhood.

GILMAN, MOTHERHOOD, AND SEX-EXPRESSION

"I always fancy I see people walking in these numerous paths and arbors, but John has cautioned me not to give way to fancy in the least. He says that with my imaginative power and habit of story-making, a nervous weakness like mine is sure to lead to all manner of excited fancies, and that I ought to use my will and good sense to check the tendency. So I try" (see p. 46). The isolation of motherhood leads the heroine to imagine alternatives, including the company of strangers at the house and even within the wallpaper. Because Gilman believed that modern culture isolated individuals by sexualizing industrial relations and commercializing sex-relations, thereby destroying the seriousness of the home and the maternal function (*Woman and Economics* 121), she advocated collective responsibility on the part of a community for childrearing.

Gilman wrote "The Yellow Wallpaper" at about the time that America imported sexology — the scientific study of sex that Richard von Krafft-Ebing, Havelock Ellis, and Sigmund Freud, among others, initiated (see Part Two, Chapter 3). As many critics have noted, Gilman's story reveals her resentment toward the medical establishment in general and its pathologizing of women's bodies in particular. A.J. Bloch's "Sexual Perversion in the Female" suggests that many doctors at the turn of the century were suspicious of women's sexuality and their reasons for consulting physicians (see Part Two, Chapter 3). Gilman resisted the efforts by the new sexologists and psychologists to regulate women's sexuality. Yet she did not advocate the complete liberation of women's sexual impulses. She felt — and increasingly believed throughout her career — that the new emphasis on women's sexual freedom by "New Women" and some sex radi-

cals (see Angela Heywood, Part Two, Chapter 4) might further enslave them to a system of sex hierarchy founded on the notion of men
as the producers of the world's goods and women as mere consumers. Gilman opposed the use of female sexuality as a means of
achieving financial security through the attraction of a prosperous
male.

Gilman articulated an alternative model for women's sexual selection of men, in which women's superior attributes led them to select
the mate whose characteristics were most favorable to the advancement of the human race. She advocated a sexuality that would improve the race while deemphasizing the commodity- and pleasure-
oriented propensities of modern culture, which stressed individualism
as opposed to the collectivism she preferred. Gilman wanted to
counter "the consumer world view [which] followed the emergence
of a conviction, increasingly widespread, that each individual begins
with a polymorphous potential to desire everything" (Birken 49–50).
From Darwin to Freud, sex was being touted as the consuming passion of modern culture: the consumption of material goods was seen
as a displaced exercise of sexual options necessitated by the Victorian
prescription of proper object choice. Sexology attributed a sexual desire to women that the Victorian code of female passionlessness and
passivity had erased. Yet even as it acknowledged female desire, the
discourse of sexology sublimated and subordinated that desire to
male desire. While Gilman aligned herself with sociologists such as
Edward Alsworth Ross and Lester Frank Ward (see Part Two, Chapter 3), she rejected *any* portrayal of humans as inherently full of desire — consumer, sexual, or otherwise.

The new professional discourse of sexuality — from the first
American lectures by Freud in 1909 to Gilman's own contributions
and the sociologists' reports — announced that the sexual life of
American women was out of control. Sexology introduced the notion
that sexuality was a universal (that all men, women, and children had
it) but that it needed to be redirected — particularly in the case of
women, whose libidinal energy mass culture inevitably deflected onto
the consumption of goods. Gilman, on the contrary, wanted to return
to an older matriarchal model, designed to preserve the race against
the insults and perversions of modernity, including what she and others perceived as the assault on motherhood. She advocated social
motherhood, a collective rearing of children for the greater good of
all humans. Thus, the debates over the proper channeling of women's
sexuality might be read in the context of President Theodore

Roosevelt's paean to motherhood, delivered to the National Congress of Mothers on March 1, 1905: "the Nation is in a bad way if there is no real home, . . . if the woman has lost her sense of duty, if she is sunk in vapid self-indulgence or has let her nature be twisted so that she prefers a sterile pseudo-intellectuality to that great and beautiful development of character which comes only to those whose lives know the fullness of duty done, of effort made and self-sacrifice undergone" (see Part Two, p. 204).

Early twentieth-century debates over who was supposed to be sexual were multivocal and clamorous. Perhaps the topic that women writers most vigorously addressed, no matter what their politics, was that of "sex-expression" — the growing movement to democratize the language of sexuality and to unleash human creativity by separating sexual expression from its reproductive function. One of the most radical aspects of the discourse of sex-expression was the idea that women need not be tied to the cultural work of raising children and keeping house. Sex-expression gave women an alternative language to the discourse of domesticity in which to express their desires. In spite of the greater possibilities for women in the public sphere that it seemed to promise, Gilman opposed sex-expression and birth control for a long time, worrying that men would gain more power if women were protected from pregnancy and freed to pursue sexual gratification.

Paradoxically, the attempt to liberate female sexuality can also be read as an attempt to regulate female desire. Earlier and more overt attempts to control women's bodies had culminated in the 1873 Comstock Law, which prohibited the distribution of contraceptive information and devices and other "obscene or immoral" materials (see Part Two, Chapter 3). Under the aegis of sex-expression, a variety of new professionals — sexologists, psychologists, sociologists — took up the codifying and policing of what was to be deemed a normal, healthy, sexual life. More often than not, they posited a connection between sexual behavior and the vitality and stability of the state. American society was continuing to undergo radical transformations in its populace as well as its popular culture, including the rise of the New Woman at the turn of the century and the flapper in the 1920s, figures which came to symbolize the perceived threat to conventions of femininity. Large-scale government control of sexuality, such as Comstock's hunting down Ezra and Angela Heywood and their Free Love publications in the 1890s, was no longer possible, since sexuality had increasingly come to be associated with the private realm. The new psychiatrists, psychologists, sex therapists, and social workers had gained control over the definition of sexual norms and the codification of sexual science. They regularly employed a vocabulary of rationalism and empirical research to justify their analyses. Indeed, the new American sense of scientific expertise participated in the development of the conviction that America's sexual and social ills could be cured through attention to the psyche in large part through the professonalization of therapeutic culture. ⇒

While many New Women pursued self-gratification through the expression of their sexuality, Gilman rejected such individualistic self-expression. For her, an individual displayed "character" not through the socially sanctioned conventions of speech, dress, and behavior, but by participating in collective activism. The nineteenth-century notion of "character" emerged from the belief that virtue and integrity could substitute for capital (whether money, land, or personal property), thereby eliding the issue of social class in America. While the emphasis on public morality might have had some influence in mid-century, Gilman feared that the valorization of "character" had given way to a glorification of self-interest and personal aggrandizement by the end of the century. Gilman attributed what she saw as a decline in ethics and the "lowering of standards in sex relations" (*Living* 323) to this growing emphasis on selfish satisfactions, which included what she termed the "infantile delight in 'self-expression'" (*Living* 330). For her, self-expression, like sex-expression, was an overindulgence of individualism. Gilman's notorious hatred of fashion can be linked to her distrust of sexualized style (Seidman 71) since, for her, women's consumption of such commodities as fashionable clothing represented the exercise of limited cultural options. Gilman and other women writers at the turn of the century shared various challenges in establishing their roles as mediators of public debates about American modernity and women's place in it, as sex reformer Angela Heywood had done in the 1880s when she advocated an unrestricted sexual lexicon (see Part Two, Chapter 4). Heywood wanted, for example, to use the word *penis* in public debates in order to banish any unnecessary prudishness. Like Heywood, Gilman suffered from attacks on her character and threats. In examining how twentieth-century American women writers responded to the issue of sex-expression, we can see how, in trying to establish their authority, they perpetuated an earlier tradition of public education or social reform that they had inherited from such predecessors as Harriet Beecher Stowe and Catharine Beecher (see Part Two, Chapter 1), Gilman's own relatives.

MENTAL HEALTH, INTELLECTUAL WORK,
AND SELF-EXPRESSION

"Looked at in one way each breadth stands alone, the bloated curves and flourishes — a kind of 'debased Romanesque' with *delirium tremens* — go waddling up and down in isolated columns of fatuity" (see p. 48). It is no accident that Gilman has her narrator refer to *delirium tremens* — the "shakes," hallucinations, and disorientation often caused by alcohol consumption or withdrawal — in the context of describing the wallpaper. This allusion shows just how attuned Gilman was to the medical diagnoses of her time, and it reflects her culture's fascination with and fear of addiction and mental disorder. "The Yellow Wallpaper" elicited strong reactions when Gilman submitted it to William Dean Howells at the *Atlantic Monthly,* who passed it along to Horace E. Scudder, then editor of the *Atlantic.* Howells introduced the story to Scudder by exclaiming that "it wanted at least two generations to freeze our young blood with Mrs. Perkins Gilman's story of *The Yellow Wall Paper,*" and Scudder rejected it, claiming, according to Howells, "that it was so terribly good that it ought never to be printed" (see Part Two, Chapter 5). Both men were troubled less — if at all — by the feminist message of "The Yellow Wallpaper" than by its horrifying rendition of the heroine's mental illness. At a time when the influence of psuedo-sciences like phrenology and ethnology — the studies, respectively, of head lumps and blood heredity as indications of human character and breeding — was waning, new social sciences such as urban sociology, crowd and social psychology, and anthropology were leaving their mark on cultural debates concerning the definition of insanity. According to this new discourse, sexual license resulted in impotence or sexual mania (spermatorrhea or satyriasis) for men and in nymphomania or hysteria for women. Female sexuality in particular was pathologized and linked to mental illness. The secrecy and self-determination of Gilman's narrator would have made her suspiciously different from other women, such as Jennie, the perfect housekeeper, and her mental deterioration might, for Gilman's contemporaries, have made her sexually suspect.

Gilman was, of course, attracted to the topic of mental illness, having experienced severe depression both before and after the birth of her daughter, Katharine, on March 23, 1885. After enduring periodic bouts of anxiety as a result of S. Weir Mitchell's treatment, she came to distrust the growing popularity of the rest cure that he had pioneered for neurasthenics (see Part Two, Chapter 2). Perhaps even more, she feared the injunctions for women's health that resulted in the restriction of women's activity in the public sphere and their greater confinement in the home. Dr. John Harvey Kellogg published *The Ladies' Guide in Health and Disease* in 1882, for example (see Part Two, Chapter 2), expressly to offer advice designed to provide "escape for women from the thralldom of aches and pains and 'weaknesses' in which the sex is as a class enslaved [and to trace] the method of training by which a higher type of womanhood may be developed" (iii). His "know your body" approach helped to control women's sexuality by urging women and their physicians to maintain a strictly private knowledge of women's ailments. Kellogg's dedication to the development of a "higher type of womanhood," which for him involved "enlightening" women as to their physical weaknesses, did not coincide with Gilman's ambitions for women in the public arena. Gilman advocated broadening women's realm of activity, complaining in *Women and Economics* that the "freedom of expression has been more restricted in women than the freedom of impression, if that be possible" (66). In a passage that follows, Gilman refers to the middle-class woman's experience in terms that echo "The Yellow Wallpaper": "Something of the world she lived in she has seen from her barred windows," suggesting that women are forced to intuit the masculine sphere from their more restricted one at home. Even more disastrous than this restriction, for Gilman, was the culture's limitation on women's self-expression through writing.

Gilman publicized her writing and herself when she lectured, offering advice about such topics as "Parasitism and Civilised Vice" (see Part Two, Chapter 3), the title of an article in *Woman's Coming of Age* (1931), a volume of essays dedicated to the New Woman. She argued that women fall prey to the commodity pleasures of the culture and succumb to the mating strategy of plumage, display, and spectacle. For Gilman, "sex parasitism" was common among what she referred to as "low forms of life," mostly masculine and buglike, yet "it has remained for humanity to show us the unique spectacle of a parasitic female, a creature who economically considered, at best shares in a consortium of low-grade activities, . . . but is entirely supported by the male" (see Part Two, p. 265). Gilman's work everywhere suggests her rejection of sex-expression in favor of a more radical self-assertion, which was to take its form in the professionalization of women's work, whether domestic, maternal, pedagogical, or authorial. Gilman referred to sex as a "pathological" urge (see Part Two,

p. 277). Complaining that psychoanalysis unleashed "women of to-day, ... overcharged with sex-energy and warmly urged to use it" (see Part Two, pp. 276–77), Gilman battled to eradicate the effects of women's self-expression when it was — for her, disastrously, even parasitically — channelled into sex-expression.

One need look no farther than *Women and Economics* to find Gilman decrying women's dependence on men for their food supply. Gilman argued that this dependence had defined women's roles through most of human history, serving to increase sex-differentiation (with men as producers and women as consumers). In this treatise, Gilman laments the consumer economy, which offers the *illusion* of a genderless access to commodities and of meaningful choices for women. The marriage market was, for Gilman, the mirror image of the commodity market, as women were forced to sell themselves as "pure" commodities. Gilman feared that such a marriage market could only lead to human destruction, much as she had portrayed the marriage of the narrator of "The Yellow Wallpaper" as leading to "madness" and mutual devastation.

Gilman was a believer in social progress, who founded her hope for pragmatic social change on theories of social evolution and im-provements in education. As historian Mark Pittenger describes this world view, men would compete freely, women would choose the best mate, and the race would benefit (78). Gilman believed in women's moral superiority, given their development as nurturers of the human race, and she blamed competitive individualism on male ambition, since men fought wars and battled in capitalist arenas. Gilman advocated the importance of women in the socialist schemes she favored, arguing that once women were freed from economic de-pendence, the state would be free to progress toward socialism and "proper sex selection" — which meant, according to the principles of social Darwinism, a substantial improvement in the moral and intel-lectual qualities of the race.

IMMIGRATION, EUGENICS, AND SOCIAL CONTROL

Midway through "The Yellow Wallpaper," the narrator complains, "It is getting to be a great effort for me to think straight. Just this ner-vous weakness I suppose." John's response is telling, if understandable: "And dear John gathered me up in his arms, and just carried me up-stairs and laid me on the bed, and sat by me and read to me till it tired my head" (see p. 49). John's cure for his invalid wife involves exposing her to as little excitement as possible, and their relationship is portrayed as asexual — almost parental. Perceived as passionless, the middle-class woman was not seen as an appropriate partner for sex. As the critic William Veeder argues, since "proper" women were thought not to desire sexual activity and since doctors such as S. Weir Mitchell declared that sexual activity was dangerous for neurasthenic women, John most likely stayed late in town with "a woman [who might] take pity on his [sexual] continence" (59). Certainly "The Yellow Wall-paper" expresses Gilman's disdain for the Victorian "double standard" according to which men's sex-expression was implicitly sanctioned while women were condemned for any expression of sexuality. Gilman found support in the many female moral reform societies that flourished during the late nineteenth century, some of which supported the temperance movement, the abolition of prostitution, and even the availability of contraception. Many late-nineteenth-century American feminists, including Gilman, did not advocate sexual freedom, only the control of sex in marriage and, hence, the timing of children.

In her provocative analysis of "The Yellow Wallpaper," Susan Lanser characterizes the "psychic geography" of Anglo-American culture in Gilman's time. It is a culture not only preoccupied with sexuality, but also "obsessively preoccupied with race as the foundation of character, a culture desperate to maintain Aryan superiority in the face of massive immigrations from Southern and Eastern Europe, a culture openly anti-Semitic, anti-Asian, anti-Catholic, and Jim Crow" (236). Nativism (a term originally coined to describe anti-immigration prejudice but eventually expanded to include racism of any kind) was often a common offshoot of the socialism and Fabian-ism (a version of non-Marxist socialism that emphasized ethical advances) to which Gilman was attracted. While utopianism and Fabianism urged collectivization of individuals for the good of the country, these movements also regularly excluded blacks and Asians — categories of people Gilman worried were propagating at a faster rate than the true American "primal stock."

Such overlapping issues as eugenics, birth control, and sexual politics were addressed by sociologists like the influential University of Wisconsin professor Edward Alsworth Ross, Gilman's friend and mentor, who argued that the great changes in modern culture demanded new social engineering (see Part Two, Chapter 3). In *Changing America* (1912), Ross wrote that "race deterioration soon sets in if the successful withhold their quota while the stupid multiply like rabbits" (45). Eugenics, the study of how to improve the human race through genetic selection and control of biological heredity, was in part a response to the social changes taking place in America as a result of unlimited immigration. Sex-expression was linked by such writers as Gilman, Edith Wharton, and the California author Gertrude Atherton to the influx of supposedly unruly, bohemian, and passionate eastern and southern Europeans, as well as Asians (Gilman's most vitriolic attacks were saved for Asian women), whose foreign blood and sexual proclivities were feared to be diluting the "primal stock" in America. A number of Immigration Restriction Acts were passed to control the population and to limit the effects of the "melting pot." The 1855 Naturalization Act (which automatically naturalized foreign-born women married to U.S. citizens) had been liberal for its time. The first Restrictive Immigration Law was passed in 1875, while the 1882 Chinese Exclusion Act, which banned any new Chinese immigrants for a ten-year period, became a permanent law in 1904 until its repeal in 1943. The 1907 Expatriation Act revoked U.S. citizenship of U.S.-born women married to foreign men.

Critically linked to the question of race and immigration, sex-expression was also, for many of the sociologists and sexologists, a question of youth. Women's reproductivity, as their one claim to power, was being redefined in a pseudoscientific way as the domain of the most nubile, the most marriageable, and the most sexually attractive. One of Ross's recurring points concerns the necessity of eugenic population control to stave off "race suicide" (see Part Two, Chapter 3). He argues that such control is to be achieved in part by "the impressing of all young people with the racial offense of having progeny in case one's personal or family history makes manifest the presence of deficiencies in one's inheritance which ought not to be passed on" ("The Future Human Race" reel 34). In asserting that sex absorbs "not more than twenty per cent" of our minds and lives, Ross claimed to differ with "Freudians, popular fictionists and scenario writers" as certainly as Gilman did ("Positions and Attitudes," 7, 15). Gilman hated the new Freudian theories of her day, with their privileging of masculinity and emphasis on unconscious drives. In her writing, she denounces the unconscious and its impulses, maintaining that all life can submit to rational control and the power of the will. Gilman claims that we will advance as a civilization beyond an "over-weening masculinization" (156) when ethics and education return to their origin in the maternal (143).

Over the years, Gilman maintained an allegiance to thinkers like Ross and Ward. In "Birth Control, Religion, and the Unfit," a 1932 essay appearing in *The Nation*, she advocated birth control as a means of improving "human stock" by checking the alarming increase in numbers of the unfit and allowing "parents above the average" to "give the world as many children as they can" (109). Gilman's views confirm historian Linda Gordon's argument that early-twentieth-century eugenic propaganda defied political categories; radicals and conservatives alike shared a conviction that extravagant sex drives — what Gilman saw as excessive sexual attraction — "contributed to the subjection of women and hence limited the development of the whole civilization" (116).

DARWINISM, ECONOMICS, AND THE SEXES

The narrator of "The Yellow Wallpaper" experiences her confinement — symbolized by the wallpaper — as a kind of violence: "You think you have mastered it [the wallpaper], but just as you get well underway in following, it turns a back-somersault and there you are. It slaps you in the face, knocks you down, and tramples upon you. It is like a bad dream" (see p. 51). In order to counteract the violence she felt the patriarchal culture perpetrated upon women, Gilman became a proponent of a radical social doctrine devoted to race betterment through the achievement of women's economic independence through work. However, Gilman resisted the designation "feminist," preferring to see herself as a humanist (Lane 5). As an advertisement for one of her New York lecture series observed, "Mrs. Gilman is widely known as a feminist, but deprecates that term, claiming that her interest is in humanity, and in women only because their previous debasement has retarded the upward movement of us all" (Pond). Gilman would use her international standing as a social critic to advance her primary interests: the progress of the human race; collectivism as the final consummation of this progress; and the improved condition of women in the movement toward a collective society.

In virtually every aspect of her thought, Gilman reveals herself as belonging to the post-Darwinian age. Like many of her contemporaries, she drew, sometimes uncritically, on the three main ideas that came to be regarded as the substance of Darwin's evolutionary theory:

variation, inheritance, and natural selection — a concept that corresponded with the late-nineteenth- and early-twentieth-century faith in "progress." Herbert Spencer was the best-known exponent of Social Darwinism, the belief that conflict and competition in the public sphere lead to the survival of the superior. His was the most tenacious effort to extract from Darwinism the laws governing humankind's past, present, and future development. Spencer argued that any interference in natural evolution compromised and endangered the future of the species. His version of "survival of the fittest," an uneasy translation of Darwin's concept of natural selection, came to signify a whole set of immensely influential social ideals, including the glorification of unfettered, harsh struggle among individuals as the evolutionary route to a higher social order founded on individualism.

In sharp contrast to Spencer, Gilman viewed individualism not as the realization of the final stage of progress but as belonging to that primitive stage of development when the individual, "in the absolute economic isolation of the beast . . . profited by pure egoism" (*Women and Economics* 325). She argued, in *Women and Economics,* that society was moving inevitably toward collectivism, and that "specialization and organization," developments that increase our economic interdependence, formed the "basis of human progress" (67). To "serve each other more and more widely; to live only by such service," Gilman maintained, constituted "civilization, our human glory and race-distinction" (74). Unlike other species, human beings could be taught the "very spirit of socialism," the "sinking of personal interest in common interest," and could modify their environment to reflect these shared interests (107).

Gilman's reformism needs to be understood in the wider context of her views on human evolution and on collectivism as the measure of social progress. While she felt that the necessary changes in social organizations were "already taking place under the forces of social evolution" (*Women and Economics* 122), Gilman worried that counterforces hindered this change. Without radical changes in these "sexuo-economic" relations, she maintained, "no higher collectivity than we have to-day is possible" (*Women and Economics* 145). Gilman's career was roughly coextensive with the second, successful push for women's suffrage, and in an era that often defined women's goals in terms of obtaining legal rights, Gilman set out to expose the reigning assumptions and submerged forms of thought that contributed to women's suppression but often passed unnoticed in the quest for suffrage.

Disputing the "naturalness" of the sex differences and social arrangements on which the domestic social order was founded, Gilman based her argument in *Women and Economics* on the proposition that we are the only species in which the "female depends on the male for food, the only animal species in which the sex-relation is also an economic relation" (5). She claimed that as a result of this "abnormal" situation, "we may naturally look to find effects peculiar to our race" (23), such as unfortunate sex-differentiation and the sexual parasitism found in prostitution and harems. From her progressivist evolutionary perspective, which defined the "normal" as that which was self-preserving but also race-preserving and the "abnormal" as that which impeded the progress of the race, Gilman concluded that there were few profound "natural" differences between the sexes.

Maintained in a state of economic dependence belonging to a primitive stage of human development and denied access to the "healthful activities of racial life" that strengthened and refreshed men (43), Gilman further argued in *Women and Economics* that women manifested an "excessive" sex-distinction (30). She detected signs of such modification in virtually every aspect of early-twentieth-century womanhood: in woman's physiology, her smallness and weakness (46); in her psychology, namely the emotionalism "so intense as to override all other human faculties" (48); in her relations as wife, in which she is at once "patient Griselda" and "priestess of the temple of consumption" (218, 120), and as mother, which Gilman denounced as "pathological . . . more morbid, defective, irregular, diseased" (181).

Gilman did not find suffrage a strong enough plank for women's rights. She based her vision of reform on her hopes for social *evolution* rather than revolution (see Pittenger 72–73; Kessler 13), believing that utopian progress would emerge from a gradual shift from capitalism to socialism. Influenced by Edward Bellamy's 1888 socialist utopia and bestseller, *Looking Backward, 2000–1887* (see Part Two, Chapter 4), Gilman adopted an American version of socialism that was shorn of its radical association with anarchists. Bellamy's novel depicts the gradual resolution of class struggle and the nationalization of industry as the inevitable effects of a shift from the competitive economics of capitalism to a genteel model of non-Marxist socialism, offering a vision of humanistic collectivism as progressive rather than agonistic. Gilman joined the American nationalist movement in 1890, the year of her first publication, "Similar Cases," a poem about human progress that questions American social Darwinism. The Nationalists shared the Fabians' Christian vision of a humanitarian cooperation and communitarianism that would ensure progress in the United States (Pittenger 70, 73). Gilman structured her reform activities around nationalist clubs, politics, and events backing public education and the break-up of monopolies as well as remedies for women's poverty such as those Jane Addams had instituted in Hull-House (see Part Two, Chapter 4). Her emphasis on "the economic independence and specialization of women as essential to the improvement of marriage, motherhood, domestic industry, and racial improvement; with much on advance in child culture" (*Living* 186) distinguished her from the majority of Nationalists, but before she could advocate the reform of gender roles she needed to dramatize the state of women's dependence in marriage and isolation in motherhood, which she did in her 1892 story "The Yellow Wallpaper."

In her later, more overtly political treatises *Women and Economics* (1898) and *Human Work* (1904), Gilman advanced the proposition that work was a human, not a sex-linked, activity (see Part Two, Chapter 4), and virtually every facet of her theory that "essential" sex differences are in reality cultural sex-distinctions follows from this premise:

> All the varied activities of economic production and distribution, all our arts and industries, crafts and trades, all our growth in science, discovery, government, religion ... these are, or should be, common to both sexes. To teach, to rule, to make, to decorate, to distribute ... so inordinate is the sex-distinction of the human race that the whole field of human progress has been considered a masculine prerogative. (52)

Gilman challenged the division of labor in all aspects of life that undergirded conventional sex roles and the ideology of separate spheres. Arguing the economic issue of women's unpaid labor in the home, Gilman and Anna Shaw came to loggerheads in a public debate in the *New York Times* in 1909 that appeared under the headline "Think Husbands Aren't Mainstays" (see Part Two, Chapter 4). Gilman and Shaw represented opposing views, Gilman declaring that wives were "unpaid servants[s], merely a comfort and a luxury agreeable to have if a man can afford it" (see p. 326), and Shaw contending that women financially, spiritually, and ethically supported men. The audience was reported to have "warmly applauded" Gilman's observation that women are not "rewarded in proportion to their work" (see p. 326), but Shaw's position carried the day. The vote at the close of the debate was a "loud and emphatic 'No'" to the question "Do men support their wives?" The audience found Shaw's view of marriage as a reciprocal relationship more palatable than Gilman's provocative view of marriage as a version of prostitution.

One of the most significant products of Gilman's experience with depression and the isolation of motherhood was her view of the family. For Gilman, the family in its current form, once a necessary institution for material survival, had outlived its usefulness. In the final section of *Women and Economics,* Gilman argues that the home, considered as both a social and an economic entity, represents the single greatest obstacle to a realization of humanity's collective interests, since it fosters "an elaborate devotion to individuals and their personal needs" (119). Driven to gain financial support by securing husbands, women are pitted against one another, engaging in "primitive individual competition . . . as against the tendency of social progress to develope co-operation in its place" (110). Even in its role as cradle of future generations the isolated family fails, since the "servant-mother"'s constant attention to the child teaches him "to magnify the personal duties and minify the social ones . . . greatly retard[ing] his adjustment to larger life" (279).

Following John Stuart Mill's and Harriet Taylor's line in *The Subjection of Women* (1869) and Friedrich Engels's analogy between slavery and marriage in *The Origin of the Family,* Gilman draws the comparison between marriage and prostitution at several points in *Women and Economics.* In an era when purity campaigns and female reform societies were at the height of their influence, Gilman characterized prostitution as, at least in one sense, a lesser evil than marriage. In both cases "the female gets her food from the male by virtue of her sex-relationship," but in marriage the "evil" is compounded by a "perfect acceptance of the situation" (64). Despite her occasional references to working- and upper-class women, Gilman's analysis of the condition of women in marriage follows from a narrowly construed class perspective. Her representative woman is distinctly middle class: she spends most of her life at home with no direct relation to the market or production; her husband is an industrous capitalist in pursuit of wealth; she has enough money to participate in a compensatory consumer culture but not enough to be relieved of domestic duties.

In *The Home: Its Work and Influence* (1903), Gilman argues that the exclusion which characterizes the domestic sphere has rendered women inferior. *The Home* begins with the premise that "whosoever, man or woman, lives always in a small dark place, is always guarded, protected, directed, and restrained, will become inevitably narrowed and weakened by it" (277). *The Home* is an exhaustive inventory of the ways in which the conditions of "a small dark place" have crippled women. (When she first lectured upon the topic "Home" at the Washington Women's Congress Association, some women rejected the topic as not worth a week's discussion, but the audience overflowed its original site [*Woman's Journal,* Feb. 15, 1896].) Gilman argues that it is not that the values of the home need to reach into industry (as many female reformers had maintained) but that the principles of industry need to be applied to the home, thereby professionalizing women's work. Adamantly rejecting the claims certain of her contemporaries known as "female feminists" made for the innately different but superior contributions represented by women's influence in the home, Gilman concludes that exclusion is always and only oppressive.

In *The Man-Made World or, Our Androcentric Culture* (1911), Gilman lists the failures of patriarchal culture and provides an argument for what her intellectual guide, Lester Frank Ward, called "gynaecocentric culture" — where women, not men, are the race-type of the culture and where "common humanity" is emphasized over excessive masculinity or femininity (Kessler 60). For Gilman, "humanness" ought to be developed in three ways: mechanical, psychical, and social (*Man-Made* 15–16). In *The Man-Made World,* Gilman critiques "androcentric culture," cataloging the ills that have accumulated as a result of what she sees as an unhealthy move from earlier matriarchal communities to patriarchal society. First, beauty and health have been retarded and both men and women have become weak, inefficient, and ill, not to mention victims of fashion. What is considered beautiful in women is only the "gross overdevelopment" of certain sex characteristics or "sex ornament" (53, 59). Second, the sexual double standard has weakened the race by resulting in the transmission of sexual diseases. Third, women's "civilized art sense" has been aborted since they have not learned "applied art" — in creativity — but only fashion and fad (73, 77); finally, literature "has not given any true picture of woman's life, very little of human life, and a disproportioned section of man's life" (102). For Gilman, masculine competition and combat have overshadowed female service, the goal of her new human ethics, which is to "outgrow our androcentric culture" (162) and to overthrow the "androcracy."

By the end of her career, Gilman wholeheartedly embraced a racism undergirded by eugenics. In describing the deficiencies of Asian,

African, and Eastern European women immigrants, she succumbed to
the temptation to play to, rather than against, prevailing prejudices. In
The Living, she writes that her move to New York City in 1900 with
her second husband, Houghton Gilman, made her happy — with one
qualification: "I brought to the city a large, undiscriminating love of
Humanity, without a shadow or race-prejudice or preference. I had
much to learn" (284). What Gilman learned in New York was to divide
the world into "native Americans" — by which she meant Nordic
Protestants — and Italian, Russian, and Jewish "invaders" of America.
Whether or not she used her experiences in New York to justify a
racism she had felt all along is debatable. What is clear is that she saw
the indiscriminate breeding and inefficient households that she felt
characterized the city as a confirmation of her worst fears regarding
"alien" as opposed to "native" stock. After World War I, Gilman's
fears concerning a decline in ethics and sex-relations paled in comparison to her fear of immigration, which to her meant that "our grand-
children will belong to a minority of dwindling Americans, ruled over
by a majority of conglomerate races quite dissimilar" (*Living* 324).
Gilman feared that immigration would result in democratic rule by dys-
genic — or degenerate — mobs that would put an end to the social
progress she had spent her life imagining.

In "Parasitism and Civilised Vice" (see Part Two, Chapter 3),
Gilman employs her anti-Freudian diatribe against sex-expression
and all forms of egocentric excess in the cause of advancing her social
philosophy of race-development. This essay, as well as the end of her
autobiography, calls for the use of birth control to limit the population of "fecund foreigners" (*Living* 330). "Parasitism and Civilised
Vice" — published in a collection of other socialist pieces entitled
Woman's Coming of Age (1931) — details Gilman's argument
against women's growing dependence on men in capitalist America.
Gilman argues that like harem women, who "were fed and protected
in return for sex-service," American women are becoming "sex-
parasites" (Part Two, p. 268). Sex has become a process of economic
exchange instead of race betterment, leading to greater temptation
for men, in Gilman's terms, to "go native" by "marrying women of
frankly lower race" (Part Two, p. 273). Gilman's solution is for both
men and women to renounce sexual gratification, acknowledging that
"reproduction and improvement of the race" will bring about a
"rapid advance in health, beauty and intellectual power," and result
in joy in love as opposed to mere sex-attraction (Part Two, p. 277).

RECENT CRITICAL RECEPTION
OF "THE YELLOW WALLPAPER"

As Julie Bates Dock notes in her recent article on shifting scholarly responses to "The Yellow Wallpaper," the story's first readers frequently "identify the cause of the narrator's insanity as her husband," who is labelled by one reviewer of the 1889 Small, Maynard edition as a "'blundering, well-intentioned male murderer'" (60). At least some contemporaneous reviewers seem to have recognized the story's potentially subversive qualities, arguing that it should be kept away from young women, who presumably might avoid marriage as a result of reading it (Dock 59–61).

In 1973, the Feminist Press published an edition of "The Yellow Wallpaper," making the story available to a new generation of readers. Elaine Hedges wrote an afterword to the edition that celebrated Gilman as a feminist and cultural critic of the prevailing sexual politics of her day. Since 1973, the story has generated many responses. It has been read as Gilman's autobiographical commentary on her own depression and feelings of helplessness in her first marriage to Walter Stetson; as a critique of patriarchy and of male medical practices; as a fiction about women finding voice within the constraints of masculine language; as a reflection of the invalid women who seemed to be part of an "epidemic" of invalidism, neurasthenia, and disease in nineteenth-century, white, middle-class American culture; and as a study of one woman's attempt to free herself from social constraints.

Some critics see Gilman as an iconoclast, whose "bold, clear-eyed, commonsense stance" and "hard-hitting, straight-shooting rhetoric" took on the nineteenth-century ideology of separate spheres and attacked the sentimentalism and nostalgia which underlay dominant assumptions about sexuality and human consciousness (Fishkin 236–38). Others have seen her as a precursor of the modernist consciousness (DeKoven 38) or, as Walter Benn Michaels has it, "the triumphant omnipresence of market relations," even in the heroine's nursery (13), while Wai-Chee Dimock sees her as "a paragon of professionalism in the late nineteenth century" (88). Much recent criticism of "The Yellow Wallpaper" has focused on Gilman's racial and sexual elitism, and Jonathan Crewe interprets the story through the lens of 1990s queer theory, arguing that "it would be historically false to suppose that, in 1890, there could be no lesbian implication" in some of Gilman's narrative (280). In "'Out at Last'?: 'The Yellow

Wallpaper' after Two Decades of Feminist Criticism" (1992), Elaine Hedges argues that the shift from 1970s readings of Gilman's story to current interpretations has resulted in "the diminishment or even disavowal of the narrator's status as a feminist heroine" (326).

  While feminist literary critics in the seventies and early eighties celebrated Gilman's works as recovered "feminist" texts, more recent critics such as Susan Lanser and Ann Lane are revising such interpretations and recording Gilman's debt to the new, albeit troubling, social sciences of her time: scientific racism and scientific sexism, as well as the culture of consumption that began in the late 1800s. Reading Gilman's nonfiction — her sixty extant speeches along with her books and notebooks on her favorite topic, "Human Nature" — gives us a much more ambivalent picture of earlier critical analyses of Gilman's platform for social change and its roots in the attempt to regulate social progress at the expense of private competition and individualism. As many feminist critics of Gilman's fiction have shown, her stories focus not on the differences among women but on their common oppression as economic dependents of men.

  Whether one reads the "yellow" in "The Yellow Wallpaper" as a reference to urine and the heroine's postpartum psychosis (as William Veeder does), or to the arsenic often used in the nineteenth century to create yellow wallpaper (as Tom Lutz speculates), or to Asian ("yellow") women, suggesting the depth of Gilman's fears of the waves of Asian immigrants in the 1890s (as Lanser does), we can see how Gilman's story draws on contemporaneous anxieties about the formation of American character, whether these influences were psychological, material, or cultural. Her story crystallizes the various debates about social progress and fears of regression. Whether through feminist, New Historicist, or literary-historical lenses, Gilman's work has been interpreted and reinterpreted because of its richness and rhetorical power.

Charlotte Perkins Gilman in 1898. Courtesy of University of Wisconsin —
Madison, Memorial Library Special Collections.

Chronology of Gilman's Life and Times

1860

July 3: Charlotte Anna Perkins born in Hartford, Connecticut, second surviving child of Mary Westcott Perkins (1828–1893) and Frederick Beecher Perkins (1826–1899). Charlotte's father — a nephew of Harriet Beecher Stowe (1811–1896) and Catharine Beecher (1800–1878) — deserts the family but visits occasionally. Charlotte, her mother, and her brother (Thomas Adie, b. May 9, 1859) live in poverty, moving from relative to relative.

November: Abraham Lincoln (1809–1865) elected U.S. president.

December: South Carolina secedes from the Union, the first state to do so.

First English-language kindergarten opened in Boston by Elizabeth Palmer Peabody.

Nathaniel Hawthorne (1804–1864), *The Marble Faun*. First of Beadle's Dime Novels appear.

1861

April: Civil War begins with Confederate firing on Fort Sumter, in Charleston Harbor, South Carolina.

Rebecca Harding Davis (1831–1910), *Life in the Iron-Mills*. Harriet Jacobs (1813–1897), *Incidents in the Life of a Slave Girl*.

1863

January: Emancipation Proclamation issued, freeing slaves in territory controlled by the Confederacy.

1864

November: Abraham Lincoln elected to a second term as president.

1865

Civil War ends with Robert E. Lee's surrender at Appomattox.

Ku Klux Klan founded in Pulaski, Tennessee. Died out at the turn of the century. Reorganized in 1915 and flourished in 1920s.

1866

S. Weir Mitchell (1829–1914) publishes his first fiction about Civil War injuries, "The Case of George Dedlow."

1867

March 2: First Reconstruction Act passed by Congress.

1868

July: Fourteenth Amendment grants citizenship to African Americans.

Louisa May Alcott (1832–1888), *Little Women.*

1869

Gilman's parents separate permanently.

May: Fifteenth Amendment grants suffrage to black males.

Elizabeth Cady Stanton (1815–1902) and Susan B. Anthony (1820–1906) found the National Woman Suffrage Association (NWSA).

1871

William Dean Howells (1837–1920) begins ten-year editorship of the *Atlantic Monthly,* an influential literary and cultural magazine.

1873

Gilman's parents divorce. Charlotte, her brother, Thomas, and her mother lived in a cooperative housekeeping group in Providence, Rhode Island, where they stay until 1875.

March 3: The Comstock Law, named after Anthony Comstock (1844–1915), the secretary of the Society for the Suppression of Vice, prohibits the distribution of "obscene" literature and birth control information through the U.S. mail.

Panic of 1873: Nationwide economic depression.

1874

Women's Christian Temperance Union founded to end the sale and consumption of liquor.

1877

Gilman begins close friendship with Martha Luther (1862–1948).

1878–79

Gilman attends Rhode Island School of Design.

1882

January: Gilman meets Walter Stetson (1858–1911), a struggling artist. She rejects his marriage proposal two weeks later but continues their relationship. During this year Gilman suffers her first bout with depression.

The first Chinese Exclusion Act bars further Chinese immigration.

1883

May: Gilman accepts Walter Stetson's proposal, with a year's postponement of the wedding. Her depression continues.

Comstock, *Traps for the Young.*

1884

January: Gilman publishes her first poem, "In Duty Bound," in *Woman's Journal.*

May 2: Gilman marries Walter Stetson in Providence.

Mark Twain (1835–1910), *The Adventures of Huckleberry Finn.*

1885

March 23: Gilman gives birth to her first and only child, Katharine Beecher Stetson Chamberlin.

Fall: Gilman leaves for Pasadena without Walter to visit Grace Ellery Channing (1862–1937); she recuperates from "hysteria" and depression following Katharine's birth.

1886

Gilman's return to Providence worsens her depression. She is treated by Dr. S. Weir Mitchell for neurasthenia.

1887

April: Gilman enters Mitchell's sanitarium outside Philadelphia and is later considered cured. She returns to physical exercise and writing and decides to ask Walter for a divorce. They live together for another year after their agreement to separate.

1888

Gilman spends the summer with Grace Ellery Channing in Bristol, RI.

October: Gilman and Walter Stetson separate, and Gilman moves to Pasadena with Katharine to recuperate with Grace.

December: Walter requests a reconciliation.

Edward Bellamy (1850–1898), *Looking Backward, 2000–1887*.

1889

Walter spends a year in Pasadena and becomes engaged to Grace. Gilman suffers chronic depression.

Jane Addams (1860–1935) establishes Hull-House in Chicago with Ellen Gates Starr (1859–1940).

1890

In addition to "The Yellow Wallpaper," Gilman writes thirty-three short articles and twenty-three poems; after reading Edward Bellamy's *Looking Backward, 2000–1887* (1888), she becomes active in the Nationalist movement in California.

National American Woman Suffrage Association created, uniting two suffragist organizations: the National Woman Suffrage Association (originally founded by Elizabeth Cady Stanton and Susan B. Anthony in 1869 for a federal constitutional amendment for women's voting rights) and the American Woman Suffrage Association (also founded in 1869 by Lucy Stone, among others, for suffrage through state legislatures). Carrie Chapman Catt (1859–1947) led the NAWSA to win the right for women to vote.

April: Gilman publishes the poem "Similar Cases" in Bellamy's periodical *Nationalist;* she begins writing plays with Grace.

October: Gilman sends "The Yellow Wallpaper" to Howells, who forwards it to Horace Scudder, the new editor of the *Atlantic Monthly.*

December: Grace leaves Pasadena to join Walter Stetson on the East Coast.

William James (1842–1910), *Principles of Psychology.*

1891

Gilman publishes her story "The Giant Wisteria." She joins the Pacific Coast Women's Press Association, where she meets Adeline ("Delle" or "Dora," 1860–1909), a writer for the San Francisco *Call.*

September: Gilman moves to Oakland and shares boarding-house rooms with Adeline Knapp, Katharine, and her ailing mother. She initiates divorce proceedings against Walter Stetson.

The word *feminist* coined by the *Athenaeum* book review. The Populist Party, which advocates economic reforms such as the free coinage of silver and government ownership of railroads, launched in Ohio.

1892

January: Gilman publishes "The Yellow Wallpaper" in the *New England Magazine.*

Various newspapers announce the "scandal" of Gilman's divorce proceedings. Gilman is active in Nationalist and Populist politics, as well as various reform movements. She lectures on women's issues, advocating women's economic independence, and makes a living by running a boarding house.

Ellis Island becomes an immigrant station.

1893

March 6: Gilman's mother dies.

October: Gilman publishes her first book of poetry, *In This Our World.*

World's Columbia Exhibition opens in Chicago.

Bicycling craze hits the United States (through 1895).

1894

Gilman supports Pullman strikers and fights the monopoly of the Southern Pacific Railroad.

April: Gilman's divorce from Walter Stetson is final. She moves to San Francisco to edit the *Impress* with her friends Helen Campbell (1839–1918) and Paul Tyner (d. 1925), and writes editorials, reviews, poems, and other items. She meets Edward Alsworth Ross (1866–1951), whose friendship ensures her exposure to the new sociology of the day.

May: Gilman sends her daughter, Katharine, to live with Grace Ellery Channing and Walter Stetson.

June: Walter Stetson and Grace Ellery Channing marry.

1895

The *Impress* fails, leaving Gilman in debt. She moves to Hull-House in Chicago at Jane Addams's request, helps Helen Campbell in "Little Hell" settlement house on Chicago's north side; she lectures nationally on social evolution and economics, women's independence, and child/family culture.

Charles Dana Gibson (1867–1944) popularizes the ideal of the Gibson Girl, a slim, small-waisted American beauty with pompadour hair.

1896

January: Gilman meets Lester Frank Ward (1841–1913), a sociologist advocating a gynaecocentric theory of human evolution, at the National Woman Suffrage Convention in Washington, D.C.

July–November: Gilman attends the International Socialist and Labor Congress in London. Meets George Bernard Shaw (1856–1950) and is invited to join the Fabian Society.

In *Plessy v. Ferguson* the Supreme Court rules that "separate but equal" railroad cars for African Americans and whites are constitutional, establishing a system of legal race segregation that lasted until the 1950s.

1897

March: Gilman is reintroduced to her younger cousin, George Houghton Gilman, an attorney; they correspond from 1897 to 1900. Gilman leaves on an extended lecture tour in the United States.

Havelock Ellis (1859–1939), *Studies in the Psychology of Sex: Sexual Inversion.*

1898

Gilman writes *Women and Economics* in six weeks, and its publication brings her fame.

April: The Spanish-American War begins after the destruction of the battleship *Maine* in February and ends in August after military and naval victories; United States acquires Puerto Rico and the Philippines.

1899

Gilman attends the International Women's Congress in London and spends five months in England.

Thorstein Veblen (1857–1929), *The Theory of the Leisure Class.*
Kate Chopin (1851–1904), *The Awakening.*

1900

June 11: Gilman marries George Houghton Gilman in Detroit, and they move to the upper West Side of Manhattan; publishes *Concerning Children,* her study of children's role in social progress. From

1900–1915, she lectures extensively throughout the United States on such issues as women's education, work, suffrage, ethics, and economics.

1901

Ross, *Social Control.* Booker T. Washington (1856–1915), *Up from Slavery.*

1902

Henry James (1843–1916), *The Wings of the Dove.*

1903

Gilman publishes *The Home: Its Work and Influence.* Ward, *Pure Sociology.* W.E.B. Du Bois (1868–1963), *The Souls of Black Folk.*

1904

Gilman publishes *Human Work;* attends the International Council of Women in Berlin.

1905

Gilman goes on a lecture tour of England, Holland, Germany, Austria, and Hungary. Edith Wharton (1862–1937), *The House of Mirth.*

1906

Upton Sinclair (1878–1968) publishes *The Jungle,* which leads to the passage of the Pure Food and Drug Act.

1907

Gilman publishes *Women and Social Service.* Performance of the first Ziegfeld Follies. Shows continue for twenty-four years and eventually feature Fanny Brice and Will Rogers.

1909

Gilman founds, edits, and writes the *Forerunner,* a monthly magazine published from 1909 to 1916. Sigmund Freud lectures in the United States. The NAACP (National Association for the Advancement of Colored People), dedicated to the advancement of the rights and welfare of African Americans, founded.

1910

Gilman's novel, *What Diantha Did,* published in serial form in the *Forerunner.*

Addams, *Twenty Years at Hull-House.*

1911

Gilman's *The Man-Made World or, Our Androcentric Culture* serialized in the *Forerunner,* as are Gilman's novels *The Crux* and *Moving the Mountain.*

March: The Triangle Shirtwaist Company — a sweatshop in New York City — catches fire, and 146 people, mostly women, are killed. The outrage over the poor working conditions and safety hazards that caused so many to die increases participation in the union movement.

1912

April 14–15: The British luxury oceanliner the *Titanic* sinks on its first voyage.

1913

Gilman attends the International Woman's Suffrage Congress in Budapest, her last European conference.

1914

Gilman gives a series of lectures in New York and London.

May: First official Mother's Day is celebrated.

June: Archduke Ferdinand of Austria assassinated in Sarajevo.

July 28: World War I begins in Europe (Germany and Austria-Hungary against Britain, France, and Russia).

1915

Gilman's utopian novel, *Herland,* serialized in the *Forerunner.*

Nevada's easy divorce law signed, making the residency requirement only 6 months.

1916

Gilman supports World War I (1916–17) and reveals her anti-German sentiments; publishes sequel to *Herland: With Her in Ourland.*

Margaret Sanger (1883–1966) opens the first U.S. birth control clinic in New York City.

1917

April: United States enters World War I on the side of the Allies after German U-boats attack neutral ships and Germany proposes a German-Mexican alliance against the United States.

1918

November: "Fourteen Points" Armistice signed; President Wilson (1856–1924) attends Paris peace conference in 1919, where he urges the formation of the League of Nations.

1919

Gilman becomes a daily columnist for New York *Tribune* syndicate.

The ratification of the Eighteenth Amendment (the Volstead Act) begins Prohibition.

1920

Gilman publishes essays on urban planning (1920–21).

The Nineteenth Amendment, guaranteeing women's suffrage, ratified.

1922

Gilman moves to Norwich Town, Connecticut.

The flapper dress comes into fashion. The fascist leader, Benito Mussolini (1883–1945), also known as "*Il Duce*," comes to power in Italy.

1923

Gilman publishes *His Religion and Hers: A Study of the Faith of Our Fathers and the Work of Our Mothers.*

1925

The Scopes "Monkey Trial" pits evolution against creationism; John T. Scopes convicted of teaching evolutionary theory and fined one hundred dollars.

1926

Gilman writes a draft of her autobiography, *The Living of Charlotte Perkins Gilman* (1926–27).

April: The Book-of-the-Month Club organized and has forty thousand subscribers by the end of the first year.

1927

August: Nicóla Sacco (1891–1927) and Bartolomeo Vanzetti (1888–1927), admitted anarchists, executed for their alleged murder of a factory guard in 1920. Critics charge that they are innocent and have been convicted because of their radical beliefs and foreign birth.

December: Gilman's "Progress Through Birth Control" is published in the *North American Review*.

1929

Gilman completes a detective novel, *Unpunished*, published posthumously in 1997 by The Feminist Press.

October 29: The stock market crashes on "Black Tuesday," ushering in the Great Depression.

1930

Sinclair Lewis (1885–1951) becomes the first American to win the Nobel Prize in Literature. His works include *Main Street* (1920), *Babbitt* (1922), *Arrowsmith* (1925), and *Elmer Gantry* (1927).

1931

Jane Addams wins the Nobel Peace Prize for her work as the first president of the Women's International League for Peace and Freedom.

1932

Gilman is diagnosed with inoperable breast cancer.

March: The Lindbergh baby kidnapping case, one of the most highly publicized crimes of the century, outrages the public. The Lindbergh baby is found dead after the payment of a ransom.

May: Amelia Earhart (1897–1937) becomes the first woman to make a solo flight across the Atlantic.

1933

Prohibition repealed.

1934

May: George Houghton Gilman dies.

August: Gilman moves to Pasadena to be with her daughter. She revises her autobiography and selects pictures for it.

Adolf Hitler (1889–1945) combines presidency and chancellorship of Germany, assuming title of "*Der Führer*."

Alice James's (1848–1892) *Diary* published, after having been suppressed by the James family for many years.

1935

August 17: Gilman dies in Pasadena, committing suicide by taking an overdose of chloroform. Gilman is cremated and her ashes scattered.

October 4: Gilman's autobiography published posthumously.

Pearl Buck (1892–1973), author of the best-selling *The Good Earth* (1931), is the first U.S. woman to receive the Nobel Prize in Literature.

A Note on the Text

This volume reprints the text of "The Yellow Wallpaper" from the January 1892 issue of the *New England Magazine,* where the short story was first published. While several obvious misprints in that edition have been corrected, late-nineteenth-century usages and peculiarities of spelling and punctuation have been preserved in order to be faithful to Gilman's style. The inconsistent hyphenation of the word *wallpaper* in the 1892 edition has been retained throughout the text of the story; however, we have chosen to follow convention in omitting the hyphen from the title of the story, which appeared as "The Yellow Wall-Paper" in the *New England Magazine.*

Wherever possible, the text of the documents in Part Two is that of the original edition, and unless otherwise indicated in the headnote for a document, the text has not been modified from the copy text. Students should expect to encounter some archaic or variant spellings and punctuation conventions.

(handwritten top) how is the story multiple climactic? I don't really see any climax.

The Yellow Wallpaper

(handwritten annotations surrounding text)
does it matter that it is the summer
something too good?
word choice
History
how she views herself and her husband
thats cool they rented a summer cottage

It is very seldom that mere ordinary people like John and myself secure ancestral halls for the summer.

A colonial mansion, a hereditary estate, I would say a haunted house, and reach the height of romantic felicity — but that would be asking too much of fate! *→ something about her beliefs*

Still I will proudly declare that there is something queer about it.

Else, why should it be let so cheaply? And why have stood so long untenanted? *(handwritten: Important background info)*

(handwritten: Part of that unromantic monotony, not spontan') John laughs at me, of course, but one expects that in marriage. *(handwritten: view of marriage)* John is practical in the extreme. He has no patience with faith, an intense horror of superstition, and he scoffs openly at any talk of things not to be felt and seen and put down in figures. (intangibles) *(handwritten: it shows she views these as negative qualities)*

John is a physician, and *perhaps* — (I would not say it to a living soul, of course, but this is dead paper and a great relief to my mind) — *perhaps* that is one reason I do not get well faster. *? come back to this*

You see he does not believe I am sick!

And what can one do? *→ one, alone, no support, crazy, not*

If a physician of high standing, and one's own husband, assures friends and relatives that there is really nothing the matter with one *(handwritten: part of the multitude)*

(handwritten: She doesn't finish her thought.)

(handwritten: using "one" takes this to a new level of meaning, not just the narrator but any "one")

41

but temporary nervous depression — a slight hysterical tendency[1] —
what is one to do?

My brother is also a physician, and also of high standing, and he
says the same thing.

So I take phosphates or phosphites[2] — whichever it is, and tonics,
and journeys, and air, and exercise, and am absolutely forbidden to
"work" until I am well again.

—Personally, I disagree with their ideas.

—Personally, I believe that congenial work, with excitement and
change, would do me good.

But what is one to do?

I did write for a while in spite of them; but it *does* exhaust me a
good deal — having to be so sly about it, or else meet with heavy opposition.

I sometimes fancy that in my condition if I had less opposition and
more society and stimulus — but John says the very worst thing I can
do is to think about my condition, and I confess it always makes me
feel bad.

So I will let it alone and talk about the house.

The most beautiful place! It is quite alone, standing well back from
the road, quite three miles from the village. It makes me think of English places that you read about, for there are hedges and walls and
gates that lock, and lots of separate little houses for the gardeners and
people.

There is a *delicious* garden! I never saw such a garden — large and
shady, full of box-bordered paths, and lined with long grape-covered
arbors with seats under them.

There were greenhouses, too, but they are all broken now.

There was some legal trouble, I believe, something about the heirs
and co-heirs; anyhow, the place has been empty for years.

That spoils my ghostliness, I am afraid, but I don't care — there is
something strange about the house — I can feel it.

---

[1] *hysterical tendency:* In the nineteenth century, women's illnesses of all sorts were
generally characterized as "hysteria," although the symptoms might range from pain
to anxiety, fatigue to depression. These symptoms were presumed to have a somatic
origin. See Part Two, Chapter 2.

[2] *phosphates or phosphites:* Any salt or ester of phosphoric acid, used during the
nineteenth century to cure exhaustion of the nerve centers, neuralgia, mania, melancholia, and often sexual exhaustion.

I even said so to John one moonlight evening, but he said what I felt was a *draught*, and shut the window. → so practical, John, you jerk

[margin: recognizes her unreasonableness]

I get unreasonably angry with John sometimes. I'm sure I never used to be so sensitive. I think it is due to this nervous condition.

But John says if I feel so, I shall neglect proper self-control; so I take pains to control myself — before him, at least, and that makes me very tired. *starts out not liking it*

[margin: self suppression]

I don't like our room a bit. I wanted one downstairs that opened on the piazza and had roses all over the window, and such pretty old-fashioned chintz hangings! but John would not hear of it. *I wonder why not.*

He said there was only one window and not room for two beds, and no near room for him if he took another.

He is very careful and loving, and hardly lets me stir without special direction. → but so boring and controlling, that doesn't seem like love

I have a schedule prescription for each hour in the day; he takes all care from me, and so I feel basely ungrateful not to value it more.

He said we came here solely on my account, that I was to have perfect rest and all the air I could get. "Your exercise depends on your strength, my dear," said he, "and your food somewhat on your appetite; but air you can absorb all the time." So we took the nursery at the top of the house.

[margin: ?]

It is a big, airy room, the whole floor nearly, with windows that look all ways, and air and sunshine galore. It was nursery first and then playroom and gymnasium, I should judge; for the windows are barred for little children, and there are rings and things in the walls.

[margin: Sounds more like a loony bin than a play room]

The paint and paper look as if a boys' school had used it. It is stripped off — the paper — in great patches all around the head of my bed, about as far as I can reach, and in a great place on the other side of the room low down. I never saw a worse paper in my life.

[margin: Description of the wallpaper]

One of those sprawling flamboyant patterns committing every artistic sin.

It is dull enough to confuse the eye in following, pronounced enough to constantly irritate and provoke study, and when you follow the lame uncertain curves for a little distance they suddenly commit suicide — plunge off at outrageous angles, destroy themselves in unheard of contradictions. → is this metaphorical?

[margin: author committed suicide]

The color is repellant, almost revolting; a smouldering unclean yellow, strangely faded by the slow-turning sunlight.

It is a dull yet lurid orange in some places, a sickly sulphur tint in others. *why yellow?*

No wonder the children hated it! I should hate it myself if I had to live in this room long.

There comes John, and I must put this away, — he hates to have me write a word. *why?*

* * * * * *

2 weeks later

We have been here two weeks, and I haven't felt like writing before, since that first day.

I am sitting by the window now, up in this atrocious nursery, and there is nothing to hinder my writing as much as I please, save lack of strength.

John is away all day, and even some nights when his cases are serious.

I am glad my case is not serious! *— sarcasm?*

But these nervous troubles are dreadfully depressing.

John does not know how much I really suffer. He knows there is no *reason* to suffer, and that satisfies him. *like my friend*

Of course it is only nervousness. It does weigh on me so not to do my duty in any way! *↳ Why does she suffer?*

I meant to be such a help to John, such a real rest and comfort, and here I am a comparative burden already!

Nobody would believe what an effort it is to do what little I am able, — to dress and entertain, and order things. *Gosh this reminds me of my friend, I hope she doesn't see me*

It is fortunate Mary is so good with the baby. Such a dear baby! *as John.*

And yet I *cannot* be with him, it makes me so nervous.

weird relationship with the baby

I suppose John never was nervous in his life. He laughs at me so about this wall-paper!

At first he meant to repaper the room, but afterwards he said that I was letting it get the better of me, and that nothing was worse for a nervous patient than to give way to such fancies.

He said that after the wall-paper was changed it would be the heavy bedstead, and then the barred windows, and then that gate at the head of the stairs, and so on.

"You know the place is doing you good," he said, "and really, dear, I don't care to renovate the house just for a three months' rental."

"Then do let us go downstairs," I said, "there are such pretty rooms there." *what does that mean?*

Then he took me in his arms and called me a blessed little goose, and said he would go down cellar, if I wished, and have it white-washed into the bargain.

no, I don't think I am like John he doesn't listen or care, I do.

Between the two stars she goes

"I am sitting by the Window in this Atrocious Nursery."

Illustration by Jo. H. Hatfield from the *New England Magazine* edition of "The Yellow Wallpaper" (1892). Courtesy of the University of Wisconsin — Madison, Memorial Library Special Collections.

her putting him above

But he is right enough about the beds and windows and things.

It is an airy and comfortable room as any one need wish, and, of course, I would not be so silly as to make him uncomfortable just for a whim.

please, you are miserable you sell out, make him uncomfy for you

—I'm really getting quite fond of the big room, all but that horrid paper.

When I make myself uncomfortable to help someone I think it is good and that makes it comfortable especially one I love

Out of one window I can see the garden, those mysterious deep-shaded arbors, the riotous old-fashioned flowers, and bushes and gnarly trees.

Out of another I get a lovely view of the bay and a little private wharf belonging to the estate. There is a beautiful shaded lane that runs down there from the house. I always fancy I see people walking in these numerous paths and arbors, but John has cautioned me not to give way to fancy in the least. He says that with my imaginative power and habit of story-making, a nervous weakness like mine is sure to lead to all manner of excited fancies, and that I ought to use my will and good sense to check the tendency. So I try.

I think sometimes that if I were only well enough to write a little it would relieve the press of ideas and rest me.

But I find I get pretty tired when I try.

It is so discouraging not to have any advice and companionship about my work. When I get really well, John says we will ask Cousin Henry and Julia down for a long visit; but he says he would as soon put fireworks in my pillow-case as to let me have those stimulating people about now.

I wish I could get well faster.

But I must not think about that. This paper looks to me as if it *knew* what a vicious influence it had!

There is a recurrent spot where the pattern lolls like a broken neck and two bulbous eyes stare at you upside down.

I get positively angry with the impertinence of it and the everlastingness. Up and down and sideways they crawl, and those absurd, unblinking eyes are everywhere. There is one place where two breadths didn't match, and the eyes go all up and down the line, one a little higher than the other.

I never saw so much expression in an inanimate thing before, and we all know how much expression they have! I used to lie awake as a child and get more entertainment and terror out of blank walls and plain furniture than most children could find in a toy-store.

I remember what a kindly wink the knobs of our big, old bureau used to have, and there was one chair that always seemed like a strong friend.

I used to feel that if any of the other things looked too fierce I could always hop into that chair and be safe.

The furniture in this room is no worse than inharmonious, however, for we had to bring it all from downstairs. I suppose when this was used as a playroom they had to take the nursery things out, and no wonder! I never saw such ravages as the children have made here.

The wall-paper, as I said before, is torn off in spots, and it sticketh closer than a brother — they must have had perseverance as well as hatred.

Then the floor is scratched and gouged and splintered, the plaster itself is dug out here and there, and this great heavy bed which is all we found in the room, looks as if it had been through the wars.

But I don't mind it a bit — only the paper.

There comes John's sister. Such a dear girl as she is, and so careful of me! I must not let her find me writing. *100% perfect housekeeper of*

She is a perfect and enthusiastic housekeeper, and hopes for no *20* better profession. I verily believe she thinks it is the writing which made me sick! *I thought something like that too. Why did my friend say*

But I can write when she is out, and see her a long way off from *that she hated literature?* these windows.

There is one that commands the road, a lovely shaded winding road, and one that just looks off over the country. A lovely country, too, full of great elms and velvet meadows.

This wallpaper has a kind of sub-pattern in a different shade, a particularly irritating one, for you can only see it in certain lights, and not clearly then. *anything else?*

But in the places where it isn't faded and where the sun is just so — I can see a strange, provoking, formless sort of figure, that seems to skulk about behind that silly and conspicuous front design.

There's sister on the stairs! → *then the figure is juxtaposed textually with the sister who only will be a housekeeper*

*formless woman, not even a * * * woman, just a figure.. how can a figure be formless?*

Well, the Fourth of July is over! The people are all gone and I am tired out. John thought it might do me good to see a little company, so we just had mother and Nellie and the children down for a week.

Of course I didn't do a thing. Jennie sees to everything now.

But it tired me all the same.

John says if I don't pick up faster he shall send me to Weir Mitchell[3] in the fall. → *ooh, that's bad!*

---

[3] *S. Weir Mitchell:* Mitchell (1829–1914) was a famous Civil War doctor and later novelist, who treated shell shock during and after the Civil War. Later, he developed a "rest cure" for women and men suffering from neurasthenia. See the Introduction to Chapter 2 and the documents in Part Two, Chapter 2.

(handwritten top margin: remember Dan, this is just literature.)

But I don't want to go there at all. I had a friend who was in his hands once, and she says he is just like John and my brother, only more so!

Besides, it is such an undertaking to go so far.

I don't feel as if it was worth while to turn my hand over for anything, and I'm getting dreadfully fretful and querulous.

(handwritten: my friend) I cry at nothing, and cry most of the time.

(handwritten: but she cries when I am there) Of course I don't when John is here, or anybody else, but when I am alone.

(handwritten: more and more lovely)

And I am alone a good deal just now. John is kept in town very often by serious cases, and Jennie is good and lets me alone when I want her to.

(handwritten: ooh, so she can go outside) So I walk a little in the garden or down that lovely lane, sit on the porch under the roses, and lie down up here a good deal.

I'm getting really fond of the room in spite of the wallpaper. Perhaps *because* of the wallpaper.

It dwells in my mind so! *(handwritten: Yeah it does)*

(handwritten: Why, how awful, just follow a pointless pattern to conclusion, maybe her outlook on life) I lie here on this great immovable bed — it is nailed down, I believe — and follow that pattern about by the hour. It is as good as gymnastics, I assure you. I start, we'll say, at the bottom, down in the corner over there where it has not been touched, and I determine for the thousandth time that I *will* follow that pointless pattern to some sort of a conclusion.

I know a little of the principle of design, and I know this thing was not arranged on any laws of radiation, or alternation, or repetition, or symmetry, or anything else that I ever heard of. *(handwritten: like life)*

It is repeated, of course, by the breadths, but not otherwise.

Looked at in one way each breadth stands alone, the bloated curves and flourishes — a kind of "debased Romanesque"[4] with *delirium tremens* — go waddling up and down in isolated columns of fatuity.

(handwritten: horizontal and vertical) But, on the other hand, they connect diagonally, and the sprawling outlines run off in great slanting waves of optic horror, like a lot of wallowing seaweeds in full chase.

The whole thing goes horizontally, too, at least it seems so, and I exhaust myself in trying to distinguish the order of its going in that direction.

They have used a horizontal breadth for a frieze,[5] and that adds wonderfully to the confusion.

(handwritten: more description of + about feelings the wallpaper)

[4] *debased Romanesque:* European architectural style with elaborate ornamentation and complexity, as well as repeated motifs.

[5] *frieze:* A decorative band used as a border around a room or mantle.

[handwritten top margin: "or maybe love he does love her but it isn't expressed how she needs it."]

There is one end of the room where it is almost intact, and there, when the crosslights fade and the low sun shines directly upon it, I can almost fancy radiation after all, — the interminable grotesques seem to form around a common centre and rush off in headlong plunges of equal distraction.

It makes me tired to follow it. I will take a nap I guess. *[handwritten: rather passive, uncaring]*

* * * * * *

I don't know why I should write this. *[handwritten: why this introduction]* *[handwritten: why do it anyway?]*
I don't want to.
I don't feel able.
And I know John would think it absurd. But I *must* say what I feel and think in some way — it is such a relief!
But the effort is getting to be greater than the relief.
Half the time now I am awfully lazy, and lie down ever so much.
John says I mustn't lose my strength, and has me take cod liver oil and lots of tonics and things, to say nothing of ale and wine and rare meat. *[handwritten: I think that he does]*
Dear John! He loves me very dearly, and hates to have me sick. I tried to have a real earnest reasonable talk with him the other day, and tell him how I wish he would let me go and make a visit to Cousin Henry and Julia. *[handwritten: yeah sure sends love]*
But he said I wasn't able to go, nor able to stand it after I got there; and I did not make out a very good case for myself, for I was crying before I had finished.
It is getting to be a great effort for me to think straight. Just this nervous weakness I suppose.
And dear John gathered me up in his arms, and just carried me upstairs and laid me on the bed, and sat by me and read to me till it tired my head. *[handwritten: doh! I do that! Fuck! oh well... I think it is different]*
He said I was his darling and his comfort and all he had, and that I must take care of myself for his sake, and keep well.
He says no one but myself can help me out of it, that I must use my will and self-control and not let any silly fancies run away with me. *[handwritten: no, you can't keep yourself out of it, I know who can.]*
There's one comfort, the baby is well and happy, and does not have to occupy this nursery with the horrid wallpaper. *[handwritten: what baby?]*
If we had not used it, that blessed child would have! What a fortunate escape! Why, I wouldn't have a child of mine, an impressionable little thing, live in such a room for worlds.

I never thought of it before, but it is lucky that John kept me here after all, I can stand it so much easier than a baby, you see.

Of course I never mention it to them any more — I am too wise, — but I keep watch of it all the same.

There are things in that paper that nobody knows but me, or ever will.

Behind that outside pattern the dim shapes get clearer every day.

It is always the same shape, only very numerous.

And it is like a woman stooping down and creeping about behind that pattern. I don't like it a bit. I wonder — I begin to think — I wish John would take me away from here!

It is so hard to talk to John about my case, because he is so wise, and because he loves me so.

But I tried it last night.

It was moonlight. The moon shines in all around just as the sun does.

I hate to see it sometimes, it creeps so slowly, and always comes in by one window or another.

John was asleep and I hated to waken him, so I kept still and watched the moonlight on that undulating wallpaper till I felt creepy.

The faint figure behind seemed to shake the pattern, just as if she wanted to get out.

I got up softly and went to feel and see if the paper *did* move, and when I came back John was awake.

"What is it, little girl?" he said. "Don't go walking about like that — you'll get cold."

I thought it was a good time to talk, so I told him that I really was not gaining here, and that I wished he would take me away.

"Why, darling!" said he, "our lease will be up in three weeks, and I can't see how to leave before.

"The repairs are not done at home, and I cannot possibly leave town just now. Of course if you were in any danger, I could and would, but you really are better, dear, whether you can see it or not. I am a doctor, dear, and I know. You are gaining flesh and color, your appetite is better, I feel really much easier about you."

"I don't weigh a bit more," said I, "nor as much; and my appetite may be better in the evening when you are here, but it is worse in the morning when you are away!"

[handwritten: it is him, well or sick as he wants her to be. & she is as]

"Bless her little heart!" said he with a big hug, "she shall be as sick as she pleases! But now let's improve the shining hours[6] by going to sleep, and talk about it in the morning!"

"And you won't go away?" I asked gloomily.

"Why, how can I, dear? It is only three weeks more and then we will take a nice little trip of a few days while Jennie is getting the house ready. Really dear you are better!"

"Better in body perhaps — " I began, and stopped short, for he sat up straight and looked at me with such a stern, reproachful look that I could not say another word.

"My darling," said he, "I beg of you, for my sake and for our child's sake, as well as for your own, that you will never for one instant let that idea enter your mind! There is nothing so dangerous, so fascinating, to a temperament like yours. It is a false and foolish fancy. Can you not trust me as a physician when I tell you so?"

So of course I said no more on that score, and we went to sleep before long. He thought I was asleep first, but I wasn't, and lay there for hours trying to decide whether that front pattern and the back pattern really did move together or separately. *[handwritten: what could this symbolize]* *[handwritten signature: William A. M. Heart]*

* * * * * *

On a pattern like this, by daylight, there is a lack of sequence, a defiance of law, that is a constant irritant to a normal mind.

The color is hideous enough, and unreliable enough, and infuriating enough, but the pattern is torturing. *[handwritten: what could this symbolize]*

You think you have mastered it, but just as you get well underway in following, it turns a back-somersault and there you are. It slaps you in the face, knocks you down, and tramples upon you. It is like a bad dream. *[handwritten: — men ?]*

The outside pattern is a florid arabesque, reminding one of a fungus. If you can imagine a toadstool in joints, an interminable string of toadstools, budding and sprouting in endless convolutions — why, that is something like it.

That is, sometimes!

There is one marked peculiarity about this paper, a thing nobody seems to notice but myself, and that is that it changes as the light changes. *[handwritten: lack of consistency]*

[6] *improve the shining hours:* These lines are adapted from "Song XX" by English hymnist Isaac Watts (1674–1748): "How doth the little busy bee / Improve each shining hour, / And gather honey all the day / From every opening flower!"

When the sun shoots in through the east window — I always watch for that first long, straight ray — it changes so quickly that I never can quite believe it.

That is why I watch it always.

By moonlight — the moon shines in all night when there is a moon — I wouldn't know it was the same paper.

At night in any kind of light, in twilight, candlelight, lamplight, and worst of all by moonlight, it becomes bars! The outside pattern I mean, and the woman behind it is as plain as can be.

I didn't realize for a long time what the thing was that showed behind, that dim sub-pattern, but now I am quite sure it is a woman.

By daylight she is subdued, quiet. I fancy it is the pattern that keeps her so still. It is so puzzling. It keeps me quiet by the hour.

I lie down ever so much now. John says it is good for me, and to sleep all I can.

Indeed he started the habit by making me lie down for an hour after each meal.

It is a very bad habit I am convinced, for you see I don't sleep. And that cultivates deceit, for I don't tell them I'm awake — O no!

The fact is I am getting a little afraid of John.

He seems very queer sometimes, and even Jennie has an inexplicable look.

It strikes me occasionally, just as a scientific hypothesis, — that perhaps it is the paper!

I have watched John when he did not know I was looking, and come into the room suddenly on the most innocent excuses, and I've caught him several times *looking at the paper!* And Jennie too. I caught Jennie with her hand on it once.

She didn't know I was in the room, and when I asked her in a quiet, a very quiet voice, with the most restrained manner possible, what she was doing with the paper — she turned around as if she had been caught stealing, and looked quite angry — asked me why I should frighten her so!

Then she said that the paper stained everything it touched, that she had found yellow smooches on all my clothes and John's, and she wished we would be more careful!

Did not that sound innocent? But I know she was studying that pattern, and I am determined that nobody shall find it out but myself!

"She didn't know I was in the Room."

Illustration by Jo. H. Hatfield from the *New England Magazine* edition of "The Yellow Wallpaper" (1892). Courtesy of the University of Wisconsin — Madison, Memorial Library Special Collections.

Life is very much more exciting now than it used to be. You see I have something more to expect, to look forward to, to watch. I really do eat better, and am more quiet than I was.

John is so pleased to see me improve! He laughed a little the other day, and said I seemed to be flourishing in spite of my wall-paper.

I turned it off with a laugh. I had no intention of telling him it was *because* of the wall-paper — he would make fun of me. He might even want to take me away.

I don't want to leave now until I have found it out. There is a week more, and I think that will be enough.

*   *   *   *   *   *

I'm feeling ever so much better! I don't sleep much at night, for it is so interesting to watch developments; but I sleep a good deal in the daytime.

In the daytime it is tiresome and perplexing.

There are always new shoots on the fungus, and new shades of yellow all over it. I cannot keep count of them, though I have tried conscientiously.

It is the strangest yellow, that wall-paper! It makes me think of all the yellow things I ever saw — not beautiful ones like buttercups, but old foul, bad yellow things.

But there is something else about that paper — the smell! I noticed it the moment we came into the room, but with so much air and sun it was not bad. Now we have had a week of fog and rain, and whether the windows are open or not, the smell is here.

It creeps all over the house.

I find it hovering in the dining-room, skulking in the parlor, hiding in the hall, lying in wait for me on the stairs.

It gets into my hair.

Even when I go to ride, if I turn my head suddenly and surprise it — there is that smell!

Such a peculiar odor, too! I have spent hours in trying to analyze it, to find what it smelled like.

It is not bad — at first, and very gentle, but quite the subtlest, most enduring odor I ever met.

In this damp weather it is awful, I wake up in the night and find it hanging over me.

It used to disturb me at first. I thought seriously of burning the house — to reach the smell.

But now I am used to it. The only thing I can think of that it is like is the *color* of the paper! A yellow smell.

There is a very funny mark on this wall, low down, near the mop-board. A streak that runs round the room. It goes behind every piece of furniture, except the bed, a long, straight, even *smooch*, as if it had been rubbed over and over.

I wonder how it was done and who did it, and what they did it for. Round and round and round — round and round and round — it makes me dizzy!

*   *   *   *   *   *

I really have discovered something at last.

Through watching so much at night, when it changes so, I have finally found out.

The front pattern *does* move — and no wonder! The woman behind shakes it!

Sometimes I think there are a great many women behind, and sometimes only one, and she crawls around fast, and her crawling shakes it all over.

Then in the very bright spots she keeps still, and in the very shady spots she just takes hold of the bars and shakes them hard.

And she is all the time trying to climb through. But nobody could climb through that pattern — it strangles so; I think that is why it has so many heads.

They get through, and then the pattern strangles them off and turns them upside down, and makes their eyes white!

If those heads were covered or taken off it would not be half so bad.

*   *   *   *   *   *

I think that woman gets out in the daytime!

And I'll tell you why — privately — I've seen her!

I can see her out of every one of my windows!

It is the same woman, I know, for she is always creeping, and most women do not creep by daylight.

I see her in that long shaded lane, creeping up and down. I see her in those dark grape arbors, creeping all around the garden.

I see her on that long road under the trees, creeping along, and when a carriage comes she hides under the blackberry vines.

I don't blame her a bit. It must be very humiliating to be caught creeping by daylight!

I always lock the door when I creep by daylight. I can't do it at night, for I know John would suspect something at once.

And John is so queer now, that I don't want to irritate him. I wish he would take another room! Besides, I don't want anybody to get that woman out at night but myself.

I often wonder if I could see her out of all the windows at once.

But, turn as fast as I can, I can only see out of one at one time.

And though I always see her, she *may* be able to creep faster than I can turn!

I have watched her sometimes away off in the open country, creeping as fast as a cloud shadow in a high wind.

Woman is the shadow of man [handwritten margin note]

*   *   *   *   *   *

If only that top pattern could be gotten off from the under one! I mean to try it, little by little.

I have found out another funny thing, but I shan't tell it this time! It does not do to trust people too much.

There are only two more days to get this paper off, and I believe John is beginning to notice. I don't like the look in his eyes.

And I heard him ask Jennie a lot of professional questions about me. She had a very good report to give.

She said I slept a good deal in the daytime.

John knows I don't sleep very well at night, for all I'm so quiet!

He asked me all sorts of questions, too, and pretended to be very loving and kind.

As if I couldn't see through him!

Still, I don't wonder he acts so, sleeping under this paper for three months.

It only interests me, but I feel sure John and Jennie are secretly affected by it.

*   *   *   *   *   *

Hurrah! This is the last day, but it is enough. John to stay in town over night, and won't be out until this evening.

Jennie wanted to sleep with me — the sly thing! But I told her I should undoubtedly rest better for a night all alone.

That was clever, for really I wasn't alone a bit! As soon as it was moonlight and that poor thing began to crawl and shake the pattern, I got up and ran to help her.

I pulled and she shook, I shook and she pulled, and before morning we had peeled off yards of that paper.

A strip about as high as my head and half around the room.

And then when the sun came and that awful pattern began to laugh at me, I declared I would finish it to-day!

We go away to-morrow, and they are moving all my furniture down again to leave things as they were before.

Jennie looked at the wall in amazement, but I told her merrily that I did it out of pure spite at the vicious thing.

She laughed and said she wouldn't mind doing it herself, but I must not get tired.

How she betrayed herself that time!

But I am here, and no person touches this paper but me, — not *alive!*

She tried to get me out of the room — it was too patent! But I said it was so quiet and empty and clean now that I believed I would lie down again and sleep all I could; and not to wake me even for dinner — I would call when I woke.

So now she is gone, and the servants are gone, and the things are gone, and there is nothing left but that great bedstead nailed down, with the canvas mattress we found on it.

We shall sleep downstairs to-night, and take the boat home to-morrow.

I quite enjoy the room, now it is bare again.

How those children did tear about here!

This bedstead is fairly gnawed!

But I must get to work.

I have locked the door and thrown the key down into the front path.

I don't want to go out, and I don't want to have anybody come in, till John comes.

I want to astonish him.

I've got a rope up here that even Jennie did not find. If that woman does get out, and tries to get away, I can tie her!

But I forgot I could not reach far without anything to stand on!

This bed will *not* move!

I tried to lift and push it until I was lame, and then I got so angry I bit off a little piece at one corner — but it hurt my teeth.

Then I peeled off all the paper I could reach standing on the floor. It sticks horribly and the pattern just enjoys it! All those strangled heads and bulbous eyes and waddling fungus growths just shriek with derision!

I am getting angry enough to do something desperate. To jump out of the window would be admirable exercise, but the bars are too strong even to try.

Besides I wouldn't do it. Of course not. I know well enough that a step like that is improper and might be misconstrued.

I don't like to *look* out of the windows even — there are so many of those creeping women, and they creep so fast.

I wonder if they all come out of that wall-paper as I did?

But I am securely fastened now by my well-hidden rope — you don't get *me* out in the road there!

I suppose I shall have to get back behind the pattern when it comes night, and that is hard!

It is so pleasant to be out in this great room and creep around as I please!

I don't want to go outside. I won't, even if Jennie asks me to.

For outside you have to creep on the ground, and everything is green instead of yellow.

But here I can creep smoothly on the floor, and my shoulder just fits in that long smooch around the wall, so I cannot lose my way.

Why there's John at the door!

It is no use, young man, you can't open it!

How he does call and pound!

Now he's crying for an axe.

It would be a shame to break down that beautiful door!

"John dear!" said I in the gentlest voice, "the key is down by the front steps, under a plaintain leaf!"

That silenced him for a few moments.

Then he said — very quietly indeed, "Open the door, my darling!"

"I can't," said I. "The key is down by the front door under a plantain leaf!"

And then I said it again, several times, very gently and slowly, and said it so often that he had to go and see, and he got it of course, and came in. He stopped short by the door.

"What is the matter?" he cried. "For God's sake, what are you doing!"

I kept on creeping just the same, but I looked at him over my shoulder.

"I've got out at last," said I, "in spite of you and Jane. And I've pulled off most of the paper, so you can't put me back!"

Now why should that man have fainted? But he did, and right across my path by the wall, so that I had to creep over him every time!

Final illustration by Jo. H. Hatfield from the *New England Magazine* edition of "The Yellow Wallpaper" (1892). Courtesy of the University of Wisconsin — Madison, Memorial Library Special Collections.

Part Two

The Yellow Wallpaper
Cultural Contexts

1

Conduct Literature
and Motherhood Manuals

not exactly sure what that is

While the focus of this chapter is on late-nineteenth-century American conduct literature, the documents included reflect mid-century British concerns about women's role in culture and domesticity. The British writer Mrs. Sarah Stickney Ellis's advice books from the 1840s were popular in America, and Dr. William Acton's medical advice books, originally published in England, were widely available and immensely respected in the United States. American temperance advocate and socialist Frances Willard codified the exciting temper of the times when she advised young girls in 1888 that *"the ideal of woman's place in the world is changing in the average mind"* (see p. 110). No longer would one's gender determine one's place in the world. While such statements as Willard's might suggest that there was no longer a need for advice or conduct literature at the turn of the century — that anything was appropriate — in fact many Americans felt even more in need of guidance given the social transformations that were occurring.

Advice manuals were addressed to men, women, and children, and they helped define the emerging middle class in terms of moral values associated with the bourgeois home. At mid-century, Catharine Beecher's *A Treatise on Domestic Economy* (1841) could speak to a legion of women who worked and produced in the home, including Beecher's grandniece, Charlotte Perkins Gilman. As the century progressed, Beecher's advice gave way to more "modern" conceptions of culture and psychology. Few of these new manuals encouraged women to develop their intellectual abilities; it took the suffragists and the New Women of the early twentieth century to suggest such possibilities. Rather, advice ranged from the concrete — as in Mrs. Susan Powers's suggestion to use lettuce for the complexion — to the broad domain of women's domestic training and the assumed dangers of women overexerting their brains. Reverend Richard Heber Newton, for example, cautioned women that because belletristic writing would yield few female geniuses such as George Eliot, they had better focus their energies on the more attainable goal of the model family (122).

Many of the most popular advice books worked to shape a normative vision of the responsibilities of motherhood, instructing middle-class American women in how to raise a child to assume his or her proper place in the growing capitalist economy and the new culture of commodities. While eighteenth-century mothers taught the virtues of "republican motherhood" — of piety, loyalty, and hard work for the preservation of America — late-nineteenth-century mothers were enjoined to create a happy home for their children — the new democratic citizens. Moreover, they were expected to sacrifice willingly their personal ambitions in order to contribute to the new "modern" society through their influence in the home. Many women and men advocated such "influence," as opposed to the economic equality that Gilman desired, as a means of strengthening women's position that would complement rather than compete with men's power. Advice such as the kind Julia and Annie Thomas offered, although seemingly more liberal, also urged women to bring their physical and mental selves into harmony with the existing social order through movement, exercise, and, above all, self-control.

As we might expect, Gilman objected to attempts to offer separate advice to men and women, whether it was that of popular advice-givers like Margaret Sangster or political icons like President Theodore Roosevelt (see Part Two, Chapter 3). She saw the division of women and men into separate spheres as dangerous to *human* culture as a whole, and she sought ways to realign male and female culture to decrease the gap between the "private" domestic sphere and the public sphere of politics and the marketplace. Gilman objected to the image of the "true" mother as the uncomplaining self-sacrificer offered by writers such as Sangster and Marion Harland.

In many ways, "The Yellow Wallpaper" addresses the major tenets of the conduct and "self-help" literatures that were so popular in the 1880s and 1890s. While Gilman's narrator does not seek autonomy (as opposed to Gilman herself, who fled the restrictions of marriage and motherhood), she does try to write as a way of curing her depression. However, she admits that she gets tired when she writes, as her husband said she would. In fact, the narrator exhibits a concern with propriety even as her mental state deteriorates. Gilman's heroine tries to follow the decorum promoted by nineteenth-century advice manuals — she wants to be a helpmeet and a "comfort" to her husband — yet she can fulfill neither her maternal nor her wifely duties. She hides things from her husband, especially her "interpretations" of the wallpaper. Gilman's story registers the frustration her narrator/heroine feels in dealing with an unwitting, perhaps devious doctor-husband. Arguably, "The Yellow Wallpaper" reveals women's frustration in a culture that seemingly glorifies motherhood while it actually relegates women to nursery-prisons.

CATHARINE BEECHER

From A Treatise on Domestic Economy

Daughter of well-known Calvinist preacher Lyman Beecher and sister to Harriet Beecher Stowe (with whom she coauthored advice literature), Catharine Beecher (1800–1878) was a writer and an advocate of women's education as well as various moral reforms. In 1823, she opened the Hartford Seminary where she instructed young women in her principles of religion, health, housekeeping, and reform. In the following excerpt from one of the most influential of her many books, *A Treatise on Domestic Economy* (1841), Beecher argues that American women have a special responsibility to their country: to educate the members of their families to be productive and useful citizens. To that end, women must be efficient and careful housekeepers, despite the delicacy of their constitutions. Moreover, the demands of housework — without relief or exercise as a tonic — weigh upon women so that they are seldom healthy and vital.

The text of the following excerpt is taken from *A Treatise on Domestic Economy, for the Use of Young Ladies at Home, and at School* (Boston: Webb, 1841), 38–51.

Difficulties Peculiar to American Women

In the preceding chapter, were presented those views, which are calculated to inspire American women with a sense of their high responsibilities to their Country, and to the world; and of the excellence and grandeur of the object to which their energies may be consecrated.

But it will be found to be the law of moral action, that whatever involves great results and great benefits, is always attended with great hazards and difficulties. And as it has been shown, that American women have a loftier position, and a more elevated object of enterprise, than the females of any other nation, so it will appear, that they have greater trials and difficulties to overcome, than any other women are called to encounter.

Properly to appreciate the nature of these trials, it must be borne in mind, that the estimate of evils and privations depends, not so much on their positive nature, as on the character and habits of the person who meets them. A woman, educated in the savage state, finds it no trial to be destitute of many conveniences, which a woman, even of the lowest condition, in this Country,[1] would deem indispensable to existence. So a woman, educated with the tastes and habits of the best New England or Virginia housekeepers, would encounter many deprivations and trials, which would never occur to one reared in the log cabin of a new settlement. So, also, a woman, who has been accustomed to carry forward her arrangements with well-trained domestics, would meet a thousand trials to her feelings and temper, by the substitution of ignorant foreigners, or shiftless slaves, which would be of little account to one who had never enjoyed any better service.

Now, the larger portion of American women are the descendants of English progenitors, who, as a nation, are distinguished for systematic housekeeping, and for a great love of order, cleanliness, and comfort. And American women, to a greater or less extent, have inherited similar tastes and habits. But the prosperity and democratic tendencies of this Country produce results, materially affecting the comfort of housekeepers, which the females of monarchical and aristocratic lands are not called to meet. In such countries, all ranks and

---

[1] *savage state, . . . in this Country:* Beecher refers to the status of women in non-Christian, particularly Muslim, countries. In addition, she believed that New England women had the best domestic help and she saw the frontier as — in all matters — uncivilized. [All notes are the editor's unless identified otherwise.]

classes are fixed in a given position, and each person is educated for a particular sphere and style of living. And the dwellings, conveniences, and customs of life, remain very nearly the same, from generation to generation. This secures the preparation of all classes for their particular station, and makes the lower orders more dependent, and more subservient to employers.

But how different is the state of things in this Country. Every thing is moving and changing. Persons in poverty, are rising to opulence, and persons of wealth, are sinking to poverty. The children of common laborers, by their talents and enterprise, are becoming nobles in intellect, or wealth, or office; while the children of the wealthy, enervated by indulgence, are sinking to humbler stations. The sons of the wealthy are leaving the rich mansions of their fathers, to dwell in the log cabins of the forest, where very soon they bear away the daughters of ease and refinement, to share the privations of a new settlement. Meantime, even in the more stationary portions of the community, there is a mingling of all grades of wealth, intellect, and education. There are no distinct classes, as in aristocratic lands, whose bounds are protected by distinct and impassable lines, but all are thrown into promiscuous masses.[2] Thus, persons of humble means are brought into contact with those of vast wealth, while all intervening grades are placed side by side. Thus, too, there is a constant temptation presented to imitate the customs, and to strive for the enjoyments, of those who possess larger means.

In addition to this, the flow of wealth, among all classes, is constantly increasing the number of those who live in a style demanding much hired service, while the number of those, who are compelled to go to service, is constantly diminishing. Our manufactories, also, are making increased demands for female labor, and offering larger compensation. In consequence of these things, there is such a disproportion between those who wish to hire, and those who are willing to go to domestic service, that, in the non-slaveholding States, were it not for the supply of poverty-stricken foreigners,[3] there would not be a domestic for each family who demands one. And this resort to foreigners, poor as it is, scarcely meets the demand; while the disproportion

[2] *no distinct classes . . . promiscuous masses:* Like many of her contemporaries, Beecher believed that no rigid class system, like that prevailing in European countries with established aristocracies, existed in America.

[3] *female labor . . . poverty-stricken foreigners:* Beecher refers to the influx of immigrants to the United States, between 1840 and 1860, which was in large part due to the failure of the Irish potato crop.

must every year increase, especially if our prosperity increases. For, just in proportion as wealth rolls in upon us, the number of those, who will give up their own independent homes to serve strangers, will be diminished.

The difficulties and sufferings, which have accrued to American women, from this cause, are almost incalculable. There is nothing, which so much demands system and regularity, as the affairs of a housekeeper, made up, as they are, of ten thousand desultory and minute items; and yet, this perpetually fluctuating state of society seems forever to bar any such system and regularity. The anxieties, vexations, perplexities, and even hard labor, which come upon American women, from this state of domestic service, are endless; and many a woman has, in consequence, been disheartened, discouraged, and ruined in health. The only wonder is, that, amid so many real difficulties, American women are still able to maintain such a character for energy, fortitude, and amiableness, as is universally allowed to be their due.

But the second, and still greater difficulty, peculiar to American women, is, a delicacy of constitution, which renders them early victims to disease and decay.

The fact that the women of this Country are unusually subject to disease, and that their beauty and youthfulness are of shorter continuance than those of the women of other nations, is one which always attracts the attention of foreigners; while medical men and philanthropists are constantly giving fearful monitions as to the extent and alarming increase of this evil. Investigations make it evident, that a large proportion of young ladies, from the wealthier classes, have the incipient stages of curvature of the spine, one of the most sure and fruitful causes of future disease and decay. The writer has heard medical men, who have made extensive inquiries, say, that a very large proportion of the young women at boarding schools, are affected in this way, while many other indications of disease and debility exist, in cases where this particular evil cannot be detected.

In consequence of this enfeebled state of their constitutions, induced by a neglect of their physical education, as soon as they are called to the responsibilities and trials of domestic life, their constitution fails, and their whole existence is rendered a burden. For no woman can enjoy existence, when disease throws a dark cloud over the mind, and incapacitates her for the proper discharge of every duty.

The writer, who for some ten years has had the charge of an institution, consisting of young ladies from almost every State in the Union, since relinquishing that charge, has travelled and visited extensively in most of the non-slaveholding States. In these circuits, she has learned the domestic history, not merely of her pupils, but of many other young wives and mothers, whose sorrowful experience has come to her knowledge. And the impression, produced by the dreadful extent of this evil, has at times been almost overwhelming.

It would seem as if the primeval curse, which has written the doom of pain and sorrow on one period of a young mother's life, in this Country had been extended over all; so that the hour never arrives, when "she forgetteth her sorrow for joy that a man is born into the world." Many a mother will testify, with shuddering, that the most exquisite sufferings she ever endured, were not those appointed by Nature, but those, which, for week after week, have worn down health and spirits, when nourishing her child. And medical men teach us, that this, in most cases, results from a debility of constitution, consequent on the mismanagement of early life. And so frequent and so mournful are these, and the other distresses that result from the delicacy of the female constitution, that the writer has repeatedly heard mothers say, that they had wept tears of bitterness over their infant daughters, at the thought of the sufferings which they were destined to undergo; while they cherished the decided wish, that these daughters should never marry. At the same time, many a reflecting young woman is looking to her future prospects, with very different feelings and hopes from those which Providence designed.

A perfectly healthy woman, especially a perfectly healthy mother, is so unfrequent, in some of the wealthier classes, that those, who are so, may be regarded as the exceptions, and not as the general rule. The writer has heard some of her friends declare, that they would ride fifty miles, to see a perfectly healthy and vigorous woman, out of the laboring classes. This, although somewhat jocose, was not an entirely unfair picture of the true state of female health in the wealthier classes.

There are many causes operating, which tend to perpetuate and increase this evil. It is a well-known fact, that mental excitement tends to weaken the physical system, unless it is counterbalanced by a corresponding increase of exercise and fresh air. Now, the people of this Country are under the influence of high commercial, political, and religious stimulus, altogether greater than was ever known by any other nation; and in all this, women are made the sympathizing companions of the other sex. At the same time, young girls, in pursuing an education, have ten times greater an amount of intellectual taxation demanded, than was ever before exacted. Let any daughter, educated in our best schools at this day, compare the course of her study with that pursued in her mother's early life, and it will be seen that this estimate of the increase of mental taxation probably falls below the truth. Though, in some countries, there are small classes of females, in the higher circles, who pursue literature and science to a far greater extent than in any corresponding circles in this Country, yet, in no nation in the world are the advantages of a good intellectual education enjoyed, by so large a proportion of the females. And this education has consisted far less of accomplishments, and far more of those solid studies which demand the exercise of the various powers of mind, than the education of the women of other lands.

And when American women are called to the responsibilities of domestic life, the degree in which their minds and feelings are taxed, is altogether greater than it is in any other nation.

No women on earth have a higher sense of their moral and religious responsibilities, or better understand, not only what is demanded of them, as housekeepers, but all the claims that rest upon them as wives, mothers, and members of a social community. An American woman, who is the mistress of a family, feels her obligations, in reference to her influence over her husband, and a still greater responsibility in rearing and educating her children. She feels, too, the claims which the moral interests of her domestics have on her watchful care. In social life, she recognises the claims of hospitality, and the demands of friendly visiting.[4] Her responsibility, in reference to the institutions of benevolence and religion, is deeply realized. The regular worship of the Lord's day, and all the various religious meetings and benevolent societies which place so much dependence on female influence and example, she feels obligated to sustain. Add to these multiplied responsibilities, the perplexities and evils which have been pointed out, resulting from the fluctuating state of society, and the deficiency of domestic service, and no one can deny that American women are exposed to a far greater amount of intellectual and

---

[4] *demands of friendly visiting:* Middle-class women were expected to make philanthropic or charitable visits to working-class families in order to minister to their needs and to impart the spirit of benevolence and middle-class values in the tenements and slums.

moral excitement, than those of any other land. Of course, in order to escape the danger resulting from this, a greater amount of exercise in the fresh air, and all those methods which strengthen the constitution, are imperiously required.

But, instead of this, it will be found, that, owing to the climate and customs of this Nation, there are no women who secure so little of this healthful and protecting regimen, as ours. Walking and riding and gardening, in the open air, are practised by the women of other lands, to a far greater extent, than by American females. Most English women, in the wealthier classes, are able to walk six and eight miles, without oppressive fatigue; and when they visit this Country, always express their surprise at the inactive habits of American ladies. In England, regular exercise, in the open air, is very commonly required by the mother, as a part of daily duty, and is sought by young women, as an enjoyment. In consequence of a different physical training, English women, in those circles which enjoy competency, present an appearance which always strikes American gentlemen as a contrast to what they see at home. An English mother, at thirty, or thirty-five, is in the full bloom of perfected womanhood; as fresh and healthful as her daughters. But where are the American mothers, who can reach this period unfaded and unworn? In America, young ladies of the wealthier classes are sent to school from early childhood; and neither parents nor teachers make it a definite object to secure a proper amount of fresh air and exercise, to counterbalance this intellectual taxation. As soon as their school days are over, dressing, visiting, evening parties, and stimulating amusements, take the place of study, while the most unhealthful modes of dress add to the physical exposures. To make morning calls, or do a little shopping, is all that can be termed their exercise in the fresh air; and this, compared to what is needed, is absolutely nothing, and on some accounts is worse than nothing.[5] In consequence of these, and other evils, which will be pointed out more at large in the following pages, the young women of America grow up with such a delicacy of constitution, that probably eight out of ten become subjects of disease, either before or as soon as they are called to the responsibilities of domestic life. . . .

---

[5] So little idea have most ladies, in the wealthier classes, of what is a proper amount of exercise, that, if they should succeed in walking a mile or so, at a moderate pace, three or four times a week, they would call it taking a great deal of exercise. [Beecher's note.]

Remedies for the Preceding Difficulties

Having pointed out the peculiar responsibilities of American women, and the peculiar embarrassments which they are called to encounter, the following suggestions are offered, as remedies for their difficulties.

In the first place, the physical and domestic education of daughters should occupy the principal attention of mothers, in childhood; and the stimulation of the intellect should be very much reduced. As a general rule, daughters should not be sent to school before they are six years old; and when they are sent, far more attention should be paid to their physical development, than is usually done. They should never be confined, at any employment, more than an hour at a time; and this confinement should be followed by sports in the open air. Such accommodations should be secured, that, at all seasons, and in all weathers, the teacher can every half hour send out a portion of her school, for sports. And still more care should be given to preserve pure air in the schoolroom. The close stoves, crowded condition, and poisonous air, of most schoolrooms, act as constant drains on the health and strength of young children.

In addition to this, much less time should be given to school, and much more to domestic employments, especially in the wealthier classes. A little girl may begin, at five or six years of age, to assist her mother; and, if properly trained, by the time she is ten, she can render essential aid. From this time, until she is fourteen or fifteen, it should be the principal object of her education to secure a strong and healthy constitution, and a thorough practical knowledge of all kinds of domestic employments. During this period, though some attention ought to be paid to intellectual culture, it ought to be made altogether secondary in importance; and such a measure of study and intellectual excitement, as is now demanded in our best female seminaries, ought never to be allowed, until a young lady has passed the most critical period of her youth, and has a vigorous and healthful constitution fully established. The plan might be adopted, of having schools for young girls kept only in the afternoon; that their mornings might be occupied in domestic exercise, without interfering with school employments. Where a proper supply of domestic exercise cannot be afforded, the cultivation of flowers and fruits might be resorted to, as a delightful and unfailing promotive of pleasure and health.

And it is to that class of mothers, who have the best means of securing hired service, and who are the most tempted to allow their daughters to grow up with inactive habits, that their Country and the world must look for a reformation, in this respect. Whatever ladies in the wealthier classes decide shall be fashionable, will be followed by all the rest; but, while they persist in the aristocratic habits, now so common, and bring up their daughters to feel as if labor was degrading and unbecoming, the evils pointed out will never find a remedy. It is, therefore, the peculiar duty of ladies, who have wealth, to set a proper example, in this particular, and make it their first aim to secure a strong and healthful constitution for their daughters, by active domestic employments. All the sweeping, dusting, care of furniture and beds, the clear starching, and the nice cooking, should be done by the daughters of a family, and not by hired servants. It may cost the mother more care, and she may find it needful to hire a person for the express purpose of instructing and superintending her daughters, in these employments; but it should be regarded as indispensable to be secured, either by the mother's agency, or by a substitute.

It is in this point of view, that the dearth of good domestics in this Country may, in its results, prove a substantial blessing. If all housekeepers, who have the means, could secure good servants, there would be little hope that so important a revolution, in the domestic customs of the wealthy classes, could be effected. And so great is the natural indolence of mankind, that the amount of exercise, needful for health, will never be secured by those who are led to it through no necessity, but merely from rational considerations. Yet the pressure of domestic troubles, from the want of good domestics, has already determined many a mother, in the wealthy classes, to train her daughters to aid her in domestic service; and thus necessity is compelling mothers to do what abstract principles of expediency could never secure.

A second method of promoting the same object, is, to raise the science and practice of Domestic Economy to its appropriate place, as a regular study in female seminaries. The succeeding chapter will present the reasons for this, more at large. But it is to the mothers of our Country, that the community must look for this change. It cannot be expected, that teachers, who have their attention chiefly absorbed by the intellectual and moral interests of their pupils, should properly realize the importance of this department of education. But if mothers generally become convinced of this, their judgement and wishes will meet the respectful consideration they deserve, and the object will be accomplished.

SUSAN POWER

From The Ugly-Girl Papers

One of a multitude of late-nineteenth-century beauty manuals for women, *The Ugly-Girl Papers; or, Hints For the Toilet* (first published in "Harper's Bazar") argues that women cannot be beautiful for others unless they master beauty for themselves; to that end, the American woman's goal must be to "be pleased with herself." A woman of thirty, Susan Power observes, may lay claim to beauty — achieving physical and spiritual refinement — if she follows advice ranging from eating food to "cool the blood" to getting exercise that "relieves the nerves." Such advice is intended to increase "a woman's value," which, for Powers, "depends entirely on her use to the world and to that person who happens to have the most of her society." Powers warns prospective mothers about such potential problems as the coincidence of biting infants and breast cancer. Undertaking childrearing after reading such admonitions would be a terrifying process indeed. In another chapter, <u>Powers argues that</u> <u>"writing women" are especially susceptible to madness and depravity.</u> The text of the following excerpt is taken from *The Ugly-Girl Papers; or, Hints for the Toilet* (New York: Harper, 1874), 9–21; 224–37; 247–56.

[handwritten margin note: that seems true of all writers, actually.]

Chapter I

Woman's Business to be Beautiful. — How to Acquire a Clear Complexion. — Regimen for Purity of the Blood. — Carbonate of Ammonia and Powdered Charcoal. — Stippled Skins. — Face Masks. — Oily Complexions. — Irritations of the Skin. — Lettuce as a Cosmetic. — Cooling Drinks. — Sun Baths. — Bread and Molasses.

The first requisite in a woman toward pleasing others is that she should be pleased with herself. In no other way can she attain that self-poise, that satisfaction, which leaves her at liberty to devote herself successfully to others.

I appeal to the ugly sisterhood to know if this is not so. Could a woman be made to believe herself beautiful, it would go far toward making her so. Those hopeless, shrinking souls, alive with devotion and imagination, with hearts as fit to make passionate and worshiped lovers, or steadfast and inspiring heroines, as the fairest Venus of the

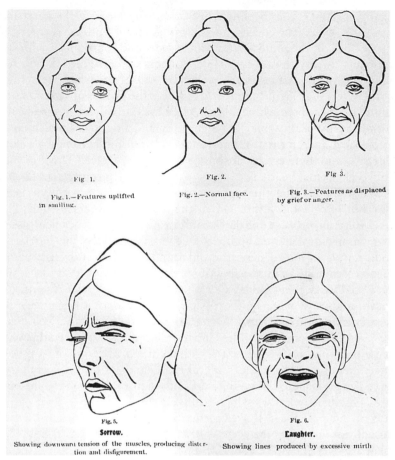

Fig. 1.

Fig. 1.—Features uplifted in smiling.

Fig. 2.

Fig. 2.—Normal face.

Fig 3.

Fig. 3.—Features as displaced by grief or anger.

Fig. 5.

Sorrow.

Showing downward tension of the muscles, producing distortion and disfigurement.

Fig. 6.

Laughter.

Showing lines produced by excessive mirth

"The Influence of Thought Upon Beauty." From *The Attainment of Womanly Beauty of Form and Features,* edited by Albert Turner (1890).

sex, need not for an instant believe there is no alleviation for their case, no chance of making face and figure more attractive and truer exponents of the spirit within.

There is scarcely any thing in the history of women more touching than the homage paid to beauty by those who have it not. No slave among her throng of adorers appreciated more keenly the beauty of Récamier[1] than the skeleton-like, irritable Madame De

[1] *Récamier:* Jeanne Francois Récamier (1777–1849), French society beauty and salon-wit.

Chateaubriand.[2] The loveliness of a rival eats into a girl's heart like corrosion; every fair curling hair, every grace of outline, is traced in lines of fire on the mind of the plainer one, and reproduced with microscopic fidelity. It is a woman's business to be beautiful. She recommends every virtue and heroism by the grace which sets them forth. Women of genius are the first to lay the crown of womanhood on the head of the most beautiful. Mere fashion of face and form are not meant by beauty, but that symmetry and brightness which come of physical and spiritual refinement. Such are the heroines of Scott, Disraeli, and Bulwer,[3] as inspiring as they are rare. Toward such ideals all women yearn.

Who will say that this most natural feeling of the feminine heart may not have some fulfillment in the first thirty years of life? This limit is given because the latest authorities in social science[4] assert that woman's prime of youth is twenty-six, moving the barriers a good ten years ahead from the old standard of the novelist, whose heroines are always in the dew of sixteen. In the very first place, one may boldly say that beauty, or rather fascination, is not a matter of youth, and no woman ought to sigh over her years till she feels the frost creeping into her heart. Men of the world understand well that a woman's wit is finest, and her heart yields the richest wealth, when experience has formed the fair and colorless material of youth. A sweet girl of seventeen and a high-bred beauty of thirty, if well preserved, may dispute the palm. I do not mean to decry rose-buds and dew. One hardly knows which to love them for most — their loveliness or their briefness. But women who look their thirties in the face should not lay down the sceptre of life, or fancy that its delights for them are over. They are young while they seem young.

Then we may boldly set about renovating the outward form, sure that Nature will respond to our efforts. The essence of beauty is health; but all apparently healthy people are not fair. The type of the system must be considered in treatment. The brunette is usually built up of much iron, and the bilious secretion is sluggish. The blonde is

---

[2] *Madame De Chateaubriand:* Celebrated wife of early-nineteenth-century French politician and ambassador.

[3] *Scott, Disraeli, Bulwer:* Sir Walter Scott (1771–1832), Benjamin Disraeli (1804–1881), and Edward Bulwer-Lytton (1803–1873), popular nineteenth-century British novelists.

[4] *latest authorities in social science:* Due to rapid industrialization after the Civil War and Reconstruction, social science as a discipline of study enjoyed success in modern universities, which attempted to disrupt the sway that religion had held over American culture until then.

apt to be dyspeptic, and subject to disturbances of the blood. From these causes result freckles, pimples, and that coarse, indented skin *stippled* with punctures, like the tissue of pig-skin — a fault of many otherwise clear complexions.

The fairest skins belong to people in the earliest stage of consumption,[5] or those of a scrofulous[6] nature. This miraculous clearness and brilliance is due to the constant purgation which wastes the consumptive, or to the issue which relieves the system of impurities by one outlet. We must secure purity of the blood by less exhaustive methods. The diet should be regulated according to the habit of the person. If stout, she should eat as little as will satisfy her appetite; never allowing herself, however, to rise from the table hungry. A few days' resolute denial will show how much really is needed to keep up the strength. When recovering from severe nervous prostration, years ago, the writer found her appetite gone. The least morsel satisfied hunger, and more produced a repugnance she never tried to overcome. She resumed study six hours a day and walked two miles every day from the suburbs to the centre of the city, and back again. Breakfast usually was a small saucer of strawberries and one Graham cracker, and was not infrequently dispensed with altogether. Lunch was half an orange — for the burden of eating the other half was not to be thought of; and at six o'clock a handful of cherries formed a plentiful dinner. Once a week she did crave something like beef-steak or soup, and took it. But, guiding herself wholly by appetite, she found with surprise that her strength remained steady, her nerves grew calm, and her ability to study was never better. This is no rule for any one, farther than to say persons of well-developed physique need not fear any limitation of diet for a time which does not tell on the strength and is approved by appetite. Never eat too much; never go hungry.

For weak digestion nothing is so relished or strengthens so much as the rich beef tea, or rather gravy, prepared from the beef-jelly sold by first-rate grocers. This is very different from the extracts of beef made by chemists. The condensed beef prepared by the same companies which send out the condensed milk is preferable, in all respects, as to taste and nourishment. A table-spoonful of this jelly, dissolved by pouring a cup of boiling water on it, and drank when cool, will give as much strength as three fourths of a pound of beef-steak

---

[5] *consumption:* A progressive wasting away of the body due to pulmonary tuberculosis, often presumed in the nineteenth century to have moral dimensions.
[6] *scrofulous:* Affected with tuberculosis or swelling of the lymph nodes.

broiled. For singers and students, who need a light but strengthening diet, nothing is so admirable.

Nervous people, and sanguine ones, should adopt a diet of eggs, fish, soups, and salads, with fruit. This cools the blood, and leaves the strength to supply the nerves instead of taxing them to digest heavy preparations. Lymphatic people should especially prefer such lively salads as cress, pepper-grass, horseradish, and mustard. These are nature's correctives, and should appear on the table from March to November, to be eaten not merely as relishes, but as stimulating and beneficial food. They stir the blood, and clear the eye and brain from the humors of spring. Nervous people should be more sparing of these fiery delights, and eat abundantly of golden lettuce, which contains opium in its most delicate and least injurious state. The question of fat meat does not seem satisfactorily settled. I should compound by using rich soups which contain the essence of meats, and supply carbon by salad oil and a free use of nuts or cream. Plump, fair people may let oily matters of all kinds carefully alone. Thin ones should eat vegetables — if they can find a cook who knows how to make them palatable. It is strange that in this country, which produces the finest vegetables, fit for the envy of foreign cooks, not one out of a hundred knows how to prepare them properly. People who are anxious to be rid of flesh should choose acids, lemons, limes, and tamarinds, eat sparingly of dry meats, with crackers instead of bread, and follow strictly the advice now given.

To clear the complexion or reduce the size, the blood must be carefully cleansed. Two simple chemicals should appear on every toilet-table — the carbonate of ammonia and powdered charcoal. No cosmetic has more frequent uses than these. The ammonia must be kept in glass, with a glass stopper, from the air. French charcoal is preferred by physicians, as it is more finely ground, and a large bottle of it should be kept on hand. In cases of debility and all wasting disorders it is valuable. To clear the complexion, take a tea-spoonful of charcoal well mixed in water or honey for three nights, then use a simple purgative to remove it from the system. It acts like calomel,[7] with no bad effects, purifying the blood more effectually than any thing else. But some simple aperient[8] must not be omitted, or the charcoal will remain in the system, a mass of festering poison, with all the impurities it absorbs. After

[7] *calomel:* Also called "blue pills"; a compound (mercurous chloride) used as a purgative and fungicide and as a remedy for syphilis and cholera.
[8] *aperient:* A medicine or food acting as a mild laxative.

this course of purification, tonics may be used. Many people seem not to know that protoxide of iron, medicated wine, and "bracing" medicines are useless when the impurities remain in the blood. The use of charcoal is daily better understood by our best physicians, and it is powerful, and simple enough to be handled by every household. The purifying process, unless the health is unusually good, must be repeated every three months. We absorb in bad food and air more unprofitable matter than nature can throw off in that time. If diet and atmosphere were perfect, no such aid would be needed; but it is the choice between a very great and a small evil in existing conditions. A free use of tomatoes and figs is, by the way, recommended, to maintain a healthy condition of the stomach, and the seeds of either should *not* be discarded.

The most troublesome task is to refine a *stippled* skin whose oil-glands are large and coarse. There may not be a pimple or freckle on the face, and the temples may be smooth, but the nose and cheeks look like a pin-cushion from which the pins have just been drawn. Patience and many applications are necessary, for one must, in fact, renew the skin.

The worst face may be softened by wearing a mask of quilted cotton wet in cold water at night. Roman ladies used poultices of bread and asses' milk for the same purpose; but water, and especially distilled water, is all that is needful. A small dose of taraxacum[9] every other night will assist in refining the skin. But it will be at least a six weeks' work to effect the desired change; and it will be a zealous girl who submits to the discomfort of the mask for that length of time. The result pays. The compress acts like a mild but imperceptible blister, and leaves a new skin, soft as an infant's. Bathing oily skins with camphor dries the oil somewhat, when the camphor would parch nice complexions. The opium found in the stalks of flowering lettuce refines the skin singularly, and may be used clear, instead of the soap which sells so high. Rub the milky juice collected from broken stems of coarse garden lettuce over the face at night, and wash with a solution of ammonia in the morning.

Blondes who are unbeautiful are apt to have divers irritations of the skin, which their darker neighbors do not know. People of this type also have a tendency to acid stomachs, the antidote for which is a dose of ammonia, say one quarter of a spoonful in half a glass of water, taken every night and morning. This also prevents decay of the

[9] *taraxacum:* Parts of a dandelion used as a diuretic, tonic, and laxative.

teeth and sweetens the breath, and is less injurious than the soda and magnesia many ladies use for acid stomachs. In summer the system should be kept cool by bathing at night and morning, and by tart drinks containing cream of tartar. Small quantities of nitre,[10] prescribed by the physician, may be taken by very sanguine persons who suffer with heat; but pale complexions should seek the sun when its power is not too great, and be careful, of all things, to avoid a chill. This deadens the skin, paints blue circles round the eyes, and leaves the hands an uncertain color.

These precautions may seem burdensome, but they all have been practiced by those who prize beauty. Nothing is so attractive, so suggestive of purity of mind and excellence of body, as a clear, fine-grained skin. Strong color is not desirable. Tints, rather than colors, best please the refined eye in the complexion. Some mothers are so anxious to secure this grace for their daughters that they are kept on the strictest diet from childhood. The most dazzling Parian[11] could not be more beautiful than the cheek of a child I once saw who was kept on oat-meal porridge for this effect. At a boarding-school, I remember, a fashionable mother gave strict injunctions that her daughter should touch nothing but brown bread and syrup. This was hard fare; but the carmine lips and magnolia brow of the young lady were the envy of her shoolmates, who, however, were not courageous enough to attempt such a régime for themselves.

Chapter XXII

Physical Education of Girls. — A Woman's Value in the World. — High-bred Figures. — Antique Races. — Inspiration of Art not Vanity. — The Trying Age. — Dress, Food, and Bathing for Young Girls. — A Veto on Close Study. — Braces and Backboards. — Never Talk of Girls' Feelings. — Exercise for the Arms. — Singing Scales with Corsets off. — Development of the Bust. — Open-work Corsets the Best. — The Bayaderes[12] of India and their Forms. — The Delicacy due Young Girls. — A Frank but Needed Caution. — Care of the Figure after Nursing.

American girls begin to make much of physical culture. As they advance in refinement they see how much of their value in society de-

---

[10] *nitre:* Saltpetre, a diuretic with an unsupported reputation of being an aphrodisiac.
[11] *Parian:* Marble from the island of Paros, often used in ancient statues.
[12] *Bayaderes:* Nineteenth-century French term for Hindu dancing girls.

pends on the nerve and spirit which accompanies thorough development. It is not enough that they know how to dance languidly, and
carry themselves in company. To distinguish herself, a young belle
must row, swim, skate, ride, and even shoot, to say nothing of lessons
in fencing, which noble ladies in Germany, and some of foreign family here, take to develop sureness of hand and agility. The heavy, flat-
footed creature who can not walk across a room without betraying
the bad terms her joints are on with each other, must have a splendid
face and fortune to keep any place in the world, no matter how good
her family, or how varied her acquirements, though she speaks seven
languages like a native, and has played sonatas since she was eight
years old. A woman's value depends entirely on her use to the world
and to that person who happens to have the most of her society. A
man likes the society of a woman who can walk a mile or two to see
an interesting view, and can take long journeys without being laid up
by them. He likes smooth motions, round arms and throat, head held
straight, and shoulders that do not bow out. When you see that a fine
figure must be a straight line from the roots of the hair to the base of
the shoulderblade, you will realize how few women approach this
high-bred ideal. Special culture, indeed, is discerned where such excellence of line meets the eye. The polished races of the East, who,
untutored and degraded, yet have the entail of antique subtlety and
art, inherit such figures along with the proverbs of sages and palace
mosaics. The best-born of all countries have this noble set of head,
this lance-like figure, and easy play of limb. As surely as one can be
educated to right thoughts and manners, so the motions and poise of
limb can be trained to correctness. The work must begin early. A girl
should be put in training as soon as she passes from the plumpness of
childhood into the ugly age of development. The mother should in-
spect her dressing to see what improvement is needed, and stimulate
the child by the desire to possess beautiful limbs and figure. The
senses are early awake to the sense of grace. There is no better way to
inspire a girl with it than to take her to picture-galleries, show the
faces of historical beauties, or the figures of Italian sculpture, and ask
her if she would not like to have the same fine points herself. This
substitutes the love of art for that of admiration, and makes self-
cultivation too deep a thing for vanity.

There is a time when girls are awkward, indolent, and capricious.
Their boisterous spirits at one time, their sickly minauderies[13] at

---

[13] *minauderies:* Coquettish, affected behavior.

another, are very trying to mothers and teachers. The cause is often set down as depravity, when it is only nature. Girls are lapsided[14] and indolent because they are weak or languid, between which and being lazy there is a vast difference. They have demanding appetites that strike grown people with wonder. They go frantic on short notice when their wishes are crossed. Mother, if such is the case, your growing girl is weak. The nursery bath Saturday night is not enough. Encourage her to take a sponge-bath every day. When she comes in heated from a long walk or play, see that she bathes her knees, elbows, and feet in cold water, to prevent her growing nervous with fatigue when the excitement is over. See that she does not suffer from cold, and that she is not too warmly dressed, remembering a plump, active child will suffer with heat under the clothes it takes to keep you comfortable. If she is thin and sensitive, care must be taken against sudden chills. Keep her on very simple but well-flavored diet, with plenty of sour fruit, if she crave it, for the young have a facility for growing bilious, which acids correct. Sweet-pickles not too highly spiced are favorites with children, and better than sweetmeats. Nuts and raisins are more wholesome than candies. New cheese and cream are to be preferred to butter with bread and vegetables. Soup and a little of the best and juiciest meat should be given at dinner. But the miscellaneous stuffing that half-grown girls are allowed to indulge in ruins their complexion, temper, and digestion. No coffee nor tea should be taken by any human being till it is full-grown. The excitement of young nerves by these drinks is ruinous. Besides, the luxury and the stimulus is greater to the adult when debarred from these things through childhood. Neither mind nor body should be worked till maturity. Children will do all they ought in study and work without much urging; and they will learn more and remember more in two hours of study to five of play, than if the order is inverted. Say to a child, Get this lesson and you may go to play — and you will be astonished to see how rapidly it learns; but if one lesson is to succeed another till six dreary hours have dragged away, it loses heart, and learns merely what can not well be helped. A girl under eighteen ought not to practice at the piano or sit at a desk more than three quarters of an hour at a time. Then she should run out-of-doors ten minutes, or exercise, to relieve the nerves. An adult never ought to study or sit more than an hour without brief change before passing to the next. This keeps the head clearer, the limbs fresher, and carries

[14] *lapsided:* Lopsided, *naut.* unevenly balanced.

one through a day with less fatigue than if one worked eight hours and then rested four.

Thoughtful teachers do not share the prejudice against braces and backboards for keeping the figure straight, especially when young. It is the instinct of barbarous nations to use such aids in compelling erectness in their children. These appliances need not be painful in the least, but rather relieve tender muscles and bones. Languid girls should take cool sitz-baths[15] to strengthen the muscles of the back and hips, which are more than ordinarily susceptible of fatigue when childhood is over. But *never* talk of a girl's feelings in mind or body before her, or suffer her to dwell on them. The effect is bad physically and mentally. See that these injunctions are obeyed implicitly; spare her the whys and wherefores. It is enough for her to know that she will feel better for them. Of all things, deliver us from valetudinarians of fifteen. Never laugh at them; never sneer; never indulge them in self-condolings. Be pitiful and sympathetic, but steadily turn their attention to something interesting outside of themselves.

Special means are essential to special growth. Throwing quoits[16] and sweeping are good exercises to develop the arms. There is nothing like three hours of house-work a day for giving a woman a good figure, and if she sleep in tight cosmetic gloves, she need not fear that her hands will be spoiled. The time to form the hands is in youth, and with thimbles for the finger-tips, and close gloves lined with cold cream, every mother might secure a good hand for her daughter. She should be particular to see that long-wristed lisle-thread gloves are drawn on every time the girl goes out. Veils she should discard, except in cold and windy weather, when they should be drawn close over the head. A broad-leafed hat for the country is protection enough for the summer; the rest of the year the complexion needs all the sun it can get.

There is commonly a want of fullness in those muscles of the shoulder which give its graceful slope. This is developed by the use of the skipping-rope, in swinging it over the head, and by battledoor, which keeps the arms extended, at the same time using the muscles of the neck and shoulders. Swinging by the hands from a rope is capital, and so is swinging from a bar. These muscles are the last to receive exercise in common modes of life, and playing ball, bean-bags, or pillow-fights are convenient ways of calling them into action. Singing

---

[15] *sitz-bath:* Hip bath; to bathe in a sitting position.
[16] *quoits:* Flattened rings or circles of rope, used in a game.

scales with corsets off, shoulders thrown back, lungs deeply inflated, mouth wide open, and breath held, is the best tuition for insuring that fullness to the upper part of the chest which gives majesty to a figure even when the bust is meager. These scales should be practiced half an hour morning and afternoon, gaining two ends at once — increase of voice and perfection of figure.

This brings us to the inquiries made by more than one correspondent for some means of developing the bust. Every mother should pay attention to this matter before her daughters think of such a thing for themselves, by seeing that their dresses are never in the least constricted across the chest, and that a foolish dressmaker never puts padding into their waists. The horrible custom of wearing pads is the ruin of natural figures, by heating and pressing down the bosom. This most delicate and sensitive part of a woman's form must always be kept cool, and well supported by a linen corset. The open-worked ones are by far the best, and the compression, if any, should not be over the heart and fixed ribs, as it generally is, but just at the waist, for not more than the width of a broad waistband. Six inches of thick coutille[17] over the heart and stomach — those parts of the body that have most vital heat — must surely disorder them and affect the bust as well. It would be better if the coutille were over the shoulders or the abdomen, and the whalebones of the corset held together by broad tapes, so that there would be less dressing over the heart, instead of more. A low, deep bosom, rather than a bold one, is a sign of grace in a full-grown woman, and a full bust is hardly admirable in an unmarried girl. Her figure should be all curves, but slender, promising a fuller beauty when maturity is reached. One is not fond of overripe pears.

Flat figures are best dissembled by puffed and shirred blouse-waists, or by corsets with a fine rattan run in the top of the bosom gore, which throws out the fullness sufficiently to look well in a plain corsage. Of all things, India-rubber pads act most injuriously by constantly sweating the skin, and ruining the bust beyond hope of restoration. To improve its outlines, wear a linen corset fitting so close at the end of the top gores as to support the bosom well. For this the corset must be fitted to the skin, and worn next the under-flannel. Night and morning wash the bust in the coldest water — sponging it upward, but never down. Madame Celnart relates that

---

[17] *coutille:* A close-woven canvas material, used in stays and corsets.

the bayaderes of India cultivate their forms by wearing a cincture of linen under the breasts, and, at night chafing them lightly with a piece of linen. The breasts should never be touched but with the utmost delicacy, as other treatment renders them weak and flaccid, and not unfrequently results in cancer. A baby's bite has more than once inflicted this disease upon its mother. But one thing is to be solemnly cautioned, that no human being — doctor, nurse, nor the mother herself — on any pretense, save in case of accident, be allowed to touch a girl's figure. It would be unnecessary to say this, were not French and Irish nurses, especially old and experienced ones, sometimes in the habit of stroking the figures of young girls committed to their charge, with the idea of developing them. This is not mentioned from hearsay. Mothers can not be too careful how they leave their children with even well-meaning servants. A young girl's body is more sensitive than any harp is to the air that plays upon it. Nature — free, uneducated, and direct — responds to every touch on that seat of the nerves, the bosom, by an excitement that is simply ruinous to a child's nervous system. This is pretty plain talking, but no plainer than the subject demands. Girls are very different in their feelings. Some affectionate, innocent, hearty natures remain through their lives as simple as when they were babes taking their bath under their mothers' hands; while others, equally innocent but more susceptible, require to be guarded and sheltered even from the violence of a caress as if from contagion and pain.

Due attention to the general health always has its effect in restoring the bust to its roundness. It is a mistake that it is irremediably injured by nursing children. A babe may be taught not to pinch and bite its mother, and the exercise of a natural function can injure her in no way, if proper care is taken to sustain the system at the same time. Cold compresses of wet linen worn over the breast are very soothing and beneficial, provided they do not strike a chill to a weak chest. At the same time, the cincture should be carefully adjusted. Weakness of any kind affects the contour of the figure, and it is useless to try to improve it in any other way than by restoring the strength where it is wanting. Tepid sitz-baths strengthen the muscles of the hips, and do away with that dragging which injures the firmness of the bosom. Bathing in water to which ammonia is added strengthens the skin, but the use of camphor to dry the milk after weaning a child is reprehensible. No drying or heating lotions of any kind should ever be applied except in illness.

Chapter XXIV

*Women's Looks and Nerves. — A Low-toned Generation. —
Children and their Ways. — Brief Madness. — Women in the
Woods. — Singing. — Work well done the Easiest. — Sleep the
Remedy for Temper. — Hours for Sleep. — The Great Medicines. —
Sunshine, Music, Work, and Sleep.*

Women's looks depend too much on the state of their nerves and
their peace of mind to pass them over. The body at best is the perfect
expression of the soul. The latter may light wasted features to brilliance, or turn a face of milk and roses dark with passion or dead
with dullness; it may destroy a healthy frame or support a failing one.
Weak nerves may prove too much for the temper of St. John, and
break down the courage of Saladin.[18] Better things are before us,
coming from a fuller appreciation of the needs of body and soul, but
the fact remains that this is a generation of weak nerves. It shows
particularly in the low tone of spirits common to men and women.
They can not bear sunshine in their houses; they find the colors of
Jacques Minot roses[19] and of Gérome's pictures[20] too deep; the waltz
in *Traviata* is too brilliant, Rossini's music is too sensuous, and Wagner's too sensational; Mendelssohn is too light, Beethoven too cold.[21]
Their work is fuss; instead of resting, they idle — and there is a wide
difference between the two things. People who drink strong tea and
smoke too many cigars, read or stay in-doors too much, find the hum
of creation too loud for them. The swell of the wind in the pines
makes them gloomy, the sweep of the storm prostrates them with terror, the everlasting beating of the surf and the noises of the streets
alike weary their worthless nerves. The happy cries of school-children
at play are a grievance to them; indeed, there are people who find the

[18] *temper of St. John, and . . . courage of Saladin:* John and his brother James, two
of the twelve disciples, were both nicknamed "sons of thunder" (Mark 3:17) because
of their tempers. Saladin was a twelfth-century Kurdish general who became legendary
for his military accomplishments and generosity.
[19] *Jacques Minot roses:* Variety of classic rose, noted for clear red, shapely pointed
buds, opening to well-formed, perfumed flowers. Also known as General Jacques-
minot, or General Jack, or Jack Rose.
[20] *Gérome's pictures:* Jean-Léon Gérôme (1824–1904), French painter of decorative and erotic subjects.
[21] *Traviata . . . too cold: La Traviata* is the most famous opera by Italian composer
Giuseppe Verdi (1813–1901); Gioacchino Rossini (1792–1868), leading composer of
Italian opera in the early nineteenth century; Wilhelm Richard Wagner (1813–1883),
nineteenth-century German composer of dramatic operas; Felix Mendelssohn
(1809–1847), nineteenth-century composer and performer; the famous German composer Ludwig von Beethoven (1770–1827) wrote both classic and romantic works.

chirp of the hearth cricket and the singing tea-kettle intolerable. But it is a sign of diseased nerves. Nature is full of noises, and only where death reigns is there silence. One wishes that the men and women who can't bear a child's voice, a singer's practice, or the passing of feet up and down stairs might be transported to silence like that which wraps the poles or the spaces beyond the stars, till they could learn to welcome sound, without which no one lives.

Children must make noise, and a great deal of it, to be healthy. The shouts, the racket, the tumble and turmoil they make, are nature's way of ventilating their bodies, of sending the breath full into the very last corner of the lungs, and the blood and nervous fluid into every cord and fibre of their muscles. Instead of quelling their riot, it would be a blessing to older folks to join it with them. There is an awful truth following this assertion. Do you know that men and women go mad after the natural stimulus which free air and bounding exercise supply? It is the lack of this most powerful inspiration, which knows no reaction, that makes them drunkards, gamesters, and flings them into every dissipation of body and soul. Men and women, especially those leading studious, repressed lives, often confess to a longing for some fierce, brief madness that would unseat the incubus of their lives. Clergymen, editors, writing women, and those who lead sedentary lives, have said in your hearing and mine that something ailed them they could not understand. They felt as if they would like to go on a spree, dance the tarantella, or scream till they were tired. They thought it the moving of some depraved impulse not yet rooted out of their natures, and to subdue it cost them hours of struggle and mortification. Poor souls! They need not have visited themselves severely if they had known the truth that this lawless longing was the cry of idle nerve and muscle, frantic through disuse. What the clergyman wanted was to leave his books and his subdued demeanor for the hill-country, for the woods, where he could not only walk, but leap, run, shout, and wrestle, and sing at the full strength of his voice. The editor needed to leave his cigar and the midnight gas-light for a wherry[22] race, or a jolly roll and tumble on the green. The woman, most of all, wanted a tent built for her on the shore, or on the dry heights of the pine forest, where she would have to take sun by day and balsamic air by night; where she would have to leap brooks, gather her own fire-wood, climb rocks, and laugh at her own mishaps. Or, if she were city-pent, she needed to take some

[22] *wherry:* Long, light rowboats; light boats such as sculls or barges.

child to the Park and play ball with it, and run as I saw an elegant girl dressed in velvet and furs run through Madison Square one winter day with her little sister. The nervous, capricious woman must be sent to swimming-school, or learn to throw quoits or jump the rope, to wrestle or to sing. There is nothing better for body and mind than learning to sing, with proper method, under a teacher who knows how to direct the force of the voice, to watch the strength, and expand the emotions at the same time. The health of many women begins to improve from the time they study music. Why? Because it furnishes an outlet for their feelings, and equally because singing exerts the lungs and muscles of the chest which lie inactive. The power for the highest as well as the lowest note is supplied by the bellows of the lungs, worked by the mighty muscles of the chest and sides. In this play the red blood goes to every tiny cell that has been white and faint for want of its food; the engorged brain and nervous centres where the blood has settled, heating and irritating them, are relieved; the head feels bright, the hands grow warm, the eyes clear, and the spirits lively. This is after singing strongly for half an hour. The same effect is gained by any other kind of brisk work that sets the lungs and muscles going, but as music brings emotion into play, and is a pleasure or a relief as it is melancholy or gay, it is preferable. The work that engages one's interest as well as strength is always the best. Per contra, whatever one does thoroughly and with dispatch seldom continues distasteful. There is more than we see at a glance in the command, "Whatsoever thy hand findeth to do, do it with thy might." The reason given, because the time is short for all the culture and all the good work we wish to accomplish, is the apparent one; but the root of it lies in the necessities of our being. Only work done with our might will satisfy our energies and keep their balance. Half the women in the world are suffering from chronic unrest, morbid ambitions, and disappointments that would flee like morning mist before an hour of hearty, tiring work.

It is not so much matter what the work is, as how it is done.

The weak should take work up by degrees, working half an hour and resting, then going at it steadily again. It is better to work a little briskly and rest than to keep on the slow drag through the day. Learn not only to do things well, but to do them quickly. It is disgraceful to loiter and drone over one's work. It is intolerable both in music and in life.

The body, like all slaves, has the power to react on its task-master. All mean passions appear born of diseased nerves. Was there ever a jealous woman who did not have dyspepsia, or a high-tempered one without a tendency to spinal irritation? Heathen tempers in young people are a sign of wrong health, and mothers should send for physician as well as priest to exorcise them. The great remedy for temper is — sleep. No child that sleeps enough will be fretful; and the same thing is nearly as true of children of larger growth. Not less than eight hours is the measure of sleep for a healthy woman under fifty. She may be able to get on with less, and do considerable work, either with mind or hands. But she could do much more, to better satisfaction, by taking one or two hours more sleep, that she can not afford to lose it. Women who use their brains — teachers, artists, writers, and housewives (whose minds are as hard wrought in overseeing a family as those of any one who works with pen or pencil) — need all the sleep they can get. From ten to six, or, for those who do not want to lose theatres and lectures altogether, from eleven to seven, are hours not to be infringed upon by women who want clear heads and steady tempers. What they gain by working at night they are sure to lose next day, or the day after. It is impossible to put the case too strongly. Unless one has taken a narcotic, and sleeps too long, one should *never* be awakened. The body rouses itself when its demands are satisfied. A warm bath on going to bed is the best aid to sleep. People often feel drowsy in the evening about eight or nine o'clock, but are wide awake at eleven. They should heed the warning. The system needs more rest than it gets, and is only able to keep up by drawing on its reserve forces. Wakefulness beyond the proper time is a sign of ill-health as much as want of appetite at meals — it is a pity that people are not as much alarmed by it. The brain is a more delicate organ than the stomach, and nothing so surely disorders it as want of sleep. In trouble or sorrow, light sedatives should be employed, like red lavender[23] or the bromate of potassa,[24] for the nerves have more to bear, and need all the rest they can get. The warm bath, I repeat, is better than either.

Sunshine, music, work, and sleep are the great medicines for women. They need more sleep than men, for they are not so strong, and their nerves perhaps are more acute. Work is the best cure for ennui and for grief. Let them sing, whether of love, longing, or sorrow, pouring out their hearts, till the love returns into their own bosoms, till the longing has spent its force, or till the sorrow has lifted itself into the sunshine, and taken the hue of trust, not of despair.

---

[23] *red lavender:* Used as a stimulant or tonic, prevents fainting and nausea.
[24] *bromate of potassa:* Potassium hydroxide, or caustic potash; used as a sedative.

JULIA AND ANNIE THOMAS

From Psycho-Physical Culture

Julia and Annie Thomas's *Psycho-Physical Culture* (1892) was one of many books to promote the values of exercise for women, including the craze for bicycling. Gilman herself profited immensely from William Blaikie's exercise manual, *How To Get Strong and How To Stay So* (1879). The Thomases advocate exercise to improve women's frailties. In their view, exercise perfects the harmony between women's bodies and souls. They present — as Gilman did in her support of women's gymnastics — a "science" of bodily movement and the "soul-force" through which women can martial their physical and mental resources. The Thomas sisters reject the definition of women's passivity or weakness as "natural"; more important, they show how women's sexual desire can be displaced onto rigorous physical activity. Their directives for healthy exercise can be contrasted with S. Weir Mitchell's advocacy of electric passive exercise (see p. 148).

The text of the following excerpt is taken from *Psycho-Physical Culture* (New York: Werner, 1892), 23–27; 228–29.

Psycho-physical culture may be defined as those exercises or movements of the body excited and sustained by soul-force, and directed by, without taxing, mental activity.

To render exercise as beneficial as possible, it should be of a nature to excite the spirits with pleasurable emotions, and to attract the mind as well as to occupy the body. The object is to employ all the muscles of the body, and to strengthen those especially which are weak. Hence exercise ought to be often varied, and always adapted to the peculiarities, and also to the state or condition of individuals.

Psycho-physical exercises for strength and grace, and for special ailments and deformities, were devised for pupils who came to the Conservatory[1] for the study of elocution, with stooping shoulders, narrow chests, protruding chins, superfluous flesh and attendant ills, and who, after practicing exercises in other systems of physical culture, were apparently little benefited. We were aware that in order to train the voice,

---

[1] *Conservatory:* Academy or institution for special instruction, such as in music or declamation (from French *Conservatoire*).

"A Correct Position for Fast Walking" from *How To Get Strong and How To Stay So* by William Blaikie (1879). The picture is of champion long-distance walker Daniel O'Leary: "with head up, shoulders well back, and working busily, and — the most noticeable thing — the whole centre of the body, from the waist to the knees, thrown, if anything, actually forward of a vertical line, instead of as far, or often much farther, back of it."

the whole body must first be put into the best possible condition. We found that pupils who "talked through their noses," as it is called, invariably turned in their toes when they walked, and with these in almost every case we found the stooping shoulders and sunken chests. Those who employed deep and harsh chest-tones lacked buoyancy of spirit and lightness of bearing. Those who used high and shrill head-tones were usually very nervous, and carried their shoulders high, or one shoulder higher than the other, and were ill from many other infirmities brought about by improper carriage. And so, after a time, we began devising special exercises for special ailments and deformities, — exercises that would not tax the brain nor weary and wear one portion of the body to the detriment of other portions. Aware of the important part the soul-force performs in exciting, sustaining, and directing muscular activity, and how difficult and inefficient muscular contraction becomes when the mind which directs it is languid, or absorbed by other ideas, and that for true and beneficial exercise there must be harmony of action between the *moving power* and the *part to be moved,* or, in other words, harmony of action between soul and body (hence the name psycho-physical), we sought for exercises that would create the most amusement and the greatest amount of mirthfulness; and so, from childhood's romps and plays we gathered some, others from work, idealized and beautified, and from the graceful movements of inanimate things, — everything to give varied and exhilarating exercise, and to excite cheerfulness and joyousness of spirit.

The great superiority of active sports as a means of exercise over mere measured movements is evident. Every kind of play interests and excites the spirit, as well as occupies the body; and by thus placing the muscles in the best position for wholesome and beneficial exertion, enables them to act without fatigue, for a length of time which, if occupied in mere measured movements, or in walking for exercise, would utterly exhaust their powers. The elastic spring, bright eye, and cheerful glow of beings thus excited form a perfect contrast to the spiritless and inanimate aspect of many of our boarding-school processions, and the result in point of health and activity is not less different. It must not, however, be supposed that a walk simply for the sake of exercise can never be beneficial. If a person be thoroughly satisfied that exercise is requisite, and is desirous to obey the call which demands it, he is from that very circumstance in a fit state for deriving benefit from it, because the desire of soul is then in perfect harmony with the muscular action.

The effect of exercise upon the organs or muscles employed is very remarkable and should be understood. When any living part is called into activity, the process of waste and renovation, which are incessantly going on in every part of the body, proceeds with greater rapidity, and in due proportion to each other. To meet this condition the vessels and nerves become excited to higher action, and the supply of arterial or nutritive blood and of nervous energy becomes greater. When the active exercise ceases, the excitement thus given to the vital function subsides, and the vessels and nerves return at length to their original state. If the exercises be resumed frequently, and at moderate intervals, the increased action of the blood-vessels and nerves becomes more permanent, and does not sink to the same low degree as formerly; *nutrition* rather *exceeds waste,* and the part gains consequently in vigor and activity. But if the exercise be resumed too often, or be carried too far, so as to fatigue and exhaust the vital powers of the part, as is often the case in heavy manual labor, or in gymnastic exercises where heavy apparatus is employed, the results become reversed; waste then exceeds nutrition, and a loss of volume and of power takes place, accompanied with a painful sense of weariness, fatigue, and exhaustion. When, on the other hand, exercise is altogether refrained from, the vital functions decay from the want of their requisite stimulus; little blood is sent to the part, and nutrition and strength fail in equal proportion. When muscular employment is neglected, the body becomes weak, dull, and unfit for powerful efforts, and all the functions languish.

When exercise is taken regularly and in due proportion, a grateful sense of activity and happiness prevails, and we feel ourselves fit for every duty, both mental and bodily. It follows, therefore, first, that, to be beneficial, exercises ought always to be proportioned to the strength and constitution, and not carried beyond the point, easily discoverable by experience, at which waste begins to exceed nutrition, and exhaustion to take the place of strength; secondly, that it ought to be regularly resumed after a sufficient interval of rest, in order to insure the permanence of the healthy impulse given to the vital powers of the muscular system; and, lastly, that it is of the utmost importance to join with it a mental and soul stimulus. . . .

No subject is so all-engrossing, so all-powerful in its influence upon the mind, affections and conduct of mankind as personal beauty. It is one of the greatest incentives to the arts and the industries of the world. It is this that keeps two-thirds of the inventive genius at work in devising methods and material for adornment, and how gigantic the systems for putting the result of the invention into the market, particularly that which goes to adorn womankind! To comprehend this, one has only to walk down the leading business avenues of our large cities and look into the shops, where is seen such an endless variety of articles and styles, from the "love of a hat" to the sweet-hued shoe; from the latest coiffure and enamel-box and other beautifiers for the human form, to the daintiest and dearest hosiery, not to mention silks, satins, plushes, etc., etc.

What a temptation all this is to one's personal pride, if not vanity, to be well dressed, to look one's best! But how at variance with the true principles and philosophy of personal beauty, and how false that education which seeks in outward adornment alone the gratification of innate or cultivated desire for beauty! Yet what can we expect when the subject is so imperfectly comprehended by the masses?

The study of physical perfection — embracing proportion, symmetry, simplicity, variety, grace, and strength, and its development — should be made a part of the curriculum of every school.

Competent judges of all civilized and cultured nations have for a long period agreed to regard the Apollo Belvedere[2] and the Venus de Medici[3] as standards of beauty for the entire human race. Although at the present time no one can be found whose physical conformation is not marked by one or more defects, yet there must have been a period in man's history when physical perfection characterized the human family. This, however, was subsequently more or less marred by over-indulgence of the passions and appetites, and the diseases and infirmities consequent thereon, which nature at every new birth endeavors to correct. The Great Architect undoubtedly intended the body to be a fitting dwelling-place for its princely occupant — the soul. But, ah! how often is this soul of ours the tenant only of a ruin, the material of which still exists in fragments, although the fair and beautiful proportions are destroyed. This person may have one portion and that another, but no one can be found in whom these glimpses of original beauty are not mixed with deformities and imperfections, the necessary consequences of wrong living. It is generally understood, however, that whatever claims to be a law or a model for living beauty must in all particulars resemble the Greek statues mentioned (Apollo and Venus).

---

[2] *Apollo Belvedere:* Marble copy of a bronze sculpture from the Hellenistic period; the most famous of the Hellenistic representations of the Greek god Apollo, now in the Vatican, it is especially noted for its aestheticization of the male body.

[3] *Venus de Medici:* Most likely a reference to the Venus de Milo, the most famous copy of which is in the Louvre Museum in Paris, France. The statue represents the goddess of love and is associated with the classicism of around 100 B.C.

MARION HARLAND

"What Shall We Do with the Mothers?"

"Marion Harland" was the pen name of Mary Virginia Terhune (1830–1922), who began writing at age nine and continued her writing career even after becoming the wife of a minister. In *Eve's Daughters, or Common Sense for Maid, Wife, and Mother* (1885), Harland argues for the home economics movement, along with women's centrality to the home. The chapter of the work that is reprinted here, "What Shall We Do with the Mothers?", describes the role of the "true mother" whose watchword is self-sacrifice and whose goal is to make her children happy. In "modern" culture, mothers become obsolete once their children are raised. Harland tries to account for a mother's place in the world once her reproductive duties are over — for the fact that the aging mother is often looked on as the last "unsightly piece of furniture" to be replaced in the new, stylish home. She appeals to the new generation to respect the self-sacrifice of mothers who seem obsolete and outdated, so that the tradition of the selfless domestic woman as ruler of the home can remain intact.

The text of the following excerpt is taken from *Eve's Daughters, or Common Sense for Maid, Wife, and Mother* (New York: Scribner, 1885), 290–302.

"The parent has, in strictest ethical sense, the first of all claims upon the child's *special benevolence; i.e.,* on his *will to do good.*"
— Frances Power Cobbe, *"Duties of Women"*[1]

The girls were coming home! Their school-days were ended; their home-life, as young ladies, was about to begin. This was the cause of the upheaval from its foundations, of the usually quiet household. The parlors were to be refurnished, the library fitted up as a music-room, where Aimée, who was musical, might practice, while Eva, who was not, entertained her friends in the apartments on the other

---

[1] *Frances Power Cobbe, "Duties of Women":* Cobbe (1822–1904), a British author, urges women who have "any margin of time or money to spare" to work in the public spirit for reform. While emphasizing women's traditional roles in this 1882 advice book (based on a course of lectures given in 1881), Cobbe recommends women's widened sphere of influence "to advance God's kingdom beyond the bounds of her home."

side of the hall. Each of the fair graduates in one sphere — the *débutantes* in another — must have her own bed-room. Hence the sewing-room on the second floor, a lightsome corner chamber heretofore devoted to mamma's work, was given up to Eva. The house that had, up to this date, seemed large to desolateness for four people, had grown suddenly almost too small.

"And where, may I ask, is mamma's nook in this stirred nest?" I ventured to ask, looking about in vain for the remembered sewing-machine, work-table, and lounging-chair.

A shadow she meant should be a smile passed over the face of my friend and hostess.

"Ah! I must show you what a snuggery[2] I have in the front basement. It is light and airy and pleasantly retired from the gay bustle that, I foresee, will fill the rest of the house. I shall be cozily comfortable there in the evenings, and during the day it is a manifest convenience to be upon the same floor with the kitchen. It was my plan throughout" — hastening to check the demur she saw hovering on my lips. "The prime object now is the girls' comfort and happiness."

"I doubt if they will agree with you. They would rather think, as I do, that the coziest, softest, prettiest place of honor should be for her who, for all these years, has spent and been spent in their service. From their birth giving has been your part. It has been all outgo. When will be the income, if not now that they are able to go alone, are able to appreciate sacrifice and endeavor, and to reward these aright and openly?"

"I ask no reward except the knowledge that they are happy," responded the true mother, softly.

The troubled smile returned. We have been friends from girlhood, and she spoke out what was in her heart.

"My day is over! As you say, they are able to go alone. Were I to drop out of their lives to-morrow, it would make no difference to them or to their brother, after the first shock was over. It is the natural lot of mothers in our day. I should be content."

She put her hand on mine impulsively.

"Don't think it blasphemous, but I know how John the Baptist felt when he said, 'He must increase, but I must decrease.'[3] Yet he loved the Lord better than he did his own life. Mine are dear, affectionate children. I am thankful that I have been permitted to rear such —

---

[2] *snuggery:* A small room; a cozy place.
[3] *John the Baptist . . . 'I must decrease':* John 3:30.

very glad and grateful! I used to pray hourly, after my early widow-hood, while they were little things about my knees, that God would spare my life until they were grown up. It came to me with a strange thrill, this morning, that I might leave that petition out *now!*"

"How old are you?" I asked abruptly, for my heart was swelling.

"Forty-seven. I was married at twenty-three."

I was silent, because indignant and impotent. This woman's mother had died at seventy, lamented by all who knew her, missed and mourned most by the sons and daughters whose pride she was. I recalled her active beneficence in neighborhood and church; her ten-der ministrations in the families of her children; her wise arbitrament in the affairs they brought to her for counsel and decision. My friend, her daughter, was morally, intellectually, and physically her equal. What had held me back from gainsaying her pathetic "My day is over!"

Should she live to her mother's age, were the twenty-three years that remained to her on earth to be such waiting as that of the husk shriveled upon the stem that bears the ripened fruit?

Ten years ago I tacked above my work-stand a card inscribed with a bit of wisdom evoked from Leslie Goldthwaite's quick, thoughtful brain — "SOMETHING MUST BE CROWDED OUT!"[4] It has helped me over many a press of seemingly equally urgent duties; consoled me for inevitable short-comings; steadied me for the work of my day. My eye fell upon the silent mentor when I returned home, still revolving the problem set for me by the morning call. In the world at large, in the history of families as in the individual life, something must give way in the warfare of "Must-haves" with "May-wants." Was this the solution of what I had just heard and seen? of the multiplying similar instances of "children to the front," "parents to the rear" that vexed my equitable soul? Is there fault, and if so, whose is it, when what has been the hub of the wheel is relegated to an unimportant place upon the circumference? To the child "mother" is authority, con-science, Bible. He dwells and develops under her shadow until such time as custom demands that he shall be consigned to tutors and governors.

When my youngest born, at five years old, came radiantly in from a walk with papa, arrayed for the first time in jacket and breeches, the faithful woman who had nursed him from his birth electrified us

---

[4] "*SOMETHING MUST BE CROWDED OUT!*": Quotation from *A Summer in Leslie Goldthwaite's Life* (1888) by Adeline Dutton Train Whitney (1824–1906).

and drew from him a howl of anguish and mortification, by falling upon her knees, clasping him in her arms and sobbing bitterly, "I have lost my baby! I have no baby now!"

The son, setting out blithely upon his journey to college, warehouse, or office, where he is to learn how to earn his bread, the daughter, whose tears drop fast into the trunk packed by "mamma's own hands" for the boarding-school that is to "finish" her, may cry as sadly and more truly, "I have lost my mother!"

Friend and comforter, boy and girl, may find at each visit to the old home "mother" — as infancy and childhood know her — infallible and well-nigh omnipotent — never, never more!

Meanwhile, what of her who has learned from Nature and through years of practice to be "mother," and that alone? The brood that went out from her, callow, chirping piteously for her care and nourishing, return in such bravery of fledging as half frightens while it fills her with pride. Their note is changed too. She listens bewildered to the talk of the girl of the period and that of the "fellow" who "keeps abreast of the times." The vital necessity of accomplishments unheard of in her day of pupilage, the cant of modern science, literature, art, and progress in general are foreign to her ears, indigestible by her comprehension. If she be very humble she may comfort, even congratulate herself that she has reared a race of demideities; may survey their brilliance in a tremor of delight from the obscure corner into which she has crept, as a bat may peer from a rock crevice or hollow tree upon the flight of eaglets in the sunshine. But, human nature being what it is, the chances are in favor of the supposition that the lowliest minded will feel aggrieved at her dethronement, albeit in favor of her natural heirs. Regarding this pang as disloyal, and a weakness, she will try to hide it, and so successfully that her most intimate friend will not divine it. Least of all will the daughter ascribe to her the possession of such wounded sensitiveness as would overcome them were they openly supplanted where they feel they have the right to rule, and their legitimate claims systematically ignored. They love her very dearly, of course, and always. Did she not bear and bring them up? Are they — her own flesh, blood, and bone — destitute of natural affection? Is she not "mother"?

Thinking and saying this, they put her, in more senses than one, upon the same floor with the kitchen, and know neither scruples or remorse for the classification then or thereafter. For — and here lies their excuse, so well understood as to be seldom clothed in words — she is, in everything, behind the age. When they were "little girls" she dictated what they should wear and how the garments should be made. If they are people of moderate means, her little hoard of trinkets and laces, her stockings, collars, cuffs, shoes, were common property to her and her great growing daughters, from the time they "got to be just my size." She had a way of complaining of this that amused them without hindering their depredations.

"The mother of such big girls has nothing of her own unless it be her skin and teeth," she would scold, so plainly elated in the fact that they were old enough to wear her clothes as to encourage the freebootery. It does not occur to the full-plumed young lady that her parent preferred to be robbed to the conviction pressed upon her by every daily incident that their interests are no longer identical, or even cognate. Their very underclothing is of different texture and fashion from hers. She is satisfied with three-button gloves. She would wear two-button, and save twenty-five cents on each pair, but for their protest. They sport six buttons in walking and visiting apparel, twelve and twenty on party gloves. Their shoes cost twice, three times as much as hers, and are worn over stockings many degrees finer, with certain prettinesses of "clocking" and embroidery she never thinks of assuming, even when "dressed." This same "dressing" is with them a continual feast — with her a hebdomadal[5] luxury. She can not bear to deny them "what other girls have," and their careless, happy eyes fail to trace any connection between the "We will try to manage it, dear," which answers their petitions, and her growing old-fashionedness. They do not analyze her motive in offering to make over for herself the black silk of which Mary is "tired to death," and to give the girl a robe of the latest and dullest tint dictated by artistic taste. Jenny's last year's street costume is frayed and shabby. Moreover, "everybody knows the old thing." Mamma, "who goes out so little" (naturally) proposes to take it off her hands, giving a new one in exchange. A series of such exchanges is not favorable to the development of "style" in the elder woman's attire, but lends freshness to that of the younger.

Mary and Jenny are bright, clever girls, ready with wit and needle. *They* "go out" a great deal and must look well. The house, if not refurnished at their *début,*[6] is gradually transformed by their agency until the only unsightly piece of furniture in it is the nominal mistress.

---

[5] *hebdomadal:* Weekly.
[6] *début:* Formal introduction of a girl to high society, usually accompanied by an elegant party (French).

She looks out of place — is growing "poky," complain the juniors. As time passes she is apt to become less lively in speech and expression, and they to wonder petulantly at her backwardness in learning new customs. The very table is set differently from "her way." The late dinners *à la Russe,* ladies' lunches, kettle-drums and high teas are a surprise and a strain to her faculties. The daughters, *au fait* to every improvement upon obsolete usages, are intolerant of what they consider her obstinacy when she hesitates to adopt them. Facile youth with difficulty receives the idea that novelty is oftenest pain to age. The sun, with the young, shines upon the landscape before them. For her who gave them birth it is the track overpast, "in purple distance fair," that draws her backward, longing glances as she walks on into the lengthening gloom of her own shadow. The usages of years, the sanction of "parents passed into the skies" make common things sacred to her.

"I'm not cross! I'm *discouraged!*" piped the little fellow who had been whipped for persistent fretting.

When our girls find mamma's temper uncertain, her mood whimsical, they can apply the anecdote.

It is disheartening, dear girls, let one tell you who has thought herself into a dull, fixed heart-ache on this subject, to be swept aside by inches, or boldly removed from the board where one was, not so very long ago, a figure of consequence. The process of grinding down from somebodies into nobodies, cuts well into nerve and soul while it may remove the excrescences of vanity and selfishness. When the chipping, and wearing, and rubbing are over, our elderly matron ought to be an angel slightly clothed in human flesh. Whereas, being your fellow-creature, she too frequently evinces little akin to angelhood except the longing to fly away and be at rest beyond the reach of the untimely and, to her notion, unseemly schooling that embitters her present existence. She likes to be consulted, and she does not like to be patronized — especially by the children whose faces she washed and whose untidy tricks she chided — it seems but yesterday! She is already sufficiently conscious of her deficiencies, her ignorance of really valuable things, without being tormented by animad-versions, implied or uttered, upon her perverseness in not sitting to learn at your feet of a thousand trivialities, momentous to you, but flint-dust in weight and in irritating properties, to eyes already used to the wider horizon of life that has no appreciable dividing line from eternity. *that sounds kind of cool or profound or something.*

"O ye poor, have charity toward the rich!" prays Parson Dale in "My Novel."

We mothers, enriched by the experience of years, grown patient and wise through the discipline of our long probation, beseech you to be charitable to our slowness and merciful to the stiff movement of mental muscles that copy with pain new postures and paces. "Let us alone! for soon our lips are dumb!" is the silent protest of many a loving parent, set to lesson-learning when she thinks school-days should be over.

"Then," murmur Mary and Jenny in concert, "if the case of the daughter be thus with the mother, we are to walk forever in the old worn-out path that tries us as sorely as the new can vex her! What, then, becomes of our æsthetic zeal, our skill in domestic art decoration — the house beautiful of our dreams?"

In another chapter I shall have somewhat to say upon this head. Now I lay down but one, and what seems to me a sound principle. Your girlhood's home, as it now stands, has been your mother's kingdom for more years than you have lived in this changing world. That it is neat, home-like and comfortable — that it *is* at all, is due to her thrift and toil abetting her husband's industry in another sphere of action. Her furnishment of her dwelling stands to her as a record of her life. That was the way in which homes were fitted up in "old times." A new bedroom carpet was an exciting incident; fresh papering and painting an event; refurnishing the parlors an era which seldom fell twice in one life-time. To accomplish any one of these required long foresight, economy, and self-denial that went toward the making up of the individuality and history of the house-mother.

Whatever may be your rights under your father's roof, while she lives, they are secondary to hers.

Should she choose to assert as much, legal and moral statutes would bear her out in it. She is not likely to do this. You smile incredulously at the suggestion. The danger lies in your selfishness or usurpation, not in her want of magnanimity; in your forgetfulness of the truth that while you may be crown-princesses, she is queen until her death, not in her disregard of your hereditary claims. What she yields to your petitions or dictation is entirely of grace. One day you will come into realms of your own. She will have no kingdom but this on earth.

One word of compassion, not of right. "Mamma" is antiquated in language and dress; in works and in ways non-progressive. Had she chosen to neglect you instead of herself; had she given to her own studies and mental culture the hours devoted to drilling you in early tasks; had she kept pace with society in place of sitting out the long evenings and bright days in the nursery; had the stitches set in small frocks, trousers, and coats gone toward the furbishing of her own wardrobe, you might have had less apparent cause to be ashamed of her. You would undoubtedly, had you survived the process, have now more and just reason to blush for your own defects.

For love's and pity's sake, then, try if this thought will not transfigure gray homeliness into seemliness and shining; if, by setting over against each lack of hers that virtue or accomplishment or physical perfection of yours of which this lack is the price, you may not grow in patient love and gratitude — even if you have not the greatness of soul that should beget, with these, admiration and reverence for the plain, time-worn creature you know now as "Only Mother."

[handwritten notes in margins: "Okay! People have said it a lot other key"; "even though mothers, they are out of fashion, so but did it for you + them"]

MARGARET E. SANGSTER

From Winsome Womanhood: Familiar Talks on Life and Conduct

[handwritten: , a little before Gilman (1860 – 1935)]

Margaret E. Sangster (1838–1912) was a poet, editor, and newspaperwoman whose name was associated with many of the notable magazines of her time. Her chapter on motherhood in *Winsome Womanhood: Familiar Talks on Life and Conduct* (1900), reprinted here, argues that training for motherhood should begin in infancy in order to develop maternal skills to the fullest. Like Harland, Sangster defines the true mother as a source of both discipline and affection. "Great men and great women, too, have had great mothers." Like a legion of other advice books, Sangster's implores women to devote themselves to the hallowed work of childraising as their God-given vocation. The self-control and willpower fostered by the domestic woman are crucial to the family and the nation alike. Unlike Harland, however, Sangster does not glorify self-sacrifice, but rather counsels a mother to develop intimate friendships with her children so as to be better able to guide and direct their futures.

The text of the following excerpt is taken from *Winsome Womanhood: Familiar Talks on Life and Conduct* (New York: Revell, 1900), 125–35.

Motherhood

"The little ones cling to their mother
And their kisses softly fall
But the babe in the wee white cradle
~~not mostly~~ dearest to mother of all."
  ~~but whole~~

The whole education of a girl from her infancy onward should be *wow*
a preparation for motherhood, and this, not because she may marry
and become a mother, but rather for the reason that the upbringing
and nurture of the race in its earliest and most impressionable years is
in the molding hands of woman. A teacher cannot perform the duties
of her high office as she ought unless she possess the maternal spirit.
An elder sister needs the mother-heart. Every girl in her relation to
those younger than herself, and to some extent in her friendships
with others, of her own sex not only, but of the opposite, is the better
for having in her nature something of the tender and brooding love
and compassion which are the mother's finest endowments. This is
beautifully brought out in a recent novel by James Lane Allen,[1] in
which the hero, storm-tossed and well nigh wrecked, harassed by
doubts and in bitter stress and strain, is beloved by the heroine with
more than the sweet surrendering love of girlhood; with the sustaining devotion and all comprehending intuitive sympathy of that maternal nature which it is the glory of woman to possess.

That is the best training of the school and of the home which makes
woman patient, gentle, forceful and spontaneous, which keeps in her,
intact amid all changes the child-heart. Except ye become as little children, said the Master, ye cannot inherit the kingdom of heaven. A little
child is quick to trust, quick to forgive, quick to serve. The small feet
run willingly on errands, the small hands tug at tasks too big for them,
the child, often wounded by thoughtless criticism, often misunderstood
by the duller adult, often unjustly punished, is swift to pardon injury
and is utterly incapable of malice. Revenge, deceit, wilful unkindness
are unchildlike; though they are fostered in children by the examples,
the blunders, and the cruelty of those who have them in charge.

Child culture has become a familiar phrase, and mothers are intent
in learning all they can about theories of education, and nursery discipline. From the cradle, which is the baby's nest, soft, warmly-lined,

[1] *James Lane Allen:* Allen (1849–1925) was an essayist and novelist, whose popular fiction was often set in Kentucky.

"Happy Childhood Days." From Margaret E. Sangster, *The Art of Home-Making* (New York: Christian Herald Bible House, 1898).

and protected from rude intrusion, guarded wisely from the indiscriminate caresses and promiscuous kisses of affectionate kindred, to the kindergarten which is the child's paradise, every step of infantile progress is most sedulously and vigilantly watched. These are the golden years of life. No one who has observed the almost miraculous facility with which children acquire ideas and grow from babyhood through the first seven years, can fail to see that most jealous attention should be given to the trend of the soul then and there, when God and the mother have the child to themselves.

No two little ones in the family are alike. To an outsider there may be great similarity; eyes, mouth, hair, may be in close resemblance as in the case of twins. Yet the mother is aware of differences vital and deep, and it is the privilege of the mother to study the individual and to adapt training to the individual need. One child is weak of will and easily bent: another is manifestly stubborn and requires gentle handling and guiding. There are still homes, more is the pity, in which obedience is a fetich,[2] and people dare attempt that diabolical thing and boast of it later, namely the breaking of a child's will. There are other homes, great is the shame, where the children are ever in the forefront, and the elders have no rights worth respecting, where misrule reigns, and order is unknown. True motherhood avoids extremes. The mother trains her children to obey, lovingly and continually, not by penalty, not by severity, not by perpetual nagging and fussing, and a hailstorm of don'ts rained on childish heads, but by firmness, by sweetness, and by consistency and calmness. Her unbroken self-control is the children's refuge and shelter: her authority always felt is never expressed in threats and harshness. Children must indeed obey, not because parents tell them to, but because obedience to the Divine Father is enjoined on us all, and together we must look for the Divine leadings and walk as God wishes us to. —> Christian Perspective,

Our little ones live in a very narrow world. They are hearing almost what we say, they are observing what we do. They are taking on our looks, our manner, our very thoughts. With the mother, the children's welfare is supreme, their health of body and their grasp of mind, their contentment or their fretfulness, their whole life story, are in her hands.

A mother may sensibly avail herself of every possible help. Her library should contain the best books which modern thought and mod-

---

[2] *fetich:* Alternate spelling for *fetish*, which Freud used to refer to an object or non-genital body part to which erotic meaning has been attributed but broadly refers to an object regarded with superstitious or excessive interest or obsession.

ern science have produced on maternal duties and children's needs. She will find great profit in association with other mothers, and the numerous societies, congresses and conventions where mothers meet will make their appeal to her and assist her with suggestions. But after all, each woman must be a law unto herself, and the ultimate comfort of every one is, that the Lord still says to the baby's mother, "Take this child and nurse it for me and I will give thee thy wages."[3] As our Lord's mother, heard a voice saying "Blessed art thou among women" so may every expectant mother hear a sweet voice in her soul, and over every crib, we may be sure that guardian angels bend. And every woman who does mother's work in this world whether or not she bear babes, is in such wise as she rears children for Christ, a sharer in the promise. That he (or she) that overcometh shall inherit all things, the hidden manna, the new name, the morning star, is the never abrogated promise of the Lord.

Before the baby comes, during the quiet months of waiting for its advent, the mother's heart should be as a cloister, hallowed and pure. No storm of passion should sweep it, no fretful reluctance should mar its peace. Of old, Hannah prayed, and God gave her Samuel,[4] a child of rare beauty consecrated from his birth. Read the story of Samuel, and observe how his whole life from infancy to venerable age was a testimony to the faithfulness of his mother, and to her dedication of him from the earliest life throb. A babe seems a mere waif on the stream of eternity, but in its little hand may lie the destinies of nations. Alexander, Cæsar, Napoleon, Washington, Lincoln, were once infants in mother's arms. Great men and great women, too, have had great mothers. A mean, petty, selfish, vain and egotistical mother will impress those traits on her child; he will draw them in with the milk which feeds his early life. For the sake of our country, let its motherhood be noble.

As the Children Are About Her

"Busy days are happy days
Brimming o'er with cares
But to each day's portal comes,
Many an angel unawares."

---

[3] *"Take this child . . .":* Exodus 2:9.
[4] *Samuel:* Son of Hannah, Samuel promised his mother to give his life over to the service of the Lord; in doing so, he became a national leader and judge. From the book of I Samuel 7:13–14, 28.

A mother around whom clustered a group of five beautiful girls and boys, their ages ranging from seven to fourteen said one day, "Life is so interesting in our home." Indeed it was, and is, wherever the children are growing up together, bringing into the household their games, their school tasks and competitions, their perpetually changing points of view, and the multitude of speculations which are inseparable from their development. What shall these little ones be? For what are we training them? How are they to meet the unknown future? Are they filling each day's measure of duty as the day comes? These boys and girls are immature men and women, men and women in the process of making, and to the mother who keeps pace with them, their characters are of the utmost, the most absorbing importance.

Mothers are sometimes aware that they are intellectually rusting, that they are lagging behind their children, and forgetting what they once knew not only, but losing the mental acuteness which keeps for them the children's confidence. That we are all our lives to remember the rules and dates and facts we learned at school is not to be expected, but it is not well for a child to feel that mother and father are ignorant persons, on whom he may look down from a superior level. Nor is it a happy thing in the struggle for subsistence that the children shall grow apart from the parents. There are homes in which there is no community of friendship. Edith has her intimates, Louise has hers, Laura has hers, but they remain distinct, and the mothers of the several girls are almost strangers. In the ideal home, mother and daughters have friends in common, and the confidence between them is unbroken. The mother is the one to whom boys and girls turn with their problems, their troubles and their doubts, she can sympathize; she can understand and decide; she knows what is best to do and say.

Whenever I notice in a young woman or young man a disinclination to confide in the mother, a dislike to consult her and a withholding of confidence, I am sure that at some moment in the home life, there was the making of a great and almost irreparable mistake. In the effort to dress the daughter daintily, the mother has not had time to be the daughter's friend. Or else, and this is a more common error and equally deplorable, the mother in her great unselfishness, deliberately effaced herself, took the second place when she was entitled to the first, wore old gowns that the girls might have new ones, and shabby gloves and hats that their finery and millinery might be resplendent, did the rough work to save their hands, took on herself the hardest burdens and walked the steepest road, that theirs might be light loads and easy paths. No mother does well to put herself too far in the background. She is the planet, her children the satellites, and she cannot step down from her proper place without disturbance to the solar system.

Perhaps life's happiest days are these of high noon, when woman is at her fullest maturity and in the radiance of her richest powers and her children are growing out of childhood and looking forward to college and to business. She must make much of herself for their sakes: she must not fall below a high standard; she must be bright, helpful, sympathetic, eager-hearted, and young with them. Blessed is that youth of the heart which abides, and is not dimmed in the heat of the day.

So swiftly fleet the years, so whirl the hours and days and weeks away, as the waves rush over onward to the sea, that "What thou doest, thou must do quickly" is the word spoken to us as we stand in the midst of our years.

We should make much of the home anniversaries, as the children are about us. Birthdays come and go. Let every birthday be a festival, a time when the gladness of the house finds expression in flowers, in gifts, in a little fête. Never should a birthday be passed over without note, or as if it were a common day, never should it cease to be a garlanded milestone in the road of life.

The wedding anniversary, the day of the son's majority, of the daughter's graduation, the day when a very sweet and beautiful thing happened, any day of the right hand of the Most High, should be fitly commemorated in the family life, and thus will help in making the family united and clannish, the latter a good thing, within due bounds. A little trouble may be taken to give such a day an air of festivity, but it is worth while.

The recurrence of Christmas, the world's gladdest day, of the New Year, and of the patriotic holidays are signalized in family annals. Thanksgiving is peculiarly a day of the home, a day when the kindred gather, and from near and far the scattered and the precious ones return to the old homestead, to the roof-tree, the table, and the fire on the hearth.

Many a little journey, many a homely jest, much merry-making, much thrift, sacrifices shared, endeavors made together for the good of all, belong to this period. If poverty comes and the skies darken, there is the more reason that the family shall cling close and stand shoulder to shoulder. Mother should not bear her solicitudes alone. Father should let his boys know that things are pressing hardly upon him. Injustice is often done to the young people in hiding from them the precise nature of the difficulties which hedge the path of parents. They would gallantly do their share if they were allowed, but they are kept in the dark, and do not know that there is trouble they might relieve.

Entire confidence, the security of love, freedom of movement, sympathy and trust in God, are the pivotal springs of home life. Never is a mother happier than when her children are about her, than when on her nightly round, she leaves a kiss on every brow, and knows each darling safe and asleep in bed, the door shut, and the little world curtained in, with Our Father watching it till the morning light. *God·*

In Mrs. Oliphant's[5] touching autobiography there is a passage which moves every mother-heart, where looking back over lonely years, the saddened elderly woman remembers how simply happy she was, when at night her babies were asleep, and with her needlework in her hand, she went down the stair to sit with her husband. The little homely scene is like a Flemish painting; and similar pictures are in our homes everywhere, the children folding dimpled hands and saying their evening prayers, the mother looking to the windows and doors and hearing the story of each childish day; then in the room below, with a sigh of full content, taking her work, her book, her mending; talking with her good man, or writing the letter she has in mind for her own distant mother. Outside the wind may blow, and the tempest beat; it matters not for the little home is as God's ark, where the tiniest birdling is safe. *Please! welcome to the 21st century!*

Every child's birthright is a happy home. No human foresight can provide for the child a happy life. The future may be full of shoals and quick-sands. But there is gladness enough to go round the whole world while the children are little and in the home nest.

a mothers/womans job is to raise children in a God fearing, devoted way.

---

[5] *Mrs. Oliphant:* Margaret Oliphant (1828–1897), extremely prolific Scottish novelist and historical writer known for her depictions of small-town life. Her autobiography details her financial struggle to support her family through writing.

From How to Win: A Book for Girls

Frances E. Willard (1939–1898) was a temperance advocate and educator, as well as the first female college president in the United States (at the Evanston College for Ladies, from 1871 to 1874). She became president of the Women's Christian Temperance Union in 1879 and served until her death; in 1883, she wrote *Women and Temperance,* a popular piece of social reformism. The injunction against novel reading in Willard's *How to Win: A Book for Girls* (1886) was a commonplace by the turn of the century, since novels were often blamed for promulgating "lies" and fantasies as well as corrupting morals. What is interesting about Willard's book is that it advocates the "New Ideal of Womanhood": that is, the "co-equal" power of men and women. According to Willard, a woman will more effectively domesticate the world if, through education and self-knowledge, she goes into it as a partner to the male. With a playful irony, Willard declares: "I shall try to show that if every young woman held in her firm little hand her own best gift, duly cultivated and made effective, society would not explode, the moon would not be darkened, the sun would still shed light" (13).

The text of the following excerpt is taken from the fifth edition of *How to Win: A Book for Girls* (New York: Funk & Wagnalls, 1888), 48–57; 102–104.

The New Ideal of Womanhood

No doubt my readers have asked ere this the inevitable question: "Why does that seem natural and fitting for a young woman to do and to aspire to now which would have been no less improper than impossible a hundred years ago?" Sweet friends, it is because *the ideal of woman's place in the world is changing in the average mind.* For as the artist's ideal precedes his picture, so the ideal woman must be transformed before the actual one can be. In an age of brute force, the warrior galloping away to his adventures waved his mailed hand to the lady fair who was enclosed for safe keeping in a grim castle with moat and drawbridge. But to-day, when spirit force grows regnant, a woman can circumnavigate the globe alone, without danger of an uncivil word, much less of violence. We shall never span a wider chasm than this change implies. All our inventions have led up to it, and have in nothing else wrought out beneficence so great as

110

they have accomplished here, purely by indirection. In brief, the barriers that have hedged women into one pathway and men into another, altogether different, are growing thin, as physical strength plays a less determining part in our life drama. All through the vegetable and animal kingdoms the fact of sex does not widely differentiate the broader fact of life, its environment and its pursuits. Hence, the immense separateness which sex is called in to explain when we reach the plane of humanity, is to be accounted for largely on artificial grounds. In Eden it did not exist, nor in the original plan of creation, as stated in these just and fatherly words: "And God said, 'Let us make man in our own image, after our own likeness. Let them have dominion.' . . . So God created man in His own image, in the image of God created he him, male and female created he them, and God blessed them, and said unto them, ' . . . replenish the earth and subdue it . . . and have dominion over every living thing.'"[1] After the fall came the curse, which may have been no part of the original design, and from which the Gospel's triumph is releasing us, for there is "neither male nor female in Christ Jesus." Who knows but that the origin of evil was contemporaneous with man's assertion of supremacy over one who was meant to be his equal comrade? If so, our Paradise regained will come only when the laureate's prophecy is realized:

> "Two heads in council, two beside the hearth,
> Two in the noisy business of the world,
> Two in the liberal offices of life;
> Two plummets dropped to sound the abyss of science
> And the secrets of the mind."[2]

The times when a new ideal is moulded, in Church, State, or society, mark the epochs of history. Amid what throes did Europe pass from that of supreme authority in the Church to the incomparably higher one of supreme liberty in conscience; from the divine right of kings to the divine right of the people! But there was to come a wider evolution of the same ideal — namely, the co-equal power of the co-partners, man and woman, in working out the problem of human destiny. This newest and noblest of ideals marks the transition from physical force ruling to spiritual force recognized. The gradual adjustment of every-day occupation, custom and law, to this new

---

[1] *And God said . . . thing:* Genesis 1:26.
[2] *"Two heads . . . of the mind":* Lines from *The Princess,* Book 2 (1847) by Alfred, Lord Tennyson (1809–1892), ll. 156–160. This much-beloved, long narrative poem included interludes with songs.

ideal, marks ours as a transition period. Those who have the most enlargement of opportunity to hope for from the change, will, in the nature of the case, move on most rapidly into the new conditions, and this helps to explain, I think, why women seem to be climbing more rapidly than men, to-day, the heights of spiritual power, with souls more open to the "skyey influences" of the oncoming age.

More women study to-day than men; a greater proportion travel abroad for purposes of culture; a larger share are moral and religious. Half of the world's wisdom, more than half its purity, and nearly all its gentleness, are to-day to be set down on woman's credit side. Weighted with the alcohol and tobacco habits, Brother Jonathan will have to make better time than he is doing now, if he keeps step with Sister Deborah across the threshold of the twentieth century. For the law of survival of the fittest will inevitably choose that member of the firm who is cleanliest, most wholesome, most accordant with God's laws of nature and of grace, to survive. To the blindness or fatuity which renders him oblivious of the fact that the coming woman is already well-nigh here, our current writer of the W. D. Howells and Henry James[3] school owes the dreary monotony of his "society novel." Not more "conventional" was the style of art known as "Byzantine," which repeated with barren iteration its placid and colorless "type," than are the pages of this dreary pair, whose books will put a period to the literary sentence of their age. The "American novel"[4] will not be written until the American woman, a type now to be found in Michigan, Boston, Cornell, and other universities, shall have taken her place, twentieth-century product that she is, beside the best survivals of young men in similar institutions, and wrought out the Home, the Church, the State that are to be. Measuring each other on all planes, these life partners will know each other's value, and no appeal to the divorce court will be made to relieve them, a few years after marriage, from an incompatibility that has ripened into open war. Happy homes will dot the country from shore to shore, in which both the man and the woman will do their best to lift the world toward God.

"Self-knowledge, self-reverence, and self-control: these three alone lead life to sovereign power,"[5] and these are fast becoming essential

---

[3] *W. D. Howells and Henry James:* See p. 352 and p. 362.

[4] *"American novel":* Howells and James, among others, sought to define a subject and a tone for indigenous fiction that would distinguish American writing from its European counterpart and model.

[5] *"Self-knowledge ... power":* Misquote of "Oenone" (1832) by Alfred, Lord Tennyson (1809–1892) l. 142: "Self-reverence, self-knowledge, and self-control . . ."

to any ideal of womanly character which the modern age will recognize as the product of its institutions. Of self-knowledge, these talks have said much. Self-reverence I would fain help you to develop in your character as a woman. If my dear mother did me one crowning kindness it was in making me believe that next to being an angel, the greatest bestowment of God is to make one a woman. With what contempt she referred to the old Jewish formula in which the less refined sex rolled out the words, "I thank Thee, O God, that Thou hast not made me a woman," and with what pathos she repeated the gentle prayer of the other, "I thank Thee, O God, that Thou hast made me as it pleased Thee," with the pithy comment, "What could have pleased Him better, I should like to know, than to make one so rare, so choice, so spiritual as woman is?" Perhaps some of you may have thought you wanted to be a boy, but I seriously doubt it. You may have wanted a boy's freedom, his independence, his healthful, unimpeding style of dress,[6] but I do not believe any true girl could ever have been coaxed to be a boy. Reverence yourself, then, if you would learn one of the first elements of "How to Win" in this great world race, with its "go-as-you-please" terms, but its relentless penalties for failure.

What will the new ideal of woman *not* be? Well, for example, she will never be written down in the hotel register by her husband after this fashion: "John Smith and Wife." He would as soon think of her writing "Mrs. John Smith and Husband." Why does it not occur to any one to designate him thus? Simply because he is so much more than that. He is a leading force in the affairs of the Church; he helps decide who shall be pastor. (So will she.) He is, perhaps, the village physician, or merchant (so she will be, perhaps — indeed, they are oftentimes in partnership, nowadays, and I have found their home a blessed one.) He is the village editor. (Very likely she will be associate.) He is a voter. (She will be, beyond a peradventure.) For the same reason you will never read of her marriage that "the minister pronounced them MAN and *wife*," for that functionary would have been just as likely to pronounce them "husband and woman," a form of expression into which the regulation reporter will be likely to fall one

---

[6] *healthful, unimpeding style of dress:* Women like Willard and Gilman protested against corsets and other frivolous apparel (including hats) which constricted women's movements and appealed to men's desires. The controversy over Amelia Bloomers's attempt, in the 1850s, to introduce a costume for women consisting of a short skirt and loose trousers gathered at the ankle, triggered efforts to get women to abandon their corsets and long skirts for more comfortable clothing.

of these days, it being, really, not one whit more idiotic than the time-worn phrase, "man and wife." The ideal woman of the future will never be designated as "the *Widow* Jones," because she will be so much more than that — "a provider" for her children, "a power" in the Church, "a felt force" in the State. I think George Eliot is the first woman to attain the post-mortem honor of having her husband called "her widower," John W. Cross having been thus indicated in English papers of the period. A turn about is fair play, and the phrase is really quite refreshing to one's sense of justice. The ideal woman will not write upon her visiting-card, nor insist on having her letters addressed, to Mrs. John Smith, or Mrs. General Smith, as the case may be, but if her maiden name were Jones, she will fling her banner to the breeze as "Mrs. Mary Jones-Smith," and will be sure to make it honorable. She will not be the lay figure made and provided to illustrate the fashions of Monsieur Worth and lesser lights of the same guild, but will insist that the goddess Hygeia[7] is the only true modiste,[8] and will dutifully obey her orders. As the Louvre Gallery proves that when men were but the parasites of the court they, too, decked themselves with earrings, high heels, powdered hair and gaudy garments, so the distorted figures in the detestable fashion-plates[9] of to-day are the irrefutable proofs of woman's fractional estate; but this will not be so to-morrow, when she finds her kingdom — which is her own true self. The ideal woman will cease to heed the cruel "Thus far and no farther," which has issued from the pinched lips of old Dame Custom, checking her ardent steps throughout all the ages past, and will be studious only to hear the kindly "Thus far and no farther" of God.

The ideal woman will play Beatrice to man's Dante[10] in the Inferno of his passions. She will give him the clew out of materialism's Labyrinth. She will be civilization's Una,[11] taming the Lion of disease

---

[7] *goddess Hygeia:* One of the daughters of Asclepius, the god of medicine; in Greek mythology, Hygeia is associated with health.

[8] *modiste:* Milliner, dress-maker; one who deals in fashion.

[9] *fashion-plates:* Advertisements and pictures in women's magazines depicting women's clothes; the term *fashion-plate* came to refer to the women wearing the clothes themselves.

[10] *Beatrice . . . Dante:* Beatrice was the beloved of the Italian poet Dante Alighieri (1265–1321); he portrays her as his intercessor in the *Inferno* and his guide through *Paradiso*.

[11] *Una:* Fair damsel in Edmund Spenser's (1552–1599) *Faerie Queene* (1590–1609), she serves as the personification of religion and truth. Married Red Cross Knight, after he slays a dragon.

and misery. The State shall no longer go limping on one foot through the years, but shall march off with steps firm and equipoised. The keen eye and deft hand of the housekeeper shall help to make its every-day walks wholesome; the skill in detail, trustworthiness in finance, motherliness in sympathy, so long extolled in private life, shall exalt public station. Indeed, if I were asked the mission of the ideal woman, I would reply: IT IS TO MAKE THE WHOLE WORLD HOMELIKE. Some one has said that "Temperament is the climate of the individual," but home is woman's climate, her vital breath, her native air. A true woman carries home with her everywhere. Its atmosphere surrounds her; its mirror is her face; its music attunes her gentle voice; its longitude may be reckoned from wherever you happen to find her. But "home's not merely four square walls."

Some people once thought it was, and they thought, also, that you might as well throw down its Lares and Penates[12] as to carry away its weaving-loom and spinning-wheel. But it survived this spoliation; and when women ceased to pick their own geese and do their own dyeing, it still serenely smiled. The sewing-machine took away much of its occupation; the French and Chinese laundries have intruded upon its domain; indeed the next generation will no doubt turn the cook-stove out of doors, and the housekeeper, standing at the telephone, will order better cooked meals than almost any one has nowadays, sent from scientific caterers by pneumatic tubes, and the debris thereof returned to a general cleaning-up establishment; while houses will be heated, as they are now lighted and supplied with water, from general reservoirs.

Women are fortunate in belonging to the less tainted half of the race. Dr. Benjamin Ward Richardson tells us that but for this conserving fact it would deteriorate to the point of failure. A bright old lady said, after viewing a brewery, distillery, and tobacco factory: "Ain't I thankful that the women folks hain't got all that stuff to chew and smoke and swallow down!" It behooves us to offset force of muscle by force of heart, that what our strong brothers have done to subdue the material world for us, who are not their equals in physical strength, may be offset by what we shall achieve for them in bringing in the reign of "Sweeter manners, purer laws." For the world is slowly making the immense discovery that not what woman *does,* but what she is, makes home a possible creation. It is the Lord's

---

[12] *Lares and Penates:* Household gods; the home in general; personal or household items.

ark, and does not need steadying; it will survive the wreck of systems and the crash of theories, for the home is but the efflorescence of woman's nature under the nurture of Christ's Gospel. She came into the college and elevated it, into literature and hallowed it, into the business world and ennobled it. She will come into government and purify it, into politics and cleanse its Stygian pool,[13] for woman will make homelike every place she enters, and she will enter every place on this round earth. Any custom, or traffic, or party on which a woman cannot look with favor is irrevocably doomed. Its welcome of her presence and her power is to be the final test of its fitness to survive. All gospel civilization is radiant with the demonstration of this truth: "It is not good for man to be alone." The most vivid object lesson on history's page is the fact that his deterioration is in exact proportion to his isolation from the home of woman's pure companionship. To my own grateful thought, the most sacred significance of woman's philanthropic work to-day lies in the fact that she occupies the outer circle in this tremendous evolution of the Christian idea of home. Ours is a high and sacred calling. Out of pure hearts fervently, let us love God and humanity; so shall we be Christ's disciples, and so shall we safely follow on to know the work whereunto we have been called. "'Tis home where'er the heart is," and no true mother, sister, daughter, or wife can fail to go in spirit after her beloved and tempted ones, as their adventurous steps enter the labyrinth of the world's temptations. We cannot call them back. "All before them lies the way."

There is but one remedy: we must bring the home to them, for they will not return to it. Still must their mothers walk beside them, sweet and serious, and clad in the garments of power. The occupations, pleasures, and ambitions of men and women must not diverge so widely from each other. Potent beyond all other facts of every-day experience is the rapidly increasing similarity between the pursuits of these two fractions that make up the human integer. When brute force reigned, this *rapport* was at zero. "Impedimenta to the rear," was the command of Cæsar and the rule of every warrior — women and children being the hindrances referred to. But to-day there is not a motto more popular than that of the inspired old German, "Come, let us live for our children;" and as for women, "the world is all before them where to choose."

---

[13] *Stygian pool:* Relating to the river Styx, in Greek underworld; dark, gloomy, hellish place.

No greater good can come to the manhood of the world than is prophesied in the increasing community of thought and works between it and the world's womanhood. The growing individuality, independence and prestige of the gentler sex steadily require from the stronger a higher standard of character and purer habits of life. This blessed consummation, so devoutly to be wished, is hastened, dear girlish hearts, by every prayer you offer, by every hymn you sing, by every loving errand of your willing feet and gentle hands. You are the true friends of tempted manhood, bewildered youth, and every little child. The steadfast faith and loyal, patient work you are to do, in the white fields of reform, will be the mightiest factor in woman's contribution to the solution of this Republic's greatest problem, and will have their final significance in the thought and purpose, not that the world shall come into the home, but that the home, embodied and impersonated in its womanhood, shall go forth into the world.

I have no fears for the women of America. They will never content themselves remaining stationary in methods or in policy, much less sound a retreat in their splendid warfare against the saloon in law and in politics. The tides of the mother's heart do not change; we can count upon them always. The voice of Miriam[14] still cheers the brave advance, and all along the line we hear the battle-cry: "Speak unto the children of Israel, that they go forward." . . .

Novel-Reading

her vision of the future of womanhood.

Much as I disliked the restriction then, I am now sincerely thankful that my Puritan father not only commanded me not to read novels, but successfully prohibited the temptation from coming in his children's way. Until I was fifteen years old I never saw a volume of the kind.

"Pilgrim's Progress"[15] was the nearest approach we made, but it seems profanation to refer to that choice English classic in this degenerate connection. (I should add that Rev. Dr. Tefft's "Shoulder Knot"[16] was also early read at our house, in the *Ladies' Repository;*

[14] *Miriam:* The prophetess Miriam (Hebrew for *bitterness*) appears in the Bible as the eldest sister of Moses and Aaron.

[15] *"Pilgrim's Progress":* A religious allegory written by John Bunyan, *The Pilgrim's Progress* (Part 1, 1678; Part 2, 1684) exemplified the Puritan religious outlook and remained immensely popular through the first half of the nineteenth century.

[16] *Rev. Dr. Tefft's "Shoulder Knot":* Benjamin Franklin Tefft (1813–1885) was the editor of the *Ladies' Repository* (Jan. 1841–Dec. 1876); "Shoulder Knot" was one of the many editorial articles, verses, and comments he wrote and published in this magazine.

but then that delightful work was an *historical* story, and even my father praised it.)

A kind and garrulous seamstress, who declared that this law of our household was "a shame," told us what she could remember of "The Children of the Abbey,"[17] and finally brought in, surreptitiously, "Jane Eyre"[18] and "Thaddeus of Warsaw."[19] But the glamor of those highly seasoned pages was unhealthful, and made "human nature's daily food," the common pastoral life we led, and nature's soothing beauty seem so tame and tasteless that the revulsion was my life's first sorrow. How evanescent and unreal was the pleasure of such reading; a sort of spiritual hasheesh-eating[20] with hard and painful waking; a benumbing of the healthful, every-day activities; a losing of so much that was simple and sweet, to gain so little that was, at best, a fevered and fantastic vision of utter unreality. In all the years since then I have believed that novel-writing, save for some high, heroic, moral aim, while the most diversified, is the most unproductive of all industries. The young people who read the greatest quantity of novels know the least, are the dullest in aspect, and the most vapid in conversation. The flavor of individuality has been burned out of them. Always imagining themselves in an artificial relation to life, always content to look through their author's glasses, they become as commonplace as pawns upon a chess-board. "Sir, we had good talk!" was Sam Johnson's[21] highest praise of those he met. But any talk save the dreariest commonplace and most tiresome reiteration is impossible with the regulation reader of novels or player of games. And this is, in my judgment, because God, by the very laws of mind, must punish those who *kill* time instead of *cultivating* it. For time is the stuff that life is made of; the crucible of character, the arena of achievement, and woe to those who fritter it away. They cannot help paying great nature's penalty, and "mediocre," "failure," or "imbe-

---

[17] *"The Children of the Abbey"*: Historical romance (1895) by Regina Maria Roche set in Ireland and England and concerning a family that rises from adversity.

[18] *"Jane Eyre"*: Psychological romance published in 1847 by Charlotte Brontë (1815–1855) about a governess who falls in love with and finally marries her employer.

[19] *"Thaddeus of Warsaw"*: Historical romance (1803) written by Jane Porter (1776–1850).

[20] *spiritual hasheesh-eating*: That is, a reading of novels for their intoxicating, sensational effect.

[21] *Sam Johnson*: Samuel Johnson (1709–1784), British literary critic and man of letters, who argued for the representation of the universal and of general nature in literature.

cile" will surely be stamped upon their foreheads. Therefore I would have each generous youth and maiden say to every story-spinner, except the few great names that can be counted on the fingers of one hand: I really cannot patronize your wares, and will not furnish you my head for a football, or my fancy for a sieve. By writing these books you get money, and a fleeting, unsubstantial fame, but by reading them I should turn my possibility of success in life to the certainty of failure. *Myself plus time* is the capital stock with which the good heavenly Father has pitted me against the world to see if I can gain some foothold. I cannot afford to be a mere spectator. I am a wrestler for the laurel in life's Olympian games. I can make history, why should I maunder in a hammock and read the endless repetitions of romance? No, find yourself a cheaper patron, for I count myself too valuable for the sponge-like use that you would put me to.

Nay, I would have our young people reach a higher key than this. Because of life's real story with its mystery and pathos; because of the romance that crowds into every year; the plot that thickens daily, and the tragedy that lies a little way beyond; because of Christ and His kingdom — the mightiest drama of the ages, let us be up and doing with a heart for any fate. Humanity is worth our while, to love, to bless, to die for if need be.

> "The cause that lacks assistance,
> The wrong that needs resistance,
> The future in the distance
> And the good that we can do,"

make up the truest epic and train the noblest heroes. Achievement, which is growth's condition, ought to be the bread of life to us, the tireless inspiration of each full day of honest toil. God meant this to be so, for only thus do we cease chasing about for happiness, and find blessedness instead.

don't read, it's a waste of time,

WILLIAM ACTON

From The Functions and Disorders of the Reproductive Organs

While Dr. Acton's writings may seem more like medical advice than conduct literature, his directives served to instruct men and women in the proper course of their domestic situations. Victorian advice literature was filled with edicts about sexuality in marriage. Marriage was supposed to be a spiritual event, and sexuality was not intended to be part of it, except for the sake of reproduction. In short, much of the advice literature of the time was devoted to making sexuality a function of social and especially familial order. Dr. William Acton (1813–1875) was a British physician and author of the influential study *The Functions and Disorders of the Reproductive Organs in Childhood, Youth, Adult Age, and Advanced Life* (1857). Acton was considered his age's authority on venereal disease, prostitution and its diseases, and masturbation. His medical manuals gave the Victorian culture genteel explanations about reproductive functions. Contrary to popular wisdom, Victorians were not prudes. They were interested in sexuality and natural urges, but in moderation. However, Acton was one of the foremost theorists of women's "passionlessness," claiming that "there are many females who never feel any excitement whatever.... The best mothers, wives, and managers of households know little or nothing of sexual indulgences."

The text of the following excerpt is taken from the sixth edition of *The Functions and Disorders of the Reproductive Organs in Childhood, Youth, Adult Age, and Advanced Life* (London: Churchill, 1875), 191–93; 210–13; 215–17; 246–47.

Marital Excesses

It is a common notion among the public, and even among professional men, that the word *excess* chiefly applies to *illicit* sexual connection. Of course, whether extravagant in degree or not, all such connection is, from one point of view, an *excess*. But any warning against sexual dangers would be very incomplete if it did not extend to the excesses too often committed by married persons in ignorance of their ill-effects. Too frequent emission of the life-giving fluid, and too frequent sexual excitement of the nervous system, are, as we have seen, in themselves most destructive. The result is the same within the marriage bond as without it. The married man who thinks that, because he is a married man, he can commit no excess, however often the act of sexual congress is repeated, will suffer as certainly and as seriously as the unmarried debauchee[1] who acts on the same principle in his indulgences — perhaps more certainly, from his very ignorance, and from his not taking those precautions and following those rules which a career of vice is apt to teach the sensualist. Many a man has, until his marriage, lived a most continent life; — so has his wife. As soon as they are wedded, intercourse is indulged in night after night; neither party having any idea that these repeated sexual acts are excesses, which the system of neither can with impunity bear, and which to the delicate man, at least, is occasionally absolute ruin. The practice is continued till health is impaired, sometimes permanently; and when a patient is at last obliged to seek medical advice, his usual surgeon may have no idea or suspicion of the excess, and treat the symptom without recommending the removal of the cause, namely, the sexual excess; hence it is that the patient experiences no relief for the indigestion, lowness of spirits, or general debility from which he may be suffering. If, however, the patient comes under the care of a medical man in the habit of treating such cases, the invalid is thunderstruck at learning that his sufferings arise from excesses unwittingly committed. Married people often appear to think that connection may be repeated just as regularly and almost as often as their meals. Till they are told of the danger, the idea never enters their heads that they have been guilty of great and almost criminal excess; nor is this to be wondered at, since the possibility of such a cause of disease is seldom hinted at.

Some years ago a young man called on me, complaining that he was unequal to sexual congress, and was suffering from spermatorrhœa, the result, he said, of self-abuse.[2] He was cauterised,[3] and I lost sight of him for some time, and when he returned he came complaining that he was scarcely able to move alone. His mind had become enfeebled, there was great pain in the back, and he wished me to repeat the operation.

---

[1] *debauchee:* One given over to seduction, intemperance, or sensuality.

[2] *spermatorrhœa . . . self-abuse:* Obsolete term for an involuntary ejaculation, "wet dream," or nocturnal emission; the involuntary loss of semen, due to "self-abuse" or masturbation.

[3] *cauterised:* To burn or sear; to destroy tissue in order to deaden pain.

On cross-examining the patient, I found that after the previous cauterization he had recovered his powers, and, having subsequently married, had been in the habit of indulging in connection (ever since I had seen him, two years previously) three times a week, without any idea that he was committing an excess, or that his present weakness could depend upon this cause. The above is far from being an isolated instance of men who, having been reduced by former excesses, still imagine themselves equal to any excitement, and when their powers are recruited, to any expenditure of vital force. Some go so far as to believe that indulgence may increase these powers, just as gymnastic exercises augment the force of the muscles. This is a popular error, and requires attention. Such patients should be told that the shock on the system, each time connection is indulged in, is very powerful, and that the expenditure of seminal fluid must be particularly injurious to organs previously debilitated. It is by this and similar excesses that premature old age and debility of the generative organs is brought on.

A few months later I again saw this young man, and all his symptoms had improved under moderated indulgence, care, and tonics. . . .

In December, 1861, a stout, florid man, about forty-five years of age, was sent to me by a distinguished provincial practitioner, in consequence of his sexual powers failing him, and one of his testes being smaller than the other. On cross-examination I found that he had been married some years, and had a family. Connection had been indulged in very freely, when, about four years ago, a feeling of nervousness insensibly came over him, and about the same time his sexual powers gradually became impaired. The real object, he avowed, which he had in coming to me was to obtain some stimulus to increase his sexual powers, rather than to gain relief for the nervousness and debility under which he was labouring. Indeed, at his own request, the efforts of the country practitioner had been made in the former direction. Instead of giving remedies to excite, I told him that his convalescence must depend upon moderate indulgence, and allowing the system time to rally, and treated him accordingly.

The lengths to which some married people carry excesses is perfectly astonishing. I lately saw a married medical man who told me that for the previous fourteen years, he believed, he had *never* allowed a night to pass without having had connection, and it was only lately, on reading my book, that he had attributed his present ailments to marital excesses. The contrast between such a case as this, where an individual for fourteen years has resisted this drain on the system, and that of a man who is, as many are, prostrated for twenty-four hours by one nocturnal emission, is most striking. . . . All experience, however, shows that, whatever may be the condition of the nervous system, as regards sexual indulgences, excesses will sooner or later tell upon any frame, and can never be indulged in with impunity. I believe general debility and impaired health dependent upon too frequent sexual relations to be much more common than is generally supposed, and that they are hardly yet sufficiently appreciated by the profession as very fruitful causes of ill-health. . . .

Impotence

Sexual Indifference among Married Men, as a temporary affection, is another cause of anxiety, which in some persons produces the greatest alarm; and well it may, because if instead of being properly treated, it be allowed to continue, it may, as will be seen further on . . . , lead to domestic differences, and even induce the wife to appeal to the Divorce Court for an order to annul the marriage.

Causes. — Men who gain their bread by the sweat of their brows or the exhausting labour of their brains, cannot be always ready to perform the sexual act. During certain periods, when occupied with other matters, a man's thoughts may dwell but little on sexual subjects, and no disposition exist to indulge anything but the favourite or absorbing pursuit, mental or physical, as the case may be. After a lapse of time, different in various individuals, sexual thoughts recur, and the man who yesterday was so indifferent to sexual feelings, as practically to be temporarily impotent, now becomes ardent and sexually disposed, remaining so until the necessary and, in fact, healthy lethargy of the organs consequent on the performance of the act, has supervened.

This quiescent condition is much more persistent in some married men than in others. There are persons (married as well as single) who only at very infrequent intervals feel any disposition for sexual intercourse, just as there are others who never feel any such desire at all. Again, there are *lethargic* men who, unless roused, will hardly do anything. It requires an effort in some men to eat. There is in some of these cases undoubtedly great sexual debility. Again the habitual drinker cares little for sexual enjoyments. I am quite certain that some excessive smokers, if very young, never acquire, and if older, rapidly lose, any keen desire for connection. The pleasures of the table so monopolise many a man's thoughts that he is indifferent to all other indulgences. In all the above cases the sexual feelings occupy a secondary position, and offer a strong contrast to that tyrannous mastery from which the thorough voluptuary suffers. In the more advanced stages of this quiescent condition, it is often difficult to say whether the sexual organisation was originally weak, whether the other tastes have overpowered the sexual appetite, or whether the individual has not early in life abused his generative faculty.

Among the married we sometimes find men taking a dislike or even a disgust to their wives, and, as a consequence, there is an entire want of desire. A first failure will sometimes so annihilate men's sexual appetite that they are never able or anxious to attempt connection a second time. In many cases this arises from wounded *amour propre*,[4] as they have succeeded with other women. Early excesses in married life will, in a certain number of cases, occasionally produce a temporary impotency later in life. Want of sympathy or want of sexual feeling, on the woman's part, again, is not an unfrequent cause of apathy, indifference, or frigidity on the part of the husband. Lastly, there are cases of amiable men who carry their consideration for the women they love to such an extent as to render themselves practically impotent for very dread of inflicting pain.

Want of Sexual Feeling in the Female a Cause of Absence of Virility. — We have already mentioned lack of sexual feeling in the female as not an uncommon cause of apparent or temporary impotence in the male. There is so much ignorance on the subject, and so many false ideas are current as to women's sexual condition, and are so productive of mischief, that I need offer no apology for giving here a plain statement that most medical men will corroborate.

I have taken pains to obtain and compare abundant evidence on this subject, and the result of my inquiries I may briefly epitomise as follows: — I should say that the majority of women (happily for society) are not very much troubled with sexual feeling of any kind. What men are habitually, women are only exceptionally. It is too true, I admit, as the Divorce Court shows, that there are some few women who have sexual desires so strong that they surpass those of men, and shock public feeling by their consequences. I admit, of course, the existence of sexual excitement terminating even in nymphomania,[5] a

---

[4] *amour propre:* Self-love.
[5] I shall probably have no other opportunity of noticing that, as excision of the clitoris has been recommended for the cure of this complaint, Köbelt thinks that it would not be necessary to remove the whole of the clitoris in nymphomania, the same results (that is destruction of venereal desire) would follow if the glans clitoridis had been

form of insanity that those accustomed to visit lunatic asylums must be fully conversant with; but, with these sad exceptions, there can be no doubt that sexual feeling in the female is in the majority of cases in abeyance, and that it requires positive and considerable excitement to be roused at all; and even if roused (which in many instances it never can be) it is very moderate compared with that of the male. Many persons, and particularly young men, form their ideas of women's sensuous feeling from what they notice early in life among loose or, at least, low and immoral women. There is always a certain number of females who, though not ostensibly in the ranks of prostitutes, make a kind of a trade of a pretty face. They are fond of admiration, they like to attract the attention of those immediately above them. Any susceptible boy is easily led to believe, whether he is altogether overcome by the syren or not, that she, and therefore all women, must have at least as strong passions as himself. Such women, however, give a very false idea of the condition of female sexual feeling in general. Association with the loose women of the London streets in casinos and other immoral haunts (who, if they have not sexual feeling, counterfeit it so well that the novice does not suspect but that it is genuine), seems to corroborate such an impression, and as I have stated above, it is from these erroneous notions that so many unmarried men imagine that the marital duties they will have to undertake are beyond their exhausted strength, and from this reason dread and avoid marriage.

Married men — medical men — or married woman themselves, would, if appealed to, tell a very different tale, and vindicate female nature from the vile aspersions cast on it by the abandoned conduct and ungoverned lusts of a few of its worst examples.

I am ready to maintain that there are many females who never feel any sexual excitement whatever. Others, again, immediately after each period, do become, to a limited degree, capable of experiencing it; but this capacity is often temporary, and may entirely cease till the next menstrual period. Many of the best mothers, wives, and managers of households, know little of or are careless

---

alone removed, as it is now considered that it is the glans alone in which the sensitive nerves expand. This view I do not agree with, as I have already stated with regard to the analogous structure of the penis. . . . I am fully convinced that in many women there is no special sexual sensation in the clitoris, and I am positive that the special sensibility dependent on the erectile tissue exists in several portions of the vaginal canal. [Acton's note.]

about sexual indulgences. Love of home, of children, and of domestic duties are the only passions they feel.[6]

As a general rule, a modest woman seldom desires any sexual gratification for herself. She submits to her husband's embraces, but principally to gratify him; and, were it not for the desire of maternity, would far rather be relieved from his attentions. No nervous or feeble young man need, therefore, be deterred from marriage by any exaggerated notion of the arduous duties required from him. Let him be well assured, on my authority backed by the opinion of many, that the married woman has no wish to be placed on the footing of a mistress. . . .

Perversion of Sexual Feeling. — Where, in addition to the indisposition to cohabitation which many modest women feel, we find a persistent aversion to it, so strong as to be invincible by entreaty or by any amount of kindness on the husband's part, a very painful suspicion may sometimes arise as to the origin of so unconquerable a frigidity.

The following is a case in which these suspicions seemed to be justified by the facts: — A gentleman came to ask my opinion on the cause of want of sexual feeling in his wife. He told me he had been married four years. His wife was about his own age (twenty-seven), and had had four children, but she evinced no sexual feeling, although a lively, healthy lady, living in the country. I suggested several causes, when he at last asked me if it was possible that a woman might lose sexual feeling from the same causes as men. "I have read your former edition, Mr. Acton," said he, "and though you only allude to the subject incidentally, yet from what I have learned since my marriage, I am led to think that my wife's want of sexual feeling may arise, if you can affirm to me that such a thing is possible, from self-abuse. She has confessed to me that at a boarding-school, in perfect ignorance of any injurious effects, she early acquired the habit. This practice still gives her gratification; not so connection, which she views with positive aversion, although it gives her no pain." I told

[6] The physiologist will not be surprised that the human female should in these respects differ but little from the female among animals. We well know it as a fact that the female animal will not allow the dog or stallion to approach her except at particular seasons. In many a human female, indeed, I believe, it is rather from the wish of pleasing or gratifying the husband than from any strong sexual feeling, that cohabitation is so habitually allowed. Certainly, during the months of gestation this holds good. I have known instances where the female has during gestation evinced positive loathing for any marital familiarity whatever. In some exceptional cases, indeed, feeling has been sacrificed to duty, and the wife has endured, with all the self-martyrdom of womanhood, what was almost worse than death. [Acton's note.]

him that medical men, who are consulted about female complaints, have not unfrequently observed cases like that of his wife. It appears that at last nothing but the morbid excitement produced by the baneful practice can give any sexual gratification, and that the natural stimulus fails to cause any pleasure whatever. A similar phenomenon occurs in men, and this state is seldom got the better of as long as self-abuse is practised. I feared, therefore, that his surmises were correct, and that the lady practised self-abuse more frequently than she was willing to admit. So ruinous is the practice of solitary vice, both in the one and other sex, so difficult is it to give it up, that I fear it may be carried on even in married life, where no excuse can be devised, and may actually come to be preferred to the natural excitement. Venereal excesses engender satiety just as certainly as any other indulgences, and satiety is followed by indifference and disgust. If the unnatural excesses of masturbation take place early in life, before the subjects who commit them have arrived at maturity, it is not surprising that we meet with women whose sexual feelings, if they ever existed, become prematurely worn out. Doubtless sexual feelings differ largely in different women, and although it is not my object to treat otherwise than incidentally of the sexual economy in women, yet I may here say that the causes which in early life induce abnormal sexual excitement in boys operate in a similar manner on girls. This tendency may be checked in girls, as in boys, by carefully moral education in early life. But no doubt can exist that hereditary predisposition has much to do with this, independently of education and early associations. It is publicly maintained by some credible persons that there are well-known families, for instance, in which chastity is not a characteristic feature among the females. We offer, I hope, no apology for light conduct when we admit that there are some *few* women who, like men, in consequence of hereditary predisposition or ill-directed moral education, find it difficult to restrain their passions, while their more fortunate sisters have never been tempted, and have, therefore, never fallen. This, however, does not alter the fact which I would venture again to impress on the reader, that, in general, women do *not* feel any great sexual tendencies. The unfortunately large numbers whose lives would seem to prove the contrary are to be otherwise accounted for. Vanity, giddiness, greediness, love of dress, distress, or hunger, make women prostitutes, but do not induce female profligacy so largely as has been supposed.

Malformation in the female is sometimes a source of non-consummation, wrongly attributed to want of power in the man. A singularly agreeable and gentlemanly, but very mild-looking man, once called on me, saying that he had been lately married, and had not succeeded in performing his marital duties. I treated him in the usual way and he got stronger, but still the act was not satisfactorily performed, and my patient said enough to induce me to believe that the failure was not to be attributed to him alone. After some little hesitation the lady consulted me. I found her a pretty, pleasing, but excessively nervous and excitable person. At first the mere application of cold water to the generative organs could not be borne, but after some time, and after a good deal of careful management, an astringent lotion was used. When the morbid excitability was somewhat reduced, the hymen was found not only entire, but very tough, presenting the appearance of the finger of a kid glove on the stretchers. Division of the hymen and dilatation of the vagina at length accustomed the parts to bear contact, and a permanent cure was effected. I have reason to believe that cases of supposed impotence arising from this cause are not uncommon; cohabitation is, under these circumstances, not likely to be followed by impregnation when the husband has been previously continent, and his natural disposition renders him particularly unwilling to distress or hurt his wife while she is in this state of unnatural and morbid sensitiveness. It is not improbable that divorces have taken place before now from such causes as these, particularly when interfering friends have exaggerated and envenomed the painful difference between the young couple. . . .

The following question has often been put to me by counsel: — "Surely, you do not pretend that a man can be otherwise than impotent who for months or years has cohabited with his wife and slept in the same bed without having had sexual relations with her?" Strange as it may appear, I am satisfied that such a state of things is not only possible, but that it often exists. The fact is, as I have already pointed out . . . , that in many women sexual feelings are either very slight or entirely dormant, at all events, until aggressively aroused. If a cold or nervous man should be married to a woman of similar disposition, I know it is quite possible that they may cohabit together and sleep in the same bed for months and years without any sexual intercourse taking place, and it is obvious that every day that passes after the marriage without consummation being attempted, decreases the probability of and even the ability (unless medical treatment is had recourse to) for sexual congress. It often happens that time passes on without the marriage having ever been consummated, and the parties live happily together untroubled by sexual thoughts. At length estrangement arises, mutual disappointment, incompatibility of temper, or poverty, or some other cause intervenes, or perhaps the lady forms an attachment for some other man, and so separation comes to be desired, a lawyer to be consulted, and a petition for nullity of marriage on the ground of the husband's impotence to be presented. In such a case the non-consummation of the marriage has clearly inflicted no hardship on the wife, and is attributable as much to her own fault as her husband's, and the wife as little deserves to be released from her contract as the husband does to be burdened with an odious stigma as the price of her freedom.

In concluding this part of the subject, I can only express the hope that greater attention, than it has received in the past, may be vouchsafed to it in the future by the medical profession. Assured as I am that just as in former days men were consigned to helpless confinement, as idiots and lunatics, whom proper treatment would have restored to society and usefulness, so now many are condemned to bear the stigma and privations of impotence who are in fact merely the victims of ailments removable by medical care and skill.

Upon these cases, which I consider have hitherto been neglected and misunderstood, I have attempted to throw new light, and I have every reason to hope that in future distinctions will be made between many of these cases of impotence which are now mixed up together, owing to the assumed inability to distinguish between the true and false complaint.

I consider these charges of alleged impotence some of the gravest that can be brought against a man. They, like some other accusations, are easily made, but not so easily disproved.

In my opinion these suits for nullity of marriage are becoming much too common,[7] and I hope the law will cease to countenance some wives in dishonouring instead of honouring the husbands they have sworn to cherish, and this the more especially as a worldly experience teaches me that a woman seldom brings these charges till she has formed another attachment.

---

[7] I have been told that the instances of woman seeking divorce on account of impotence have largely increased of late, the increase reaching the formidable proportion of about 12 to 1 in the course of the last twelve months. [Acton's note.]

2

Invalid Women

The documents assembled in this chapter provide an overview of those late-nineteenth-century assumptions about women's health and assumed frailty that Gilman set out to debunk in both "The Yellow Wallpaper" and her 1913 defense of the story (see Part Two, Chapter 5), as well as in her later fictions about the salvation of suicidal women through sympathetic female doctors and reformers. Gilman herself was urged to become pregnant in order to get over the periods of depression she suffered from as a young woman. This advice proved to be wrong, and she remained depressed through most, if not all, of her life. As part of her own struggle with depression and her experience of the ways in which women were segregated from public life as a result of their reproductivity, Gilman became more and more devoted to the professionalization of women's careers, including the professionalization of mothering.

The doctor-husband in "The Yellow Wallpaper" threatens his wife with a visit to S. Weir Mitchell if her health does not improve. He prevents her from seeing "exciting" visitors, reads to her, and controls her activities, as Dr. Mitchell and later Dr. John Harvey Kellogg would advise was a necessary precaution in "ante-natal life." Arguably, the heroine's madness is a form of the "puerperal mania" — what is now called postpartum depression — that Kellogg had diagnosed or another bout of the neurasthenia that Mitchell discusses in his analyses of nervous women.

Many of the selections included here illustrate the contemporaneous thinking about puerperal mania, as well as women's illnesses in general. Puerperal mania was considered to be a physical and mental reaction to the traumas of childbirth, manifesting itself in symptoms such as obscene language, psychotic breaks with reality, and resistance to the needs of the baby. As both Alfred Meadows's "Puerperal Mania" (1871) and Fordyce Barker's *The Puerperal Diseases* (1874) suggest, "melancholic depression" is the hardest to cure. In dramatizing the melancholic condition of a doctor's wife, Gilman's story reflected a common occurrence, for, as Dr. Barker states, "Since 1855, I have seen thirteen cases of puerperal mania in the wives of physicians, nine in this city, and four in the adjoining cities. All but one were primaparæ. It has struck me as very extraordinary, that so large a number should have occurred in one special class" (see p. 184). Doctors' wives, he contends, are usually intellectual and have read their husbands' medical books. They are susceptible, therefore, to the suggestions they have read and internalized. Nineteenth-century conduct literature, as we have seen, gave little attention to women's intellectual development (see the documents in Part Two, Chapter 1), and some medical texts attributed real health problems to women's intellectual activities.

In the late nineteenth century, more than at any other time in American history, attention was focused on the effects of industrialization on mental health, so much so that former Civil War physician S. Weir Mitchell developed a series of remedies first administered to veterans and later — with some modification — to victims of the stress and "wear and tear" of modern culture. Mitchell's rest cure was not always the same for men as it was for women. While men might be told to seek physical exercise — fishing or hiking — to reenergize themselves, Mitchell's remedy for the female neurasthenic was rest, forced feeding, and seclusion, a treatment designed to infantilize the patient so that she acknowledged the paternal authority of the doctor (Lutz 32).

The emphasis of the new consumer culture on the exercise of desire proved to be enervating, for it left many people spiritually "weightless" in a society where scientific and medical experts had replaced the previous moral anchors of religion, community, and extended family. Earlier in the century, the individualistic desire for material success had been distrusted and viewed as antagonistic to the commonwealth, or greater good of the country. By the turn of the century, desire was coming to be seen as the great personal motivator

for work, for ambition, and for life in general. A new emphasis on individual "style" was formed and bolstered by the commodity culture,
which emphasized self-improvement through exercise, psycho-physical
growth, exposure to stimulating activities (such as stereopticons,
lyceum or lecture events, and concerts), or merely through the acqui-
sition of the "proper" household objects. The documents in this section testify to the relationship of the debate in Gilman's time about
physical and mental health to the development of industrial capitalism at the turn of the century. While the shift from a primarily agrar-
ian society to an urban, industrial culture occurred over the course of
the nineteenth century, occasioning all kinds of changes in demo-
graphics and the American class system, it took until the 1880s and
1890s for Americans to address the psychic and somatic transfigura-
tions that the new commercial culture had ushered in.

Gilman worried about the consumer culture's emphasis on sexual
pleasure and on individual sex attraction. She lamented that women
had long been competing over men in a system of oppression that had
its roots in precapitalist culture. Only men could promise economic
security in a world which would not employ women. Middle-class
women were generally excluded from the workplace and relegated to
the monotony of housework, the intellectual void of the home, the
obligation of caring for others, and the minutae of domestic management. Any of these tedious conditions could, in themselves, bring
about nervousness. In contrast to the emphasis many doctors placed
on the biological and physical aspects of mental disorders, Sigmund
Freud's work on hysteria — the late-nineteenth century catch-phrase
for a variety of nervous disorders attributed primarily to women —
would define the disease as a psychological affair, stemming from
childhood experiences. Freud traced hysteria to the patient's repressed memories of a "premature sexual experience" that constituted the "scene" from which the hysterical symptoms first arose.

The 1880s and 1890s saw the rise of "therapy" as a way to cure
this sense of "dis-ease" in American culture. Exercise and calisthenics
were also promoted as remedies for women's nervous disorders.
Gilman herself endorsed regular exercise, but she went much further
in her recommendations for women, advocating their independence
through writing and, above all, through freedom from the drudgery
of housework. As we will see in her 1915 story, "Dr. Clair's Place"
(see Part Two, Chapter 4), Gilman believed in "busyness" and intellectual stimulation as antidotes for modern psychological dilemmas.

S. WEIR MITCHELL

From Wear and Tear, or Hints for the Overworked

From "Nervousness and Its Influence on Character"

From "The Evolution of the Rest Treatment"

S. Weir Mitchell (1829–1914), expert on neurology and inventor of the rest cure for neurasthenics and invalid women, began his career as a Civil War doctor. He wrote fiction based on his experiences with Civil War casualties and clinical medicine, and his first story, "The Case of George Dedlow," was published in the *Atlantic Monthly* in 1866. In 1871, Mitchell published *Wear and Tear, or Hints for the Overworked*, which contains his most famous medical statements about nervous maladies, or what was termed "neurasthenia." In this book, which was a popular success, Mitchell documented the increase of nervous disorders in America, arguing that Americans devoted too little time to leisure activities and that incessant work was ruining the mental health of the country's citizens. The text reprinted here is taken from the fifth edition of *Wear and Tear, or Hints for the Overworked* (Philadelphia: Lippincott, 1887), 30–37; 42–48; 56–57.

The next volume of Mitchell's studies of American mental health, *Fat and Blood* (1877), cautioned the American public about the dangers of modernity and industrialization. In 1887, Mitchell published *Doctor and Patient*, in which he gives the following description of modern women: "As women, their lives are likely, nay certain, to bring them a variety of physical discomforts, and perhaps pain in its gravest forms. For man, pain is accidental, and depends much on the chances of life. Certainly, many men go through existence here with but little pain. With women it is incidental, and a far more probable possibility." The text of "Nervousness and Its Influence on Character," reprinted here, is taken from *Doctor and Patient* (Philadelphia: Lippincott [1887], 1904), 6–13; 115–20.

In "The Evolution of the Rest Treatment" (1904), first given as a lecture at the twentieth anniversary of the founding of the Philadelphia Neurological Society (celebrated in January 1904) and published that same year, Mitchell charts the reasoning that led him to develop the rest cure for nervous diseases, which he first used to treat Civil War cases of acute exhaustion. The cure involved not only rest, but also overfeeding and massage ("exercise without exertion"). The study of "hysteria" was at its peak in the decades from 1870 through 1910, when Mitchell's career was at its height and Freud was beginning his study of hysterics and his ground-breaking treatment through psychoanalysis. The text from "The Evolution of the Rest Treatment" reprinted here is taken from *The Journal of Nervous and Mental Disease* 31. 6 (June 1904): 368–73.

From Wear and Tear, or Hints for the Overworked

If I have made myself understood, we are now prepared to apply some of our knowledge to the solution of certain awkward questions which force themselves daily upon the attention of every thoughtful and observant physician, and have thus opened a way to the discussion of the causes which, as I believe, are deeply affecting the mental and physical health of working Americans. Some of these are due to the climatic conditions under which all work must be done in this country, some are outgrowths of our modes of labor, and some go back to social habitudes and defective methods of early educational training.

In studying this subject, it will not answer to look only at the causes of sickness and weakness which affect the male sex. If the mothers of a people are sickly and weak, the sad inheritance falls upon their offspring, and this is why I must deal first, however briefly, with the health of our girls, because it is here, as the doctor well knows, that the trouble begins. Ask any physician of your acquaintance to sum up thoughtfully the young girls he knows, and to tell you how many in each score are fit to be healthy wives and mothers, or in fact to be wives and mothers at all. I have been asked this question myself very often, and I have heard it asked of others. The answers I am not going to give, chiefly because I should not be believed — a disagreeable position, in which I shall not deliberately place myself. Perhaps I ought to add that the replies I have heard given by others were appalling.

Next, I ask you to note carefully the expression and figures of the young girls whom you may chance to meet in your walks, or whom you may observe at a concert or in the ball-room. You will see many very charming faces, the like of which the world cannot match — figures somewhat too spare of flesh, and, especially south of Rhode Island, a marvellous littleness of hand and foot. But look further, and

S. Weir Mitchell, ca. 1910. Courtesy of the Library of College of Physicians of Philadelphia.

especially among New England young girls: you will be struck with a certain hardness of line in form and feature which should not be seen between thirteen and eighteen, at least; and if you have an eye which rejoices in the tints of health, you will too often miss them on the cheeks we are now so daringly criticising. I do not want to do more than is needed of this ungracious talk: suffice it to say that multitudes of our young girls are merely pretty to look at, or not that; that their destiny is the shawl and the sofa, neuralgia, weak backs, and the varied forms of hysteria, — that domestic demon which has produced untold discomfort in many a household, and, I am almost ready to say, as much unhappiness as the husband's dram. My phrase may seem outrageously strong, but only the doctor knows what one of these self-made invalids can do to make a household wretched. Mrs. Gradgrind[1] is, in fiction, the only successful portrait of this type of misery, of the woman who wears out and destroys generations of nursing relatives, and who, as Wendell Holmes[2] has said, is like a vampire, sucking slowly the blood of every healthy, helpful creature within reach of her demands.

If any reader doubts my statement as to the physical failure of our city-bred women to fulfil all the natural functions of mothers, let him contrast the power of the recently imported Irish or Germans[3] to nurse their babies a full term or longer, with that of the native women even of our mechanic classes. It is difficult to get at full statistics as to those of a higher social degree, but I suspect that not over one-half are competent to nurse their children a full year without themselves suffering gravely. I ought to add that our women, unlike ladies abroad, are usually anxious to nurse their own children, and merely cannot. The numerous artificial infant foods now for sale singularly prove the truth of this latter statement. Many physicians, with whom I have talked of this matter, believe that I do not overstate the evil; others think that two-thirds may be found reliable as nurses; while the rural doctors, who have replied to my queries, state that only from one-tenth to three-tenths of farmers' wives are unequal to this natural demand. There is indeed little doubt that the mass of our women possess that peculiar nervous organization which is associated with great excitability, and, unfortunately, with less physical vigor than is to be found, for example, in the sturdy English dames at whom Hawthorne sneered so bitterly. And what are the causes to which these peculiarities are to be laid? There are many who will say

[1] *Mrs. Gradgrind:* In Charles Dickens's 1854 novel *Hard Times,* Mrs. Gradgrind is married to the proprietor of an experimental school who worships "facts" and insists that they are superior to the imagination. She is a sickly woman who is incapable of physical or mental exertion and who provides no moral guidance for her two children, Louisa and Tom.

[2] *Wendell Holmes:* Oliver Wendell Holmes (1809–1894), man of letters and professor of medicine; best known for his occasional poetry.

[3] *imported Irish or Germans:* Irish and German immigrants were generally employed as unskilled workers or domestics.

that late hours, styles of dress, prolonged dancing, etc., are to blame; while really, with rare exceptions, the newer fashions have been more healthy than those they superseded, people are better clad and better warmed than ever, and, save in rare cases, late hours and overexertion in the dance are utterly incapable of alone explaining the mischief. I am far more inclined to believe that climatic peculiarities have formed the groundwork of the evil, and enabled every injurious agency to produce an effect which would not in some other countries be so severe. I am quite persuaded, indeed, that the development of a nervous temperament is one of the many race-changes[4] which are also giving us facial, vocal, and other peculiarities derived from none of our ancestral stocks. If, as I believe, this change of temperament in a people coming largely from the phlegmatic races[5] is to be seen most remarkably in the more nervous sex, it will not surprise us that it should be fostered by many causes which are fully within our own control. Given such a tendency, disease will find in it a ready prey, want of exercise will fatally increase it, and all the follies of fashion will aid in the work of ruin.

While a part of the mischief lies with climatic conditions which are utterly mysterious, the obstacles to physical exercise, arising from extremes of temperature, constitute at least one obvious cause of ill health among women in our country. The great heat of summer, and the slush and ice of winter, interfere with women who wish to take exercise, but whose arrangements to go out-of-doors involve wonderful changes of dress and an amount of preparation appalling to the masculine creature.

The time taken for the more serious instruction of girls extends to the age of nineteen, and rarely over this. During some of these years they are undergoing such organic development as renders them remarkably sensitive. At seventeen I presume that healthy girls are as well able to *study, with proper precautions,*[6] as men; but before

---

[4] *race-changes:* Mitchell refers to the supposed degeneration of "native stock" — from western Europe and England — due to modernization, industrialization, and immigration.

[5] *phlegmatic races:* A reference to Slavic immigrants (including Poles, Lithuanians, and Bulgarians), who were categorized by sociologists such as Edward Alsworth Ross in *The Old World in the New* (New York: Century, 1914) as possessing a slow and stolid temperament.

[6] *study, with proper precautions:* A reference to such works as Dr. E. A. Clarke's *Sex in Education* (1873), which argued that girls could be educated only if their feminine bodies and reproductive systems were taken into account and not irreparably harmed by too much instruction.

this time overuse, or even a very steady use, of the brain is in many dangerous to health and to every probability of <u>future womanly usefulness</u>. hmm...

In most of our schools the hours are too many, for both girls and boys. From nine until two is, with us, the common school-time in private seminaries. The usual recess is twenty minutes or half an hour, and it is not as a rule filled by enforced exercise. In certain schools — would it were common! — ten minutes' recess is given after every hour; and in the Blind Asylum of Philadelphia this time is taken up by light gymnastics, which are obligatory. To these hours we must add the time spent in study out of school. This, for some reason, nearly always exceeds the time stated by teachers to be necessary; and most girls of our common schools and normal schools between the ages of thirteen and seventeen thus expend two or three hours. Does any physician believe that it is good for a growing girl to be so occupied seven or eight hours a day? or that it is right for her to use her brains as long a time as the mechanic employs his muscles? But this is only a part of the evil. The multiplicity of studies, the number of teachers, — each eager to get the most he can out of his pupil, — the severer drill of our day, and the greater intensity of application demanded, produce effects on the growing brain which, in a vast number of causes, can be only disastrous.

My remarks apply of course chiefly to public school life. I am glad to say that of late in all of our best school States more thought is now being given to this subject, but we have much to do before an evil which is partly a school difficulty and partly a home difficulty shall have been fully provided against.

Careful reading of our Pennsylvania reports and of those of Massachusetts convinces me that while in the country schools overwork is rare, in those of the cities it is more common, and that the system of pushing, — of competitive examinations, — of ranking, etc., is in a measure responsible for that worry which adds a dangerous element to work. . . .

In private schools for girls of what I may call the leisure class of society overwork is of course much more rare than in our normal schools for girls, but the precocious claims of social life and the indifference of parents as to hours and systematic living needlessly add to the ever-present difficulties of the school-teacher, whose control ceases when the pupil passes out of her house.

As to the school in which both sexes are educated together a word may be said. Surely no system can be worse than that which complicates a difficult problem by taking two sets of beings of different gifts, and of unlike physiological needs and construction, and forcing them into the same educational mould.

It is a wrong for both sexes. Not much unlike the boy in childhood, there comes a time when in the rapid evolution of puberty the girl becomes for a while more than the equal of the lad, and, owing to her consciousness, his moral superior, but at this era of her life she is weighted by periodical disabilities which become needlessly hard to consider in a school meant to be both home and school for both sexes. Finally, there comes a time when the matured man certainly surpasses the woman in persistent energy and capacity for unbroken brain-work. If then she matches herself against him, it will be, with some exceptions, at bitter cost.

It is sad to think that the demands of civilized life are making this contest almost unavoidable. Even if we admit equality of intellect, the struggle with man is cruelly unequal and is to be avoided whenever it is possible. *Wi*

The colleges for women, such as Vassar,[7] are nowadays more careful than they were. Indeed, their machinery for guarding health while education of a high class goes on is admirable. What they still lack is a correct public feeling. The standard for health and endurance is too much that which would be normal for young men, and the sentiment of these groups of women is silently opposed to admitting that the feminine life has necessities which do not cumber that of man. Thus the unwritten code remains in a measure hostile to the accepted laws which are supposed to rule.

As concerns our colleges for young men I have little to say. The cases I see of breakdown among women between sixteen and nineteen who belong to normal schools or female colleges are out of all proportion larger than the number of like failures among young men of the same ages, and yet, as I have hinted, the arrangements for watching the health of these groups of women are usually better than such as the colleges for young men provide. The system of professional guardianship at Johns Hopkins is an admirable exception, and at some other institutions the physical examination on matriculation becomes of the utmost value, when followed up as it is in certain of these schools by compulsory physical training and occasional re-examinations of the state of health.

I do not see why the whole matter could not in all colleges be systematically made part of the examinations on entry upon studies. It

---

[7] *Vassar:* Founded in 1865, one of the first women's colleges.

would at least point out to the thoughtful student his weak points, and enable him to do his work and take his exercise with some regard to consequences. I have over and over seen young men with weak hearts or unsuspected valvular troubles who had suffered from having been allowed to play foot-ball. Cases of cerebral trouble in students, due to the use of defective eyes, are common, and I have known many valuable lives among male and female students crippled hopelessly owing to the fact that no college pre-examination of their state had taught them their true condition, and that no one had pointed out to them the necessity of such correction by glasses as would have enabled them as workers to compete on even terms with their fellows.

In a somewhat discursive fashion I have dwelt upon the mischief which is pressing today upon our girls of every class in life. The doctor knows how often and how earnestly he is called upon to remonstrate against this growing evil. He is, of course, well enough aware that many sturdy girls stand the strain, but he knows also that very many do not, and that the brain, sick with multiplied studies and unwholesome home life, plods on, doing poor work, until somebody wonders what is the matter with that girl; or she is left to scramble through, or break down with weak eyes, headaches, neuralgias,[8] or what not. I am perfectly confident that I shall be told here that girls ought to be able to study hard between fourteen and eighteen years without injury, if boys can do it. Practically, however, the boys of today are getting their toughest education later and later in life, while girls leave school at the same age as they did thirty years ago. It used to be common for boys to enter college at fourteen: at present, eighteen is a usual age of admission at Harvard or Yale. Now, let any one compare the scale of studies for both sexes employed half a century ago with that of to-day. He will find that its demands are vastly more exacting than they were, — a difference fraught with no evil for men, who attack the graver studies later in life, but most perilous for girls, who are still expected to leave school at eighteen or earlier.

I firmly believe — and I am not alone in this opinion — that as concerns the physical future of women they would do far better if the brain were very lightly tasked and the school hours but three or four a day until they reach the age of seventeen at least. Anything, indeed, were better than loss of health; and if it be in any case a question of doubt, the school should be unhesitatingly abandoned or its hours

---

[8] *neuralgias:* Acute paroxysmal pain radiating through a nerve.

lessened, as at least in part the source of very many of the nervous maladies with which our women are troubled. I am almost ashamed to defend a position which is held by many competent physicians, but an intelligent friend, who has read this page, still asks me why it is that overwork of brain should be so serious an evil to women at the age of womanly development. My best reply would be the experience and opinions of those of us who are called upon to see how many school-girls are suffering in health from confinement, want of exercise at the time of day when they most incline to it, bad ventilation,[9] and too steady occupation of mind. At no other time of life is the nervous system so sensitive, — so irritable, I might say, — and at no other are abundant fresh air and exercise so important. To show more precisely how the growing girl is injured by the causes just mentioned would lead me to speak of subjects unfit for full discussion in these pages, but no thoughtful reader can be much at a loss as to my meaning. . . .

It were better not to educate girls at all between the ages of fourteen and eighteen, unless it can be done with careful reference to their bodily health. To-day, the American woman is, to speak plainly, too often physically unfit for her duties as woman, and is perhaps of all civilized females the least qualified to undertake those weightier tasks which tax so heavily the nervous system of man. She is not fairly up to what nature asks from her as wife and mother. How will she sustain herself under the pressure of those yet more exacting duties which nowadays she is eager to share with the man?

While making these stringent criticisms, I am anxious not to be misunderstood. The point which above all others I wish to make is this, that owing chiefly to peculiarities of climate, our growing girls are endowed with organizations so highly sensitive and impressionable that we expose them to needless dangers when we attempt to overtax them mentally. In any country the effects of such a course must be evil, but in America I believe it to be most disastrous.

[9] In the city where this is written there is, so far as I know, not one private girls' school in a building planned for a school-house. As a consequence, we hear endless complaints from young ladies of overheated or chilly rooms. If the teacher be old, the room is kept too warm; if she be young, and much afoot about her school, the apartment is apt to be cold. [Mitchell's note.]

From "Nervousness and Its Influence on Character"

There are two questions often put to me which I desire to use as texts for the brief essay or advice of which nervousness[10] is the heading. As concerns this matter, I shall here deal with women alone, and with women as I see and know them. I have elsewhere written at some length as to nervousness in the male, for he, too, in a minor degree, and less frequently, may become the victim of this form of disability.

So much has been written on this subject by myself and others, that I should hesitate to treat it anew from a mere didactic point of view. But, perhaps, if I can bring home to the sufferer some more individualized advice, if I can speak here in a friendly and familiar way, I may be of more service than if I were to repeat, even in the fullest manner, all that is to be said or has been said of nervousness from a scientific point of view.

The two questions referred to above are these: The woman who consults you says, "I am nervous. I did not use to be. What can I do to overcome it?" Once well again, she asks you, — and the query is common enough from the thoughtful, — "What can I do to keep my girls from being nervous?"

Observe, now, that this woman has other distresses, in the way of aches and feebleness. The prominent thing in her mind, nervousness, is but one of the symptomatic results of her condition. She feels that to be the greatest evil, and that it is which she puts forward. What does she mean by nervousness, and what does it do with her which makes it so unpleasant? Remark also that this is not one of the feebler sisters who accept this ill as a natural result, and who condone for themselves the moral and social consequences as things over which they have little or no reasonable control. The person who asks

---

[10] Neither *nerves* nor *nervousness* are words to be found in the Bible or Shakespeare. The latter uses the word nerve at least seven times in the sense of sinewy. *Nervy*, which is obsolete, he employs as full of nerves, sinewy, strong. It is still heard in America, but I am sure would be classed as slang. Writers, of course, still employ nerve and nervous in the old sense, as a nervous style. Bailey's dictionary, 1734, has nervous, — sinewy, strongly made. Robt. Whytte, Edin., in the preface to his work on certain maladies, 1765, says, "Of late these have also got the name of nervous," and this is the earliest use of the word in the modern meaning I have found. Richardson has it in both its modern meanings, "vigorous," or "sensitive in nerves, and consequently weak, diseased." Hysteria is not in the Bible, and is found once in Shakespeare; as, "Hysterica passio, down," Lear ii. 4. It was common in Sydenham's day, — *i.e.*, Charles II. and Cromwell's time, — but he classified under hysteria many disorders no longer considered as of this nature. [Mitchell's note.]

142

this fertile question has once been well, and resents as unnatural the weaknesses and incapacities which now she feels. She wants to be helped, and will help you to help her. You have an active ally, not a passive fool who, too, desires to be made well, but can give you no potent aid. There are many kinds of fool, from the mindless fool to the fiend-fool, but for the most entire capacity to make a household wretched there is no more complete human receipt than a silly woman who is to a high degree nervous and feeble, and who craves pity and likes power. But to go back to the more helpful case. If you are wise, you ask what she means by nervousness. You soon learn that she suffers in one of two, or probably in both of two, ways. The parentage is always mental in a large sense, the results either mental or physical or both. She has become doubtful and fearful, where formerly she was ready-minded and courageous. Once decisive, she is now indecisive. When well, unemotional, she is now too readily disturbed by a sad tale or a startling newspaper-paragraph. A telegram alarms her; even an unopened letter makes her hesitate and conjure up dreams of disaster. Very likely she is irritable and recognizes the unreasonableness of her temper. Her daily tasks distress her sorely. She can no longer sit still and sew or read. Conversation no longer interests, or it even troubles her. Noises, especially sudden noises, startle her, and the cries and laughter of children have become distresses of which she is ashamed, and of which she complains or not, as her nature is weak or enduring. Perhaps, too, she is so restless as to want to be in constant motion, but that seems to tire her as it once did not. Her sense of moral proportion becomes impaired. Trifles grow large to her; the grasshopper is a burden. With all this, and in a measure out of all this, come certain bodily disabilities. The telegram or any cause of emotion sets her to shaking. She cries for no cause; the least alarm makes her hand shake, and even her writing, if she should chance to become the subject of observation when at the desk, betrays her state of tremor. What caused all this trouble? What made her, as she says, good for nothing? I have, of course, put an extreme case. We may, as a rule, be pretty sure, as to this condition, that the woman has had some sudden shock, some severe domestic trial, some long strain, or that it is the outcome of acute illness or of one of the forms of chronic disturbance of nutrition which result in what we now call general neurasthenia or nervous weakness, — a condition which has a most varied parentage. With the ultimate medical causation of these disorderly states of body I do not mean to concern myself here, except to add also that the great physiological revolutions of a woman's life are often responsible for the physical failures which create nervousness.

If she is at the worst she becomes a ready victim of hysteria.[11] The emotions so easily called into activity give rise to tears. Too weak for wholesome restraint, she yields. The little convulsive act we call crying brings uncontrollable, or what seems to her to be uncontrollable, twitching of the face. The jaw and hands get rigid, and she has a hysterical convulsion, and is on the way to worse perils. The intelligent despotism of self-control is at an end, and every new attack upon its normal prerogatives leaves her less and less able to resist.

From "The Evolution of the Rest Treatment"

I have been asked to come here to-night to speak to you on some subject connected with nervous disease. I had hoped to have had ready a fitting paper for so notable an occasion, but have been prevented by public engagements and private business so as to make it quite impossible. I have, therefore, been driven to ask whether it would be agreeable if I should speak in regard to the mode in which the treatment of disease by rest was evolved. This being favorably received, I am here this evening to say a few words on that subject.

You all know full well that the art of cure rests upon a number of sciences, and that what we do in medicine, we cannot always explain, and that our methods are far from having the accuracy involved in the term scientific. Very often, however, it is found that what comes to us through some accident or popular use and proves of value, is defensible in the end by scientific explanatory research. This was the case as regards the treatment I shall briefly consider for you to-night.

The first indication I ever had of the great value of mere rest in disease, was during the Civil War, when there fell into the hands of Doctors Morehouse, Keen and myself, a great many cases of what we called acute exhaustion. These were men, who, being tired by much marching, gave out suddenly at the end of some unusual exertion, and remained for weeks, perhaps months, in a pitiable state of what

---

[11] *hysteria:* The general term in the nineteenth century for a variety of nervous disorders, ranging from seizures to schizophrenia, attributed primarily to women. The Victorian medical and scientific communities linked women's sexual organs — their "wandering wombs" — to a propensity for insanity. (Thus the use of the term *hysteria,* which derives from the Latin and Greek for *womb.*)

S. Weir Mitchell in consultation, ca. 1890. Courtesy of the Library of College of Physicians of Philadelphia.

we should call today, Neurasthenia. In these war cases, it came on with strange abruptness. It was more extreme and also more certainly curable than are most of the graver male cases which now we are called on to treat.

I have seen nothing exactly like it in civil experience, but the combination of malaria, excessive exertion, and exposure provided cases such as no one sees today. Complete rest and plentiful diet usually brought these men up again and in many instances enabled them to return to the front.

In 1872 I had charge of a man who had locomotor ataxia[12] with extreme pain in the extremities, and while making some unusual exertion, he broke his right thigh. This confined him to his bed for three months, and the day he got up, he broke his left thigh. This involved another three months of rest. At the end of that time he confessed with satisfaction that his ataxia was better, and that he was, as he remained thereafter, free from pain. I learned from this, and two other cases, that in ataxia the bones are brittle, and I learned also that rest

[12] *ataxia:* A lack of coordination of the muscles which is a symptom of some nervous disorders.

in bed is valuable in a proportion of such cases. You may perceive that my attention was thus twice drawn towards the fact that mere rest had certain therapeutic values.

In 1874 Mrs. G., of B——, Maine, came to see me in the month of January. I have described her case elsewhere, so that it is needless to go into detail here, except to say that she was a lady of ample means, with no special troubles or annoyances, but completely exhausted by having had children in rapid succession and from having undertaken to do charitable and other work to an extent far beyond her strength. When first I saw this tall woman, large, gaunt, weighing under a hundred pounds, her complexion pale and acneous, and heard her story, I was for a time in a state of such therapeutic despair as usually fell upon physicians of that day when called upon to treat such cases. She had been to Spas,[13] to physicians of the utmost eminence, passed through the hands of gynecologists,[14] worn spinal supporters, and taken every tonic known to the books.[15] When I saw her she was unable to walk up stairs. Her exercise was limited to moving feebly up and down her room, a dozen times a day. She slept little and, being very intelligent, felt deeply her inability to read or write. Any such use of the eyes caused headache and nausea. Con-

versation tired her, and she had by degrees accepted a life of isolation. She was able partially to digest and retain her meals if she lay down in a noiseless and darkened room. Any disturbance or the least excitement, in short, any effort, caused nausea and immediate rejection of her meal. With care she could retain enough food to preserve her life and hardly to do more. Anemia, which we had then no accurate means of measuring, had been met by half a dozen forms of iron, all of which were said to produce headache, and generally to disagree with her. Naturally enough, her case had been pronounced to be hysteria, but calling names may relieve a doctor and comfort him in failure, but does not always assist the patient, and to my mind there was more of a general condition of nervous excitability due to

---

[13] *Spas:* Many women and some men went to spas for restorative treatment and care; treatments involved bathing, wet compresses, steam, massage, exercise, electricity, cold water, and new diets.

[14] *gynecologists:* Gynecology as a science grew after the Civil War, when physicians were given some education on midwifery and sexual organs. Yet women were still urged to abjure "local examination" of their bodies in order to preserve their modesty.

[15] *spinal supporters . . . the books:* Spinal supporters were often marketed as substitutes for stays and corsets. Tonics were patented medicines or remedies which often contained high percentages of alcohol or opiates.

the extreme of weakness than I should have been satisfied to label with the apologetic label hysteria.

I sat beside this woman day after day, hearing her pitiful story, and distressed that a woman, young, once handsome, and with every means of enjoyment in life should be condemned to what she had been told was a state of hopeless invalidism.[16] After my third or fourth visit, with a deep sense that everything had been done for her that able men could with reason suggest, and many things which reason never could have suggested, she said to me that I appeared to have nothing to offer which had not been tried over and over again. I asked her for another day before she gave up the hope which had brought her to me. The night brought counsel. The following morning I said to her, if you are at rest you appear to digest your meals better. "Yes," she said. "I have been told that on that account I ought to lie in bed. It has been tried, but when I remain in bed for a few days, I lose all appetite, have intense constipation, and get up feeling weaker than when I went to bed. Please do not ask me to go to bed." Nevertheless, I did, and a week in bed justified her statements. She threw up her meals undigested, and was manifestly worse for my experiment. Sometimes the emesis[17] was mere regurgitation, sometimes there was nausea and violent straining, with consequent extreme exhaustion. She declared that unless she had the small exercise of walking up and down her room, she was infallibly worse. I was here between two difficulties. That she needed rest I saw, that she required some form of exercise I also saw. How could I unite the two?

As I sat beside her, with a keen sense of defeat, it suddenly occurred to me that some time before, I had seen a man, known as a layer on of hands, use very rough rubbing for a gentleman who was in a state of general paresis.[18] Mr. S. had asked me if I objected to this man rubbing him. I said no, and that I should like to see him do so, as he had relieved, to my knowledge, cases of rheumatic stiffness. I was present at two sittings and saw this man rub my patient. He kept him sitting in a chair at the time and was very rough and violent like the quacks now known as osteopaths. I told him he had injured my patient by his extreme roughness, and that if he rubbed him at all

---

[16] *invalidism:* During the nineteenth century, *invalidism* referred to the state of being afflicted — as many white, middle-class women appeared to be — with chronic illnesses.

[17] *emesis:* Vomiting.

[18] *paresis:* Also called brain syphilis. A psychosis caused by widespread destruction of brain tissue, usually in a case of syphilis, resulting in general paralysis.

he must be more gentle. He took the hint and as a result there was every time a notable but temporary gain. Struck with this, I tried to have rubbing used on spinal cases, but those who tried to do the work were inefficient, and I made no constant use of it. It remained, however, on my mind, and recurred to me as I sat beside this wreck of a useful and once vigorous woman. The thought was fertile. I asked myself why rubbing might not prove competent to do for the muscles and tardy circulation what voluntary exercise does. I said to myself, this may be exercise without exertion, and wondered why I had not long before had this pregnant view of the matter.

Suffice it to say that I brought a young woman to Mrs. G.'s bedside and told her how I thought she ought to be rubbed. The girl was clever, and developed talent in that direction, and afterwards became the first of that great number of people who have since made a livelihood by massage. I watched the rubbing two or three times, giving instructions, in fact developing out of the clumsy massage I had seen, the manual of a therapeutic means, at that time entirely new to me. A few days later I fell upon the idea of giving electric passive exercise[19] and cautiously added this second agency. Meanwhile, as she had always done best when secluded, I insisted on entire rest and shut out friends, relatives, books and letters. I had some faith that I should succeed. In ten days I was sure the woman had found a new tonic, hope, and blossomed like a rose. Her symptoms passed away one by one. I was soon able to add to her diet, to feed her between meals, to give her malt daily, and, after a time, to conceal in it full doses of pyro-phosphates of iron. First, then, I had found two means which enabled me to use rest in bed without causing the injurious effects of unassisted rest; secondly, I had discovered that massage was a tonic of extraordinary value: thirdly, I had learned that with this combination of seclusion, massage and electricity, I could overfeed[20] the patient until I had brought her into a state of entire health. I learned later the care which had to be exercised in getting these patients out of bed. But this does not concern us now. In two months she gained forty pounds and was a cheerful, blooming woman, fit to do as she pleased. She has remained, save for time's ravage, what I made her.

It may strike you as interesting that for a while I was not fully aware of the enormous value of a therapeutic discovery which em-

---

[19] *electric passive exercise:* The application of electricity to parts of the body to offset the effects of prolonged confinement or immobility.

[20] *overfeed:* Gaining weight was associated with good health and an increase in blood; surplus fat was believed to help fight moral or mental strain.

ployed no new agents, but owed its usefulness to a combination of means more or less well known.

Simple rest as a treatment had been suggested, but not in this class of cases. Massage has a long history. Used, I think, as a luxury by the Orientals for ages, it was employed by Ling in 1813. It never attained perfection in the hands of the Swedes, nor do they to-day understand the proper use of this agent. It was over and over recognized in Germany, but never generally accepted. In France, at a later period, Dreyfus, in 1841, wrote upon it and advised its use, as did Recamier and Lainé in 1868. Two at least of these authors thought it useful as a general agent, but no one seems to have accepted their views, nor was its value as a tonic spoken of in the books on therapeutics or recommended on any text-book as a powerful toning agent. It was used here in the Rest Treatment, and this, I think, gave it vogue and caused the familiar use of this invaluable therapeutic measure.

A word before I close. My first case left me in May, 1874, and shortly afterwards I began to employ the same method in other cases, being careful to choose only those which seemed best suited to it. My first mention in print of the treatment was in 1875, in the Sequin Lectures, Vol. 1., No. 4, "Rest in the Treatment of Disease." In that paper I first described Mrs. G.'s case. My second paper was in 1877, an address before the Medico-Chirurgical[21] faculty of Maryland, and the same year I printed my book on "Rest Treatment." The one mistake in the book was the title. I was, however, so impressed at the time by the extraordinary gain in flesh and blood under this treatment that I made it too prominent in the title of the book. Let me say that for a long time the new treatment was received with the utmost incredulity. When I spoke in my papers of the people who had gained half a pound a day or more, my results were questioned and ridiculed in this city as approaching charlatanism. At a later date in England some physicians were equally wanting in foresight and courtesy. It seems incredible that any man who was a member of the British Medical Association could have said that he would rather see his patients not get well than have them cured by such a method as that. It was several years before it was taken up by Professor Goodell, and it was a longer time in making its way in Europe when by mere accident it came to be first used by Professor William Playfair.

[21] *Medico-Chirurgical:* From the Greek for one who works with his or her hands; old term for *surgical.*

I suffered keenly at that time from this unfair criticism, as any sensitive man must have done, for some who were eminent in the profession said of it and of me things which were most inconsiderate. Over and over in consultation I was rejected with ill-concealed scorn. I made no reply to my critics. I knew that time would justify me: I have added a long since accepted means of helping those whom before my day few helped. This is a sufficient reward for silence, patience and self-faith. I fancy that there are in this room many who have profited for themselves and their patients by the thought which evolved the Rest Treatment as I sat by the beside of my first rest case in 1874. Playfair said of it at the British Association that he had nothing to add to it and nothing to omit, and to this day no one has differed as to his verdict.

How fully the use of massage has been justified by the later scientific studies of Lauder Brunton, myself, and others you all know. It is one of the most scientific of remedial methods.

William H. M. Weir

PRUDENCE B. SAUR

From Maternity; A Book for Every Wife and Mother

The advice given by Mrs. Prudence B. Saur, M.D., in *Maternity; A Book for Every Wife and Mother,* published in 1887, is representative of the counsel given to women at the turn of the century about achieving domestic and familial bliss. During a decade when one of the central social issues was the Woman Question, several authors attempted to educate women about their physical natures and their contribution to the future of the "race." Like Beecher (see Part Two, Chapter 1), Dr. Saur begins by assuming that most American women are unhealthy; she then prescribes exercise and counsels moderation in everything. She argues that women should return to activity after childbirth, since idleness leads to unhealthiness. Women's physical condition determines their destiny and the future of the race, and greater knowledge of their physiological and psychological attributes can alleviate women's moral burdens. Saur's book is dedicated to "the enlightenment of mothers and daughters upon this, and all topics pertaining to the physical, mental and moral conditions of women, as the surest means of correcting the glaring evils which to-day embitter the lives of our sex" (iv).

The text of the following excerpt is taken from the revised and enlarged edition of *Maternity; A Book for Every Wife and Mother* (Chicago: Miller, 1891), 11–16; 247–49.

[handwritten: everything of hers is for him]

A good wife is heaven's last, <u>best gift to man</u> — <u>his</u> angel and minister of graces innumerable — <u>his</u> gem of many virtues — <u>his</u> casket of jewels; her voice is sweet music — her smiles, his brightest day — her kiss, the guardian of his innocence — her arms, the pale of his safety, the balm of his health, the balsam of his life — her industry, his surest wealth — her economy, his safest steward — her lips, his faithful counselors — her bosom, the softest pillow of his cares — and her prayers, the ablest advocate of heaven's blessedness on his head.

[handwritten: remember to ask why and see] — Jeremy Taylor.[1] *[handwritten: Jaddr's subject]*

[handwritten: it is all for men, not for the woman herself]

To be the ideal woman here <u>portrayed</u>, perfect health is essential. My subject then, is health, the care, the restoration, and the preservation of health — one of the most important themes that can be brought before a human being, one that should engross much of our time and attention, and one that cannot be secured unless properly inquired into and attended to. The human frame is, as every one knows, constantly liable to be out of order; it would be strange, indeed, if a beautiful and complex instrument like the human body were not occasionally out of tune. *[handwritten: Stopped here]*

The advice I am about to offer my reader is of the greatest importance, and demands her deepest attention. How many wives are there with broken health, with feeble constitutions, and with childless homes. Their number is legion. It is painful to contemplate that, in our country, there are far more unhealthy, than healthy wives. There must surely be numerous causes for such a state of things. It will in the following pages, be my object to point out many of the causes of so much ill-health among women, and to suggest remedies both for the prevention and for the cure of such cases.

If a wife is to be healthy and strong, she must use the means — she must sow the seeds of health before she can reach a full harvest of health; health will not come by merely wishing for it. The means are not always at first pleasant, but, like many other things, habit makes

---

[1] *Jeremy Taylor:* Jeremy Taylor (1613–1667), English bishop and devotional writer; author of *Holy Living* (1650) and *Holy Dying* (1651).

them so. Life without health is a burden, life with health is a joy and gladness.

The judicious spending of the first year of married life is of the greatest importance in the making and in the strengthening of a wife's constitution.

The first year of married life generally determines whether, for the remainder of a woman's existence, she shall be healthy and strong, or shall be delicate and weak; whether she shall be the mother of fine, healthy children or of sickly, undersized offspring.

A young married woman ought at once to commence taking regular and systematic *out-door exercise,* which may be done without in the least interfering with her household duties. There are few things more conducive to health than walking exercise; and one advantage of our climate is, that there are but few days in the year in which, at some period of the day, it might not be taken. Walking — I mean a walk, not a stroll — is a glorious exercise; it expands the chest and throws back the shoulders; it strengthens the muscles; it promotes digestion, making a person digest almost any kind of food; it tends to open the bowels, and is better than any aperient pill[2] ever invented; it clears the complexion, giving roses to the cheeks and brilliancy to the eye, and, in point of fact, is one of the greatest beautifiers in the world. If women would walk more than they do, there would be fewer useless, complaining wives than at present. Walking is worthy of commendation, and is indispensable to contentment, health, strength, and comeliness. During pregnancy walking must be cautiously pursued; but still, walking in moderation is even then absolutely necessary, and tends to keep off many of the wretchedly depressing symptoms often accompanying that state. I am quite sure that there is nothing more conducive to health than the wearing out of lots of shoe leather, and leather is cheaper than physic.

Do not let me be misunderstood: I am not advocating that a delicate woman, unaccustomed to exercise, should at once take violent and long-continued exercise; certainly not. Let a delicate lady *learn* to take exercise as a young child would *learn* to walk — by degrees; let her creep, and then go; let her gradually increase her exercise, and let her do nothing either rashly or unadvisedly. If a child attempted to run before he could walk, he would stumble and fall. A delicate lady requires just as much care in the training to take exercise as a child

---

[2] *aperient pill:* Laxative.

does in learning to walk, but exercise must be learned and must be practiced, if a lady, or any one else, is to be healthy and strong.

A lady should walk *early* in the morning and not *late* in the evening. The dews of evening are dangerous, and are apt to give severe colds, fevers, and other diseases. Dew is more likely than rain to give cold.

Does a wife desire to be strong? Then let her take exercise. Does she hope to retain her bloom and her youthful appearance and still look charming in the eyes of her husband? Then let her take exercise. Does she wish to banish nervousness and low spirits? Then let her take exercise. There is nothing standing still in nature; if it were, creation would languish and die. There is a perpetual motion. And so must we be constantly employed, if we are to be healthy and strong. Nature will not be trifled with; these are her laws — immutable and unchangeable, and we cannot infringe them with impunity.

Let me strongly caution the young wife against the evil effects of *tight lacing.*[3] The waist ought to be from twenty-seven to twenty-nine inches in circumference; should she lace until she is only twenty-three or in some cases, only twenty-one inches, it must be done at the expense of comfort, of health, and happiness. If stays are worn tightly, they press down the lower part of the abdomen, which may either prevent a lady from having a family, or produce a miscarriage. Tight lacing is also a frequent cause of displacement of the womb. Let the dress be loose, and adapted to the season.

Pleasure to a certain degree is as necessary to the health of a young wife, and every one else, as the sun is to the earth — to warm, to cheer, and to invigorate it, and to bring out its verdure. Pleasure, in moderation, rejuvenates, humanizes, and improves the character, and expands and exercises the good qualities of the mind; but, like the sun in its intensity, it oppresseth, drieth up, and withereth. Pleasures, kept within due bounds, are good, but in excess are utterly subversive of health and happiness. A wife who lives in a whirl of pleasure and excitement is always sickly and nervous, and utterly unfitted for her

---

[3] *tight lacing:* Corset wearing, or tight lacing, was one of the most contested fashion rituals of the mid- to late nineteenth century. Tight lacing kept the form erect, with the waist contracted two-and-a-half to six inches. The stays — often made of bones — kept the upper abdomen and waist compressed as tightly as possible, so that the corsetted figure emphasized the mammary and pelvic areas of the woman's body. Both women's dress reform activists and the medical establishment opposed tight lacing, the former because of its constriction of women's movements and the latter because of its effects on the health of future mothers.

duties and responsibilities; and the misfortune of it is, the more pleasure she takes, the more she craves.

A wife's life is made up of little pleasures, of little tasks, of little cares, and little duties, but which, when added together, make a grand total of human happiness; she is not expected to do any grand work; her province lies in a contrary direction, in gentleness, in cheerfulness, in contentment, in housewifery, in care and management of her children, in sweetening her husband's cup of life, when it is, as it often is, a bitter one, in abnegation of self; these are emphatically a heritage, her jewels, which help to make up her crown of glory.

The quiet retirement of her own home ought to be her greatest pleasure and her most precious privilege. Home is the kingdom of woman, and she should be the reigning potentate. A father, a mother, children, a house and its belongings, constitute a home — the most delightful place in the world — where affections spring up, take root and flourish, and where happiness loves to take up its abode.

Cheerfulness, contentment, occupation, and healthy activity of mind cannot be too strongly recommended. A cheerful, happy temper is one of the most valuable attributes a wife can have. The possession of such a virtue not only makes herself, but every one around her, happy. It gilds with sunshine the humblest dwelling, and often converts an indifferent husband into a good one. Contentment is the finest medicine in the world; it not only frequently prevents disease, but, if disease is present, it assists in curing it. Happy is the man who has a contented wife! . . .

Some persons have an idea that a wife, for some months after child-birth, should be treated as an invalid — should lead an idle life. This is an error; for of all people in the world, a nursing mother should remember that "employment is Nature's physician, and is essential to human happiness." The best nurses and the healthiest mothers, are wives who are employed from morning until night — who have no spare time unemployed to feel nervous, or to make complaints of aches and of pains — to make a fuss about; indeed, so well does employment usually make them feel that they have really no aches or pains — either real or imaginary — to complain of, but are hearty and strong, happy and contented; indeed, the days are too short for them. . . .

A mother ought not, unless she intends to devote herself to her baby, to undertake to nurse him. She must make up her mind to forego the so-called pleasures of a fashionable life. There ought to be no half-and-half measures; she should either give up her helpless babe to the tender mercies of a wet nurse, or she must devote her whole time and energy to his welfare — to the greatest treasure that God hath given her.

If a mother is blessed with health and strength, and has a good breast of milk, *it is most unnatural and very cruel for her not to nurse her child.*

A mother who does not nurse her child is very likely soon to be in the family way again. This is an important consideration, as frequent child-bearing is much more weakening to the constitution than is the nursing of children. Indeed nursing, as a rule, instead of weakening, strengthens the mother's frame exceedingly, and assists her muscular development.

JOHN HARVEY KELLOGG

From The Household Monitor of Health

From The Ladies' Guide in Health and Disease

Focusing much of his career on ways to eradicate sexual excess and obsessions in American culture, Dr. John Harvey Kellogg (1852–1943) attacked the "secret sin" of masturbation, which he associated primarily with males. He wrote several success manuals for boys on how to struggle against such "self-abuse" or "self-pollution," and he urged both men and women to control their sexual impulses and avoid overindulgences. Sexual excess and cultural consumption were related for Kellogg, who saw the vast array of new products and leisure possibilities as leading to the decline of American culture — a decline which took the form of mental and physical weakness. In the excerpt reprinted here from Kellogg's *The Household Monitor of Health* (1891), he warns against such potential dangers as that of poison in the wallpaper. The text is taken from *The Household Monitor of Health* (Battle Creek, MI: Good Health Publishing, 1891), 67–68.

In addition to founding the famous Battle Creek Sanatarium in 1866, a place dedicated to "all known rational remedies," Kellogg published the *Ladies' Guide in Health and Disease, Girlhood, Maidenhood, Wifehood, Motherhood* in 1882, in which he proposed to treat the "diseases of women" which, according to him, were increasing in modern America.

His advice to ladies of more "civilized" temperament was to renounce "chronic invalidism" as a fashionable complaint and, instead, embrace health through physical and mental self-control. The excerpts included here are from "The Young Lady" (about female education and reading) and "The Mother" (about "true womanhood"). Kellogg advocates careful attention to heredity and to antenatal treatment. He warns against any excessive behavior, which for him includes intercourse on the part of the expectant mother. His description of "puerperal mania" — or postpartum depression — is especially relevant to "The Yellow Wallpaper." The text of the following excerpt is taken from *Ladies' Guide in Health and Disease, Girlhood, Maidenhood, Wifehood, Motherhood* (Battle Creek, MI: Modern Medicine Publishing, 1893), 207–11; 381–89; 420–26; 482–85.

From The Household Monitor of Health

Poisonous Paper. — Many cases of poisoning, some of which were fatal, have been traced to the arsenic contained in several of the colors of wall paper. The most dangerous color is green. It is almost impossible to find a green paper which does not contain arsenic. Green window curtains are especially dangerous. The green dust which can be rubbed off from them is deadly poison. In rolling and unrolling the curtain it is thrown into the air, and is breathed. The same poison is brushed off the surface of arsenical wall paper into the air, by the rubbing of pictures, garments, etc., which come in contact with it.

It is very easy to test papers of this kind before buying, and it would be wise always to take this precaution. Take a piece of the paper, hold it over a saucer, and pour upon it strong aqua ammonia. If there is any arsenic present, this will dissolve it. Collect the liquid in a vial or tube, and drop in a crystal of nitrate of silver. If there is arsenic present, little yellow crystals will make their appearance about the nitrate of silver. Arsenical green, when washed with aqua ammonia, either changes to blue, or fades.

From The Ladies' Guide in Health and Disease

Preface

The author of this volume was induced to undertake its preparation by the belief that there was a real and urgent demand for such a work, and the hope that the effort would do something at least toward supplying that demand. The very remarkable increase in the number and frequency of that very large class of maladies familiarly known as "diseases of women" observable in modern times, especially among the women of the more civilized nations, and those of this country in particular, has attracted the attention of many intelligent physicians. The ailments from which women suffer constitute a large part of the practice of the majority of physicians, and probably contribute more to the support of the medical profession than any other class of maladies. So numerous and complicated has this class of diseases become in recent times, that a new race of specialists has sprung up, who confine themselves exclusively to this branch of practice; and many a fashionable woman has her favorite gynecologist as well as her favorite milliner or dress-maker, and is as much dependent upon the first to keep her internal arrangements in proper order as upon the second and third to regulate her head-gear and garments in accordance with the ruling fashion. We have no sympathy with that large class who seem to consider chronic invalidism necessary to gentility; and it is not the purpose of this work in any way to increase or exaggerate the tendency in this direction which is so apparent among civilized women at the present time. What we hope to do is in some degree to mitigate this growing evil by calling attention to the causes out of which it springs, and pointing out the remedy. . . .

The Young Lady

. . . Much of the weakness and failure of girls during school-life is due to improper habits of dress, improper food, want of regular habits of rest, attendance at theaters, evening parties, dances, etc., too little physical exercise, confinement in close and unventilated school-

Pages 158–59: Testimonials for Dr. Pierce's "Golden Medical Discovery," a tonic designed "to cleanse the blood, tone the system, increase its nutrition, and establish a healthy condition." From R.V. Pierce, M.D., *The People's Common Sense Medical Adviser in Plain English: or, Medicine Simplified* (1895).

TESTIMONIALS.

While we have a great cloud of witnesses testifying to the efficacy of our treatment of the diseases described in this volume, yet for lack of space we can here introduce only the few following :

"LIVER COMPLAINT."

WORLD'S DISPENSARY MEDICAL ASSOCIATION,
Buffalo, N. Y.:

Gentlemen—In the year 1889 I was taken with disease which the doctors called "liver complaint." I tried three different doctors. They did me no good. They tried about one year; I was not able to work for two years. At last I thought I would try Dr. Pierce's medicines, and I wrote to Dr. Pierce, and he wrote to me to take his "Golden Medical Discovery," and I bought two bottles, and when I took it, I saw it was improving me, and I got five more, and before I had taken all I was well, and I haven't felt the symptoms since. I had a continued hurting in my bowels for about two years. I feel as if the cure is worth thousands of dollars to me.   Yours truly,
J. H. MAY,
Potts' Station, Pope Co., Ark.

J. H. MAY, ESQ.

DYSPEPSIA AND WOMB DISEASE.

WORLD'S DISPENSARY MEDICAL ASSOCIATION,
Buffalo, N. Y.:

Dear Sirs—When first taking Dr. Pierce's Favorite Prescription I was nervous and would have sour stomach and distress after eating, and when I would rise after stooping over everything would turn dark before me and I would feel dizzy. I suffered a great deal of pain at each monthly period. I took one bottle and a half of the "Favorite Prescription," one teaspoonful three times a day, and the "Pellets" as directions called for. I gained in health and strength so rapidly that I have been able to work very hard the past summer, and my back never troubles me; and when I have my monthly periods I never feel the least bit of pain. In fact I consider myself in excellent health.
Very truly yours,
MRS. INEZ V. CARR RANSOM,
Panama, Chaut. Co., N. Y.

MRS. RANSOM.

INFLAMMATION OF LIVER.

WORLD'S DISPENSARY MEDICAL ASSOCIATION,
Buffalo, N. Y.:

Gentlemen—I was taken sick with inflammation of the liver and could get no relief from the doctors of this place—Randolph, N.Y. I was induced to use Dr. Pierce's Golden Medical Discovery, and "Pleasant Pellets," and after using five bottles of the medicine, I regained my health, and now I am a well man. I weighed 185 pounds before taken sick, and I was reduced to 135 pounds in sixty days' time. I suffered greatly from headache, pain in my right shoulder, poor appetite, constipation and a sleepy feeling all the time. My health is now very good, and I weigh 170 pounds, and I am able to do a good day's work without any trouble at all. Thanks to these valuable medicines.
Yours truly,
THOMAS J. BENTLEY,
Randolph, Catt. Co., N. Y.

T. J. BENTLEY, ESQ.

TESTIMONIALS.   587

MRS. HART.

LIVER DISEASE AND DYSPEPSIA.

WORLD'S DISPENSARY MEDICAL ASSOCIATION,
Buffalo, N. Y.:

Dear Sirs—I am enjoying excellent health. After taking a bottle of Dr. Pierce's Golden Medical Discovery and several bottles of "Pellets," I am a different person. Only weighed 119 pounds when I began taking your medicine, now weigh 160. My symptoms were pain under the left shoulder, distress after eating, headache, dizziness, constipation, and, in fact, my system was "out of sorts generally." I tell every one your medicine has done more for me than any other.

I remain, yours truly,
MRS. CHARLES H. HART.
San Ardo, Monterey Co.,
California.

LIVER COMPLAINT AND CATARRH.

Dear Sirs—After suffering for several years with nasal catarrh and liver complaint, and having become greatly reduced in health, as a last resort I placed myself in your hands for treatment. My improvement began almost immediately after entering your institution. I was enabled to leave at the end of one month, having experienced great benefit. The treatment was continued at home for a few months, after which my cure was complete. At the present time, I am able for office work, and feel that I am completely cured of the catarrh and have but little if any trouble with my liver. I shall lose no opportunity to recommend your institution or your medicines to the afflicted. I do most unhesitatingly recommend chronic sufferers to visit your institution or take your remedies at home.
Sincerely yours,
WILLIAM KING,
Rose Bud,
Pope Co., Ills.

WM. KING, ESQ.

MRS. RADEMAKER.

A COMPLICATED CASE OF STOMACH, LUNG, AND UTERINE DISEASE.

Dear Sirs—Some six years ago I was taken sick with chills; I would have a very bad chill and then I would begin to sweat and vomit; I had no appetite; I had the catarrh very bad; I had inward troubles of different kinds; my back ached all the time; I had sores gather and break inside; I had a lung trouble; I was very bad off; I could sit up only long enough to have my bed made; my husband sent for our family doctor; he came three times a week for three months; I was not so well at the end of three months as when he first came, but kept growing worse; he gave me up to die, and said I had consumption. I had heard of Dr. Pierce's medicines doing a good deal of good, so I made up my mind to try them. I sent and got one bottle of "Favorite Prescription" and one bottle of "Golden Medical Discovery"; also one bottle of "Pellets," and commenced taking them. In a few days I commenced to gain, and in two weeks' time I could sit up most all day, and in five weeks' time I could do my work with the help of two small girls. After taking four bottles of "Favorite Prescription," six bottles of "Discovery," and three of "Pellets," I was well enough to get along without any medicine. I can do a good day's work, and I owe my life to Dr. Pierce. With God's will and the use of Dr. Pierce's medicine I am still alive and well. Yours respectfully,
MRS. CLARA A. RADEMAKER,
Addison Point, Washington Co., Me.

rooms, sitting upon hard and improperly made seats, bending over desks which are equally improper and unsuitable in construction, — all of these causes and many more among which may be included the vicious habit to which we have called attention in a previous section, are really the chief causes of the numerous breakdowns which are so common among school girls.

Novel-Reading. — The reading of works of fiction is one of the most pernicious habits to which a young lady can become devoted. When the habit is once thoroughly fixed, it becomes as inveterate as the use of liquor or opium. The novel-devotee is as much a slave as the opium-eater or the inebriate. The reading of fictitious literature destroys the taste for sober, wholesome reading and imparts an unhealthy stimulus to the mind, the effect of which is in the highest degree damaging.

novel reading is like taking opium.

When we add to this the fact that a large share of the popular novels of the day contain more or less matter of a directly depraving character, presented in such gilded form and specious guise that the work of contamination may be completed before suspicion is aroused, it should become apparent to every careful mother that her daughters should be vigilantly guarded against this dangerous source of injury and possible ruin. We have dilated quite fully upon this subject in a preceding section, and will not enlarge upon it here. We wish, however, to put ourself upon record as believing firmly that the practice of novel reading is one of the greatest causes of uterine disease in young women. There is no doubt that the influence of the mind upon the sexual organs and functions is such that disease may be produced in this way. As remarked in the consideration of the physiology of the reproductive organs, it is a common observation that the menstrual function may be suspended suddenly as the result of grief or some other strong emotion experienced by the individual. Hemorrhage or profuse menstruation may result from a similar cause. These facts demonstrate beyond the possibility of question that the circulation in the uterus and its appendages is greatly subject to changes through the influence of the mind. Reading of a character to stimulate the emotions and rouse the passions may produce or increase a tendency to uterine congestion, which may in turn give rise to a great variety of maladies, including all the different forms of displacement, the presence of which is indicated by weak backs, painful menstruation, leucorrhoea,[1] etc.

okay..

---

[1] *leucorrhoea:* A whitish fungal vaginal discharge.

We do not insist that nothing should ever be read but history, biography, or perfectly authentic accounts of experiences in real life. There are undoubtedly novels, such as Uncle Tom's Cabin,[2] and one or two others which we might mention, which have been active agents in the accomplishment of great and good results. Such novels are not likely to do anybody any harm; but the number of harmless works of fiction is very limited indeed. Many works which are considered among the standards of literature are wholly unfit for the perusal of young ladies who wish to retain their simplicity of mind and purity of thought. We have felt our cheeks burn more than once when we have seen young school-girls intently poring over the vulgar poems of Chaucer[3] or the amorous ditties of Burns or Byron.[4] Still worse than any of these are the low witticisms of Rabelais and Boccaccio;[5] and yet we have not infrequently seen these volumes in the book-cases of family libraries readily accessible to the young daughters or growing sons of the family. The growing influence of this kind of literature is far more extensive than can be readily demonstrated. Thousands of women whose natural love for purity leads them to shun and abhor everything of an immoral tendency, yet find themselves obliged to wage a painful warfare for years to banish from their minds the impure imagery generated by the perusal of books of this character. We have met cases of disease in which painful maladies could be traced directly to this source.

Impurity of Speech. — It is not to be supposed that young ladies are by any means so remiss in this particular as the majority of young men, and yet we have had painful evidence of the fact that too often even young ladies who are looked upon as in the highest degree respectable allow themselves to indulge in conversation of a character which they would not like to have overheard by their mothers. We would not say that every young woman who indulges in loose conversations is guilty of vicious habits; but it is certain that a young

<hr/>

[2] *Uncle Tom's Cabin:* 1852 abolitionist best-selling novel written by Harriet Beecher Stowe (1811–1896).

[3] *vulgar poems of Chaucer:* Geoffrey Chaucer (ca. 1340–1400), best known for his *Canterbury Tales* and their bawdiness, also wrote "songs and lecherous lays" to which he confessed in his Retractions.

[4] *Burns or Byron:* Robert Burns (1759–1796), Scottish poet who often wrote about his love affairs and liaisons; George Gordon, Lord Byron (1788–1824), Romantic poet.

[5] *Rabelais and Boccaccio:* François Rabelais (ca. 1490–1553), French writer, whose humor is considered bawdy and grotesque; Giovanni Boccaccio (1313–1375), Italian writer and author of the *Decameron* (1348–53), a series of one hundred tales, many of which are bawdy.

woman who allows herself to utter unchaste words and joins with others in conversation upon impure subjects, if not already impure, is in the way to become so should a strong temptation present itself under favorable circumstances.

The habit which many girls have of talking familiarly about the boys, is an exceedingly detrimental one. It leads in the same direction as the habit indulged in by many coarse and vulgar young men who stand upon the street corners making lewd criticisms upon every passing female. "Out of the abundance of the heart the mouth speaketh," are the words of an inspired writer, and it is fair to conclude that a young woman who delights in conversation upon unchaste subjects is poorly fortified against the temptation to overt acts of unchastity.

Women of mature age as well as young girls are often guilty of this same practice. In one form or another this "ghost of vice" often haunts the sewing-circle and the boudoir. Women who consider themselves immaculate often seem to enjoy nothing more thoroughly than the retailing of scandal and gossiping about the lapses from virtue of the sons and daughters of their neighbors.

Lapses from virtue, in women as well as men, begin with mental impurity. A young woman who allows her imagination to run riot in lewdness is in a fair way to become impure in deed as well as thought. Man, even when most debased, loves to regard woman as chaste and pure in mind as well as body, and a woman cannot consider herself in the strictest sense pure unless she reaches this high ideal. Even listening to impure conversation without participation in it is demoralizing and destructive to purity, as the mind accustomed to hear words of unchaste and impure meaning unconsciously acquires some tolerance not only of the language but of the actions which it signifies. The society of women whether young or old who indulge in unchaste conversation, should be shunned as one would avoid the vicinity of a rattlesnake or a man sick with the plague. The moral disease engendered by this contagion of vice is far more deadly than any physical malady from which the body can suffer, yet these inoculators of vice are often admitted to the best circles of society, and the moral vaccination to which girls and young women who come under their influence are subjected, is much more certain to "work" and to develop in some foul disease in the victims than a vaccine inoculation for kine-pox.[6] . . .

---

[6] *kine-pox:* Also cowpox; a mild but contagious disease in cows that, when communicated to humans, protects against smallpox.

The Mother

The motherly instinct is without doubt the ruling passion in the heart of the true woman. The sexual nature of woman finds expression in this channel when her life is a normal one, rather than in the grosser forms of sexual activity. In modern times there seems to be a tendency to the obliteration of the instinct which makes motherhood desirable and regards it with respect; but every true woman will recognize the demoralizing nature of this unhallowed influence, and will lift her voice in solemn protest against it. In no sphere does woman so well display her Eden-born graces of character so excellently as when fulfilling her duties in nurturing and training for usefulness the plastic minds and forms which have been intrusted to her care. We behold with admiration the canvass of a Raphael or a Michael Angelo;[7] we stand with speechless wonderment before the recovered marble of a Phidias or a Praxiteles;[8] we are almost ready to bend the knee in adoration of the lofty genius which gave birth to these marvelous works of art which have immortalized their creators; but which of all of these can for a moment compare with the work intrusted to the mother, the task of molding a mind, of modeling a character, not for time only, but for eternity.

Let the purity and dignity of motherhood be magnified. Let woman be taught that in the performance of her Heaven-intrusted task she is fulfilling a mission so lofty and so sacred that none other can ever approach to it. We do not say that woman should never aspire to any calling outside the province of the domestic circle; but we do most emphatically denounce as false and in the highest degree perverting in its tendency, the notion that the mother's mission is a lowly one, unsuited to the capabilities of a brilliant intellect. Such teaching is in the highest degree mischievous. Any mother may find within the scope of her own family circle ample opportunity for the full employment of the noblest endowments of mind and soul which have ever been bestowed upon a human being.

The Prospective Mother. — The woman who for the first time recognizes the fact that she will in the natural course of events in a few

---

[7] *Raphael or a Michael Angelo:* Raphael Santi (1483–1520), Florentine painter and architect of the High Renaissance; Michelangelo Buonarroti (1475–1564), one of the greatest Italian Renaissance artists.

[8] *Phidias . . . Praxiteles:* Phidias (c. 490–430 B.C.), Greek sculptor, most famous for the Parthenon. Both Phidias and Praxiteles (ca. 370–330 B.C.) were known through Roman copies of their work and were the most noted artists of the ancient world.

months become a mother, naturally finds her mind occupied with new thoughts and curious questions on a variety of themes which may never have interested her before. If she possesses the true mother's instincts she will earnestly inquire how her own habits of life, her thoughts and actions, may affect the well-being of her developing child. Possibly she may never have heard of the marvelous influence of heredity in molding not only the form but the character of the unborn; but instinct teaches her that her own conditions in some way affect those of her child, and that for a period she must think, act, and live for another besides herself. One of the most powerful means of impressing indelibly upon the mind the necessity for care and proper training, mental and moral, as well as physical, during the period of pregnancy and lactation, is a presentation of the principles and facts of

Heredity.[9]

We have not space here to enter into the details of this somewhat intricate department of biology, and can only call attention to a few of its leading features which are of special practical value in this connection.

"Like father like son," is a homely adage, the correctness of which is rarely questioned; and "like mother like daughter" would be equally true. A careful study of the subject of heredity has established as a scientific fact the principle that sons as a rule most resemble the father, and daughters the mother, although there are often observed marked exceptions to the rule. The degree to which this hereditary tendency exists, and how it may be utilized to the improvement of the race is a question of interest which we may profitably consider. Unfortunately, the question of "pedigree" receives very little attention so far as human beings are concerned. If a man is about to expend a thousand dollars for a fine horse, he inquires with great care into the ancestry of the animal. The owner must be able to show a record of lineal and unmixed descent from parents of pure stock, or its value will be greatly depreciated in the eyes of the purchaser.

---

[9] *heredity:* The Austrian monk and botanist Gregor Johann Mendel (1822–1884) argued in 1865 that heredity was dominant and environment of little or no consequence in shaping individuals, thus proving genetics more powerful than culture. Mendel's laws of heredity were used by scientific racists as justification for their claims that Nordics, Aryans, or those of "pure" American stock were natural leaders and cultural elites.

Stock raisers appreciate in the highest degree the fact that "blood" is a thing of market value, and not to be ignored in the slightest degree. In matters which relate to the welfare of their own race, however, eternal as well as temporal, human beings seem to ignore the principles which they so readily recognize in lower species.

A young man seeking a wife, or a young woman considering the eligibility of a young man to become her husband, asks no questions about pedigree. The question, At what age did your father or mother, or grandfather or grandmother die, or of what disease, is rarely if ever asked as having any bearing on the subject of marriage. Family tendencies to scrofula, consumption, insanity, epilepsy, or any one of numerous other lines of physical degeneracy, to say nothing of vicious moral and mental tendencies, are never taken into consideration.

Race Deterioration.[10] — In consequence of this neglect of one of the primary conditions of healthy parentage, the race is daily deteriorating in spite of the efforts of sanitarians and health teachers. Sanitary laws respecting the care of cities and of individuals may be ever so thorough and complete, and may be enforced with the most scrupulous rigor, yet the race will continue to degenerate so long as this matter of heredity is neglected; for "blood will tell," whether good or bad, and the great preponderance of "bad blood" is the fatal element at work undermining the constitution of the race and destined ultimately to destroy it, if some means is not taken to prevent its baneful influence.

We are fully aware that this view of the prospects of the race is a very unpopular one; but considerable study of the subject has convinced us that the conclusion we have drawn is the only correct one. Defects of body and mind, as well as of morals, are growing yearly more abundant. Two persons possessing these defects unite in marriage, and their defects are many times increased in intensity in their children.

A quaint writer in speaking on the subject of heredity and indiscriminate marriage, utters the truth in the following very forcible words: —

---

[10] *race deterioration:* Anxieties about the flood of new immigrants from southern and eastern Europe in the late nineteenth and early twentieth centuries increased the nativist discussion of "pure" races and also led to anti-immigrant legislation, including the 1924 Sullivan Act, which restricted the immigration of various ethnic and racial groups.

"By our too much facility in this kind, in giving way for all to marry that will, too much liberty and indulgence in tolerating all sorts, there is a vast confusion of breed and diseases, no family secure, no man almost free from some grievous infirmity or other, when no choice is had, but still the eldest must marry. . . . or, if rich, be they fools or dizzards,[11] lame or maimed, unable, intemperate, dissolute, exhaust through riot, as it is said, *jure hæreditatis sapere jubentur,* they must be wise and able by inheritance; it comes to pass that our generation is corrupt, we have many weak persons, both in body and mind, many feral diseases raging amongst us, crazed families, *parentes peremptores;*[12] our fathers bad, and we are like to be worse."[13] . . .

Mr. Francis Galton,[14] who has probably made the most careful study of the hereditary influences which produce men of genius, tells us that nearly all men of great talent, jurists, statesmen, commanders, artists, scientists, poets, and clergymen, have had parents of marked ability. Of the two parents, the father has the precedence in the proportion of seven to three; but this is no greater difference in favor of the male than would naturally result from the superior advantages afforded men for the development of genius.

One curious fact is that eminent divines seem to inherit their ability from their mothers much more frequently than their fathers, the proportion being nearly three to one in favor of mothers, from which he concludes that mothers transmit piety to their children in a larger measure than fathers.

If true, this certainly speaks well for the piety of women; but we question the correctness of the conclusion, for we are by no means certain that the qualities which contribute the most largely to the eminence of distinguished divines are not other than those which constitute piety. Learning, eloquence, and other traits which make men famous in other callings are more often the chief factors.

The difference in the aptitude for acquiring knowledge, which is very apparent between the negro and the caucasian races, is almost equally marked when the children of the ignorant and the cultivated classes of the white race are compared. In both cases the influence of heredity is apparent.

---

[11] *dizzards:* Idiots.
[12] *parentes peremptores:* The preemption of a parent, taking the place of a parent (Latin).
[13] Burton's Anatomy of Melancholy. [Kellogg's note.]
[14] *Mr. Francis Galton* (1822–1911): Explorer, anthropologist, and early eugenicist, famous for his works on human intelligence and heredity.

That moral as well as mental qualities are transmitted from parent to child[15] is also evident from the observation of what are known as the criminal classes, in whom the hereditary tendency to crime is so apparent that in England, institutions have been organized to provide for the care of the children of criminals in the hope that by correct early training something may be done toward reclaiming them.

The habit or vice of the parent becomes in the child an almost irresistible tendency. This is apparent in the children of drunkards, thieves, libertines, and prostitutes, and we do not doubt that farther investigation and careful study of the subject will show that the tobacco, opium, chloral, and other similar habits, and possibly also the excessive use by parents of tea and coffee and of stimulating condiments, stamp the progeny with vicious tendencies which either lead directly to the formation of similar habits or worse ones, or establish diseased conditions which sooner or later develop into serious or even fatal maladies.

No better illustration of the fact of the inheritance of a tendency to vice could be asked than is afforded by the notorious Juke family[16] of New York. From five unchaste sisters have sprung a family of 1200 persons, nearly all of whom, at least of those living, are the occupants of jails, work-houses, poor-houses, or houses of bad repute. . . .

Hygiene of Ante-Natal Life. — The influence of the mother upon the child during gestation has already been referred to under the head of "Heredity," and the facts there presented need not be repeated here. We wish, however, to impress still further a few points, and especially to call attention to the fact that since it is evident that accidental influences and circumstances acting upon the mother affect the child either favorably or unfavorably, it becomes the duty of the mother to surround herself with such influences and to supply such conditions and circumstances as she knows will be for the best good of her developing infant. In this work she should be aided so far as possible by her husband and by all those about her who have an opportunity to render her assistance. Work of so important a character

---

[15] *qualities are transmitted from parent to child:* Kellogg and others believed that all mental traits and habits of mind were the result of evolutionary inheritance and, thus, part of one's physical structure. Hence, cultural traits were assumed to have racial origins.

[16] *Juke family:* One of the first studies of the purportedly "degenerate" clans, written by Richard L. Dugdale (184?–1883) and reporting that inferior heredity accounted for feeblemindedness, criminality, alcoholism, and other social vices: *"The Jukes": A Study in Crime, Pauperism, Disease and Heredity* (1877).

as this, the influence of which can only be estimated in eternity, such work demands the earnest and prayerful attention of every prospective mother. The self-denial which must be exercised, the subordination of the appetites, desires, tastes, and convenience to the interests of another being which the duties of the mother involve, afford a moral discipline which if rightly appreciated must result in good to the mother as well as to the child, and, like every act of duty in life, no matter how remotely relating to the individual, reacts upon the doer through the reflex influence of mental and moral discipline.

The special influence of the mother begins with the moment of conception. In fact it is possible that the mental condition at the time of the generative act has much to do with determining the character of the child, though it is generally conceded that at this time the influence of the father is greater than that of the mother. Any number of instances have occurred in which a drunken father has impressed upon his child the condition of his nervous system to such a degree as to render permanent in the child the staggering gait and maudlin manner which in his own case was a transient condition induced by the poisonous influence of alcohol. A child born as the result of a union in which both parents were in a state of beastly intoxication was idiotic.

Another fact might be added to impress the importance that the new being should be supplied from the very beginning of its existence with the very best conditions possible. Indeed, it is desirable to go back still further, and secure a proper preparation for the important function of maternity. The qualities which go to make up individuality of character are the result of the summing up of a long line of influences, too subtle and too varied to admit of full control, but still, to some degree at least, subject to management. The dominance of law is nowhere more evident than in the relation of ante-natal influences to character.

The hap-hazard way in which human beings are generated leaves no room for surprise that the race should deteriorate. No stock-breeder would expect anything but ruin should he allow his animals to propagate with no attention to their physical conditions or previous preparation.

Finding herself in a pregnant condition, the mother should not yield to the depressing influences which often crowd upon her. The anxieties and fears which women sometimes yield themselves to, grow with encouragement, until they become so absorbed as to be capable of producing a profoundly evil impression on the child. The true mother who is prepared for the functions of maternity, will welcome the evidence of pregnancy, and joyfully enter upon the Heaven-given task of molding a human character, of bringing into the world a new being whose life-history may involve the destinies of nations, or change the current of human thought for generations to come.

The pregnant mother should cultivate cheerfulness of mind and calmness of temper, but should avoid excitements of all kinds, such as theatrical performances, public contests of various descriptions, etc. Anger, envy, irritability of temper, and, in fact, all the passions and propensities should be held in check. The fickleness of desire and the constantly varying whims which characterize the pregnant state in some women should not be regarded as uncontrollable, and to be yielded to as the only means of appeasing them. The mother should be gently encouraged to resist such tendencies when they become at all marked, and to assist her in the effort, her husband should endeavor to engage her mind by interesting conversation, reading, and various harmless and pleasant diversions.

If it is desired that the child should possess a special aptitude for any particular art or pursuit, during the period of pregnancy the mother's mind should be constantly directed in this channel. If artistic taste or skill is the trait desired, the mother should be surrounded by works of art of a high order of merit. She should read art, think art, talk, and write about art, and if possible, herself engage in the close practical study of some one or more branches of art, as painting, drawing, etching, or modeling. If ability for authorship is desired, then the mother should devote herself assiduously to literature. It is not claimed that by following these suggestions any mother can make of her children great artists or authors at will; but it is certain that by this means the greatest possibilities in individual cases can be attained; and it is certain that decided results have been secured by close attention to the principles laid down. It should be understood, however, that not merely a formal and desultory effort on the part of the mother is what is required. The theme selected must completely absorb her mind. It must be the one idea of her waking thoughts and the model on which is formed the dreams of her sleeping hours.

The question of diet during pregnancy as before stated is a vitally important one as regards the interests of the child. A diet into which enters largely such unwholesome articles as mustard, pepper, hot sauces, spices, and other stimulating condiments, engenders a love for stimulants in the disposition of the infant. Tea and coffee, especially if used to excess, undoubtedly tend in the same direction. We firmly believe that we have, in the facts first stated, the key to the constant increase in the consumption of ardent spirits. The children of the present generation inherit from their condiment-consuming, tea-, coffee-, and liquor-drinking, and tobacco-using parents, not simply a readiness for the acquirement of the habits mentioned, but a propensity for the use of stimulants which in persons of weak will-power and those whose circumstances are not the most favorable, becomes irresistible.

The present generation is also suffering in consequence of the impoverished diet of its parents. The modern custom of bolting the flour from the different grains has deprived millions of infants and children of the necessary supply of bone-making material, thus giving rise to a greatly increased frequency of the various diseases which arise from imperfect bony structure, as rickets, caries, premature decay of the teeth, etc. The proper remedy is the disuse of fine-flour bread and all other bolted grain preparations. Graham-flour bread, oatmeal, cracked wheat, and similar preparations, should be relied upon as the leading articles of diet. Supplemented by milk, the whole-grain preparations constitute a complete form of nourishment, and render a large amount of animal food not only unnecessary but really harmful on account of its stimulating character. It is by no means so necessary as is generally supposed that meat, fish, fowl, and flesh in various forms should constitute a large element of the dietary of the pregnant or nursing mother in order to furnish adequate nourishment for the developing child. We have seen the happiest results follow the employment of a strictly vegetarian dietary, and do not hesitate to advise moderation in the use of flesh food, though we do not recommend the entire discontinuance of its use by the pregnant mother who has been accustomed to use it freely.

A nursing mother should at once suspend nursing if she discovers that pregnancy has again occurred. The continuance of nursing under such circumstances is to the disadvantage of three individuals, the mother, the infant at the breast, and the developing child.

Sexual indulgence during pregnancy may be suspended with decided benefit to both mother and child. The most ancient medical writers call attention to the fact that by the practice of continence[17] during gestation, the pains of childbirth are greatly mitigated. The injurious influences upon the child of the gratification of the passions during the period when its character is being formed, is undoubtedly

[17] *continence:* Chastity, abstinence, or restraint.

much greater than is usually supposed. We have no doubt that this is a common cause of the transmission of libidinous tendencies to the child; and that the tendency to abortion is induced by sexual indulgence has long been a well established fact. The females of most animals resolutely resist the advances of the males during this period, being guided in harmony with natural law by their natural instincts which have been less perverted in them than in human beings. The practice of continence during pregnancy is also enforced in the harems of the East, which fact leads to the practice of abortion among women of this class who are desirous of remaining the special favorites of the common husband.

The general health of the mother must be kept up in every way. It is especially important that the regularity of the bowels should be maintained. Proper diet and as much physical exercise as can be taken are the best means for accomplishing this. When constipation is allowed to exist, the infant as well as the mother suffers. The effete products which should be promptly removed from the body, being long retained, are certain to find their way back into the system again, poisoning not only the blood of the mother but that of the developing fœtus. . . .

Puerperal Mania.— This form of mental disease is most apt to show itself about two weeks after delivery. Although, fortunately, of not very frequent occurrence, it is a most serious disorder when it does occur, and hence we may with propriety introduce the following somewhat lengthy, but most graphic description of the disease from the pen of Dr. Ramsbotham, an eminent English physician: —

"In mania there is almost always, at the very commencement, a troubled, agitated, and hurried manner, a restless eye, an unnaturally anxious, suspicious, and unpleasing expression of face; — sometimes it is pallid, at others more flushed than usual; — an unaccustomed irritability of temper, and impatience of control or contradiction; a vacillation of purpose, or loss of memory; sometimes a rapid succession of contradictory orders are issued, or a paroxysm of excessive anger is excited about the merest trifle. Occasionally, one of the first indications will be a sullen obstinacy, or listlessness and stubborn silence. The patient lies on her back, and can by no means be persuaded to reply to the questions of her attendants, or she will repeat them, as an echo, until, all at once, without any apparent cause, she will break out into a torrent of language more or less incoherent, and her words will follow each other with surprising rapidity. These symptoms will sometimes show themselves rather suddenly, on the patient's awakening from a disturbed and unrefreshing sleep, or they may supervene more slowly when she has been harassed with wakefulness for three or four previous nights in succession, or perhaps ever since her delivery. She will very likely then become impressed with the idea that some evil has befallen her husband, or, what is still more usual, her child; that it is dead or stolen; and if it be brought to her, nothing can persuade her it is her own; she supposes it to belong to somebody else; or she will fancy that her husband is unfaithful to her, or that he and those about her have conspired to poison her. Those persons who are naturally the objects of her deepest and most devout affection, are regarded by her with jealousy, suspicion, and hatred. This is particularly remarkable with regard to her newly born infant; and I have known many instances where attempts have been made to destroy it when it has been incautiously left within her power. Sometimes, though rarely, may be observed a great anxiety regarding the termination of her own case, or a firm conviction that she is speedily about to die. I have observed upon occasions a constant movement of the lips, while the mouth was shut; or the patient is incessantly rubbing the inside of her lips with her fingers, or thrusting them far back into her mouth; and if questions are asked, particularly if she be desired to put out her tongue, she will often compress the lips forcibly together, as if with an obstinate determination of resistance. One peculiarity attending some cases of puerperal mania is the immorality and obscenity of the expressions uttered; they are often such, indeed, as to excite our astonishment that women in a respectable station of society could ever have become acquainted with such language."

The insanity of childbirth differs from that of pregnancy in that in the latter cases the patient is almost always melancholy,[18] while in the former there is active mania. Derangement of the digestive organs is a constant accompaniment of the disease.

If the patient has no previous or hereditary tendency to insanity, the prospect of a quite speedy recovery is good. The result is seldom immediately fatal, but the patient not infrequently remains in a condition of mental unsoundness for months or even years, and sometimes permanently.

Treatment: When there is reason to suspect a liability to puerperal mania from previous mental disease or from hereditary influence,

---

[18] *melancholy:* Mental state characterized by severe depression, somatic problems, and hallucinations or delusions.

much can be done to ward off an attack. Special attention must be paid to the digestive organs, which should be regulated by proper food and simple means to aid digestion. The tendency to sleeplessness must be combatted by careful nursing, light massage at night, rubbing of the spine, alternate hot and cold applications to the spine, cooling the head by cloths wrung out of cold water, and the use of the warm bath at bed time. These measures are often successful in securing sleep when all other measures fail.

The patient must be kept very quiet. Visitors, even if near relatives, must not be allowed when the patient is at all nervous or disturbed, and it is best to exclude nearly every one from the sick-room with the exception of the nurse, who should be a competent and experienced person.

When the attack has really begun, the patient must have the most vigilant watchcare, not being left alone for a moment. It is much better to care for the patient at home, when possible to do so efficiently, than to take her to an asylum.[19]

When evidences of returning rationality appear, the greatest care must be exercised to prevent too great excitement. Sometimes a change of air, if the patient is sufficiently strong, physically, will at this period prove eminently beneficial. A visit from a dear friend will sometimes afford a needed stimulus to the dormant faculties. Such cases as these of course require intelligent medical supervision.

ALFRED MEADOWS

"Puerperal Mania"

Of especial significance in relation to "The Yellow Wallpaper" are the symptoms associated with the nineteenth-century diagnosis of "puerperal mania," excessive manic or depressive behavior after giving birth. Alfred Meadows (1823–1887) suggests in the following chapter that after labor and delivery a mother may develop acute "mania" in which her restlessness overcomes her reason. In the words of one nineteenth-century physician: "In women of certain temperaments, habits, and education, pregnancy so modifies the nervous system as to produce morbid appetites,

---

[19] *asylum:* Large, custodial institutions for the mentally ill; later replaced by hospitals.

changes of temper and disposition, sometimes moral perversion, unnatural sadness, or a settled conviction of impending death." The following excerpt is taken from *A Manual of Midwifery, Including the Signs and Symptoms of Pregnancy, Obstetric Operations, Diseases of the Puerperal State, etc. etc.* (Philadelphia: Lindsay, 1871), 437–43.

Though not very often, indeed very seldom in itself, a fatal disease, there are few if any diseases more painful to witness or at times more alarming in their appearance than puerperal mania or insanity. At one time it was supposed, and pretty generally maintained, that this disease never ended fatally. This, however, is quite a mistake. There is doubtless one form, the melancholic, which is generally unattended with any feverish or inflammatory symptoms, is usually of a chronic character, and seldom terminates in death; but then it often leads to permanent fatuity; and it is clearly proved that in the case of the acute and inflammatory form the mortality is by no means inconsiderable.

As regards the frequency of these affections, out of 1644 women in the Bethlehem Hospital, 84 were cases of puerperal origin, and of 1119 cases in La Salpêtrière[1] 94 were cases of this kind.

There are probably two, if not three, different varieties of this affection, but obstetric writers are not agreed either as to their number or indeed as to the nature of the several varieties. Dr. Rigby described three distinct kinds: the first, characterized by cerebral congestion or inflammation, occurring either as simple phrenitis,[2] or in the course of, and associated with, puerperal fever; the second, arising from gastro-enteric irritation; and the third, resulting from general debility and anæmia, the adynamic form of puerperal mania, as described by Gooch. Montgomery gave the name of puerperal mania to that state of mental excitement which frequently attends the expulsion of the child, when the external parts are being most painfully dilated, when the uterus is acting vigorously, and when everything conspires to

---

[1] *Bethlehem Hospital . . . La Salpêtrière:* The Hospital of St. Mary of Bethlehem Hospital came to be known as Bedlam, the first asylum for the insane in England and infamous for the brutal mistreatment of patients; it was given by Henry VIII in 1547 to the city of London and later moved in 1815 to St. George's Fields in Southeast London. La Salpêtrière was the Paris Hospital that Jean-Martin Charcot (1825–1893), founder of modern neurology with Guillaume Duchenne, opened in 1882. It became the greatest neurological clinic of its time. In 1885, Freud became one of Charcot's students there.

[2] *phrenitis:* Inflammation of the diaphragm.

make the time one of intense anguish and suffering to the patient. At such a time, however, it can hardly be wondered at that patients are "not aware of what the exact nature of their observations may have been," even if they are "conscious that they have been wandering." But this scarcely justifies the title of puerperal mania. As Dr. Ramsbotham observes, "It is the delirium — the phrenzy — of high excitement, produced by intense pain. It is neither inflammatory nor maniacal."

Practically the division of puerperal mania into two classes is the simplest and most satisfactory. Each of these may vary as to the time and cause of its appearance. The one is characterized by violent delirium, high fever, and great constitutional disturbance, the evident indications of acute inflammation; the other is marked rather by depression and melancholia. The former occurs either immediately after delivery or at the commencement of lactation; the latter more often after suckling has been continued some time, and where the patient is becoming debilitated by it. The one is acute, both in its onset and progress, the other insidious and protracted. Death is a not infrequent result of the one, but it seldom happens in the other.

Symptoms of acute mania. — Very frequently this form of mania is ushered in by certain premonitory symptoms, which begin within a few days after labor. According to Dr. Haslam, "the first symptoms of the approach of this disease after delivery are, want of sleep, the countenance becomes flushed, a constrictive pain is often felt in the head, the eyes assume a morbid lustre, and wildly glance at objects in rapid succession; the milk is afterwards secreted in less quantity, and when the mind becomes more violently disordered it is totally suppressed." There is often great irritability of temper, wakefulness, pain in the head, a restless, anxious expression of countenance, and transient loss of memory and consciousness; the patient may either sink into obstinate sullenness, occasionally interrupted by violent outbursts of passion, or she may become furiously maniacal and threaten destruction to all around her. She generally takes a fatal dislike to her child; indeed, this is often one of the first things which attracts attention, following, as it often does, on the most devoted affection. With all this there is great excitement of the circulation, throbbing of the temples, a small and quick pulse; the skin is bedewed with perspiration, the tongue is coated and somewhat dry, the bowels probably confined, and the excretions very offensive.

Very often there is a total want of sleep, occasionally convulsions, and the ordinary symptoms of puerperal fever may be superadded with suppression of the lochia and milk. The character of the pulse varies a good deal; in some, though rarely, it is quick, full, and hard; in others slow, small, and soft. Dr. Gooch laid great stress upon this difference in the pulse; indeed he made it the basis of his classification. But it is not the pulse alone which thus varies, for in the one case the system generally gives evidence of the existence of violent inflammatory action; while in the other, the symptoms are those rather of a low form of fever; "there is less excitement, but there is also less strength; the powers of the system are rapidly giving way, not so much under the effects of the local disease, as under those of the general affection by which the local disease has been produced."

Sometimes, and especially when the disease is accompanied by puerperal fever, there is great fulness and tenderness over the abdomen. The bowels are very confined, the breath is offensive, the tongue coated with a thick, dirty-white fur, the urine is turbid and passed in small quantities, and the motions are often very knotty and dark.

The *Course* which the acute form of the disease may take varies a good deal; those cases are most fatal which come on suddenly, are more violent, and attended with a greater amount of fever and nervous disturbance. Where the symptoms are really caused by inflammation within the cranium, a fatal result is generally to be anticipated. "Mania soon after delivery is more dangerous to life than melancholia beginning several months afterwards" (Gooch); and he adds, "in the cases which I have seen terminate fatally, the patient has died with symptoms of exhaustion, not with those of oppressed brain, excepting only one case."

Where the symptoms are dependent, as they sometimes appear to be, upon a disordered state of the intestinal excretions, the chances of a successful issue are certainly much greater.

Of the *Causes* of acute mania very little really is known. In many cases, probably at least one-half, there seems to have been an hereditary tendency; in most there is a high degree of nervous development. The sleeplessness, which some have thought was a cause of the disorder, is more likely to be an early indication of the disease itself. Others have enumerated as causes, cold, mental emotion, deranged bowels, and certain moral conditions. The latter, Esquirol thought, was the cause of more than half the cases, and this opinion arose from the fact that mania occurs much more often in unmarried puerperal women than in the married. Diseases of the uterus or ovaries are said sometimes to act as exciting causes, and though this may be so occasionally, it is certainly not always; still there are many cases recorded in which undoubted disease existed in those parts and no other, and it is fair therefore to assume that this had somewhat to do with the mental disturbance, especially when we remember the varieties of mental excitement which occur in women as the result of sexual derangement and development, "witness the hysteric affections of puberty, the nervous susceptibility which occurs during every menstrual period, the nervous affections of breeding, and the nervous susceptibility of lying-in women" (Gooch). Some believe that the disease is simply inflammation of the brain or its membranes. Gooch thought that the disease is not one of congestion or inflammation, but rather of excitement without power. Nevertheless there can be no doubt that, though very rare, yet phrenitis does sometimes occur in puerperal mania. Marshall Hall considered that it was due to "the united influences of intestinal irritation and loss of blood."

The *Diagnosis* of this affection is not usually very difficult; it is, however, likely to be confounded either with simple phrenitis, or with the low muttering delirium of typhoid or any similar fever. From the former it is distinguished by the *absence* of that hard, full, bounding pulse, the intolerance of light and sound, the excruciating pain in the head, the constant vomiting, and suffusion of the eyes, all which are present, generally in a very marked degree, in phrenitis, and "conspicuous by their absence" in mania. The inflammatory fever, too, if it exists in the latter, is much less in degree than in the former. From low fever mania is distinguished by the history and progress of the case, and by the greater preponderance of the nervous as compared with the general constitutional disturbance.

As regards the *Prognosis,* Dr. Burrows gives 35 recoveries out of 37, Dr. Haslam 50 out of 80, and Esquirol 55 out of 92. Thus of a total of 209, 145 recovered; but it is curious to note that the proportion of recoveries given by these three observers, varies greatly. Of the total recoveries, by far the greater number occur before six months.

The *Treatment* of puerperal mania is of the simplest kind, but requiring at the same time the exercise of great judgment. There are three things requiring special attention: 1. To remove all supposed sources of irritation; 2. To quiet the nervous system; 3. To support the strength of the patient.

To fulfil the first indication it is necessary to find out whence the irritation comes. If there be a history of previously disordered bowels with constipation, nothing will do so much good as free purgation; a scruple or half a drachm of jalap powder,[3] with five or ten grains of calomel, will be of great service, and this may, with advantage, be followed by saline aperients. Dr. Rigby advised the use of antimony[4] in combination with calomel and ipecacuanha;[5] "it is too speedy in its operation to depress the patient much by nausea, and has the additional advantage of acting as a rapid and effectual purge; when its action is over she usually falls into a sound sleep, perspires freely, and wakes greatly refreshed."

When the bowels have acted well, and the evacuations have assumed a more healthy appearance, the second indication should, if necessary, be attended to, but opiates ought as a rule to be eschewed; they rather increase the irritability, and if there be any tendency to cerebral congestion will assuredly favor it. Some authorities say that they have derived great benefit from large doses of opium, but in many cases it undoubtedly does harm. A safer and more efficacious remedy is the hydrate of chloral;[6] it may be given in doses of from twenty to sixty grains, and while very useful in inducing sleep, it does not excite, as opium often does, nor does it produce any corresponding depression; henbane[7] is also a useful remedy, and chloroform is of great service; these may be repeated as often as seems desirable. Several cases have lately been published in which chloroform acted most admirably, it should be given so as to produce its full effects. White hellebore[8] has also been strongly recommended in America, and Indian hemp[9] has occasionally been tried with benefit. Hydrocyanic acid[10] is another sedative remedy which has been tried and found to possess great value; it requires to be given in fair doses of 5 minims of the dilute acid every four hours. Camphor[11] has also been highly extolled; Gooch and Campbell observed much benefit from its employment.

---

[3] *jalap powder:* A root of the climbing plant *Ipomae purga,* used medicinally as a purgative.

[4] *antimony:* Silvery-white crystalline, brittle metal, doses of which were given as an emetic.

[5] *ipecacuanha:* Small, emetic plant from South America; ipecac.

[6] *chloral:* Mixture of chlorine and alcohol; a hypnotic drug.

[7] *henbane:* Herb of the nightshade family, yielding alkaloid drugs such as scopolamine; a strong sedative.

[8] *White hellebore:* Source of drug veratrum, a sedative; once considered a cure for insanity.

[9] *Indian hemp:* Brazilian jaborandi root used as a stimulant, expectorant, sialagogue, and antivenomous tonic; the root causes profuse perspiration and was also used as a laxative and emetic.

[10] *Hydrocyanic acid:* Also known as prussic acid; a poisonous compound.

[11] *camphor:* Used as a mild analgesic.

The third indication requires great vigilance, for the patient's strength very soon becomes exhausted under this disease, and requires to be carefully supported. With this object in view, strong beef-tea, jellies, a little wine, and a generally tonic plan of treatment will be necessary.

In all cases of puerperal mania the condition of the uterine functions should be carefully inquired into, and any deviation from health corrected.

The second form of mania, that characterized by debility and anæmia, differs very much from the preceding. It may come on a few days after delivery, where there has been considerable flooding, and where the strength of the patient has been sorely tried by the labor; or it may come on some months later from debility consequent on long-continued nursing. There is generally a total absence of everything like excitement, the patient being rather in a state of melancholic depression. "There was a peculiarity," Dr. Gooch says, "about the commencement of the disease which I have seldom or never noticed at the commencement of acute mania; there was an incipient stage, in which the mind was wrong, yet right enough to recognize that it was wrong." Patients subject to this disease are generally thin, weakly, and delicate, and depressed in spirits.

This form of mania or melancholia is much more tedious than the other, and there is some danger of its becoming chronic and ending in complete fatuity; this, however, is happily a very rare result when once the patient has recovered her lost health and strength; it seldom or never ends fatally. The disease is apt to occur in those who have a strong hereditary tendency to insanity, and also in those cases "where hysteria has existed in an unusual degree during the latter part of pregnancy."

The *Treatment* is just that which common sense would suggest; the patient is suffering entirely from debility, therefore her physical condition is to be improved by a good, nourishing, and slightly stimulating diet — beef-tea, eggs, or even meat — anything, in fact, which will improve the condition of the blood. As medicines, tonics, the mineral acids, quinine, and steel, will be of great service. Gentle aperients will also be needed, and they should, if possible, be combined with some vegetable bitter. The Mist. Gen. Co. of the old London Pharmacopœia is a very good form.

Another indication to be fulfilled is the calming of the nervous system, and for this purpose no drug is likely to be so useful as opium;

the Liq. Opii. Sedat, is the most suitable form; but if opiates disagree then the hydrate of chloral, or henbane, camphor, or Indian hemp will be of service.

FORDYCE BARKER

From The Puerperal Diseases

Many of the clinical accounts of postpartum "insanity" cite obscenity of language as one of the symptoms of the disease. Other symptoms are listed by Fordyce Barker (1819–1891) in his manual *The Puerperal Diseases,* first published in 1883, which details the effects of postpartum illness. In this work, Barker maintains that "fully seven per cent of the insanity which occurs among women, in civilized and Christian communities that support insane hospitals, is due to causes connected with child-bearing" (167). Like many of his colleagues, Barker notes that an invalid suffering from the delusions associated with puerperal mania often believes that they are caused by some strange mysterious power. The symptoms of puerperal mania closely resemble those of *delirium tremens.* The invalid cannot sleep, refuses to eat, may have odd cravings, and may shy away from others. Chronic insanity, rather than death, is likely to be the outcome, except in extreme cases where patients commit suicide. Interestingly, Barker contends that the disease often befalls the wives of physicians, as in Gilman's "The Yellow Wallpaper." Barker's last suggested cure for puerperal mania — the "moral treatment" — is also relevant to Gilman's tale. The treatment is intended to help the new mother to establish self-control over her "moral perversion or mental eccentricity." Besides seculsion and restraint, the patient must submit to constant supervision, as well as warm baths, forced feedings, and — in severe cases — opium, morphine, chloroform, or sedatives.

The text of the following excerpt is taken from the third edition of *The Puerperal Diseases: Clinical Lectures Delivered at Bellevue Hospital by Dr. Fordyce Barker* (New York: Appleton, 1883), 172–84; 189–91.

Puerperal mania is the form with which obstetricians have most frequently to deal. In some few rare cases, it is suddenly developed without any forewarning symptoms, but, in by far a larger number, there are very characteristic prodromic[1] symptoms, sometimes con-

---

[1] *prodromic:* Indication or symptom of onset of disease.

tinuing for a few days and in other instances only a few hours before the explosion. There is generally an unusual excitement of manner, although, in a few, a morbid melancholy air first attracts attention. A sudden aversion is displayed toward those who have been before best loved; an excessive loquacity, or an obstinate silence, weeping or laughing equally without a motive, a morbid sensibility to light, to noises, to odors, a suspicious watchful expression of the eye, and sleeplessness, are symptoms, which, occurring in a woman who has been confined within ten or fifteen days, indicate an impending attack of puerperal mania. There are often muscular movements of the eyelids, the face, and the hands, very much resembling the appearance of a patient on the brink of delirium tremens.[2] Indeed, the general symptoms are often wonderfully like those which are characteristic of the beginning of delirium tremens, and, in the case of the wife of a medical friend, which I shall presently relate to you, a painful suspicion existed in the mind of her husband at first that the real disease was delirium tremens.

There are certain symptoms which very generally characterize the moment of the attack, but these are usually of short duration. The facial expression is very peculiar, and, having once been seen, will always be remembered. The features are drawn, pallid, the cheeks and forehead are covered with little drops of perspiration, and the whole air of the expression is unsettled, indicative of fright or fury.

When the malady is fully developed, the patient becomes very boisterous and noisy, incoherent in her language and in her gestures. She stares wildly at imaginary objects in the air, seizes any word spoken by those near, and repeats it with "damnable iteration," clutches at every thing and every one near her, throws off all covering, jumps from the bed, and even the most refined and religious women, when possessed with the demon of puerperal mania, will scream out oaths and obscenity with a volubility perfectly astounding. Erotic manifestations occur in a majority of cases. Masturbation is sometimes noticed, but I believe, as Dr. Tuke suggests, that this is more the result of a wish to allay than to excite irritation. Nearly one-half of these cases manifest a suicidal tendency, but rather as a sudden impulse than as a settled determination.

[2] *delirium tremens:* State of mental agitation and incoherence, often due to excessive and prolonged use of alcohol.

While many of these appearances are very like those of delirium tremens, the physical symptoms are in striking contrast with those of this disease. The patient is pale, cold, clammy, with a quick, small, irritable pulse; the features are pinched, at times almost collapsed-looking. There is usually great muscular weakness, with now and then a momentary spasmodic display of unusual strength.

I wish especially to urge it upon your attention, that other grave diseases may exist in a latent form, coincident with the mania, the manifestations of which are masked by the mental symptoms. In this hospital, one patient has died with pelvic peritonitis, another, with pneumonia, and a third, with pericarditis and endocarditis; and in neither, was the disease suspected until revealed by the autopsy. All recent authors agree that phrenitis[3] connected with puerperal mania is excessively rare.

Prognosis. — This involves the three questions, of the duration of the disease, the mental recovery, and the recovery of the general health. Dr. Tuke says: "Puerperal mania of itself does not kill, and when you have to combat it alone, not only death is not to be dreaded, but, in the very large proportion of cases, a return to sanity may be prognosticated. It is, perhaps, *the* most curable form of insanity. This statement is made advisedly, but does not extend to those cases which are placed under asylum treatment as a *dernier ressort.*" As to the duration of the disease, in some, but comparatively few cases, it entirely disappears in a few days. I have been struck with the fact that, in all the cases which I have seen, where the mania has followed puerperal convulsions, the duration of the mania has been limited to three or four days, and the patient has speedily recovered, or she has died within this period. I only mention the fact, without attempting to offer any theory to explain it.

In a majority of cases, the mania gradually subsides within a period of three weeks, more frequently earlier, and is followed by a condition of partial dementia, with some delusions, especially as regards personal identity. These gradually disappear, leaving a kind of intellectual barrenness, like one waking from a dream. From this condition, you may confidently hope for ultimate recovery. In some cases, the malady is prolonged two or three or more months; but, if beyond six months, the chances of recovery are very small. When death is the result, it is almost invariably due to some associated disease, as peritonitis, or cellulitis, pneumonia, and in some exceedingly rare cases, phrenitis, the fatal result usually occurring in a very few days.

[3] *phrenitis:* Inflammation of the diaphragm.

Causes. — Among the predisposing causes, hereditary tendency is the most prominent, especially traceable to the female side of the family, much more frequently than to the male. This was proven to exist in 22 of the 57 cases of Dr. Tuke; Esquirol, 1 in 2.8; Marcé, 24 in 56; Helftt, of Berlin, 51 in 131.

The next cause which I shall mention as predisposing to this malady is dystocia. In the 73 cases of Dr. Tuke (including both mania and melancholia), the labor was complicated in 23. Dr. Tuke remarks: "The various irregularities of labor doubtless operate in different ways, those where the suffering has been long continued depressing the nervous system directly, those in which large quantities of blood have been lost producing anæmia of the brain, and, in the case of the child being still-born, a moral shock acting on the mind naturally predisposed to this affection." I shall add, to those causes that I have mentioned, anæmia and eclampsia. Moral causes are no doubt among the most frequent of the predisposing causes, but they are also exciting causes.

Exciting Causes. — It is my firm conviction that mental emotions constitute the exciting cause of puerperal mania infinitely more frequently than all other causes combined. The relative frequency of puerperal mania is just in proportion to the susceptibility to the influence of emotional causes. In Würzburg, the proportion of cases of mania to the whole number of confinements was 1 in 1,487; in Prague, 1 in 1,228. It is not strange that Scanzoni, studying the malady in this field, should regard the frequency of mania as exaggerated, at the same time that he admits that hospital records probably do not accurately represent the relative frequency in private, as it is notoriously more common in the well-to-do classes. Now, while this is undoubtedly true in Scanzoni's field of observation, the exact reverse of this statement is true with us. I have visited the lying-in hospitals of Würzburg, Prague, Munich, and many others in Germany, and I have conversed with Scanzoni on this very subject. From him I learned that with most patients in these hospitals, there is no sacrifice of domestic ties or social position in going to the hospital, but, on the contrary, many are in every way better off than when out of the hospital. They have never before been so well cared for. For most of them, there is no stigma of disgrace in being there, and no consciousness of moral wrong or loss of position among their associates by becoming a mother without being a wife. Among the lower classes in some parts of Germany, I believe it is considered a perfectly legitimate business for young girls to become pregnant to qualify themselves for the position of wet-nurse and earn some money. There is, then, an entire absence of those moral causes of puerperal mania, which exist in tremendous force in this hospital, as I shall presently show you.

Then contrast the difference in frequency between the patients in the lying-in wards of St. Giles's Infirmary, where, in one series, there was one case of mania in 1,888 confinements, and the patients of Queen Charlotte's Lying-in Hospital,[4] where there was one of mania in 182 of labor.

Now, mark the difference between the moral condition of the patients in this hospital and those whose statistics I have given. A large majority of patients in our lying-in-wards are of foreign birth. They have come to a new country, leaving friends behind, with the hope of improving their condition, and many are disappointed in this respect. A large proportion, probably more than one-half, are unmarried. It is impossible to ascertain the truth on this point, for many represent themselves as married and deserted by their husbands, and some of these are subsequently found to be single. But this very deceit shows a moral sense on this point. Then many, who have been wronged and abandoned by their seducers, prefer to die in the hospital rather than have their disgrace known to their relatives. In addition to this, I am well convinced that our climate has a marked influence in developing the nervous susceptibilities of Europeans who come here. Then, again, there is no part of the world where the lapse from virtue in women is so severely punished by social ostracism as in New England, and she contributes her quota of poor girls who rush to a great city to hide themselves, and are at last driven to the hospital as their only resource.

Now, in view of all these facts, I think that you will agree with me that, if statistics ever prove any thing in regard to the causes of disease, they prove that moral emotions are the great exciting cause of puerperal mania.

I will mention a curious fact that has occurred in my experience: Since 1855, I have seen thirteen cases of puerperal mania in the wives of physicians, nine in this city, and four in the adjoining cities. All but one were primiparæ.[5] It has struck me as very extraordinary, that so large a number should have occurred in one special class, and I think

---

[4] *St. Giles's Infirmary . . . Queen Charlotte's Lying-in Hospital:* Founded in the Middle Ages, St. Giles's Infirmary was located in Norwich, England, and established as a charity hospital in 1249.

[5] *primiparæ:* Women bearing or having delivered a first child (Latin).

the following is the probable explanation: All of these were ladies of education and more than usual quickness of intellect, and, beginning a new experience in life, and having access to their husband's books, they probably had read just enough on midwifery to fill their minds with apprehensions as to the horrors which might be in store for them, and thus developed the cerebral disturbances, just as any other moral emotions may. . . .

Treatment. — Dr. Tuke says: "To shave and apply cold to the head, administer tartar-emetic, purge, and blister, are not uncommon remedies (!) applied where mania exists. In puerperal insanity this bad treatment insures a lapse into dementia — the patient can resist the disease, but not the remedy; each dose of antimony, each cold application, each blister, puts the case further and further beyond the control of the physician." As regards my own experience and observation, I am heartily in accord with Dr. Tuke.

The most recent article on puerperal mania, which has been probably more generally read than any other by the profession now in practice in this country, is the lecture by Sir James Simpson, in the volume of "Clinical Lectures on Diseases of Women." The warm admiration for his genius, the great respect for his remarkable talents and industry, and the deep-felt sorrow for the loss which the profession and the world sustained in his comparatively early death, combine to add force to the intrinsic weight of his suggestions. But his remarks on the treatment of puerperal mania leave the strong impression on my mind that he could not have had the personal supervision of many cases, although he probably saw a great many in consultation. I refer more especially to his remarks on "nervous sedatives," "specifics," and "depurants," which bear the stamp of theoretical suggestions, rather than of practical deductions from clinical observation.

Bleeding, once so much in vogue, it is now settled, is not only useless, but positively injurious in all but very exceptional cases. A vast majority of cases are undoubtedly associated with anæmia and nervous exhaustion. In one case only, have I seen venesection[6] positively beneficial. The patient was in a sthenic condition. She had lost very little blood at the time of labor, and the symptoms of phrenitis were very marked.

[6] *bleeding . . . venesection:* Until the mid-nineteenth century, it was generally believed that many diseases were due to an excess of blood and that, therefore, a bloodletting would give relief.

Vascular sedatives are equally useless, except when the mania is complicated with evident symptoms of some latent local inflammation, a complication which cannot be too sedulously watched for.

Laxatives and emetics should never be given, except when there are positive indications of their necessity.

As insomnia is one of the most striking features of puerperal mania, opiates[7] are naturally suggested, and I have found, in the cases that I have seen in consultation, that they have generally been tried. Dr. Tuke says: "Drugs seem of no avail; opiates, more especially, do more harm than good. A large dose, given at the very first indication of insanity, is said to have the effect of cutting short the attack; this I cannot speak to, but repeat the statement previously made: that when it has fairly established itself, although large doses of opium may moderate the intensity, they tend to prolong the period of mania."

For my own part, I have never seen opium in any doses cut short the attack, although I have often known it to be tried. I think I have seen opiates prove of great service, in some few cases, where I have believed that the mania was complicated with latent pelvic peritonitis. But it is only in such cases that I have ever found them apparently useful. Mind you, I am now speaking of mania, not of melancholia.

It is obvious that the leading indication is to allay the brain-excitement. The question is, How best to accomplish this? My answer would be:

1. By restoring exhausted nerve-power:

(a.) By improving the nutrition of the brain. I look upon good food, a plenty of such as is easily assimilated, to be one of the most important points in the treatment of this malady. Some obstinately refuse to take any thing, but, by management, tact, and perseverance, this difficulty is generally overcome after a time. Then, in many cases, even in the early periods of mania, you will find that tonics are of great service. Those which I most frequently recommend are, the tincture of the chloride of iron, the chlorate of potash, and the sulphate of bebeerine.[8] The latter is greatly to be preferred to quinine, from the fact that it has much less tendency to induce cerebral congestion.

(b.) By inducing sleep. This is nearly as important in puerperal mania as in delirium tremens, but there is this difference: In delirium

---

[7] *opiates:* Any preparation of opium that is used to produce sleep or a deadening effect.

[8] *tincture . . . bebeerine:* In the nineteenth century, the first was used as an astringent or hematinic, the second as an antiseptic, and the third as a tonic for malaria (a substitute for quinine).

tremens, when we have secured for our patient some hours of refreshing sleep, we ordinarily find that the disease is essentially overcome. But this is not the case in puerperal mania; for I have often seen patients, in whom good sleep has been secured for nights; and yet, when awake, the maniacal condition has continued for some days as before. Still, there is no doubt that every hour of good, sound sleep contributes something toward the patient's recovery. Now, neither opium nor the bromide of potassium[9] will produce sleep in maniacal patients, as a general rule. I have used the latter largely for this purpose in puerperal mania. I have often found it very useful under certain circumstances, to which I shall presently allude, but not as an hypnotic in mania. . . .

3. By such moral treatment[10] as will best secure the patient against all causes of nervous excitement, and will tend to excite in her a desire to obtain self-control:

This is difficult to define in words, and still more difficult to secure. It implies the greatest kindness, but no demonstrations of excessive solicitude; firmness, but no appearance of governing or controlling; incessant care and watchfulness, concealed by an air of indifference; a ready tact in turning the current of thought or will, but no contradiction or impatience. Few nurses, and still fewer friends, are able to exercise all these combined qualities. The physician will better teach them to the attendants, by his own manner when with the patient, than by didactic instructions.

If the moral treatment can be secured in a great measure at home, and the patient begin to show unequivocal signs of improvement within two or three weeks of the commencement of the attack, it is better that she should remain at home. But if she cannot have the advantage of proper moral treatment, and especially if the malady be not positively mitigated within the puerperal month, I have no doubt that the chances of recovery will be greatly increased by placing her in an asylum, where all the benefits of moral treatment are certain to be secured. This should not be delayed too long; as all physicians to these institutions are agreed in saying that the probabilities of cure are diminished just in proportion to the duration of the disease.

There is not the same objection to the removal to insane hospitals of those who suffer from puerperal mania, as exists in other forms of

---

[9] *bromide of potassium:* An alternative to opiates, bromide of potassium was used as a sedative to treat nervous disorders.

[10] *moral treatment:* Moral reeducation; meant to teach the patient philosophical resignation and consolation, including how to manage and control emotions.

insanity, because this removal does not suggest the same loss of family or social position. The public are ready to accept the puerperal state, which does not imply previous weakness of intellect or mental disease, as the specific cause of the overthrow of the mind, and therefore they have sound reasons for anticipating a perfect recovery.

I shall only add by way of caution that, in my observation, even those who are perfectly cured generally manifest some little occasional signs of moral perversion or mental eccentricity for months, and sometimes for a year or more.

I have nothing to add in regard to puerperal melancholia, because I have literally no clinical experience in this malady. I have seen but one case in private practice. In this hospital, we frequently have cases of this form of the disease, although it is very much more rare than mania, but, as it is generally developed the latter half of the puerperal month, and as it is more chronic in its type, the patients either die of some intercurrent disease, which is often the case, or are transferred to the asylum on Blackwell's Island.[11]

[11] *Blackwell's Island:* Opened in 1825 as an almshouse and prison complex for the insane poor (later called Welfare Island).

3

Sexuality, Race, and Social Control

The term *desire* had become a catchphrase in American culture by the turn of the century, when people came to believe that the promise of America meant the freedom to choose the commodities or sexual objects that they desired. Politicians and others came to fear that the excuse of such free-floating desires might deter Americans from devoting themselves to the principles of work and family or to the greater good of the country. While sexual desire was difficult to control, commodities could be presented as a substitute for the exercise of sexuality, sublimation could be offered as a way to delay or defer gratification, and sexuality could be regulated by medical practitioners who could shape — if not police — the "normal" exercise of sexual behavior.

A host of medical authorities — from physicians to sexologists — sought to define the "proper" boundaries of pleasurable sex in order to preserve the propagation of the race. As we can see from the treatises by leading psychologists and sexologists of the day that are included in this chapter, women's sexuality was often pathologized, declared abnormal, or otherwise subjected to the dictates of so-called "experts" on women's depraved or potentially dangerous nature. Middle- and upper-class women's "passionlessness" had been assumed in the early and mid-nineteenth century, whereas working-class women had exercised their sexuality under far less surveillance than the home-bound wife. Now, in Gilman's day, women across class lines were diagnosed as too appetitive and pleasure-seeking.

It may be surprising to notice how much President Theodore Roosevelt's 1905 address to the National Congress of Mothers resembles the conduct manuals included in Chapter 1. His advice to mothers to subordinate their own desires for the good of the "race," however, was his own ideological contribution to advice literature. Roosevelt advocated "the strenuous life" for men as an antidote to what was considered the general "feminization" of American culture in the nineteenth century, a feminization that was attributed to women's growing influence over religion, moral reform, the social gospel, and the socialization of children. Women's "influence," if not their legal or political power, had grown, and Roosevelt wanted to channel that energy into race preservation. His audience consisted of white, middle-class women whose energies could be put to use in increasing "native stock" and maintaining the dominance of Anglo culture against that of what Gilman was to call the "fecund foreigners." Gilman celebrated women's role in race preservation through procreation as part of the legitimate gendered division of labor, but she also thought that women should return to work in the public sphere after giving birth, leaving childrearing to experts. "The Yellow Wallpaper" can be seen as a negative portrayal of the effects of a gendered division of labor: John goes off to work each morning, and when the narrator-heroine collapses from depression, John's sister, Jennie, oversees the domestic scene, enabling the doctor-husband to pursue the profession which he shares with both his wife's brother and the renowned S. Weir Mitchell.

It is no coincidence that women were the special targets of the new discourses of medicine and the social sciences that became popular at the turn of the century. Psychology, sociology, and anthropology were devoted in large part to analyzing female behavior and then prescribing the physiological and psychological norms for women whose newfound (or newly won) freedoms threatened the social order of the recent Victorian past. The Comstock Law (passed in 1873) sought to restrict the availability of sexually explicit materials, including birth control guides and abortion advertisements, which Anthony Comstock, the fanatic special agent for the U.S. Post Office, had come to see as out of control. Comstock's second book, *Traps for the Young* (1883), targeted "Evil Reading" as the Devil's tool. The passing of a series of Immigration Restriction Acts was concurrent with the tightening of obscenity laws, since foreigners were often, albeit unfairly, associated with exotic sex practices and sexual licentiousness. Gilman herself, in "Parasitism and Civilised Vice" (1931), links Asian women with the tendency of American men to "go native" and engage in unhealthy sex activities. Women's sexual liberation — embodied and symbolized by the New Woman whose very presence was seen as an affront to Victorian sexual mores — brought an unsettling reminder that sexuality was no longer exercised for reproduction alone. Female sexual passion was frequently displaced onto the bodies of foreign women; as Susan Lanser has argued, the narrator's obsession with "yellowness" in Gilman's short story can be related to the larger cultural anxiety about Asian immigration that resulted in the agitation against and ultimate prohibition of Chinese immigration.

The new "sex experts" who began publishing in the 1880s and 1890s took it as their mission to categorize sexual impulses and define the boundaries of "normal" sexuality. George M. Beard's *Sexual Neurasthenia* (1903) was one of the most popular sex handbooks of the period. Beard often prescribed electric treatments as cures, since he saw nervous diseases as depleting the "bank" of energy available for sustained work or pleasure. Excessive sexual dissipation would lead to a general debility, and Beard agreed that the "highly sensitive and nervous class" (that is, the upper and middle classes) was particularly susceptible. Beard's diagnoses were followed by the even larger claims of doctor-scientists such as Havelock Ellis and Richard von Krafft-Ebing, whose case studies of hypochondriacs and hysterics were famous. With the emphasis in marriage shifting from the ideal of a productive and reproductive partnership to a companionate sex-relation, Ellis and Krafft-Ebing emphasized the importance of sexual knowledge and mutual satisfaction. Women had once been considered passionless by nature; now, their sexual satisfaction became a prime topic for study and analysis. Sex was seen as being essential to modern marriage, where it had once been seen as serving only reproductive purposes or male desires. Only by studying the sex drives and impulses, these authorities argued, would we come to understand human behavior and learn how to control it for the maximum benefit of the human race. The silence about marital sexuality in "The Yellow Wallpaper" is certainly telling, given Gilman and her culture's near obsession with discussing and documenting human needs and impulses.

Gilman's prescriptions for a culture based on sexual equality, which were influenced by Lester Frank Ward's essay on "gynæcocentric theory," oddly go hand-in-hand with the overwhelming injunctions in her culture to make race and sex into quantifiable, identifiable sciences. Scientific racism held that one people might be superior to another because of biological and racial differences, and scientific sexism held that one's sex determined one's place in the social hierarchy. Perhaps the strongest statement of scientific racism came from sociologist Edward Alsworth Ross, whose work on social engineering — the doctrine that sought to "manage" society through eugenics, cooperation, and the restraining of individual self-interest — influenced the development of Gilman's own economic theories. In one of her last and most virulent statements, "Parasitism and Civilised Vice," Gilman provides a "scientific" account of how women have developed into "sexual parasites," dependent on men for economic security.

There is a strain of scientific racism and sexism in Gilman's essay. Like many social scientists of her day, Gilman came to believe that criminality, sexual licentiousness, and excessive individualism — among other social crimes — were inheritable character traits that could only be controlled through population- and sex-management. A range of thinkers — from psychologists to physiologists — had developed the pseudoscience of measuring racial and sexual characteristics. Their work influenced Gilman's thinking about the value of the individual will and the social forces threatening to undermine individual self-restraint. By the time she wrote "Parasitism and Civilised Vice," Gilman had come to reject vehemently all sorts of dependence as enforced parasitism, and she saw Asian women who had been trained to become sex slaves as the ultimate embodiment of such parasitism. Playing as it does to racial stereotypes, Gilman's rhetoric shows how much she was influenced by the violent anti-immigration sentiment of her day, which blamed "lesser races" for the "baser passions" that consumed the vital energies of those she wished to convert to her utopian vision of social collectivism.

1873 Comstock Law

Until 1873, contraceptives were both advertised and distributed through the mail. In 1873, Anthony Comstock (see p. 195) launched a campaign to prohibit the traffic in "obscene" literature: both pornography and birth control advice, and anything advertised as "preventing conception." The resulting Comstock Law was officially called the "act for the Suppression of Trade in, and Circulation of, Obscene Literature and Articles of Immoral Use." After the law was passed, Comstock became a special agent for the U.S. Post Office, a position which enabled him to turn his private battle against vice into a public war on reproductive and sensationalist literature.

The text of the following excerpt is taken from *The Statutes at Large and Proclamations of the United States of America, From March 1871 to March 1873*, vol. 17 (Boston: Little, 1873), 598–600.

APPROVED, March 3, 1873.

An Act for the Suppression of Trade in, and Circulation of, obscene Literature and Articles of immoral Use.

Be it enacted by the Senate and House of Representatives of the United States of America in Congress assembled, That whoever, within the District of Columbia or any of the Territories of the United States, or other place within the exclusive jurisdiction of the United States, shall sell, or lend, or give away, or in any manner exhibit, or shall offer to sell, or to lend, or to give away, or in any manner to exhibit, or shall otherwise publish or offer to publish in any manner, or shall have in his possession, for any such purpose or purposes, any obscene book, pamphlet, paper, writing, advertisement, circular, print, picture, drawing or other representation, figure, or image on or of paper or other material, or any cast, instrument, or other article of an immoral nature, or any drug or medicine, or any article whatever, for the prevention of conception, or for causing unlawful abortion, or shall advertize the same for sale, or shall write or print, or cause to be written or printed, any card, circular, book, pamphlet, advertisement, or notice of any kind, stating when, where, how, or of whom, or by what means, any of the articles in this section hereinbefore mentioned, can be purchased or obtained, or shall manufacture, draw, or print, or in any wise make any of such articles, shall be deemed guilty of a misdemeanor, and, on conviction thereof in any court of the United States having criminal jurisdiction in the District of Columbia, or in any Territory or place within the exclusive jurisdiction of the United States, where such misdemeanor shall have been committed; and on conviction thereof, he shall be imprisoned at hard labor in the penitentiary for not less than six months nor more than five years for each offense, or fined not less than one hundred dollars nor more than two thousand dollars, with costs of apart.

SEC. 2. That section one hundred and forty-eight of the act to revise, consolidate, and amend the statutes relating to the Post-office Department, approved June eighth, eighteen hundred and seventy-two, be amended to read as follows:

"SEC. 148. That no obscene, lewd, or lascivious book, pamphlet, picture, paper, print, or other publication of an indecent character, or any article or thing designed or intended for the prevention of conception or procuring of abortion, nor any article or thing intended or adapted for any indecent or immoral use or nature, nor any written or printed card, circular, book, pamphlet, advertisement or notice of any kind giving information, directly or indirectly, where, or how, or of whom, or by what means either of the things before mentioned may be obtained or made, nor any letter upon the envelope of which, or postal-card upon which indecent or scurrilous epithets may be written or printed, shall be carried in the mail, and any person who shall knowingly deposit, or cause to be deposited, for mailing or delivery, any of the hereinbefore-mentioned articles or things, or any notice, or paper containing any advertisement relating to the aforesaid articles or things, and any person who, in pursuance of any plan or scheme for disposing of any of the hereinbefore-mentioned articles or things, shall take, or cause to be taken, from the mail any such letter or package, shall be deemed guilty of a misdemeanor, and, on conviction thereof, shall, for every offense, be fined not less than one hundred dollars nor more than five thousand dollars, or imprisoned at hard labor not less than one year nor more than ten years, or both, in the discretion of the judge."

SEC. 3. That all persons are prohibited from importing into the United States, from any foreign country, any of the hereinbefore-mentioned articles or things, except the drugs hereinbefore-mentioned when imported in bulk, and not put up for any of the purposes before mentioned; and all such prohibited articles in the course of importation shall be detained by the officer of customs, and proceedings taken against the same under section five of this act.

SEC. 4. That whoever, being an officer, agent, or employee of the government of the United States, shall knowingly aid or abet any person engaged in any violation of this act, shall be deemed guilty of a misdemeanor, and, on conviction thereof, shall, for every offense, be punished as provided in section two of this act.

SEC. 5. That any judge of any district or circuit court of the United States, within the proper district, before whom complaint in writing of any violation of this act shall be made, to the satisfaction of such judge, and founded on knowledge or belief, and, if upon belief, setting forth the grounds of such belief, and supported by oath or affirmation of the complainant, may issue, conformably to the Constitution, a warrant directed to the marshal, or any deputy marshal, in the proper district, directing him to search for, seize, and take possession of any such article or thing hereinbefore mentioned, and to make due and immediate return thereof, to the end that the same may be condemned and destroyed by proceedings, which shall be conducted in the same manner as other proceedings in case of municipal seizure, and with the same right of appeal or writ of error. *Provided,* That nothing in this section shall be construed as repealing the one hundred and forty-eighth section of the act of which this act is amendatory, or to affect any indictments heretofore found for offenses against the same, but the said indictments may be prosecuted to judgment as if this section had not been enacted.

APPROVED, March 3, 1873.

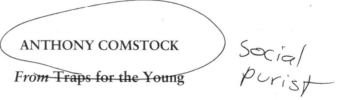

ANTHONY COMSTOCK

From Traps for the Young

Social purist

Anthony Comstock (1844–1915) was one of the most fervent nineteenth-century opponents of gambling, alcohol, and whatever else he regarded as obscene: whether it was contraception, prostitution, sensationalist literature, or erotica. He was a crusader extraordinaire, battling to suppress all forms of vice in the name of the "social purity" movements that burgeoned in the post–Civil War decades. Comstock himself founded the Society for the Suppression of Vice in 1872. Comstock's *Traps for the Young* (1883) identifies pool, gambling, sensational reading, free love, classical art, and advertisements as the invaders of moral society. In this work, Comstock ignores social and economic issues such as poverty and crime in order to foreground the ethical dangers of those vices he sees as posing the greatest threat to American society.

The text of the following excerpt is taken from *Traps for the Young* (New York: Funk & Wagnalls, 1883), 5–12.

Preface

Each birth begins a history. The pages are filled out, one by one, by the records of daily life. The mind is the source of action. Thoughts are the aliment upon which it feeds. We assimilate what we read. The pages of printed matter become our companions. Memory unites them indissolubly, so that, unlike an enemy, we cannot get away from them. They are constant attendants to quicken thought and influence action.

Good reading refines, elevates, ennobles, and stimulates the ambition to lofty purposes. It points upward. Evil reading debases, degrades, perverts, and turns away from lofty aims to follow examples of corruption and criminality.

This book is designed to awaken thought upon the subject of *Evil Reading*, and to expose to the minds of parents, teachers, guardians, and pastors, some of the mighty forces for evil that are to-day exerting a controlling influence over the young. There is a shameful recklessness in many homes as to what the children read.

The community is cursed by pernicious literature. Ignorance as to its debasing character in numerous instances, and an indifference that is disgraceful in others, tolerate and sanction this evil.

Parents send their beloved children to school, and text-books are placed in their hands, while lesson after lesson and precept after precept are drilled into them. But through criminal indifference to other reading for the children than their text-books, the grand possibilities locked up in the future of every child, if kept pure, and all the appetites and passions controlled, are often circumscribed and defeated at its threshold of life. This book is a plea for the moral purity of children. It is an appeal for greater watchfulness on the part of those whose duty it is to think, act, and speak for that very large portion in the community who have neither intellect nor judgment to decide what is wisest and best for themselves. It brings to parents the question of their responsibility for the future welfare of their offspring.

If a contagious disease be imported to these shores in some ship, at once the vessel and her passengers are quarantined. The port is promptly closed to the disease. The agent that brings it is estopped from entering the harbor until the contagion has been removed. It is the author's purpose to send a message in advance to parents, so that they may avert from their homes a worse evil than yellow fever or small-pox. Read the facts, and let them speak words of warning.

"The Modern News Stand and Its Results." Frontispiece for Anthony Comstock's *Traps for the Young* (1883).

The author, during an experience of nearly eleven years, has seen the effects of the evils herein discussed. If strong language is used, it is because no other can do the subject justice.

This work represents facts as they are found to exist. If it shall be the means of arousing parents as to what their children read, of checking evil reading among the young, or of awakening a public sentiment against the prevailing wickedness of the day, the writer will be content.

If any one doubts the startling facts stated, let me here place on record my entire readiness to sustain my assertions with proofs.

Because men will deny, scoff, and curse is no reason why these truths should not be laid before the minds of thinking men and women. But few have had the opportunity of seeing and knowing the facts concerning the evils discussed in this book. For the sake of the thousands of children in the land, I appeal to every good citizen to carefully read the following pages, not to criticise, but to see what can be done to remedy the evils discussed.

Our youth are in danger; mentally and morally they are cursed by a literature that is a disgrace to the nineteenth century. The spirit of evil environs them.

Let no man be henceforth indifferent. Read, reflect, act.

ANTHONY COMSTOCK.

NEW YORK, OCT. 15, 1883.

Chapter I
Household Traps

It is in the home that we must look for first impressions. Here the foundation of the character of the future man or woman is laid. Here the parent exerts an incalculable influence upon the offspring. Bright looks and sunny smiles beget joy and delight. Coarse expressions and hasty speech are closely followed. Anecdotes and stories are remembered and repeated as marvellous to tell, and anything that father or mother does is not questioned. What the parent allows is at once regarded by the child as "just the thing to do." Associations of good or evil nature are thus fixed in the mind in almost permanent character.

Evil thoughts, like bees, go in swarms. A single one may present itself before the mind. If entertainment be extended, or place be given it, at once this vile fellow is found to have an immense train in following. I repeat: their approach may be so secret and insidious, that but one may be discerned at first, and yet from all sides they will flock, darkening the eyes of the understanding, filling the ears of reason, until the danger signals can no longer be seen nor heard, and the poor victim swiftly becomes insensible to purity and virtue.

There is something wonderfully strange in the rapidity with which youthful minds take up lewd thoughts and suggestions. With almost equal ease they throw them off again, in the hearing and presence of others. Lewd thoughts soon overcome native innocence. Once the mind becomes familiar with foul stories and criminal deeds, self-respect at length is lost, and vile suggestions flow freely from lips that before would have scorned them.

"Evil communications corrupt good manners."

Locke[1] writes: "I think I may say, that of all the men we meet with, nine parts of ten are what they are, good or evil, useful or not, by their education. It is that which makes the great difference in mankind. Little or almost insensible impressions on our tender infancies have very important consequences; and there it is, as in the fountains of rivers, where a gentle application of the hand turns the flexible waters into channels that make them take quite contrary courses; and, by this little direction given them at first in the source, they receive different tendencies, and arrive at last at very remote and distant places. Imagine the minds of children as easily turned this way or that, as water itself."

Parents who are vacillating in principle, who give up conviction to expediency, who have no sense of honor, but let self-interest control in place of right, cannot expect their tender ones to develop into moral heroes under such influences. As well attempt to secure the perfection of the rose, in tint and odor, by placing a plant in a dark cellar where no light may come.

By means of judicious education our capacities of enjoyment may be enlarged and multiplied. Daily experience shows how susceptible the infant mind is of deep impressions.

Children of strong affections, lively imaginations, and animated characters are more easily dazzled and drawn away by the opinions and expressions of those with whom they come in contact, than those possessing more sluggish natures.

---

[1] *Locke:* John Locke (1632–1704), English philosopher whose most influential work was the *Essay Concerning Human Understanding* (1690), in which he argued that the mind was a *tabula rasa* (blank slate).

Hazlitt[2] wrote that "intellect only is immortal, and words the only things that last forever." Such a reflection weighs with terrible force when we consider that one cannot get away from a book that has once been read. The companionship of thought is more constant than the closest friend. At all times memory may bring it back. Unlike a visible enemy, it cannot be avoided, but once admitted to the shrine of our minds, it is there forever. The thought of the power of printed matter for good or evil is startling, and at times overwhelming. Authors who, for love of greed or love of sensation, publish to the world from their prurient imaginations impure and debasing thoughts — the noxious offspring of vice and immorality — have a terrible responsibility to answer for.

Consider some of the devices to capture the minds and imaginations of the young; some of the influences thrust upon the rising generations; some of the companions of the home; some of the traps which the spirit of evil is allowed to set in the home circle.

After more than eleven years' experience contending for the moral purity of the children of the land, and seeking to prevent certain evils from being brought in contact with this ever-susceptible class, I have one clear conviction, viz., that *Satan lays the snare, and children are his victims*. His traps, like all others, are baited to allure the human soul.

There is a great variety of traps used by mankind. These differ in their nature, form, and in methods of setting. For instance, the fox-trap, made of steel, with its saw-teeth jaws, is set with mouth wide open at the entrance of a burrow or in the path of sly Reynard, and covered from view with loose earth, in order to catch him as he goes for his daily food.

The box-trap, so easily constructed by every country boy, must be baited with a sweet apple to tempt the rabbit or squirrel.

The partridge snare must be suspended over the rotten trunk of some fallen tree, along which the festive bird drums his wings, or suspended over an opening in a bush fence with a cleared path strewn with squawberries to allure this sly bird into the fowler's hands.

A huge piece of tempting meat must be fastened in the bear-trap to entice bruin from his cave in the rocks and secure him as the trapper's prey.

The farmer places a chicken near the aperture in the foundation wall of the house or outbuilding, after he has concealed the trap for

---

[2] *Hazlitt:* William Hazlitt (1778–1830), English essayist, journalist, and critic, especially on poetry and drama.

the mink or odoriferous chicken-thief, who sleeps by day and commits depredations by night if he would effect a capture. The housemaid knows that the trap requires a bait of fragrant cheese for the mouse or rat.

Satan adopts similar devices to capture our youth and secure the ruin of immortal souls. Some of these traps do not of necessity cause absolute ruin, others do. Some are comparatively harmless, others are dangerous in the extreme. Those referred to in this chapter are the weakest. They are not always vicious or criminal, except so far as they pervert the taste of the young and rob the child of a desire for study. Of this class the love story and cheap work of fiction captivate fancy and pervert taste. They defraud the future man or woman by capturing and enslaving the young imagination. The wild fancies and exaggerations of the unreal in the story supplant aspirations for that which ennobles and exalts. In brief, these stories, that make day-dreamers of our children and castle-builders of the student, are harmful just in proportion as these results are produced. In the home, at school and even in the sanctuary during the solemn hours of worship on the Sabbath day, the day-dreamer wanders away in thought from all that is real and of highest importance, captivated by pictures and scenes that never can be realized. To one thus beguiled in youth the future has many sorrows; for while the victim seeks to realize his ideals in business prosperity, home, and wealth, the realities of life constantly bring disappointment and sorrow. They forget the sweet poet's admonition,

"Life is real, life is earnest."

Nourish a generation on this sort of mental food, and it must be apparent to any candid mind that it will be a generation devoid of taste for that which is pure and noble. This kind begets vapid, shallow-minded sentimentalists. The lofty thought they cannot understand. They would rate the most interesting history as distasteful, the choicest essay or finest poetry as dry and uninteresting.

To capture at the threshold of life the fancies and hold them in bondage until fiction supplants the real and study becomes irksome, is cruel and evil. Proper ambition is stunted, and the inspiration of lofty aims is supplanted by the vain imaginings suggested by this kind of light literature.

Parents mourn that the child's mind does not go out after noble things. They cannot understand why it is thus. The companion of the child's mind is exerting its sway, and the evil one is spreading his

kingdom. What I have said applies more directly to the deluge of cheap sensational stories[3] than to the higher grades of novel reading.

In novel reading, however, in general, the tendency is from the higher to the lower rather than from the lower to the higher. There are grave questions in the minds of some of our best writers, and of our most thoughtful men and women, whether novel reading at its best does not tend downward rather than upward. Some have questioned whether persons reading such authors as Mrs. Southworth[4] and Alexander Dumas[5] advance in time to George Eliot[6] and Sir Walter Scott.[7] This grade is not discussed here. We consider only the purely sensational works of fiction. These create an appetite that is seldom surfeited. The mind grows by what it feeds upon. Something more highly colored and exaggerated is sought after. The imagination is walled in like a canal, and thoughts run down the grade until the mind is emptied of lofty aims and ambitions, and the soul is shrivelled.

As the evening moth disappears at the approach of day and returns at night to flutter about the lighted lamp, so these bats of fancy may disappear when the mind is occupied, only to return in the solitary hour to besiege the imagination, calling the thoughts away from the important things of life. The fancies, once turned in this direction, wear a channel, down which dash the thoughts, gathering force like a river as they move away from the fountain-head.

How many parents ever stop and reflect, in sober earnest, that the minds of their children are active and open to anything exciting; that the bright budding intellect grasps with eagerness every topic of thought that fancy paints? How often we hear from children, "Oh, tell us a story!" How frequently the group of romping boys and girls are subdued by a story, and how charmed a child becomes with but a simple tale or anecdote! Anything marvellous or exciting is quickly appropriated. Parents forget that they are expected and designed by an all-wise Providence to think and decide in these matters for their children.

---

[3] *sensational stories:* Refers to a series of popular fictions about mysterious women, secrets, hidden crime, and insanity.

[4] *Mrs. Southworth:* E.D.E.N. Southworth (1819–1899), prolific author of sensational novels, including *The Hidden Hand* (1859); one of the most marketed of all nineteenth-century women writers.

[5] *Alexander Dumas:* Both Alexander Dumas *père* (1802–1870) and *fils* (1824–1895) were French novelists and dramatists.

[6] *George Eliot:* Pen name of Mary Ann Evans (1819–1880), famous Victorian novelist.

[7] *Sir Walter Scott* (1771–1832): Scottish poet, novelist, historian, and biographer.

Light literature, then, is a devil-trap to captivate the child by perverting taste and fancy. It turns aside from the pursuit of useful knowledge and prevents the full development in man or woman of the wonderful possibilities locked up in the child! Why rob the future ages of the high order of men and women, which would of necessity appear if the children of to-day were properly cared for and developed in keenest intellect and highest morals?

Aside from the enslavements to imagination and taste from this class of publications, alarmingly prevalent, many of the stories, though free from crime, lack a moral, contain insinuations against truth, justice, and religion, and favor deceit and lying. The tone is not elevating. They pave the way for that which is worse. If children must have stories, let parents provide those that have a high moral tone — stories where the hero is not a thief, murderer, or desperado, but a *moral hero*, whose chief trait of character is standing for the right. Teach the children to emulate deeds of heroism; to stand for the right even though the heavens fall; never to be sneered or laughed into doing a mean thing, nor neglecting duty.

THEODORE ROOSEVELT

Address to the National Congress of Mothers, March 13, 1905

Theodore Roosevelt (1858–1919) became the twenty-sixth President of the United States in 1901, after William McKinley's assassination. Before serving as McKinley's vice president, he had been a soldier, a history writer, and a politician. He served two terms as president, advocating such diverse issues as meat, food, and drug inspections; conservation; and an end to American isolationism. His writings popularized the idea of the West as Frontier, especially his four-volume *The Winning of the West* (1889–1896), as well as his progressive politics. While Roosevelt's 1905 speech in favor of Mother's Day did not contain any radically new ideas, his voice gave official support to the glorification of motherhood as necessary to the survival of good American "stock." Roosevelt argued that such survival depended on the existence of "real homes," whose moral head and heart was the American mother. Only such "healthy" homes, not based on what Thorstein Veblen termed "conspicuous consumption" or what Roosevelt called "pseudo-intellectuality," would save

America from "race suicide." Gilman would surely have approved of Roosevelt's speech where it glorifies the role of motherhood in cultural and social progress; however, while Roosevelt praises the virtues of individual, self-sacrificing good mothers, Gilman argued for the professionalization of "motherhood," which would leave the majority of women free to pursue other careers. Roosevelt's speech adds an ideological and political legitimacy to the cultural advice offered by women like Frances Willard and Margaret Sangster (see Part Two, Chapter 1).

The text of the following excerpt is taken from the *Theodore Roosevelt Papers* (Washington: Government Printing Office, 1905).

In our modern industrial civilization there are many and grave dangers to counterbalance the splendors and the triumphs. It is not a good thing to see cities grow at disproportionate speed relative to the country; for the small landowners, the men who own their little homes, and therefore to a very large extent the men who till farms, the men of the soil, have hitherto made the foundation of lasting national life in every State; and, if the foundation becomes either too weak or too narrow, the superstructure, no matter how attractive, is in imminent danger of failing.

But far more important than the question of the occupation of our citizens is the question of how their family life is conducted. No matter what that occupation may be, as long as there is a real home and as long as those who make up that home do their duty to one another, to their neighbors and to the state, it is of minor consequence whether the man's trade is plied in the country or the city, whether it calls for the work of the hands or for the work of the head.

But the Nation is in a bad way if there is no real home, if the family is not of the right kind; if the man is not a good husband and father, if he is brutal or cowardly or selfish, if the woman has lost her sense of duty, if she is sunk in vapid self-indulgence or has let her nature be twisted so that she prefers a sterile pseudo-intellectuality to that great and beautiful development of character which comes only to those whose lives know the fullness of duty done, of effort made and self-sacrifice undergone.

In the last analysis the welfare of the state depends absolutely upon whether or not the average family, the average man and woman and their children, represent the kind of citizenship fit for the foundation of a great nation; and if we fail to appreciate this we fail to appreciate the root morality upon which all healthy civilization is based.

No piled-up wealth, no splendor of material growth, no brilliance of artistic development, will permanently avail any people unless its home life is healthy, unless the average man possesses honesty, courage, common sense, and decency, unless he works hard and is willing at need to fight hard; and unless the average woman is a good wife, a good mother, able and willing to perform the first and greatest duty of womanhood, able and willing to bear, and to bring up as they should be brought up, healthy children, sound in body, mind, and character, and numerous enough so that the race shall increase and not decrease.

There are certain old truths which will be true as long as this world endures, and which no amount of progress can alter. One of these is the truth that the primary duty of the husband is to be the home-maker, the bread-winner for his wife and children, and that the primary duty of the woman is to be the helpmeet, the housewife, and mother. The woman should have ample educational advantages; but save in exceptional cases the man must be, and she need not be, and generally ought not to be, trained for a lifelong career as the family bread-winner; and, therefore, after a certain point the training of the two must normally be different because the duties of the two are normally different. This does not mean inequality of function, but it does mean that normally there must be dissimilarity of function. On the whole, I think the duty of the woman the more important, the more difficult, and the more honorable of the two; on the whole I respect the woman who does her duty even more than I respect the man who does his.

No ordinary work done by man is either as hard or as responsible as the work of a woman who is bringing up a family of small children; for upon her time and strength demands are made not only every hour of the day but often every hour of the night. She may have to get up night after night to take care of a sick child, and yet must by day continue to do all her household duties as well; and if the family means are scant she must usually enjoy even her rare holidays taking her whole brood of children with her. The birth pangs make all men the debtors of all women. Above all our sympathy and regard are due to the struggling wives among those whom Abraham Lincoln called the plain people, and whom he so loved and trusted; for the lives of these women are often led on the lonely heights of quiet, self-sacrificing heroism.

Just as the happiest and most honorable and most useful task that can be set any man is to earn enough for the support of his wife and family, for the bringing up and starting in life of his children, so the most important, the most honorable and desirable task which can be set any woman is to be a good and wise mother in a home marked by self-respect and mutual forbearance, by willingness to perform duty, and by refusal to sink into self-indulgence or avoid that which entails effort and self-sacrifice. Of course there are exceptional men and exceptional women who can do and ought to do much more than this, who can lead and ought to lead great careers of outside usefulness in addition to — not as substitutes for — their home work; but I am not speaking of exceptions; I am speaking of the primary duties. I am speaking of the average citizens, the average men and women who make up the Nation.

Inasmuch as I am speaking to an assemblage of mothers I shall have nothing whatever to say in praise of an easy life. Yours is the work which is never ended. No mother has an easy time, and most mothers have very hard times; and yet what true mother would barter her experience of joy and sorrow in exchange for a life of cold selfishness, which insists upon perpetual amusement and the avoidance of care, and which often finds its fit dwelling place in some flat designed to furnish with the least possible expenditure of effort the maximum of comfort and of luxury, but in which there is literally no place for children?

The woman who is a good wife, a good mother, is entitled to our respect as is no one else; but she is entitled to it only because, and so long as, she is worthy of it. Effort and self-sacrifice are the laws of worthy life for the man as for the woman; though neither the effort nor the self-sacrifice may be the same for the one as for the other. I do not in the least believe in the patient Griselda[1] type of woman, in the woman who submits to gross and long continued ill treatment, any more than I believe in a man who tamely submits to wrongful aggression. No wrongdoing is so abhorrent as wrongdoing by a man towards the wife and the children who should arouse every tender feeling in his nature. Selfishness toward them, lack of tenderness towards them, lack of consideration for them, above all, brutality in any form towards them, should arouse the heartiest scorn and indignation in every upright soul.

---

[1] *the patient Griselda:* Griselda is a folk-tale character noted for the patience with which she submitted to the most cruel ordeals as a wife and mother. This folk tale is given literary expression by Boccaccio in the *Decameron* (1348–1353) and Chaucer in "The Clerk's Tale" (1380s–1390s).

I believe in the woman's keeping her self-respect just as I believe in the man's doing so. I believe in her rights just as much as I believe in the man's and indeed a little more; and I regard marriage as a partnership, in which each partner is in honor bound to think of the rights of the other as well as of his or her own. But I think that the duties are even more important than the rights; and in the long run I think that the reward is ampler and greater for duty well done, than for the insistence upon individual rights, necessary though this, too, must often be. Your duty is hard, your responsibility great; but greatest of all is your reward. I do not pity you in the least. On the contrary, I feel respect and admiration for you.

Into the woman's keeping is committed the destiny of the generations to come after us. In bringing up your children you mothers must remember that while it is essential to be loving and tender, it is no less essential to be wise and firm. Foolishness and affection must not be treated as interchangeable terms; and besides training your sons and daughters in the softer and milder virtues you must seek to give them those stern and hardy qualities which in after life they will surely need. Some children will go wrong in spite of the best training; and some will go right even when their surroundings are most unfortunate; nevertheless an immense amount depends upon the family training. If you mothers through weakness bring up your sons to be selfish and to think only of themselves, you will be responsible for much sadness among the women who are to be their wives in the future. If you let your daughters grow up idle, perhaps under the mistaken impression that as you yourselves have had to work hard they shall know only enjoyment, you are preparing them to be useless to others and burdens to themselves. Teach boys and girls alike that they are not to look forward to lives spent in avoiding difficulties but to lives spent in overcoming difficulties. Teach them that work, for themselves and also for others, is not a curse but a blessing; seek to make them happy, to make them enjoy life, but seek also to make them face life with the steadfast resolution to wrest success from labor and adversity, and to do their whole duty before God and to man. Surely she who can thus train her sons and her daughters is thrice fortunate among women.

There are many good people who are denied the supreme blessing of children, and for these we have the respect and sympathy always due to those who, from no fault of their own, are denied any of the other great blessings of life. But the man or woman who deliberately forgoes these blessings, whether from viciousness, coldness, shallowheartedness, self-indulgence, or mere failure to appreciate aright the difference between the all-important and the unimportant — why, such a creature merits contempt as hearty as any visited upon the soldier who runs away in battle, or upon the man who refuses to work for the support of those dependent upon him, and who though ablebodied is yet content to eat in idleness the bread which others provide.

The existence of women of this type forms one of the most unpleasant and unwholesome features of modern life. If anyone is so dim of vision as to fail to see what a thoroughly unlovely creature such a woman is I wish they would read Judge Robert Grant's novel *Unleavened Bread*,[2] ponder seriously the character of Selma, and think of the fate that would surely overcome any nation which developed its average and typical woman along such lines. Unfortunately it would be untrue to say that this type exists only in American novels. That it also exists in American life is made unpleasantly evident by the statistics as to the dwindling families in some localities. It is made evident in equally sinister fashion by the census statistics as to divorce,[3] which are fairly appalling; for easy divorce is now as it ever has been, a bane to any nation, a curse to society, a menace to the home, an incitement to married unhappiness and to immorality, an evil thing for men and a still more hideous evil for women. These unpleasant tendencies in our American life are made evident by articles such as those which I actually read not long ago in a certain paper, where a clergyman was quoted, seemingly with approval, as expressing the general American attitude when he said that the ambition of any save a rich man should be to rear two children only, so as to give his children an opportunity "to taste a few of the good things of life."

This man, whose profession and calling should have made him a moral teacher, actually set before others the ideal, not of training children to do their duty, not of sending them forth with stout hearts and ready minds to win triumphs for themselves and their country, not of allowing them the opportunity, and giving them the privilege of making their own place in the world, but, forsooth, of keeping the number of children so limited that they might "taste a few good things!" The way to give a child a fair chance in life is not to bring it up in luxury, but to see that it has the kind of training that will give it

---

[2] *Judge Robert Grant's novel Unleavened Bread:* Grant's (1852–1940) heralded novel, published in 1900, about an ambitious, unprincipled woman.

[3] *divorce:* Divorce rates increased dramatically after the Civil War for a number of reasons, including a lessening of the legal restraints and "conditions" for divorce.

strength of character. Even apart from the vital question of national life, and regarding only the individual interest of the children themselves, happiness in the true sense is a hundredfold more apt to come to any given member of a healthy family of healthy-minded children, well brought up, well educated, but taught that they must shift for themselves, must win their own way, and by their own exertions make their own positions of usefulness, than it is apt to come to those whose parents themselves have acted on and have trained their children to act on the selfish and sordid theory that the whole end of life is "to taste a few good things."

The intelligence of the remark is on a par with its morality, for the most rudimentary mental process would have shown the speaker that if the average family in which there are children contained but two children the Nation as a whole would decrease in population so rapidly that in two or three generations it would very deservedly be on the point of extinction, so that the people who had acted on this base and selfish doctrine would be giving place to others with braver and more robust ideals. Nor would such a result be in any way regrettable; for a race that practiced such doctrine — that is, a race that practiced race suicide[4] — would thereby conclusively show that is was unfit to exist, and that it had better give place to people who had not forgotten the primary laws of their being.

To sum up, then, the whole matter is simple enough. If either a race or an individual prefers the pleasures of mere effortless ease, of self-indulgence, to the infinitely deeper, the infinitely higher pleasures that come to those who know the toil and the weariness, but also the joy, of hard duty well done, why, that race or that individual must inevitably in the end pay the penalty of leading a life both vapid and ignoble. No man and no woman really worthy of the name can care for the life spent solely or chiefly in the avoidance of risk and trouble and labor. Save in exceptional cases the prizes worth having in life must be paid for, and the life worth living must be a life of work for a worthy end, and ordinarily of work more for others than for oneself.

The man is but a poor creature whose effort is not rather for the betterment of his wife and children than for himself; and as for the mother, her very name stands for loving unselfishness and self-abnegation, and, in any society fit to exist, is fraught with associations which render it holy.

---

[4] *race suicide:* Roosevelt quickly adopted Edward Alsworth Ross's phrase to warn against the "dangerous" assimilation and proliferation of "foreigners" into U.S. culture.

The woman's task is not easy — no task worth doing is easy — but in doing it, and when she has done it, there shall come to her the highest and holiest joy known to mankind; and having done it, she shall have the reward prophesied in Scripture; for her husband and her children, yes, and all people who realize that her work lies at the foundation of all national happiness and greatness, shall rise up and call her blessed.

EDWARD ALSWORTH ROSS

From "The Causes of Race Superiority"

Edward Alsworth Ross (1866–1951), professor of sociology at the University of Wisconsin, was both friend and mentor to Gilman. Ross was influenced by reading the English philosopher Herbert Spencer (1820–1903), who adapted Charles Darwin's theory of evolution to social relations in general, using the metaphor of society as a jungle in which the "fittest" survived and prospered, and arguing that progress and peace would be reached once the evolutionary process was complete. Spencer's *The Principles of Sociology* became popular in the United States in the 1870s, since his work could be used to sanction the general rise in American laissez-faire business practices and unrestrained competition. In addition, the concept of natural selection was used to justify U.S. prejudices against "evolutionarily-stunted" African Americans, Native Americans, and Chinese.

In 1901, Ross wrote an influential book called *Social Control* that codified his thinking about the ways to manage society and control the environment. This study was dedicated to explaining the need for social engineering in the newly pluralistic American culture, which Ross characterized not as a "melting pot" but as a "polyglot boarding house." Along with other sociologists, such as Lester Frank Ward, Ross sought to superintend the social hierarchies and classes in the United States. He helped to introduce sociology as a science devoted to studying human "types," the individual in mass culture, and the most effective ways of organizing society for the greatest good of the greatest number. According to one eugenics scholar the term *race suicide* first appears in the following 1901 essay by Ross (Haller 217 n. 6); the term was generally used by eugenicists to lament the falling birth rate of those of "native stock" as compared to immigrant peoples. Ross's sociology, which we would now consider exclusionary, was designed to keep the upheavals of modern, industrialized society in check and reflected his culture's anxieties about immigration, rural and urban demographic changes, and economic and cultural instability.

The text of the following excerpt is taken from *Annals of the American Academy of Political and Social Science* 18 (Philadelphia: American Academy of Political and Social Science, July 1901–December 1901), 86–89.

One question remains. Is the Superior Race[1] as we have portrayed it, able to survive all competitions and expand under all circumstances? There is, I am convinced, one respect in which the very foresight and will power that mark the higher race dig a pit beneath its feet.

In the presence of the plenty produced by its triumphant energy the superior race forms what the economists call "a Standard of Comfort," and refuses to multiply save upon this plane. With his native ambition stimulated by the opportunity to rise and his natural foresight reinforced by education, the American, for example, overrules his strongest instincts and refrains from marrying or from increasing his family until he can realize his subjective standard of comfort or decency. The power to form and cling to such a standard is not only one of the noblest triumphs of reason over passion, but is, in sooth, the only sure hope for the elevation of the mass of men from the abyss of want and struggle. The progress of invention held out such a hope but it has proven a mockery. Steam and machinery, it is true, ease for a little the strain of population on resources; but if the birth-rate starts forward and the slack is soon taken up by the increase of mouths, the final result is simply more people living on the old plane. The rosy glow thrown upon the future by progress in the industrial arts proves but a false dawn unless the common people acquire new wants and raise the plane upon which they multiply.

Now, this rising standard, which alone can pilot us toward the Golden Age, is a fatal weakness when a race comes to compete industrially with a capable race that multiplies on a lower plane. Suppose,

[1] *Superior Race:* Ross believed that many group distinctions — such as heredity and temperament — were rooted in biology, and that white, northern European Christians constituted the healthiest, purest racial group. Social psychology explained how people arrived at their tastes, beliefs, and standards or values.

for example, Asiatics flock to this country and, enjoying equal opportunities under our laws, learn our methods and compete actively with Americans. They may be able to produce and therefore earn in the ordinary occupations, say three-fourths as much as Americans; but if their standard of life is only half as high, the Asiatic will marry before the American feels able to marry. The Asiatic will rear two children while his competitor feels able to rear but one. The Asiatic will increase his children to six under conditions that will not encourage the American to raise more than four. Both, perhaps, are forward-looking and influenced by the worldly prospects of their children; but where the Oriental is satisfied with the outlook the American, who expects to school his children longer and place them better, shakes his head.

Now, to such a competition there are three possible results. First, the American, becoming discouraged, may relinquish his exacting standard of decency and begin to multiply as freely as the Asiatic. This, however, is likely to occur only among the more reckless and worthless elements of our population. Second, the Asiatic may catch up our wants as well as our arts, and acquire the higher standard and lower rate of increase of the American. This is just what contact and education are doing for the French Canadians in New England, for the immigrants in the West, and for the negro in some parts of the South; but the members of a great culture race like the Chinese show no disposition, even when scattered sparsely among us, to assimilate to us or to adopt our standards. Not until their self-complacency has been undermined at home and an extensive intellectual ferment has taken place in China itself will the Chinese become assimilable elements. Thirdly, the standards may remain distinct, the rates of increase unequal, and the silent replacement of Americans by Asiatics go on unopposed until the latter monopolize all industrial occupations, and the Americans shrink to a superior caste able perhaps by virtue of its genius, its organization, and its vantage of position to retain for a while its hold on government, education, finance, and the direction of industry, but hopelessly beaten and displaced as a race. In other words, the American farm hand, mechanic and operative might wither away before the heavy influx of a prolific race from the Orient, just as in classic times the Latin husbandman vanished before the endless stream of slaves poured into Italy by her triumphant generals."

For a case like this I can find no words so apt as "race suicide." There is no bloodshed, no violence, no assault of the race that waxes upon the race that wanes. The higher race quietly and unmurmuringly eliminates itself rather than endure individually the bitter competition it has failed to ward off from itself by collective action. The working classes gradually delay marriage and restrict the size of the family as the opportunities hitherto reserved for their children are eagerly snapped up by the numerous progeny of the foreigner. The prudent, self-respecting natives first cease to expand, and then, as the struggle for existence grows sterner and the outlook for their children darker, they fail even to recruit their own numbers. It is probably the visible narrowing of the circle of opportunity through the infiltration of Irish and French Canadians that has brought so low the native birth-rate in New England.

However this may be, it is certain that if we venture to apply to the American people of to-day the series of tests of superiority I have set forth to you at such length, the result is most gratifying to our pride. It is true that our average of energy and character is lowered by the presence in the South of several millions of an inferior race. It is true that the last twenty years have diluted us with masses of fecund but beaten humanity from the hovels of far Lombardy and Galicia. It is true that our free land is gone and our opportunities will henceforth attract immigrants chiefly from the humbler strata of East European peoples. Yet, while there are here problems that only high statesmanship can solve, I believe there is at the present moment no people in the world that is, man for man, equal to the Americans in capacity and efficiency. We stand now at the moment when the gradual westward migration has done its work. The tonic selections of the frontier have brought us as far as they can bring us. The testing individualizing struggle with the wilderness has developed in us what it would of body, brain and character.

Moreover, free institutions and universal education have keyed to the highest tension the ambitions of the American. He has been chiefly farmer and is only beginning to expose himself to the deteriorating influences of city and factory. He is now probably at the climax of his energy and everything promises that in the centuries to come he is destined to play a brilliant and leading rôle on the stage of history.

GEORGE M. BEARD

From American Nervousness

George M. Beard (1839–1883) was the father of the study of neurasthenia, a diagnosis that meant one's "nerve force" or energy was depleted. Beard labelled neurasthenia "American nervousness," writing in his 1881 work of that title that the disease was particularly American because it accompanied the ever-quickening pace of modern civilization and industrialization: "steam power, the periodical press, the telegraph, the sciences, and the mental activity of women." According to Beard, this nervous weakness afflicted only the most sensitive and "civilized" of bodies, as opposed to Catholics or others deemed less refined. In fact, neurasthenia could be seen as the marker of American exceptionalism, as proof that America was indeed the superior place it claimed to be; Beard declared that "Without civilization there can be no nervousness; there is no race, no climate, no environment that can make nervousness and nervous disease possible and common save when re-enforced by brain-work and worry and indoor life" (*Sexual Neurasthenia* 193). In *Sexual Neurasthenia*, published in 1884, Beard argued that sexual indulgence led to nervous exhaustion, an argument coincident with the antimasturbation tracts by such doctors as John Harvey Kellogg (see Part Two, Chapter 2).

The following excerpt is taken from *American Nervousness* (New York: Putnam, 1881), 55–57; 64–68; 75–80; 82–84; 90–93; 171–77; 184–85.

Evolution of Nervousness. — Nervous Exhaustion (Neurasthenia)

More specifically, and to the eye of some, perhaps, more interesting than all, is the increase of neurasthenia, or nervous exhaustion, and effects allied to and correlated with it. Out of the soil of nerve-sensitiveness springs the nervous diathesis[1] which runs into neurasthenia, or nervous exhaustion. Among the many branches of this neurological tree are, in the order in which they are very likely to develop in many cases — nervous dyspepsia,[2] sick-headache, near-sightedness, chorea,[3] insomnia, asthenopia,[4] hay-fever, hypochondria,

---

[1] *diathesis:* Predisposition toward an abnormal or diseased state.
[2] *dyspepsia:* Indigestion.
[3] *chorea:* Involuntary, irregular muscle movements.
[4] *asthenopia:* Subjective symptoms of ocular fatigue, sometimes due to organic nervous disease.

hysteria, nervous exhaustion in its varieties, and in the extreme cases — epilepsy, inebriety, insanity [see p. 216]. The disease, state, or condition to which the term neurasthenia is applied is subdivisible just as insanity is subdivided into general paresis[5] or general paralysis of the insane, epileptic insanity, hysterical, climatic, and puerperal insanity; just as the disease or condition that we call trance is subdivided into clinical varieties, such as intellectual trance, induced trance, cataleptic trance, somnambulistic trance, emotional trance, ecstatic trance, etc.; just so neurasthenia has sub-varieties, or clinical varieties, the cerebral, the spinal, the sexual, the digestive varieties, and so forth. These varieties of nervous exhaustion are nowhere experienced, nowhere known, as they are here; and even here they have been known in great abundance only within the past quarter of a century; and they are even now but just beginning to be scientifically and discriminately recognized and differentiated. The fathers and mothers — the grandfathers and grandmothers — of our neurasthenic parents of both sexes suffered from rheumatism, from gout,[6] from lung fever, from all forms of colds, from insanity now and then, and from epilepsy quite often; but they were not neurasthenic.

The influences and conditions that excite the gout in the phlegmatic and strong develop to nervousness in the sensitive and weak; neurasthenia is more abundant in America, gout and rheumatism in Europe. Lately I was consulted by a very nervous patient who comes from a line of gouty ancestors reaching back through several generations, the morbific force in his case having changed to the symptoms of insomnia, mental depression, and neuralgia.

The excessive nervousness of Americans seems to act as an antidote and preventive of gout and rheumatism, as well as of other inflammatory diseases. Many of the gouty and rheumatic patients in Europe are troubled with indigestion, and it happens very often indeed that attacks of rheumatism and gout — such as are familiar to the English and Germans — are preceded by so-called "bilious attacks," that is, symptoms of indigestion. The antagonism of disease to disease, and the force and value of disease in the treatment of disease, are illustrated very well by the frequency of functional nervous diseases in America, and the infrequency of gout and rheumatic troubles; and it would be most interesting to know whether as Europe becomes Americanized, and neurasthenia, with its train of symptoms invades Great Britain and the Continent, there shall take

[5] *paresis:* A partial or general paralysis; sometimes connected to syphilis.
[6] *gout:* Painful disease marked by inflammation of the joints.

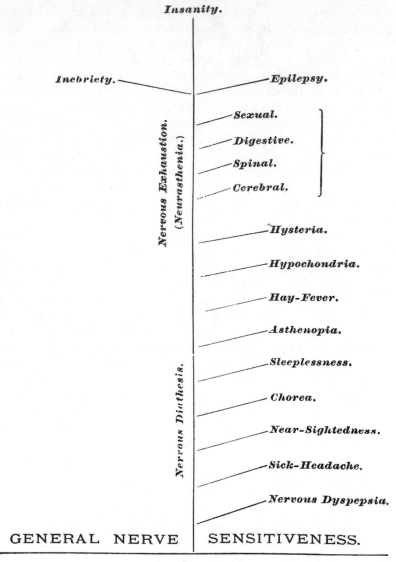

EVOLUTION OF NERVOUSNESS.
The tree of nervous illness from George M. Beard's *American Nervousness* (1881).

place a corresponding diminution in the frequency and severity of gout and rheumatism. . . .

Habit of Taking Drugs

America is a nation of drug-takers. Nowhere else shall we find such extensive, gorgeous, and richly supplied chemical establishments as here; nowhere else is there such general patronage of such establishments. Not only in proprietary medicines, but in physicians' prescriptions, as well as in self-doctoring, this continent leads the world; a physician can live here on half the number of families that would be needed to support him in Europe, on the same terms.

But with all our drug-taking we are, as a people, sensitive to medicine. The difference between American and European constitutions, on the side of the nervous system, is illustrated in the different treatment that our nervous patients receive when they consult European physicians of distinction and skill. American physicians whose patients go abroad are astonished at the powerful medicines and the largeness of the doses ordered by the best authorities in Great Britain and on the Continent; and on the other hand, English and Continental physicians are astonished at the sensitiveness of Americans to strong remedies given in ordinary doses.

An American physician, long afflicted with severe neurasthenia, who for some time had been under my professional care, on reaching London, consulted a medical gentleman whom I knew to be familiar with those conditions as they exist in Europe, and who is judicious in their treatment. In this case he ordered a combination, such as he was accustomed constantly to give in his own practice in London, which produced not only a powerful but poisonous, and almost fatal effect; so that, indeed, for some hours it was a question whether the patient would survive.

I remarked to the London physician, when I saw him, not long after, that I should not have dared to have given such a dose to that patient in America; he said, however, that it was a very common draught with him. When my patient returned, I put him on drop doses of Fowler's Solution and Tincture of Cantharides,[7] with most excellent results.

---

[7] *Fowler's Solution and Tincture of Cantharides:* Thomas Fowler (1736–1801), an English physician who developed the potassium arsenite solution; the Tincture was a preparation of Spanish fly, used as a stomachic and general tonic promoting the appetite and digestion and, among other uses, as a general stimulant.

Relation of Nervousness to Beauty

The phenomenal beauty of the American girl of the highest type, is a subject of the greatest interest both to the psychologist and the sociologist, since it has no precedent, in recorded history, at least; and it is very instructive in its relation to the character and the diseases of America.

This entrancing beauty, remarkable at once for its intensity and its extent among the comfortable classes of America, appears to be a resultant of two factors; the peculiarities of climate, to be hereafter referred to, and the unusual social position of women in America.

The same climatic peculiarities that make us nervous also make us handsome; for fineness of organization is the first element in all human beauty, in either sex.

In no other country are the daughters pushed forward so rapidly, so early sent to school, so quickly admitted into society; the yoke of social observance (if it may be called such), must be borne by them much sooner than by their transatlantic sisters — long before marriage they have had much experience in conversation and in entertainment, and have served as queens in social life, and assumed many of the responsibilities and activities connected therewith. Their mental faculties in the middle range being thus drawn upon, constantly from childhood, they develop rapidly a cerebral activity both of an emotional and an intellectual nature, that speaks in the eyes and forms the countenance; thus, fineness of organization, the first element of beauty, is supplemented by expressiveness of features — which is its second element; by the union of these two, human beauty reaches its highest.

Among the higher classes of America, the diminution of the friction of daily life, by avoiding the responsibility of housekeeping, united with generous living and all comforts, have assisted in adding the third element of beauty — that is, a moderate degree of embonpoint,[8] a feature which, in the extreme, and not re-enforced by these preceding elements — fineness of type and sprightliness of countenance, becomes the worst element of ugliness.

Handsome women are found here and there in Great Britain, and rarely in Germany; more frequently in France and in Austria, in Italy and Spain; and in all these countries one may find individuals that approximate the highest type of American beauty; but in America, it is the extent — the commonness of this beauty, which is so remarkably,

[8] *embonpoint:* Plumpness, stoutness.

unprecedentedly, and scientifically interesting. It is not possible to go to an opera in any of our large cities without seeing more of the representatives of the highest type of female beauty than can be found in months of travel in any part of Europe.

Among the middle and lower orders of the old world, beauty is kept down by labor. A woman who works all day in the field is not likely to be very handsome, nor to be the mother of handsome daughters; for, while mental and intellectual activity in the middle range heightens beauty, muscular toil, out-doors or in-doors, destroys it.

One cause, perhaps, of the almost universal homeliness of female faces among European works of art is, the fact that the best of the masters never saw a handsome woman. One can scarcely believe that Rubens[9] had he lived in America, or even in England, at the present time, would have given us such imposing and terrible types of female countenances. If Raphael[10] had been wont to see every day in Rome or Naples what he would now see every day in New York, Baltimore, or Chicago, it would seem probable that, in his Sistine Madonna he would have preferred a face of, at least, moderate beauty, to the neurasthenic and anemic type that is there represented.

To the first and inevitable objection that will be made to all here said — namely, that beauty is a relative thing, the standard of which varies with age, race, and individual — the answer is found in the fact that the American type is to-day more adored in Europe than in America; that American girls are more in demand for foreign marriages than any other nationality; and that the professional beauties of London that stand highest are those who, in appearance and in character have come nearest the American type. . . .

Dentition, Puberty, and Change of Life

Another evidence of the nervousness of our time is the difficulty which we experience in teething, at puberty, and change of life. These normal physiological processes in recent times, make so important a draft upon the nervous system that various sorts of illness result therefrom. During dentition, stomach and bowel difficulties arise; at

[9] *Rubens:* Sir Peter Paul Rubens (1577-1640), great Flemish painter of the seventeenth century, whose paintings were of large decorative schemes, often with large, nude women in them.
[10] *Raphael:* The Italian painter Raphael Santi (1483–1520) worked in Rome, decorating the Vatican from 1508 until his death; he is especially known for his paintings in the Stanzas.

puberty chorea, chlorosis,[11] sick-headache and hysteria oftentimes appear; and at change of life, a vast array of cerebral symptoms, and many of the above described symptoms of neurasthenia appear, and cause great disturbance, continuing sometimes for years. The system has an insufficient quantity of nervous force, and the draft which is made upon it by these processes exhausts it.

Cholera infantum has a nervous factor in its causation, and it is pre-eminently an American disease and is most prevalent during the excessive heats of our summer.

Parturition, Nursing, and Diseases of Women

The process of parturition[12] is everywhere the measure of nerve-strength. Had we no other barometer than this, we should know that civilization was paid for by nervousness, and that our cities are builded out of the life-force of their populations.

I was consulted, not long ago, by a Spanish lady of middle life, who had children to the number of fourteen, and always was up and about on the following day.

A case of this kind, in private practice, I have never before seen; certainly not among our in-door living classes.

For our savage ancestors, parturition was but a trifle more exhausting, either in time or expenditure of nerve-force than an attack of vomiting. On the march, an Indian woman, when taken with the pains of labor, would delay the company but half an hour.

All modern civilization demands prolonged rest for the parturient female; and how many there are in our own land, for whom the conventional nine days is extended to double that time; how many, also, to whom the simple act of giving birth to a child opens the door to unnumbered woes; beginning with lacerations and relaxations, extending to displacements and ovarian imprisonments, and ending by setting the whole system on fire with neuralgias, tremors, etc., and compelling a life-long slavery to sleeplessness, hysteria, or insanity.

One of the most amazing of all sights on the Continent of Europe and Ireland is that of the women toiling in the fields — mowing, raking, digging, driving carts, chopping wood, carrying water, which the same class on landing in this country rarely if ever do. Custom, which is the resultant of many and hard-to-be-traced influences, in part explains this difference; but in the second and third generations, the

---

[11] *chlorosis:* A disease linked to adolescent girls around 1850; a form of anemia.
[12] *parturition:* Giving birth.

force of climate is potent and imperious. Our women cannot endure such exposure to heat or to cold, and soon become unable to bear the muscular strain that such labor makes necessary. The direst straits of poverty American women, even of direct German and English descent, will endure rather than labor at the hard, muscular employments of men. Subject a part of the year to the tyranny of heat, and a part to the tyranny of cold, they grow unused to leaving the house; to live in-doors is the rule; it is a rarity to go out, as with those of Continental Europe it is to go in.

How many thousands of mothers there are who cannot, if they would, nurse their own infants, who have not sufficient milk for them, and who cannot bear the fatigue and drain upon the nervous system that nursing causes. It is not so much the dislike as the impossibility of nursing that makes wet nurses in such demand. So also the processes of gestation and child-bearing are borne in a most unsatisfactory way by large numbers in American society. In a state of perfect or almost perfect health, these processes are physiological; but for the last half century, among the upper classes of this country, they have become pathological; they have become signs of disease.

Lacerations of the Womb and Perineum

The large numbers of cases of laceration in childbirth, and the prolonged, and sometimes even life-enduring illnesses resulting from them, are good reason for the terror which the process of parturition inspires in the minds of many American women today.

The womb and perineum tear at childbirth because they have previously been reduced to the tearing point by general nervous exhaustion.

When Dr. Pallen and Dr. Sims discussed this subject of the laceration of the cervix at the last meeting of the British Medical Association, in Cambridge, and spoke of the operations of Emmet[13] for the cure of that condition, the European surgeons expressed astonishment and doubt in regard to the frequency if not the existence or importance of the disease. Allowing for imperfect observation — the confounding of ulceration with laceration, it is probable that the

---

[13] *Dr. Sims...Emmet:* James Marion Sims (1813-1883) was considered the founder of American gynecology, having developed surgery for repairs in the tears of bladders after childbirth. The Virginian Thomas Addis Emmet (1828-1919) practiced operative gynecology and pelvic surgery in Europe and was also Sims's assistant in New York.

disease is more frequent in American women, and also more likely to cause reflex constitutional disturbance among them.

The difference between an average of a half-dozen children in a family, which obtained fifty years ago, and an average of less than four which obtains now, is very great, and, abating certain obvious qualifying facts, pretty accurately measures the child-bearing and child-rearing power of the woman of the past and the woman of to-day. But on this subject statistics are scarcely needed. Consider the large number of childless households, the many families that have but two or three children, or but one, and with them contrast the families that prevailed at the beginning of this century. The contrast, also, between the higher and lower orders in this respect, cannot, it would seem, be entirely explained by excess of prudence on the one hand, or want of it on the other.

American children cry more than other children — they are more nervous, more fretful, more easily annoyed by heat, or by irritating clothing, by indigestible food, as well as by nervous and emotional influences. The generalization that children in civilization cry and worry more than children in savagery seems to be sustained by the experiences of all travellers who are trustworthy reporters on these matters. Thus Miss Bird — whose observations are always worthy of attention, and in the main, in harmony with facts — states in her work on "Unbeaten Tracks in Japan,"[14] that the children are more calm and quiet, and less troublesome than the children of higher civilizations.

Travellers in Brazil make the same report in regard to the children of the dark or mixed races in that country. In our own land the contrast between the black and the white children in this respect is very noticeable indeed; and that Indian children are cold, phlegmatic, and enduring is well known to all who have studied Indian life. . . .

Philosophy of American Humor

The power to create or to appreciate humor requires a fine organization. American humor, both in its peculiarities and in its abundance, takes its origin, in part, in American nervousness. It is an inevitable reaction from the excessive strain of mental and physical life; people who toil and worry less have less need than we for abandon-

---

[14] *Miss Bird . . . in Japan:* Isabella Lucy Bird (1831–1904) gives an account of her travels on horseback in the interior, including visits to the aborigines of Yezo and the shrines of Nikko and Ise (1880–1881).

ment — of nonsense, exaggeration, and fun. Both the supply of and demand for humor of a grotesque and exaggerated form are maintained by this increasing requirement for recreation; not the vulgar, the untrained alone, but the disciplined, the intellectual, the finely organized man and woman of position, dignity, responsibility and genius, of strong and solid acquisitions, enjoy and follow up and sustain those amusements which are in our land so very common, and which are looked upon, and rightly so, as American — such as the negro minstrels or experiments in induced or mesmeric trance.[15]

"The Gilded Age,"[16] the most popular play ever written on this continent, owes its success to those elements of exaggeration and nonsense, of absurdity and grotesqueness, that made it fail in Great Britain. Pinafore,[17] popular as it was in Great Britain, was incomparably more so in America, where great numbers of troupes were playing it simultaneously, and in New York five theatres kept it running for weeks and months: its success at home was partly a reflex of its success here. In this country at present, no lecturer can attract very large crowds unless he be a humorist and makes his hearers laugh as well as cry; and the lectures of the humorists — now a class by themselves — are more required than those of philosophers or men of science, or of fame in literature. Americans, who are themselves capable of originating thought in science or letters, scholarly, sober, and mature, prefer nonsense to science for an evening's employment; and so, with the increase of our nervousness and intelligence there has been a fading away in the popularity of the instructive and dignified lecturers for whom our lyceums[18] were first organized. . . .

Change in Type of Disease

The question often agitated is, Whether diseases have changed their type in modern times? This is a question which so far as *chronic* disease is concerned should not be discussed; to raise it, is to answer

[15] *negro minstrels . . . mesmeric trance:* Blackface minstrelsy was a nineteenth-century American entertainment, mostly in the North, where white performers would caricature black cultural forms. Mesmeric trances were part of a fad demonstrating the "new sciences" of phrenology, Mesmerism, and theories of animal magnetism, popular after 1836.

[16] *"The Gilded Age":* Originally published in 1873 as a novel by Samuel Clemens and C.D. Warner and dramatized in 1874 by G.S. Densmore; it satirizes unscrupulous competition in a world of speculation and finance.

[17] *Pinafore:* HMS Pinafore (1878), popular operetta by English playwright Sir William Gilbert (1836–1911) and English composer Sir Arthur Sullivan (1842–1900).

[18] *lyceums:* Popular societies for literary and scientific education.

it. There is no doubt that chronic diseases have changed their type in the last half century. The only question is, What are the degrees of the change, and what are the causes which produce these results? *Acute* diseases, like pneumonia, may perhaps have been but little changed in type, but it is easily demonstrable that chronic nervous diseases have increased in recent periods, and that, with this increase of nervous symptoms, there has been also an increase in the asthenic forms of disease, and a decrease in the sthenic[19] forms; and, correspondingly, that there has been a change in the methods of treatment of diseases; neurasthenia — nervous susceptibility — has affected all, or nearly all, diseases, so that nearly all illnesses occurring among the better class of people — the brain-workers — require a different kind of treatment from that which our fathers employed for the same diseases.

The four ways by which we determine these facts are — *first*, by studying the literature of medicine of the past centuries; *secondly*, by conversation with very old and experienced practitioners — men between the ages of seventy and ninety — who link the past with the present generation, and remember their own personal experience and the practice of medicine as it was fifty years ago; *thirdly*, from our own individual experience and observation; *fourthly*, by studying the habits and diseases of savages and barbarians of all climes and ages, and of the lower orders about us. Statistics on this subject are of very little value, for reasons that will be clear to those who are used to statistics, and who know how they can be handled.

We do not bear blood-letting now as our fathers did, for the same reasons that we do not bear alcohol, tobacco, coffee, opium, as they could. The change in the treatment of disease is a necessary result of the change in the modern constitution. The old-fashioned constitution yet survives in numbers of people; and in such cases, the old treatment is oftentimes better than the modern treatment.

The diseases of savages can be learned from books of travel and from conversations with travellers. Many of these books, it is true, are of a non-expert character, but some of them are written by physicians and scientific men of various degrees of eminence, whose observations on a large scale, compared together, enable us to arrive at the approximate

---

[19] *asthenic . . . sthenic:* In the eighteenth century, John Brown expounded his view that there were only two diseases, asthenic (weak) and sthenic (strong) and two corresponding treatments: stimulant and sedative. Remedies were opium and alcohol.

truth. In the study of this subject, I have compared a very large number of books of travel, and I have arrived at this fact, in regard to which there can be no doubt whatever, namely, that nervous disease of a *physical* character, scarcely exists among savages or barbarians, or semi-barbarians or partially civilized people. Likewise, in the lower orders in our great cities, and among the peasantry in the rural districts, muscle-workers, as distinguished from brain-workers — those who represent the habits and mode of life and diseases of our ancestors of the last century — functional nervous diseases, except those of a malarial or syphilitic character, are about as rare as they were among all classes during the last century. These people frequently need more violent and severe purging, more blood-letting, more frequent blistering than the higher orders would endure. If we would compare the nervous diseases of our time with those of the past, we have only to look about us among those classes of people whose temperaments take us back a half or three quarters of a century; in these classes such diseases as neurasthenia, heavy fever, sick-headache are very rare indeed; so that it is very difficult for a hospital for nervous diseases to succeed in getting a sufficient number of patients of this character. On the other hand, hospitals for inflammatory and febrile diseases are enormously patronized among them. It is partly for this reason that the literature for nervous functional diseases is so poor and unsatisfactory; our medical books and lectures are made up far too often of hospital, charity, and dispensary practice.

In regard to the incapacity for observing, which has been so often charged upon all the physicians who were so unfortunate as to be born prior to the last half century, I may say, that even conceding the general truth of the charge, as applied to the mass of the profession, it certainly does not apply to all the great leaders in medical thought. The greatest medical minds of the last century were, to use the most measured language, the equals of those who lead the profession of our day, and were capable of observing, and did observe, and they recorded their observations; some of the grandest discoveries of all time were made by them. . . .

Recapitulation of Causes of Nervous Exhaustion

The series of causes which result in a case of nervous exhaustion or general nervousness may be thus tabulated:

First, the predisposing causes. Under this head comes —

1. Modern Civilization

This is placed at the head, because none of the predisposing or exciting causes that follow it are competent to produce functional nervous disease of the class described in this work unless civilization prepares the way. The nervous diseases from which savages suffer, and the lower orders of peasantry, are largely of a subjective, psychical character, being caused by the emotions, and assume very different phases, whatever their names be, from those herein described. Civilization is, then, the one constant factor, the foundation of all these neuroses, wherever they exist. Other factors are inconstant; climate varies, special occupations vary; hygienic habits vary, but civilization of some form, with its attendant brain-work and worry, with its indoor life, is an inevitable factor in the causation of all these neuroses.

2. Climate

That climate must take a secondary, not a primary place among predisposing causes of nervous exhaustion, the history of our country alone proves. The American aborigines were the least nervous of all people; but the climate in which they lived was not much different from that in which are now living the most nervous people in the world.

3. Race

In limited, historic time, race is, in some sociological aspects, more potent than climate, since the strong races, like the Hebrews and Anglo-Saxons, succeed in nearly all climates, and are dominant wherever they go; but in unlimited or very extended time, race is a result of climate and environment. We have seen already that these neuroses may be developed in almost any race, in two or three generations, as is proved almost constantly in our climate, under which are gathered so many different races.

The two great factors in climate which are of most import in their relation to the nervous system are, dryness and moisture, heat and cold. But there had been extremes of temperature and dryness of the atmosphere for ages before modern nervousness appeared.

4. The Nervous Diathesis

The nervous diathesis can only be developed to its full expression under the combined influences of race and climate. That this is a predisposing, more perhaps than an exciting cause, is proved by the fact that very many persons have this nervous diathesis without developing to any very great extent nervous diseases.

Among the *exciting* causes are the following:

First, *functional excess* of any kind, as of the brain, the spine, the digestive, the muscular, and the reproductive systems.

Under this head must be classed all excesses in eating or drinking, the use of stimulants and narcotics, financial and domestic trouble.

None of these factors are competent to produce these neuroses, unless the way is prepared by the predisposing causes. Savages may go to the most furious excesses without developing any nervous disease; they may gorge themselves, or they may go without eating for a week, they may rest in camp or they may go upon laborious campaigns, and yet never have nervous dyspepsia, sick-headache, hayfever, or neuralgia. These exciting causes have usually been regarded as the sole causes of nervous diseases; although a philosophical study of this subject shows that of themselves they have but little power. They can only sow a crop of nervous diseases in a soil that has been prepared by civilization.

No people in the world are so careful of their diet, the quality and quantity of their food, and in regard to their habits of drinking, as the very class of Americans who suffer most from these neuroses.

At this point a query may be raised: Did not the eating, drinking, and smoking of our ancestors prepare the way for our nervousness? Is not modern nervousness the remote effect of ancient dissipation?

The answer is, that where there is no civilization there is no nervousness, no matter what the personal habits may be, even though the experiment be made, as in Africa, for centuries.

It would be impossible for an American Indian by any degree of recklessness or excess to make himself nervous. Alcohol only produces inebriety when it acts on a nervous system previously made sensitive. Alcoholism and inebriety are the products not of alcohol, but of alcohol plus a certain grade of nerve degeneration.

When a nervous American is shut up in bad and overheated air, he becomes more nervous; his face perhaps flushes, his head aches, there is a sensation of suffocation and vague misery that finds quick relief on getting into the open air, and in all directions there is an unshaken belief in the injuriousness of breathing bad air; and injunctions to live as much as possible out of doors, and to get away from cities and city-life are among the truisms of sanitary science. But bad air, that is, air simply made impure by the presence of human beings, without any special contagion, seems powerless to produce disease of any kind, unless the system be prepared for it. Not only bad air, but bad air and filth combined, the Chinese of the lower orders endure both in this country and their own, and are not demonstrably harmed thereby — certainly not in their nervous systems; but impure air, plus a constitution drawn upon and weakened by civilization, is an exciting cause of nervous disease of immense force. The Chinese huddled and herded together like sheep, of course breathe, by day as well as by night, an atmosphere as vile as it can be made by human breathing and human emanations, but seem to develop therefrom no form of nervous disease, and not always, any form of acute and inflammatory disease; and the savage tribes of the extreme North, and in cold regions everywhere, imprison themselves in their filthy houses without receiving any injury that can be easily traced, and if injury does result it is manifested otherwise than through the nervous system.

It cannot be too strongly enforced in all our thoughts, and controversies, and arguments on this complex theme of the causation of nervous disease, that not tobacco, nor alcohol, nor digestive, nor sexual excess, nor foul air, nor deprivation, nor indulgence in any form, can produce nervous disease unless they act upon a constitution predisposed by civilization. *American nervousness is the product of American civilization.* All the other influences — climate, nervous diathesis, evil habits, worry and overtoil — are either secondary or tertiary. The philosophy of the causation of American nervousness may be expressed in algebraic formula as follows: civilization in general + American civilization in particular (young and rapidly growing nation, with civil, religious, and social liberty) + exhausting climate (extremes of heat and cold, and dryness) + the nervous diathesis (itself a result of previously named factors) + overwork or overworry, or excessive indulgence of appetites or passions = an attack of neurasthenia or nervous exhaustion. A philosophic study of this question requires us to consider the whole equation, and not portions of it. To look exclusively to the bad habits or excesses, whether in use of food or alcohol or tobacco, or to special worry or excitement, or to any severe drafts on the nervous system that come from parturition or lactation in women, or to puberty or change of life, is as illogical, in the study of this subject, as it would be in the study of algebra. Climate is powerless without civilization; the nervous diathesis can only exist in civilization, and excesses of the most extreme kind, excitements of the most violent nature, of themselves, without the addition of civilization, cannot equal a case of nervousness. . . .

Physique of Woman in the Savage State

Woman in the savage state is not delicate, sensitive, or weak. Like man, she is strong, well developed, and muscular, with capacity for enduring toil, as well as child-bearing. The weakness of woman is all modern, and it is pre-eminently American. Among the Indians the girls, like the boys, are brought up to toil and out-door life; they are expected to tear limbs and boughs from trees and break sticks for fires. So different are the squaws from the tender and beautiful women of the white races, that they seem to belong to another order of creatures. The young wife of an Indian, having quarrelled one day with her husband, seized him by both ears and the hair, as he was raising his hand to strike her, threw him on the ground, as one would throw a child, and raising his head with her hands, beat it upon the hard ground until he begged for his life. In the same tribe (the Apaches) there was a young wife who prepared a meal for her husband and his friend, cooking the food and bringing it on the table. While they were eating, she went away, and in less than an hour returned, dressed in the finest apparel and ornaments and apparently very pleased and happy about something. Pressed for an explanation, she took her husband away down to the spring in a thicket near by, and there in a bed of moss, wrapped in finest skins, was a beautiful new-born child. Within the short period of less than an hour all this had been accomplished, and the mother was as lively and strong as though nothing had happened.

A.J. BLOCH

From *"Sexual Perversion in the Female"*

By the 1890s, a new trend had influenced discussions of intimate life: the eroticization of marriage, or what was often termed the goal of sex-expression. The new science of sexology sought to create norms for sexual behavior in modern American culture. New forms of intimacy — even outside of the cultural institution of marriage — were gaining legitimacy. New Women — epitomized in popular literature such as Grant Allen's *The Woman Who Did* (1895) — were seeking sexual pleasure and social freedom outside of the domestic sphere, which had once bound them to self-sacrificing service to their families. These New

Women were also pivotal in agitating for social reform, as Jane Addams did in the settlement houses (see p. 297), and for female suffrage. While some of the new sexologists, such as Beard, Ellis, and Krafft-Ebing, became famous for their pronouncements concerning "normal" sexual behavior, the work of others, such as A.J. Bloch, reflects the general passion of the times for codifying sexual conventions and expectations. Bloch's 1894 essay, "Sexual Perversion in the Female," is an example of late-nineteenth-century medical-moral discussions of women's increasingly visible sexuality. His case studies reveal that clitoridectomy, or surgical removal of the clitoris, was often considered a "cure" for women's "self-abuse," or masturbation.

The text of the following excerpt is taken from *New Orleans Medical and Surgical Journal* 22.1 (July 1894): 1–7.

Mr. President and Gentlemen — The subject of sexual perversion, which I present to you to-night, though full of horror and disgust, must receive from our hands as physicians and surgeons the same attention as would be shown to those diseases with which we are more familiar. This moral leprosy is progressively increasing; its taint is entering into the homes of our most elegant and refined; this contagion exists in our schools, seminaries and asylums; its handiwork is shown by our many obscure and unrecognized nervous disorders. It is not only necessary that we pursue a curative course, but prophylactic measures should be used, and to us belongs this responsibility.

To-night I shall limit myself to those conditions of perversion occurring only among females, but in dealing with this subject much that I will say will apply to both sexes.

Of the cerebral varieties, classified by Krafft-Ebing, I will speak only of the following:

A — "Paradoxia — *i.e.,* sexual excitement occurring independently of the period of the physiological processes in the generative organs."

B — "Hyperæsthesia — increased desire, intense libido, lustfulness, lasciviousness." "This may be of central origin, as nymphomania, satyriasis,[1] or peripheral, functional or organic."

C — "Paræsthesia (perversion of the sexual instinct — *i.e.,* excitability of the sexual functions to inadequate stimuli)."

---

[1] *satyriasis:* Derived from the Greek for *satyr;* the condition of excessive, unmanageable male sexual desire.

Of the first classification, paradoxia, our most common form, is found in all places where children are segregated. Titillation of the clitoris is the most frequent form of this perversion. Though inherited in some cases, it is often acquired, the older ones teaching the younger ones; in both cases the depravity continues in after years. The cases which I will present to you will fully illustrate this perversion.

CASE 1. — Miss A. K., aged 14, school girl, neurasthenic, menstruated one year previous. Was consulted by mother March last for nervousness and pallor, which were both extreme. Gave tonics, prescribed exercise, with negative results. Suspecting that self-abuse might be the factor I asked for an examination of the external organs of generation, which was readily acquiesced to by both mother and daughter. The vulva was slightly reddish in character, the clitoris bound down by its labia and almost obliterated. In touching the clitoris with my index finger I could see a slight tremor come over my patient. I suggested a separation of the folds, telling the mother of my suspicions. A week later the mother returned, telling me my suspicions were well founded; the daughter had acknowledged to the evil, which she had been practising for four years. The following day I liberated the clitoris from its adhesions, had the girl remain away from school, and corrected by lectures, etc., since which time she has been steadily progressing in health.

CASE 2. — J. W., æt. 2 1/2 years, was referred to me, February 3, by Dr. J., oculist, for some obscure nervous disorder of eight months' duration. The mother is a neurasthenic, of great nervous irritability, anæmic and inclined to be melancholic.

When 9 years old she, the mother, began to practise masturbation, which has progressively increased with age, and now, though married, resorts to self-abuse as the only palliative to her inordinate sexual desires. While pregnant she abstained from this perversion, though her thoughts would dwell upon it; she feared the perversion might be transmitted to her unborn child. The maternal grandmother died in an insane asylum, insanity having been induced, it is thought, by masturbation. The paternal grandfather is of an irascible disposition, morose and taciturn. Little J. is unusually bright for her age, though exceedingly shy. She is disposed to be taciturn and avoids the society of other children as much as possible. She was first seen masturbating by her mother six months before, since which time it has been uninterrupted, though every precaution was taken to effect a cure by medical corrective measures, and moral and physical persuasion.

Though precocious in intellect, the patient does not present any unusual physical developments. The legs are symmetrically formed, but childish in character, the nipples corresponding with those of other children of her age, there being no signs whatever of approaching puberty. The eyes are crossed, she suffers from insomnia, lying awake hours at night, and sleep is often interrupted by nervous twitchings. She has a strong predilection for vulgar language and often astonishes her hearers by such remarks as would do credit to the vilest steamboat captains. Inspection of the external organs of generation shows complete obliteration of the labia minora and clitoris by adhesions; the vaginal outlet is red and the hymen intact. On February 20, under an anæsthetic, I separated the adhesions, liberated the clitoris, removing a quantity of smegma, which had accumulated between the folds of the labia minora and clitoris. Two weeks later the mother brought the child to me, stating that no relief had been experienced from the operation. To assure myself before resorting to a more heroic measure that masturbation really existed as represented, and in order to be able to define if such were true, the pleasure centre, I determined to put the child to a practical test. Having her undressed and put on the bed, I first touched the external orifice of the vagina, then the labia minora, without any appreciable excitement on the part of the child.

However, as soon as I reached the clitoris, the true phenomena developed. The legs were thrown widely open, the face became pale, the breathing short and rapid, the body twitched from excitement, slight groans would come from the patient. Being fully satisfied that the clitoris alone was responsible for this growing perversion, I decided to excise this organ. Assisted by my friend Dr. H.S. Lewis, I dissected up the clitoris and amputated it almost to its attachment to the pubes. Hæmorrhage was controlled by simple pressure, the denuded surfaces of the labiæ minoræ were brought together by two silk sutures. The patient was allowed to get up and play as soon as the chloroform had worn away; she never experiencing any pain. The sutures were removed on the sixth day, with perfect union.

The result has been a very happy one. The mother writes the cure is complete, the nervous condition has entirely disappeared, the child eats and sleeps well, the eyes are rarely crossed. She has grown stouter, more playful, and has ceased masturbating entirely.

Within the last few years Robert Morris, Geo. Rohé and others have recognized nervous conditions in the female, analogous to those in the male, depending on a phimosis[2] of the glans clitoridis, which were en-

---

[2] *phimosis:* Narrowed opening in foreskin so that it cannot be drawn back over glans penis; similar condition in the clitoris.

tirely relieved by removing the cause. Acting upon their observations and results they strenuously urge the importance of an examination of the external organs of generation in all neurotic troubles, which might be of reflex origin. Prior to this, Baker Brown had practised clitoridictomy with great success, but meeting with little response from the medical fraternity this operation was finally abandoned. It might be superfluous to say that the milder methods should be the selective one, but when this proves inadequate, as it did prove in Case 2, it becomes imperative to resort to the more heroic procedure.

CLASS B. — Hyperæsthesia may be the sequelæ of paradoxia, or it may be acquired after full maturity. This is the form of perversion so frequently seen in gynecological practice, where the patient insists upon being treated for an imaginary ailment, experiencing a great pleasure from vaginal examinations. Howe relates a case, occurring in his practice in Bellevue Hospital,[3] of a young girl who complained of retention of urine, so as to invite the introduction of a catheter into the bladder. He soon noticed that the retention was not true, but *pari passu* with the introduction of the catheter an orgasm would take place. Catheterization was discontinued, and with it the retention was relieved. She subsequently went to a gynecologist, but he too soon discovered her perversion and dismissed her.

CASE 1. — Female, white, age about 18, given to masturbation with hair pin through urethra. Five years ago the Charity Hospital ambulance was summoned to remove this foreign body from the urethra, where it had become impacted.

I regret that I have been unable to collect any more data on this case; however, it represents a type of this perversion which is by no means infrequent.

CASE 2. — Mrs. W., æt. 28, mother of one child æt. 2 1/2 years, consulted me February 25 for a nervous disorder. When 5 years old began to have sexual connection with little boys, but is unable to say whether penetration ever took place. When 9 years old was sent to a convent, where she was taught digital masturbation by the older girls, since which time this perversion has been uninterrupted. Was married at 24, legitimate sexual intercourse was unsatisfactory, she merely submitting to satisfy her husband, and would often leave his side to masturbate. She says she has masturbated as often as fourteen times a day, the excesses being during her menstrual periods. Her mother

[3] *Bellevue Hospital:* An important early public hospital, founded in 1736 as an almshouse.

died in a lunatic asylum, she thinks masturbation was the cause of her insanity.

Patient was exceedingly anæmic, excitable and had a tendency to be melancholic. She avoided social relations with other people; did not care to make friends, preferring the seclusion of her room. The external organs of generation presented almost a negative appearance; the clitoris was free of adhesions, there being but a slight redness about the external orifice of the vagina, which I attributed to a slight leucorrhœa[4] from which she suffered. The uterus was slightly enlarged. The left ovary was about the size of an apple and cystic, the right ovary enlarged and very sensitive. Both seemed to be firmly bound down by adhesions. Thinking that her perversion was of reflex origin, I suggested a removal of the diseased ovaries as a probable curative measure. She and her husband readily assented, as they were willing to accept anything that might offer a reasonable chance of recovery. On March 20, assisted by my friends, Drs. H. S. Lewis and S. P. Delaup, I opened the abdominal cavity. I found the omentum[5] firmly bound to the intestines, uterus and ovaries, which I managed to break up after some perseverance. The ovaries were equally adherent, so much, in fact, that I almost despaired of removing them. The tubes were very short and thickened, the uterus almost immovable. I finally managed to separate the adhesion and remove the appendages, which I found to be as I had diagnosed. I next ligated the omentum, which reached to the middle third of the thigh, and amputated it. Hæmorrhage from the adhesions was very troublesome, the patient was so hydræmic[6] that the blood refused to coagulate. The time consumed was already fifty minutes from the beginning of the operation, and at the suggestion of Dr. Delaup, who was administering the anæsthetic, I closed the abdomen, though oozing was still apparent.

The recovery was uninterrupted, the patient reacted well, the pulse was always regular and even, and the temperature normal. On the eighth day she sat up and on the fifteenth left the sanitarium. My notes show the following:

April 10. Entirely recovered from operation, feels stronger and happier, and delights in the fact that she is cured of her perversion.

April 20. Color returning to face, is able to go anywhere without pain. Has no thought of masturbating, delights in going out and is anxious to meet people and make friends.

[4] *leucorrhœa:* A whitish, fungal vaginal discharge.
[5] *omentum:* A fold of peritoneum connecting or supporting abdominal structures.
[6] *hydræmic:* Excess of water in the blood.

May 5. Continues to improve. The perversion entirely removed.

June 2. I will quote from a letter which I have received: "My condition is all I could desire. I know and feel that I am well; I never think of self-abuse — it is foreign and positively distasteful to me."

Krafft-Ebing, G. Frank Lydston and others state that such conditions frequently depend upon some disturbance of the generative apparatus. It is also manifest during pregnancy, the former terminating with the latter. Case No. 2 is a true type of the diseased sexual organs, the perversion was solely of reflex origin, as the results show. I can not urge too strongly upon all gynecologists the necessity of watching for this class of sexual perverts. Inadvertently we may be the means of assisting and promoting this offensive habit, and not infrequently will it develop in our practice. It may be true that many of these moral lepers may have true disease; in such cases we must use more than ordinary care in our technique.

CLASS C. — Paræsthesia or perversion of the sexual instinct is common among prostitutes who pander to the diseased traits of man. With them oral masturbation is exceedingly common, and, although the majority are passive subjects, the act being actuated by pecuniary gain, many experience a great sexual delight. If in our city to-day an open book were kept of those men who delight in being the active subject in such practices, a social upheaval would take place which would only rival the great social scandal of London some few years back. I have seen but one case which might be classified under this heading.

CASE 1. — Mrs. G., æt. 36, consulted me January last for a slight tumefaction of breast. While manipulating this organ I noticed a pallor about the face, which was followed shortly by a slight cry. I attributed this at the time to pain, which I thought I might have induced. Though I had expressly stated that she should return in one week, she came to my office the next day and asked that I make another examination, stating that she had suffered more pain that night. This time I was exceedingly careful in handling her breast, and though I was unusually gentle she went through the same phenomena. I now became suspicious, and in order to put her to a final test asked her to return the next day. This time was but a repetition of the two previous days. I had no doubt now that she was a sexual pervert and that each manipulation of the breast was attended with an orgasm. She returned several times, but I scarcely touched the organ; finally she and the swelling both disappeared. The swelling I think harmonized with the perversion; it was the result of active irritation.

This condition is frequently seen in mothers who are very eager to put their nursing babies to their breasts, and if such subjects were not so delicate to handle we undoubtedly could add much more such cases to our medical literature.

HAVELOCK ELLIS

From "Sexual Inversion in Women"

Havelock Ellis (1859–1939), an English psychologist and writer, championed various movements for sexual reform in his day, advocating sex education for children, the use of contraception, the liberalization of divorce laws, emancipation for women, experimental premarital sex, and the decriminalization of homosexual acts. Ellis's classic work, the seven-volume series *Studies in the Psychology of Sex*, was written between 1896 and 1928. While this study was not generally distributed in America until 1936, Ellis was considered one of the major "sex experts" of his day. He argued that sexual life deeply influenced the daily actions and thoughts of all social relations, and he sought to provide a "psychopathology" of sexual life. Ellis's *Psychology of Sex*, an investigation of sex life, was controversial and influential. He acknowledged sexual inversion and perversion, describing women's same-sex love as "inversion," a term which suggested that lesbians often adopted masculine behavior and manners, as well as dress. Advice writers had urged the individual to conform to prevailing sexual mores, but few authors until Ellis had suggested that sexuality was a product of such social or cultural norms and practices. Ellis's analyses provided a new understanding of sexuality, which served to open up sexual "norms" for debate. The essay excerpted here, which includes a case study of a homosexual woman, is one of Ellis's early published works on inversion. It was originally published in the journal *Alienist and Neurologist* 16 (1895), 141–58. While less moralistic than Bloch, Ellis treats aberrant sexuality as pathological. His scientific labeling of homosexuals might have been of special concern to Gilman because of her passionate friendships with women.

Many of Gilman's stories follow the logic of the case study, documenting patients and their illnesses. This is true of "Dr. Clair's Place" (Chapter 4) and even of the "The Yellow Wallpaper" itself.

Homosexuality has been observed in women from very early times, and in very wide-spread regions. Refraining from any attempt to trace its history, and coming down to Europe in the seventeenth century, we find a case of sexual inversion in a woman, which seems to be recorded in greater detail than any case in a man had yet been recorded.[1] Moreover Westphal's first notable case, which may be said to inaugurate the scientific study of sexual inversion, was in a woman. This passion of women for women has, also, formed a favorite subject with the novelist, who has usually been careful to avoid the same subject as presented in the male.[2] It seems probable

[1] This is the case of Catherina Margaretha Lincken, who married another woman, somewhat after the manner of the Hungarian Countess V., in our own day; she was condemned to death for sodomy, and executed in 1721, at the age of 27. (F. C. Muller, "Ein weiterer Fall von contrarer Sexualempfindung." *Friedrich's Blatter*, Heft iv, 1891.) This was in Germany. I have found a notice of a similar case in France, nearly two centuries earlier in Montaigne's *Journal du Voyage en Italie en 1580* (written by his secretary), it took place near Vitry le Francais. Seven or eight girls belonging to Chaumont, we are told, resolved to dress and to work as men; one of these came to Vitry to work as a weaver, and was looked upon as a well-conditioned young man, whom everyone liked. At Vitry she became betrothed to a woman, but a quarrel arising no marriage took place. Afterwards "she fell in love with a woman whom she married, and with whom she lived for four or five months, to the wife's great contentment, it is said: but having been recognized by some one from Chaumont, and brought to justice, she was condemned to be hanged: she said she would prefer this to living again as a girl, and was hanged for using illicit inventions to supply the defects of her sex." (*Journal* ed. by D'Ancona, 1889, p.11.) [Ellis's note.]

[2] Diderot's famous novel, *La Religieuse*, which when first published, was thought to have been actually written by a nun, deals with the torture to which a nun was put by the perverse lubricity of her abbess, for whom it is said Diderot found a model in the Abbesse de Chelles, a daughter of the Regent, whose other daughter, the Queen of Spain, is said to have made the most violent love to her maids of honor. Balzac, who treated so many psychological aspects of love in a more or less veiled manner, has touched on this in *La Fille aux Yeux d'or*. Gautier (using some slight foundation in fact), made the adventures of a woman who was predisposed to homosexuality and slowly realizes the fact, the central motive of his wonderfully beautiful romance, *Mademoiselle de Maupin;* he approached the subject purely as an artist and poet, but his handling of it shows remarkable insight. Zola has described sexual inversion with characteristic frankness in *Nana* and elsewhere. Some fifteen years ago, a popular novelist, A. Belot, published a novel, called *Mademoiselle Giraud, ma Femme,* which was much read; the novelist took the attitude of a moralist who is bound to treat frankly but with all decorous propriety a subject of increasing social gravity; the story is that of a man whose bride will not allow his approach on account of her own *liaison* with a female friend continued after marriage. This book appears to have given origin to a large number of novels which I have not read but some of which are said to touch the question with considerably less affectation of propriety. Among other novelists of higher rank who have dealt with the matter may be mentioned Guy de Maupassant, Bourget, Daudet and Catulle Mendes. Among poets who have used the motive of homosexuality in women with more or less boldness, may be found Lamartine, (*Regina*), Swinburne (first series of *Poems [and] Ballads*) and Verlaine (*Parallelement*). [Ellis's note.]

that homo-sexuality is little if at all less common in woman than in man.[3]

Yet we know comparatively little of sexual inversion in woman; of the total number of recorded cases of this abnormality, now very considerable, but a small proportion are in women, and the chief monographs on the subject devote but little space to women.

I think there are several reasons for this. Notwithstanding the severity with which homosexuality in women has been visited in a few cases, for the most part men seem to have been indifferent towards it; when it has been made a crime or a cause for divorce in men, it has usually been considered as no offence at all in women.[4] Another reason is that it is less easy to detect in women; we are accustomed to a much greater familiarity and intimacy between women than between men, and we are less apt to suspect the existence of any abnormal passion. And allied with this cause we have also to bear in mind the extreme ignorance and the extreme reticence of women regarding any abnormal or even normal manifestation of their sexual life. A woman may feel a high degree of sexual attraction for another woman without realizing that her affection is sexual, and when she does realize it she is nearly always very unwilling to reveal the nature of her intimate experience, even with the adoption of precautions, and although the fact may be present to her that by helping to reveal the nature of her abnormality she may be helping to lighten the burden of it on other women. Among the numerous confessions voluntarily sent to Krafft-Ebing[5] there is not one by a woman. There is, I think, one other reason why sexual inversion is less obvious in a woman. We have some reason to believe that while a slight degree of homosexuality is commoner in women than in men, and is favored by the conditions under which women live, well marked and fully developed cases of inversion are rarer in women than in men. This result would be in harmony with what we know as to the greater plas-

---

[3] As regards Germany III *Moll Die Contrare Sexual empfindung*, 2nd ed. p. 315. [Ellis's note.]

[4] The popular opinion is, perhaps, represented by the remark of a young man of the last century (concerning the Lesbian friend of the woman he wishes to marry), quoted, in the *Souvenirs du Comte de Tilly*: *"J'avoue que c'est un genre of rivalite qui ne me donne aucune humeur; au, contraire cela m'amuse et j'ai l'immoralite d'en rire."* [Ellis's note.] [Translated from the French, this sentence reads: "I confess that this is a type of rivalry that doesn't put me in a bad mood; on the contrary, it amuses me, and I have the immorality to laugh at it."—Ed.]

[5] *Krafft-Ebing:* See pages 247–52.

ticity of the feminine organism to slight stimuli, and its less liability to serious variation.[6]

The same kind of aberrations that are found among men in lower races are also seen in woman though they are less frequently recorded. In New Zealand it is stated on the authority of Moerenhout[7] (though I have not been able to find the reference) that the women practised Lesbianism. In South America where inversion is common among men we find similar phenomena in women. Among Brazilian tribes Gandavo[8] wrote: "There are certain among these Indians who determine to be chaste and know no man. These leave every womanly occupation and imitate the men. They wear their hair in the same way as the men, they go to war with them or hunting, bearing their bows: they continue always in the company of the men, and each has a woman who serves her and with whom she lives."[9] This has some analogy with the phenomena seen among South American men. Dr. Holder, however, who has carefully studied the *bote*,[10] tells me that he has met with no corresponding phenomena in women.

Among Arab women, according to Kocher, homosexual practices are rare, though very common among Arab men. In Egypt, according to Godard and others, it is almost fashionable, and every woman in the harem has a "friend." Among the negroes and mulattoes of French Creole countries, according to Corre,[11] homosexuality is very common. "I know a lady of great beauty," he remarks, "a stranger in Guadalupe and the mother of a family, who is obliged to stay away from the markets and certain shops because of the excessive admiration of mulatto women and negresses, and the impudent invitations which they dare to address to her."[12] He refers to several cases of more or less violent sexual attempts on young colored girls of 12 or 14, and observes that such attempts by men on children of their own sex are much rarer.

---

[6] See H. Ellis, *Man and Woman*, Chs. xiii and xvi. [Ellis's note.]

[7] *Moerenhout:* Jacques Antoine Moerenhout (1796–1879), born in Belgium; merchant adventurer and reporter and later the U.S. counsul general to the Oceanic Islands; he wrote *Travels to the Islands of the Pacific Ocean* (1835).

[8] *Gandavo:* Pero de Magalhães de Gandavo wrote (c. 1540–1580?) *The Histories of Brazil* in Portuguese (1576), an anthropological and cultural account of the peoples and rituals.

[9] Gandavo, quoted by Lomacco, *Archives per l'Antropologia,* 1889, fasc 1. [Ellis's note.]

[10] *bote:* In old law, compensation or amends, especially for a murder.

[11] *Holder . . . Corre:* Joseph Holder, zoologist; Adolphe Kocher, criminologist and anthropologist; Pliny Godard, anthropologist; Armand-Marie Corre, sociologist.

[12] Corre, *Crime en Pays Creoles,* 1889. [Ellis's note.]

In prisons and lunatic asylums homosexual practices flourish among the women fully as much, it may probably be said, as among the men. There is, indeed, some reason for supposing that these phenomena are here even more decisively marked than among men.[13] Such manifestations are often very morbid, and doubtless often very vicious; I have no light to throw upon them and I do not propose to consider them.

With girls as with boys it is in the school, at the evolution of puberty, that homosexuality first shows itself. It may originate either peripherally or centrally. In the first case two children, perhaps when close to each other in bed, more or less unintentionally generate in each other a certain amount of sexual irritation, which they foster by mutual touching and kissing. This is a spurious kind of homosexuality; it is merely the often precocious play of the normal instinct, and has no necessary relation to true sexual inversion. In the girl who is congenitally predisposed to homosexuality it will continue and develop; in the majority it will be forgotten as quickly as possible, not without shame, in the presence of the normal object of sexual love. It is specially fostered by those employments which keep women in constant association, not only by day but often at night also, without the company of men. This is for instance the case with the female servants in large hotels, among whom homosexual practices have been found very common.[14] Laycock many years ago noted the prevalence

[13] In a Spanish prison, not many years ago, when a new governor endeavored to reform the homosexual manners of the women, the latter made his post so uncomfortable that he was compelled to resign. Salillas in his *Vida Penal en Espana,* asserts that all the evidence shows the extraordinary expansion of Lesbian love in prisons. The *mujeres bombrunas* receive masculine names — Pepe, Chulo, Bernardo, Valiente, etc., new comers are surrounded in the court-yard by a crowd of lascivious women who overwhelm them with honeyed compliments and gallantries and promises of protection, the most robust virago having most success; a single day and night complete the initiation. The frequency of sexual manifestations in insane women is well recognized. With reference to homosexual manifestations, I will merely quote the experience of Dr. Venturi in Italy: "In the asylums which I have directed I have found inverted tendencies even more common than have other observers: and that the vice is not peculiar to any disease or age, for nearly all insane women, except in acute forms of insanity, are subject to it. Tribadism must thus be regarded as without doubt a real equivalent and substitute for coitus, as these persons frankly regard it, in this unlike poederasty which does not satisfy in insane men the normal sexual desires." (Venturi, *Le Degenerazione sichosessuale,* 1892, p. 148.) [Ellis's note.]

[14] I quote the following from a private letter written on the Continent: "An English resident has told me that his wife has lately had to send away her parlor-maid (a pretty girl) because she was always taking in strange women to sleep with her. I asked if she had been taken from hotel service and found, as I expected, that she had. But neither my friend nor his wife suspected the real cause of these nocturnal visits." [Ellis's note.]

of manifestations of this kind, which he regarded as hysterical, among seamstresses, lacemakers, etc., confined for long hours in close contact to one another in heated rooms. The circumstances under which numbers of young women are employed during the day in large shops and stores and sleep in the establishment, two in a room or even two in a bed, are favorable to the development of homosexual practices.

The cases in which the source is central rather than peripheral are equally common. In such a case a school girl or young woman forms an ardent attachment for another girl, probably somewhat older than herself, often a school-fellow, sometimes her school-mistress, upon whom she will lavish an astonishing amount of affection and devotion. This affection may or may not be returned; usually the return consists of a gracious acceptance of the affectionate services. The girl who expends this wealth of devotion is surcharged with emotion, but she is often unconscious of or ignorant of the sexual impulse and she seeks for no form of sexual satisfaction. Kissing and the privilege of sleeping with the friend are, however, sought, and at such times it often happens that even the comparatively unresponsive friend feels more or less definite sexual emotion (pudendal turgescence[15] with secretion of mucus and involuntary twitching of the neighboring muscles), though little or no attention may be paid to this phenomenon, and in the common ignorance of girls concerning sex matters it may not be understood. In some cases there is an attempt, either instinctive or intuitional, to develop the sexual feeling by close embraces and kissing. This rudimentary kind of homosexual relationship is, I believe, more common among girls than among boys, and for this there are several reasons: (1) A boy more often has some acquaintance with sexual phenomena and would frequently regard such a relationship as unmanly; (2) the girl has a stranger need of affection and self-devotion to another person than a boy has; (3) she has not, under our existing social conditions, which compel young women to hold the opposite sex at arm's length, the same opportunities of finding an outlet for her sexual emotions while (4) conventional propriety recognizes a considerable degree of physical intimacy between girls, thus at once encouraging and cloaking the manifestations of homosexuality.

These passionate friendships, of a more or less unconsciously sexual character, are certainly common. It frequently happens that a

---

[15] *pudendal turgescence:* Swelling of the external sex organs or genitalia.

period during which a young woman falls in love at a distance with some young man of her acquaintance alternates with periods of intimate attachment to a friend of her own sex. No congenital inversion is usually involved. It generally happens in the end either that relationship with a man brings the normal impulse into permanent play, or the steadying of the emotions in the stress of practical life, leads to a knowledge of the real nature of such feelings and a consequent distaste for them. In some cases, on the other hand, such relationships, especially when formed after school life, are fairly permanent. An energetic emotional woman, not usually beautiful, will perhaps be devoted to another who may have found some rather specialized life-work but who may be very unpractical and who has probably a very feeble sexual instinct; she is grateful for her friend's devotion but does not actively reciprocate it. The actual specific sexual phenomena generated in such cases vary very greatly. The emotion may be latent or unconscious; it may be all on one side; it is often more or less recognized and shared. Such cases are on the borderland of true sexual inversion, but they cannot be included within its region. Sex in these relationships is scarcely the essential and fundamental element; it is more or less subordinate and parasitic. There is often a semblance of a sex relationship from the marked divergence of the friends in physical and psychic qualities, and the nervous development of one or both the friends is often slightly abnormal. We have to regard such relationships as hypertrophied friendships, the hypertrophy being due to unemployed sexual instinct.[16]

For many of the remarks which I have to make regarding true inversion in women I am not able to bring forward the justificatory individ-

---

[16] In such cases there is often considerable or complete indifference to men. This may be due to general sexual coldness, but is occasionally acquired as the result of experience. I may refer to a case mentioned by Krafft-Ebing, (*Psychopathia Sexualis*, 1893, p. 195), which at the first glance might be taken for true congenital inversion. A Hungarian lady at the age of 18 had a very passionate relationship with a man and after separation from him she adopted men's clothing to obtain her living as a tutor and subsequently showed sexual affection for her own sex. She was highly neuropathic, and congenital inversion is suggested. Her own account, however, renders her actions coherent and reduces the organic factor to a minimum. She declared that she had no man-like feelings, her first and only deep love had been a woman's for a man. But she had become disillusioned concerning this man and when in earning her living in men's clothes she mixed with men (to avoid suspicion even accompanying her male companions to brothels) she acquired an unconquerable aversion to men in general. To satisfy her passionate nature and her longing to devote herself to another person (after practicing masturbation at first) she had begun to make sexual advances to women and girls, especially those of more than usual intelligence. [Ellis's note.]

ual instances. I possess a considerable amount of information but owing to the tendencies already mentioned this information is for the most part more or less fragmentary and I am not always free to use it.

A class of women to be first mentioned, a class in which homosexuality, while fairly distinct, is only slightly marked, is formed by the women to whom the actively inverted woman is most attracted. These women differ in the first place from the normal or average woman in that they are not repelled or disgusted by lover-like advances from persons of their own sex. They are not usually attractive to the average man, though to this rule there are many exceptions. Their faces may be plain or ill-made but not seldom they possess good figures, a point which is apt to carry more weight with the inverted woman than beauty of face. Their sexual impulses are seldom well marked but they are of strongly affectionate nature. On the whole, they are women who are not very robust and well-developed, physically or nervously, and who are not well adopted for childbearing but who still possess many excellent qualities, and they are always womanly. One may perhaps say that they are the pick of the women whom the average man would pass by. No doubt this is often the reason why they are open to homosexual advances but I do not think it is the sole reason. So far as they may be said to constitute a class they seem to possess a genuine, though not precisely sexual, preference for women over men, and it is this coldness rather than lack of charm which often renders men rather indifferent to them.

The actively inverted woman differs from the woman of the class just mentioned in one fairly essential character: a more or less distinct trace of masculinity. She may not be, and frequently is not, what would be called a "mannish" woman, for the latter may imitate men on grounds of taste and habit unconnected with sexual perversion while in the inverted woman the masculine traits are part of an organic instinct which she by no means always wishes to accentuate. The inverted woman's masculine element may in the least degree consist only in the fact that she makes advances to the woman to whom she is attracted and treats all men in a cool direct manner which may not exclude comradeship but which excludes every sexual relationship, whether of passion or merely of coquetry. As a rule the inverted woman feels absolute indifference towards men, and not seldom repulsion. And this feeling as a rule is instinctively reciprocated by men.

The following case is one where the inversion is scarcely developed but still present: Miss B., age 26; father German, mother English, a sister neurotic, a brother sexually inverted.

She has no repugnance to men, and would, she says, like to try marriage on a lease, but she has never experienced sexual feeling in the slightest degree.

She is attracted towards women of different kinds, casually towards very feminine women, but in a stronger degree to women who are themselves somewhat inverted. She recognizes, however, that there are "men's women" and "women's women." She likes to kiss and embrace the women she is attracted to, though she feels no specific sexual emotion towards them, and is indignant at the exaggerated importance which, she considers, is attached to the sexual instinct. Women are not usually attracted to her in the same degree.

She has never felt any attraction whatever to men, is completely indifferent; her behavior towards them has no sexual shyness. Men are not attracted to her.

There is nothing striking in her appearance, and except for a certain careless energy and downrightness her person and manners are not conspicuously man-like. She is fond of exercise, and smokes a good deal, has artistic tastes, is indifferent to dress. . . .

The chief characteristic of the sexually inverted woman is a certain degree of masculinity. As I have already pointed out, a woman who is inclined to adopt the ways and garments of men is by no means necessarily inverted. In the volume of *Women Adventurers,* edited by Mrs. Norman[17] for the Adventure Series, there is no trace of inversion; in most of these cases, indeed, love for a man was precisely the motive for adopting male garments and manners. Again, Colley Cibber's daughter, Charlotte Charke,[18] a boyish and vivacious woman who spent much of her life in men's clothes and ultimately wrote a lively volume of memoirs, appears never to have been attracted to women though women were often attracted to her, believing her to be a man; it is, indeed, noteworthy that women, seem with special frequency to fall in love with disguised persons of their own sex. There is, however, a very pronounced tendency among sexually inverted women to adopt male attire when practicable. In such cases male garments are not usually regarded as desirable chiefly on account of practical convenience, nor even in order to make an impression on other women, but because the wearer feels more at home in them. . . .

[17] Women Adventurers, *edited by Mrs. Norman:* Menie Muriel Dowie (1866–1945), later Mrs. Henry Norman; prominent New Women author and traveler; her nonfiction book, *Women Adventurers* (1893), was a profeminist tract.

[18] *Colley Cibber's daughter, Charlotte Charke:* Famous eighteenth-century crossdressing actress, who often "played" her father, the actor Colley Cibber.

It has been stated by many observers who are able to speak with some authority — in America, in France, in Germany, in England — that homosexuality is increasing among women. It seems probable that this is true. There are many influences in our civilization to-day which encourage such manifestations. The modern movement of emancipation — the movement to obtain the same rights and duties, the same freedom and responsibility, the same education and the same work — must be regarded as on the whole a wholesome and inevitable movement. But it carries with it certain disadvantages. It has involved an increase in feminine criminality and in feminine insanity, which are being elevated towards the masculine standard. In connection with these we can scarcely be surprised to find an increase in homosexuality which has always been regarded as belonging to an allied, if not the same, group of phenomena. Women are, very justly, coming to look upon knowledge and experience generally as their right as much as their brothers' right. But when this doctrine is applied to the sexual sphere it finds certain fixed limitations. Intimacies of any kind between young men and young women are as much discouraged socially now as ever they were; as regards higher education the mere association of the sexes in the lecture-room or the laboratory or the hospital is discouraged in England and in America. The sexual field of women is usually restricted to trivial flirtation with the opposite sex and to intimacy with their own sex; having been taught independence of men and disdain for the old theory which placed women in the moated grange of the home to sigh for a man who never comes, a tendency develops for women to carry this independence still further and to find love where they find work. I do not say that these unquestionable influences of modern movements can directly cause sexual inversion, though they may indirectly, in so far as they promote hereditary neurosis; but they develop the germs of it, and they probably cause a spurious imitation. This spurious imitation is due to the fact that the congenital anomaly occurs with special frequency in women of high intelligence who, voluntarily or involuntarily, influence others. . . .

I do not propose to investigate here the pathological associations of sexual inversion in women. In this respect congenital feminine inversion is entirely on a level with masculine inversion. That is to say, it is an anomaly which even when the subject herself is fairly healthy, may be connected with neurotic heredity, and which is often associated with neurasthenia, hysteria and occasionally epilepsy and other more pronounced forms of nervous disintegration.

In the treatment of sexual inversion it is to these associated nervous disorders that our attention may best be devoted. In the absence of such symptoms the sexual invert will not as a rule appear before the physician. And this may be as well, for in such cases by mistaken assurances of permanent cure, and by encouraging marriage, it is easily possible to bring about very disastrous results, to the patient, to her husband and to the probably neurotic offspring. The physician would do well in such cases to cherish a certain judicious scepticism concerning his own powers. It is sometimes not difficult by "suggestion" or actual hypnotism (as practiced by Schrenck-Notzing) to persuade the patient that she is cured. In this way she may be plunged into a position that is falser and more miserable, more degrading to herself and dangerous to others, than her original position. It is too often forgotten that, as Raffalovitch has pointed out, to the congenitally inverted person the normal instinct is just as unnatural and vicious as homosexuality is to the normal man or woman; so that in a truly congenital case "cure" may simply mean perversion, involving the general demoralization that usually accompanies perversion. The best ideal to hold out in such cases — even although the ideal may not be perfectly reached — is not the ideal of normal love but the ideal of sexual abstinence in so far as indulgence may be doing injury to others. Very great and permanent benefit may be imparted by treating the associated neurotic conditions and general impairment of health. By a wholesome and prolonged course of physical and mental hygiene the patient may be enabled to overcome the morbid fears and suspicions which have sometimes been fostered by excessive sympathy and coddling, and the mind may thus indirectly be brought into a tonic condition of self-control. The inversion will not thus be removed but it may be rendered comparatively harmless, both to the patient herself and to those who surround her. If the physician is not satisfied with this result he will need all the tact and judgement and caution he possesses to avoid disaster.

RICHARD VON KRAFFT-EBING

From Psychopathia Sexualis

Richard von Krafft-Ebing (1840–1902), who practiced at the University of Vienna, was a neurologist specializing in forensic psychiatry. His major treatise, *Psychopathia Sexualis* (1886), counteracted the prevailing Victorian mores and traced the "hidden laws of nature" and "progress" that lead to sex impulses and the propagation of the race. According to Krafft-Ebing, the more private and sacred a society's conception of the sexual act, the more refined the society. Krafft-Ebing's tract also suggests the differences in sexual feelings between men and women: women are more passive than men, love with their whole soul, and tend toward monogamy: "Misfortune in love bruises the heart of man; but it ruins the life of woman and wrecks her happiness" (15). Moreover, woman's infidelity has greater social consequences, insofar as it might call into question the legitimacy of the heirs to a husband's property. Thus, for Krafft-Ebing, a woman's unfaithfulness "should always meet with severer punishment at the hands of the law" (15). Krafft-Ebing described the sexual lives of "perverts" as "urnings." Along with other psychopathologists, he diagnosed such sexual activities as sadism, masochism, lesbianism, nymphomania, and satyriasis. His "scientific" pronouncements came to be used as weapons against women's greater political and sexual freedom in modern America.

The text of the following excerpt is taken from *Psychopathia Sexualis, with Especial Reference to Antipathic Sexual Instinct: A Medico-Forensic Study* (New York: Rebman, 1906), 1–7.

I. Fragments of a System of Psychology of Sexual Life

The propagation of the human race is not left to mere accident or the caprices of the individual, but is guaranteed by the hidden laws of nature which are enforced by a mighty, irresistible impulse. Sensual enjoyment and physical fitness are not the only conditions for the enforcement of these laws, but higher motives and aims, such as the desire to continue the species or the individuality of mental and physical qualities beyond time and space, exert a considerable influence. Man puts himself at once on a level with the beast if he seeks to gratify lust alone, but he elevates his superior position when by curbing the animal desire he combines with the sexual functions ideas of morality, of the sublime, and the beautiful.

Placed upon this lofty pedestal he stands far above nature and draws from inexhaustible sources material for nobler enjoyments, for serious work and for the realisation of ideal aims. *Maudsley*[1] ("Deutsche Klinik," 1873, 2, 3) justly claims that sexual feeling is the basis upon which social advancement is developed.

If man were deprived of sexual distinction and the nobler enjoyments arising therefrom, all poetry and probably all moral tendency would be eliminated from his life.

Sexual life no doubt is the one mighty factor in the individual and social relations of man which disclose his powers of activity, of acquiring property, of establishing a home, of awakening altruistic sentiments towards a person of the opposite sex, and towards his own issue as well as towards the whole human race.

Sexual feeling is really the root of all ethics, and no doubt of aestheticism and religion.

The sublimest virtues, even the sacrifice of self, may spring from sexual life, which, however, on account of its sensual power, may easily degenerate into the lowest passion and basest vice.

Love unbridled is a volcano that burns down and lays waste all around it; it is an abyss that devours all — honour, substance and health.

It is of great psychological interest to follow up the gradual development of civilisation and the influence exerted by sexual life upon habits and morality.[2] The gratification of the sexual instinct seems to be the primary motive in man as well as in beast. Sexual intercourse is done openly, and man and woman are not ashamed of their nakedness. The savage races, *e.g.*, Australasians, Polynesians, Malays of the Philippines are still in this stage (*vide Ploss*). Woman is the common property of man, the spoil of the strongest and mightiest, who chooses the most winsome for his own, a sort of instinctive sexual selection of the fittest.

---

[1] *Maudsley:* Henry Maudsley (1835–1918), English psychologist and author of studies on mental illness and heredity.
[2] *Cf. Lombroso.* "The Criminal"; *Westermarck,* "The History of Marriage"; *Ploss,* "Das Weib in der Natur-und Völkerkunde," third edition, vol. ii., p. 413–90. *Joseph Müller,* "Das sexuelle Leben der Naturvölkur," 2 Aufl. 1902; *derselbe,* "Das sexuelle Leben der alten Kulturvülker," 1902 (Leipzig, Grieben). [Krafft-Ebing's note.]

Woman is a "chattel," an article of commerce, exchange or gift, a vessel for sensual gratification, an implement for toil. The presence of shame in the manifestations and exercise of the sexual functions, and of modesty in the mutual relations between the sexes are the foundations of morality. Thence arises the desire to cover the nakedness ("and they saw that they were naked") and to perform the act in private.

The development of this grade of civilisation is furthered by the conditions of frigid climes which necessitate the protection of the whole body against the cold. It is an anthropological fact that modesty can be traced to much earlier periods among northern races.[3]

Another element which tends to promote the refined development of sexual life is the fact that woman ceases to be a "chattel." She becomes an individual being, and, although socially still far below man, she gradually acquires rights, independence of action, and the privilege to bestow her favours where she inclines. She is wooed by man. Traces of ethical sentiments pervade the rude sensual appetite, idealisation begins and community of woman ceases. The sexes are drawn to each other by mental and physical merits and exchange favours of preference. In this stage woman is conscious of the fact that her charms belong only to the man of her choice. She seeks to hide them from others. This forms the foundation of modesty, chastity and sexual fidelity so long as love endures.

This development is hastened wherever nomadic habits yield to the spirit of colonisation, where man establishes a household. He feels the necessity for a companion in life, a housewife in a settled home.

The *Egyptians,* the *Israelites,* and the *Greeks* reached this level at early periods, so did the *Teutonic* races. Its principal characteristics are high appreciation of virginity, chastity, modesty and sexual fidelity in strong contrast to the habits of other peoples where the host places the personal charms of the wife at the disposal of the guest.

The history of Japan furnishes a striking proof that this high grade of civilisation is often the last stage of moral development, for in that country to within twenty years ago prostitution was not considered to impair in any way the social status of the future wife.

Christianity raised the union of the sexes to a sublime position by making woman socially the equal of man and by elevating the bond

---

[3] According to *Westermarck, op. cit.,* it was "not the feeling of shame which suggested the garment, but the garment engendered shame. The desire to make themselves more attractive originated the habit among men and women to cover their nakedness." [Krafft-Ebing's note.]

of love to a moral and religious institution.[4] Thence emanates the fact
that the love of man, if considered from the standpoint of advanced
civilisation, can only be of a monogamic nature and must rest upon a
staple basis. Even though nature should claim merely the law of
propagation, a community (family or state) cannot subsist without
the guarantee that the offspring thrive physically, morally and intellectually. From the moment when woman was recognised the peer of
man, when monogamy became a law and was consolidated by legal,
religious and moral conditions, the Christian nations obtained a mental and material superiority over the polygamic races, and especially
over Islam.

Mohammed strove to raise woman from the position of the slave
and mere handmaid of enjoyment, to a higher social and matrimonial

[4] This assertion may be modified in so far that the symbolical and sacramental character of matrimony was clearly defined only by the Council of Trent, although the
spirit of Christianity always tended to raise woman from the inferior position which
she occupied in previous centuries and in the Old Testament.

The tradition that woman was created from the rib of the sleeping man (see Genesis) is one of the causes of delay in this direction, for after the fall she is told "thy will
shall be subject to man." According to the Old Testament, woman is responsible for
the fall of man, and this became the corner-stone of Christian teaching. Thus the social
position of woman had to be neglected, as it were, until the spirit of Christianity had
conquered tradition and scholastic tenets.

It is a remarkable fact that the gospels (barring divorce, Matt. xix. 9) contain not a
word in favour of woman. The clemency shown towards the adulteress and the peni-
tent Magdalen do not affect the position of woman in general. The epistles of St. Paul
definitely insist that no change can be permitted in the position of woman (2 Cor. xi,
3–12; Eph. V. 22, "woman shall be subject to man," and 23, "woman shall fear
man").

How much the fathers of the Church are prejudiced against woman on account of
Eve's part in the temptation may be easily learned from *Tertullian*. "Woman, thou
shouldst ever go in mourning and sackcloth, thy eyes filled with tears. Thou has
brought about the ruin of mankind." *St. Jerome* has aught but good to say about
woman. "Woman is the gate of the devil, the road of evil, the sting of the scorpion"
("De Cultu Feminarum," i. 1).

Canon law declares: "Man only is created to the image of God, not woman; therefore woman shall serve him and be his handmaid."

The Provincial Council of Macon (sixth century) seriously discussed the question
whether woman had a soul at all.

These opinions of the Church had a sympathetic influence upon the peoples who
embraced Christianity. Among the converted Germanic races the *dower value* of
woman fell considerably (J. *Falke*, "Die ritterliche Gesellschaft," Berlin, 1862, p. 49.
Re the valuation of the two sexes among the Jews, cf. 3 Moses, xxvii, 3–4).

Even polygamy, which is distinctly recognised in the Old Testament, (Deut. xxi. 15)
is nowhere in the New Testament definitely prohibited. In fact many Christian princes
(*e.g.* the Merovingian kings: Chlotar I., Charibert I., Pippin I. and other Frankish nobles) indulged in polygamy without a protest being raised by the Church at the time
(*Weinhold*, "Die deutschen Frauen im Mittelalter," ii., p. 15; *cf. Unger*, "Marriage,"
etc., and *Louis Bridel*, "La Femme et le Droit," Paris, 1884). [Krafft-Ebing's note.]

grade; yet she remained still far below man, who alone could obtain divorce, and that on the easiest terms.

Above all things Islamism excludes woman from public life and enterprise, and stifles her intellectual and moral advancement. The Mohammedan woman is simply a means for sensual gratification and the propagation of the species; whilst in the sunny balm of Christian doctrine, blossom forth her divine virtues and her qualities of housewife, companion and mother. What a contrast!

Compare the two religions and their standard of future happiness. The Christian expects a heaven of spiritual bliss absolutely free from carnal pleasure; the Mohammadan an eternal harem, a paradise among lovely houris.[5] Yet, in spite of the aid which religion, law, education and the moral code offer him, the Christian (to subdue his sensual inclination) often drags pure and chaste love from its sublime pedestal and wallows in the quagmire of sensual enjoyment and lust.

Life is a never-ceasing duel between the animal instinct and morality. Only will-power and a strong character can emancipate man from the meanness of his corrupt nature, and teach him how to enjoy the pure pleasures of love and pluck the noble fruits of earthly existence.

It is an open question whether the moral status of mankind has undergone an improvement in our times. No doubt society at large shows a greater veneer of modesty and virtue, and vice is not as flagrantly practised as of yore.

The reader of *Scherr* ("Deutsche Culturgeschichte") will gain the impression that our moral code is not so gross as was that of the middle ages, even if only more refined manners have taken the place of former coarseness.

In comparing the various stages of civilisation it becomes evident that, despite periodical relapses, public morality has made steady progress, and that Christianity is the chief factor in this advance.

We are certainly far beyond sodomitic idolatry,[6] the public life, legislation and religious exercises of ancient Greece, not to speak of the worship of Phallus and Priapus[7] in vogue among the Athenians

---

[5] *houris:* Voluptuous young women.

[6] *sodomitic idolatry:* Generally, any noncoital sexual act, including oral and anal sex, as well as sex with animals; the term is derived from the biblical story of Sodom and Gomorrah.

[7] *Phallus and Priapus:* Symbols of the penis as procreative agent and of generative power, esp. in Greek Dionysian rituals. In Latin, Priapus is the god of procreation.

and Babylonians[8] or the Bacchanalian feasts[9] of the Romans and the privileged position held by the courtesans of those days.

There are stagnant and fluctuating periods in this slow progress, but they are only like the ebb- and flood-tide of sexual life in the individual.

LESTER FRANK WARD

From Pure Sociology

Lester Frank Ward (1841–1913), considered one of the best-known American social scientists and the founder of sociology, advocated improving society through controlling the environment. He described what he referred to as the "chaos" of American society in his *Pure Sociology* (1903), and he advocated self-improvement and economic and moral progress. Particularly important to Gilman was Ward's "gynæcocentric" theory, his argument for women's superiority on "scientific" grounds. As Gilman writes in her autobiography, Ward's theories of sex development influenced her immensely: "His Gynæcocentric Theory, first set forth in a *Forum* article in 1888, is the greatest single contribution to the world's thought since Evolution" (*Living* 187).

The text of the following excerpt is taken from *Pure Sociology: A Treatise on the Origin and Spontaneous Development of Society* (New York: Kelley, 1907) (Cambridge, MA: MIT P, 1970), 296–302.

A glance at the history and condition of the world in general is sufficient to show how small has been and is the rôle of woman in the most important affairs of life. None of the great business interests of mankind are or ever have been headed by women. In political affairs she has been practically a cipher, except where hereditary descent has chanced to place a crown upon her head. In such cases, however, no one can say that it has not usually rested easily. But from a certain

[8] *Athenians and Babylonians:* The ancient Greeks and the inhabitants of Babylonia, an ancient empire in Southwest Asia, in the lower Euphrates valley.
[9] *Bacchanalian feasts:* Feasts and celebrations of Bacchus (in Greek Mythology, Dionysus), god of wine; these rituals were characterized by drunkenness, disorder, and orgies.

point of view it almost seems as if everything was done by men, and woman was only a means of continuing the race.

The Gynæcocentric Theory

The gynæcocentric theory is the view that the female sex is primary and the male secondary in the organic scheme, that originally and normally all things center, as it were, about the female, and that the male, though not necessary in carrying out the scheme, was developed under the operation of the principle of advantage to secure organic progress through the crossing of strains. The theory further claims that the apparent male superiority in the human race and in certain of the higher animals and birds is the result of specialization in extra-normal directions due to adventitious causes which have nothing to do with the general scheme, but which can be explained on biological and psychological principles; that it only applies to certain characters, and to a relatively small number of genera and families. It accounts for the prevalence of the androcentric[1] theory by the superficial character of human knowledge of such subjects, chiefly influenced by the illusion of the near, but largely, in the case of man at least, by tradition, convention, and prejudice.

History of the Theory. — As this theory is not only new but novel, and perhaps somewhat startling, it seems proper to give a brief account of its inception and history, if it can be said to have such. As the theory, so far as I have ever heard, is wholly my own, no one else having proposed or even defended it, scarcely any one accepting it, and no one certainly coveting it, it would be folly for me to pretend indifference to it. At the same time it must rest on facts that cannot be disputed, and the question of its acceptance or rejection must become one of interpreting the facts.

In the year 1888 there existed in Washington what was called the Six O'Clock Club, which consisted of a dinner at a hotel followed by speeches by the members of the Club according to a programme. The Fourteenth Dinner of the Club took place on April 26, 1888, at Willard's Hotel. It was known to the managers that certain distinguished women would be in Washington on that day, and they were invited to the Club. Among these were Mrs. Elizabeth Cady Stanton, Miss Phebe Couzins, Mrs. Croly (Jennie June), Mrs. N. P. Willis,[2]

---

[1] *androcentric:* Male-centered.

[2] *Mrs. Elizabeth Cady Stanton, Miss Phoebe Couzins, Mrs. Croly (Jennie June), Mrs. N. P. Willis:* Elizabeth Cady Stanton (1815–1902), suffragist, journalist, and lec-

and a number of others equally well known. On their account the subject of Sex Equality was selected for discussion, and I was appointed to open the debate. Although in a humorous vein, I set forth the greater part of the principles and many of the facts of what I now call the gynæcocentric theory. Professor C. V. Riley was present and, I think, took part in the discussion. Many of my facts were drawn from insect life, and especially interested him. I mention this because a long time afterward he brought me a newspaper clipping from the *Household Companion* for June, 1888, containing a brief report of my remarks copied from the *St. Louis Globe,* but crediting them to him; and he apologized for its appearance saying that he could not explain the mistake. The reporter had fairly seized the salient points of the theory and presented them in a manner to which I could not object. This, therefore, was the first time the theory can be said to have been stated in print. The exact date at which it appeared in the *Globe* I have not yet learned, but presume it was shortly after the meeting of the Club. Professor Riley did not hesitate to announce himself a convert to the theory, and we often discussed it together.

I had long been reflecting along this line, and these events only heightened my interest in the subject. The editor of the *Forum* had solicited an article from me, and I decided to devote it to a popular but serious presentation of the idea. The result was my article entitled, "Our Better Halves."[3] That article, therefore, constitutes the first authorized statement of the gynæcocentric theory that was published, and as a matter of fact it is almost the only one. Mr. Grant Allen[4] answered my argument on certain points in the same magazine,[5] and I was asked to put in a rejoinder, which I did,[6] but these discussions related chiefly to certain differences between the mind of man and

---

turer. Phoebe Couzins was one of the signers of the Declaration of the Rights of Women in Philadelphia, the headquarters for the National Woman Suffrage Association in 1876. Jane Cunningham Croly (1829–1901), newspaper journalist and fashion editor, was the forerunner of today's advice, fashion, and consumer columnist. Cornelia Grinnell Willis came to know escaped slave Harriet Jacobs (famous for her autobiography, *Incidents in the Life of a Slave Girl)* after Willis's husband hired Jacobs (1825–1904) to care for their baby; she later purchased Jacobs's freedom.

[3] The *Forum,* New York, Vol. VI, November, 1888, pp. 266–275. [Ward's note.]

[4] *Mr. Grant Allen:* Evolutionary science writer and novelist, Allen (1848–1899) wrote one of the most notorious of the antimarriage New Women novels, *The Woman Who Did* (1895).

[5] "Woman's Place in Nature," by Grant Allen, the *Forum,* Vol. VII, May, 1889, pp. 258–263. [Ward's note.]

[6] "Genius and Woman's Intuition," the *Forum,* Vol. IX, June, 1890, pp. 401–408. [Ward's note.]

woman and did not deal with the question of origin. I alluded to it in my first presidential address before the Biological Society of Washington,[7] and it came up several times in writing the "Psychic Factors."

Such is the exceeding brief history of the gynæcocentric theory, and if it is entirely personal to myself, this is no fault of mine. Nothing pleases me more than to see in the writings of others any intimation, however vague and obscure, that the principle has been perceived, and I have faithfully searched for such indications and noted all I have seen. The idea has not wholly escaped the human mind, but it is never presented in any systematic way. It is only occasionally shadowed forth in connection with certain specific facts that call forth some passing reflection looking in this general direction. In introducing a few of these adumbrations I omit the facts, which will be considered under the several heads into which the subject will naturally fall, and confine myself for the most part to the reflections to which they have given rise. Many of these latter, however, are of a very general character, and not based on specific facts. In fact thus far the theory has had rather the form of a prophetic idea than of a scientific hypothesis. We may begin as far back as Condorcet,[8] who brushed aside the conventional error that intellect and the power of abstract reasoning are the only marks of superiority and caught a glimpse of the truth that lies below them when he said: —

> If we try to compare the moral energy of women with that of men, taking into consideration the necessary effect of the inequality with which the two sexes have been treated by laws, institutions, customs, and prejudices, and fix our attention on the numerous examples that they have furnished of contempt for death and suffering, of constancy in their resolutions and their convictions, of courage and intrepidity, and of greatness of mind, we shall see that we are far from having the proof of their alleged inferiority. Only through new observations can a true light be shed upon the question of the natural inequality of the two sexes.[9]

Comte,[10] as all know, changed his attitude toward women after his experiences with Clotilde de Vaux, but even in his "Positive Philoso-

---

[7] "The Course of Biologic Evolution," Proc. Biol. Soc., Washington, Vol. V, pp. 23–55. See pp. 49–52. [Ward's note.]

[8] *Condorcet:* The Marquis de Condorcet (1743–1794), French philosopher, mathematician, and politician.

[9] "Tableau Historique des Progrès de l'Esprit Humain," Paris, 1900, pp. 444–445. [Ward's note.]

[10] *Comte:* Auguste Comte (1798–1857), French mathematician and philosopher; founder of positivism.

phy," in which he declared them to be in a state of "perpetual infancy," and of "fundamental inferiority," he admitted that they had a "secondary superiority considered from the social point of view."[11] In his "Positive Polity" he expressed himself much more strongly, saying that the female sex "is certainly superior to ours in the most fundamental attribute of the human species, the tendency to make sociability prevail over personality."[12] He also says that "feminine supremacy becomes evident when we consider the spontaneous disposition of the affectionate sex (*sexe aimant*) always to further morality, the sole end of all our conceptions."[13]

Of all modern writers the one most free from the androcentric bias, so far as I am aware, is Mr. Havelock Ellis. In his excellent book "Man and Woman," he has pointed out many of the fallacies of that Weltanschauung,[14] and without apparent leaning toward anything but the truth has placed woman in a far more favorable light than it is customary to view her. While usually confining himself to the facts, he occasionally indicates that their deeper meaning has not escaped him. Thus he says: "The female is the mother of the new generation, and has a closer and more permanent connection with the care of the young; she is thus of greater importance than the male from Nature's point of view." To him is also due the complete refutation of the "arrested development" theory, above mentioned, by showing that the child, and the young generally, represent the most advanced type of development, while the adult male represents a reversion to an inferior early type, and this in man is a more bestial type.

In the sayings quoted thus far we have little more than opinions, or general philosophical tenets, of which it would be much easier to find passages with the opposite import. In fact statements of the androcentric theory are to be met with everywhere. Not only do philosophers and popular writers never tire of repeating its main propositions, but anthropologists and biologists will go out of their way to defend it while at the same time heaping up facts that really contradict it and strongly support the gynæcocentric theory. This is due entirely to the power of a predominant world view (*Weltanschauung*). The androcentric theory is such a world view that is deeply stamped upon the popular mind, and the history of human

[11] "Philosophie Positive," Vol. IV, Paris, 1839, pp. 405, 406. [Ward's note.]
[12] "Système de Politique Positive," Vol. I, 1851, p. 210. [Ward's note.]
[13] *Op. cit.*, Vol. IV, 1854, p. 63. [Ward's note.]
[14] *Weltanschauung:* "World view" (German).

thought has demonstrated many times that scarcely any number of facts opposed to such a world view can shake it. It amounts to a social structure and has the attribute of stability in common with other social structures. Only occasionally will a thinking investigator pause to consider the true import of the facts he is himself bringing to light.

Bachofen, McLennan, Morgan,[15] and the other ethnologists who have contributed to our knowledge of the remarkable institution or historic phase called the matriarchate,[16] all stop short of stating the full significance of these phenomena, and the facts of amazonism[17] that are so often referred to as so many singular anomalies and reversals of the natural order of things, are never looked at philosophically as residual facts that must be explained even if they overthrow many current beliefs. Occasionally some one will take such facts seriously and dare to intimate a doubt as to the prevailing theory. Thus I find in Ratzenhofer's work the following remark: —

> It is probable that in the horde there existed a certain individual equality between man and woman; the results of our investigation leave it doubtful whether the man always had a superior position. There is much to indicate that the woman was the uniting element in the community; the mode of development of reproduction in the animal world and the latest investigations into the natural differences between man and woman give rise to the assumption that the woman of to-day is the atavistic[18] product of the race, while the man varies more frequently and more widely. This view agrees perfectly with the nature of the social process, for in the horde, as the social form out of which the human race has developed, there existed an individual equality which has only been removed by social disturbances which chiefly concern the man. All the secondary sexual differences in men are undoubtedly explained by the struggle for existence and the position of man in the community as conditioned thereby. Even the security of the horde from predatory animals, and still more the necessity of fighting with other men for the preservation of the group, developed individual superiority in general, both mental and physical, and especially in man.

[15] *Bachofen, McLennan, Morgan:* Early ethnologists and anthropologists who published influential books about "primitive" societies: *Das Mutter-recht* (1861), *Primitive Marriage* (1865), and *Ancient Society* (1877), respectively. Ethnology is a science that deals with the division of people into races and their origins.

[16] *matriarchate:* The belief that mother-right societies based on descent through the mother, as opposed to patriarchal societies, were once historically and culturally predominant.

[17] *amazonism:* The belief in all-powerful women who rule through mother-right, advocated by Bachofen.

[18] *atavistic:* Involving a throwback or reversion to ancestral traits.

But any individual superiority disturbed the equality existing in the elements of the horde; woman from her sexual nature took only a passive part in these disturbances. The sexual life as well as the mode of subsistence no longer has its former peaceful character. Disturbances due to the demands of superior individuals thrive up to a certain point, beyond which the differentiation of the group into several takes place.[19]

Among biologists the philosophical significance of residual facts opposed to current beliefs is still less frequently reflected upon. I have stated that Professor Riley fully accepted the view that I set forth and admitted that the facts of entomology[20] sustained it, yet, although somewhat of a philosopher himself, and living in the midst of the facts, the idea had not previously occurred to him. Among botanists, Professor Meehan was the only one in whose writings I have found an adumbration of the gynæcocentric theory. He several times called attention to a certain form of female superiority in plants. In describing certain peculiarities in the Early Meadow Rue and comparing the development of the male and female flowers he observed differences due to sex. After describing the female flowers he says: —

> By turning to the male flowers we see a much greater number of bracts or small leaves scattered through the panicle, and find the pedicels longer than in the female; and this shows a much slighter effort — a less expenditure of force — to be required in forming male than female flowers. A male flower, as we see clearly here, is an intermediate stage between a perfect leaf and a perfect, or we may say, a female flower. It seems as if there might be as much truth as poetry in the expression of Burns —
>
> > Her 'prentice han' she tried on man,
> > An' then she made the lasses, O,
>
> at least in so far as the flowers are concerned, and in the sense of a higher effort of vital power.[21]

It is singular, but suggestive that he should have quoted the lines from Burns in this connection, as they are an undoubted echo of the androcentric world view, a mere variation upon the Biblical myth of the rib. Of course he could find nothing on his side in the classic liter-

---

[19] "Die Sociologische Erkenntnis," von Gustav Ratzenhofer, Leipzig, 1898, p. 127. [Ward's note.]

[20] *entomology:* The study of insects.

[21] "The Native Flowers and Ferns of the United States," by Thomas Meehan, Vol. I, Boston, 1878, p. 47. [Ward's note.]

ature of the world, but wishing to embellish the idea in a popular work, he tried to make these somewhat ambiguous lines do duty in this capacity. The fact cited is only one of thousands that stand out clearly before the botanist, but not according with the accepted view of the relations of the sexes they are brushed aside as worthless anomalies and "exceptions that prove the rule." In fact in all branches of biology the progress of truth has been greatly impeded by this spirit. All modern anatomists know how the facts that are now regarded as demonstrating the horizontal position of the ancestors of man, and in general those that establish the doctrine of evolution, were treated by the older students of the human body — rejected, ignored, and disliked, as intruders that interfered with their investigations. It is exactly so now with gynæcocentric facts, and we are probably in about the same position and stage with reference to the questions of sex as were the men of the eighteenth century with reference to the question of evolution. Indeed, the androcentric theory may be profitably compared with the geocentric theory, and the gynæcocentric with the heliocentric. The advancement of truth has always been in the direction of supplanting the superficial and apparent by the fundamental and real, and the gynæcocentric truth may be classed among the "paradoxes of nature."[22]

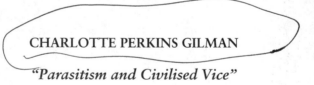

CHARLOTTE PERKINS GILMAN

"Parasitism and Civilised Vice"

While Gilman's early work concentrated on white, middle-class women, it did not, as some of her later work does, veer into outright racism or nativism. She remarks in her autobiography that her views on immigration changed when she saw the immigrant masses in New York City, and she came to blame them for the degeneration of the social climate. In "Parasitism and Civilised Vice," published in 1931, four years before her death, Gilman describes the dependence of women upon men as a "sex parasitism," which is destructive to both parties. She bitterly suggests that "many men have found satisfaction in marrying women of frankly lower race, and in their company it is not uncommon for the man

[22] "Dynamic Sociology," Vol. I, pp. 47–53. [Ward's note.]

Charlotte Perkins Gilman in 1925. Reproduced by permission of the Schlesinger Library, Radcliffe College.

to 'go native.'" Such "vices" lead, for Gilman, to the devastation of culture and the suspension of social progress.

The text of the following excerpt is taken from *Woman's Coming of Age: A Symposium*, ed. Samuel D. Schmalhausen and V. F. Calverton (New York: Liveright, 1931), 110–26.

To be called a parasite is no compliment.

"Originally," says the dictionary, "from the Greek, one who frequents the tables of the rich and earns his welcome by flattery, hence a hanger-on, a fawning flatterer, a sycophant."

The term, with its offensive connotation, has been so used long before our biological knowledge showed how common, how universal is parasitism, both vegetable and animal. As a natural process it carries in itself no reproach, and is often applicable to some periods in the life of creatures later quite independent, as with the larvæ of many insects, and in the fœtal stage of the young of viviparous[1] animals.

The fœtus may be called an endoparasite, drawing its life from the mother internally; the suckling an ectoparasite, a free individual but still nourished from her body. So long as supported by parents the life of the child is still parasitic, and in this sense the woman who does not earn her own living may be so classed.

From protozoan to vertebrate appear parasites, some familiar and pretty, as the dodder[2] and mistletoe; familiar and ugly, as many a fungus; familiar and heartily disliked, as the lively flea and the inert hookworm; but there are millions of others we never hear of. They are as numerous as independent life-forms if not more so, and various beyond measure, with the one common characteristic of drawing nutrition from some other creature known as the "host."

Hardly any animal but serves as "host" to parasites, some of which are themselves hosts to other parasites, as we long since recorded in well-known rhyme —

> "*Big bugs have little bugs and these have less to bite 'em*
> *Lesser bugs have smaller bugs and so ad infinitum.*"

These livers-upon-others are by no means to be classified as a genus or species. Parasitism is merely a process of getting a living which may be undertaken by almost anything as "the easiest way." Nevertheless there are some creatures which seem specially adapted to this process, some orders, and even classes, of worms are entirely parasitic. Worms and lice are the most common and offensive, sometimes dangerous, to man and to domestic animals.

The flea and louse, as well as the domestic pest known in New York as "crimson ramblers," are ectoparasites, moving about upon

---

[1] *viviparous:* Mammals and some reptiles who produce living young instead of eggs.

[2] *dodder:* Any one of the several parastic plants from the genus *Cuscuta*.

their hosts; the worm is an endoparasite, living inside and so ensuring not only food but protection. No early bird or prospective fisherman threatens their safety. Helpless themselves they command the services of a highly organised host, and are provided for for life; these are "true parasites."

There are many partial degrees of parasitism. Some are called "commensals" or "inqualines," which are co-inhabitants with the host in one body, but neither at the expense of the other; such are the tiny red crabs found in oysters. There is "consortium," a fellowship more intimate and necessary than that of the commensals, but differing sharply from true parasitism in that each organism needs the other for its well-being. This may be paralleled by the relation of the hard-working farmer's wife and her husband. The farmer could not make a living and raise a family without a woman to work for him without pay, the woman could not get a living and raise a family without some man to feed her and the children. The term "consort" is correctly applied to either.

Among the deadliest parasites are the young of those remorseless mother-insects which lay their eggs in living bodies, where they hatch and eat, causing acute distress and sometimes destroying outright their helpless host. A creature living on a dead host is called a saprophyte, one of which is that pale translucent forest growth the "Indian pipe"; and all the mosses and fungi thriving on dead wood. A "facultative saprophyte" is an organism normally in all stages a parasite on a living host, but which can, if put to it, thrive on a dead one, as a supported wife continues to flourish as a well-insured widow.

The epiphyte lives on a tree but not from it, like the typical orchid, with many a vine and creeper. In the dark crowding tropical jungle there is quite a garden of growth on the treetops, getting the advantage of sunlight.

Still further we learn of the "motœcious" or "metoxenous" parasite, which passes through the successive stages of its existence on different hosts. Many of the bacilli of disease are of this sort, lodging first in some "intermediate host" and then transferred to our bodies, by the mosquito or rat previously entertaining them. With no such evil connotation the term may be applied to the life of a woman, supported from the fœtal stage, first by mother, then by father, then by husband, and lastly as a saprophytic widow.

The internal processes of living consist in the absorption of air and nutriment, the assimilation of necessary material and the discharge of waste; with, for the mother, the nourishing of the unborn; all carried on unconsciously.

The external processes involve varied activity, and, in higher creatures, intelligence. It is to the wide range of exertion required in mating, in making shelter, in defence, and in securing nutrition, that we owe most of the variation of living things. From the chance contact and absorption of the amœba to the elaborate activities of the ant, the highly ingenious efforts of the fox, and the intricate international production and exchange of society, is a long road, in following which numerous and varied faculties appear.

Animals were modified to sex, with variations and improvements until order mammalia was reached, since which further improvements have been in nurture and education; physiologically there is no generic difference between the sex processes of a mouse and those of an elephant. There is also modification to climate, to escaping or resisting enemies, to the environment generally; but the most conspicuous modification of living things is by their means of getting a living. Therefore they are classified by their teeth, or lack of them, and we find, as in grass-eaters, meat-eaters, ant-eaters, the whole body of the beast mainly organised to get its dinner.

The immediate necessity, as organisms developed from a mere floating stomach to a more complicated structure with different functions, was to distribute to all the other parts the nourishment obtained by the mouth and digested by the stomach. Under this vital requirement we find in plant and animal a fluid embodying this nourishment and distributing it throughout the organism, sap or blood.

Here is the very juice of life, produced by the inner labours of various organs, of consummate ease of absorption. If any creature could establish contact with this supply in another creature no further effort was needed, and no organs required aside from the reproductive, save those wherewith to hold on and suck. Hence the popularity of parasitism. It is the softest job there is, nature's "easiest way."

The disadvantage of parasitism is in its arrest of development. The ectoparasites, hopping and crawling about on their hosts, or moving from a vacant flat to a full one, as they do in New York, show some ability, but the endoparasites, snugly fixed within, are assured of a steady climate, no enemies, and unlimited food. It is an ideal position for the unambitious.

As all animals live on other living things it seems perhaps less evil to eat without killing than to kill and eat; the evil indeed is less to the host than to the stunted hanger-on, unless there are too many of them. A tree is a marvellous engine, intricate and strong, searching food with myriad roots and distributing it to myriad leaves. Dodder is but a hank of yellow string, blossoming to be sure, but needing neither roots, trunk nor leaves.

Eating grass is a simple process, but the beast so supported must have large abdominal machinery to assimilate such raw material and competent legs to carry the large body about. The fat tick on its neck has only to hold on and suck. The one great distinction between parasites and the other forms of life is that all the others work for their livings, the parasite lives on the labour of some one else. If too numerous and too greedy these suckers sometimes destroy their hosts; many a man has sunk under a too-demanding wife and daughters.

If the production and distribution of sap or blood is so essential to the development of physical organic life, how much more necessary, in the world-circling organic life of society, is such a potent extract, carrying nutrition to the uttermost parts. The farmer, the grazier, the fisherman, furnish food; all the other people must have it to eat. Very early appeared the need of a circulating medium, in clumsy forms of hides or wampum, through the heavy metals, up to the physical convenience of paper and the psychic machinery of credit.

Money is society's blood, and its blood-suckers appear as promptly as elsewhere. Against the energising upward pressure that develops power and skill in the economic processes of society is found this reversionary tendency to live without such processes, making the "supported" human being say proudly, "I do not have to work."

The most patent and offensive social parasite is the beggar. He is a very low form, having no organs of attachment to his passing host. Since sympathy is his only hope, and that weakens with overdraft, professional beggary resorts to the simulation of revolting disease and deformity. This is distinctly a civilised vice. It can only obtain where there is a high degree of social consciousness, feeling another's pain; and as that sensitiveness is advantageous, "charity" has long been considered a virtue. It is not, it maintains, a diseased condition. Society needs the healthy distribution of nutrition to all its parts; charity is osmosis — a soaking through the tissues instead of normal circulation.

Criminals prey upon society like savage beasts or vermin, offensive and dangerous but at least active; the beggar sucks. The essential evil of social parasitism is that it involves members of the same race. Except for the technical comparison of the dependence of the young, or the primitive males of early organisms, the innumerable parasites of the lower world are of different species from their hosts. The injury to the host is mainly in loss of nutrition, and sometimes in toxic deposits or in the ramblings of trichinæ and the like, while the injury to the parasite in the abortion of all higher faculties is no consequence to the host.

Social parasitism is an infinitely greater evil, its exponents being also human. In proportion to their prevalence is our social evolution delayed, the parasite being denied all progressive powers and purposes, while maintaining unabated the primitive faculties and appetites of sub-human egotism.

In our complex social life we find the widest variation and distinction in degrees of parasitism, from the coarse and simple form of beggary to the subtlest relations of dependence, from an open and undeniable condition to those confused by so many relations and emotions that it is hard to differentiate them. Among others we have developed a unique form of sex parasitism, in which the female is dependent upon the economic activities of the male.

Sex parasitism is well known among many low forms of life, but it is masculine. In the early stages of the introduction of sex distinction there are many instances in which the tiny transient one-functioned male lives in or on the body of the female. More familiar to us in present instance, are the dependent males of insects, born in wasteful profusion for scant use, as the helpless drones feeding on the honey made by working bees until one of them achieves his only purpose and the rest are killed off; and the similar brief service of the male ant and his countless deaths.

Dr. Jordan of Stanford University, an icthyologist of world reputation, has in the *Scientific Monthly,* April, 1926, an amusing account of a deep-sea fish known as the Sea Devil, of which until lately no males were discovered. It is a fish of rather elaborate development, having a luminous-tipped fishpole of its own, projecting over its wide well-toothed jaws to attract its prey. The male has no fishpole, nor even a mouth. He is about one-thirtieth the weight of the female, and hangs on beneath. "The skin of the snout is continuous with that of the female, and no one can tell where one fish leaves off and the other begins." He is doubtless effective as a fertiliser, but otherwise a poor fish.

It has remained for humanity to show us the unique spectacle of a parasitic female, a creature who economically considered, at best shares in a consortium of low-grade activities, and at worst has no industrial faculties, but is entirely supported by the male.

This condition is not as clearly marked as with the parasitic male, who is of a low undeveloped type, made, as Kipling mistakenly remarked of the female, "for one purpose only, armed and engined for the same." The parasitic male is a case of limited function, of arrested development, remaining at a low stage while the female carries on all racial activities. This is evidently a hindrance to race progress, as all higher species have a free male, gradually developing into equality with the female.

The peculiarity of our female parasitism is that it appears in a highly developed species, and the arrest in development is mainly psychic.

Social progress is two-fold, involving the higher mental faculties which distinguish our race and the varied products of those faculties. "The material world," so deprecated by some thinkers, is as essential to the life of a society as the physical body is to the spirit inhabiting it.

At the level of squaw-labour the human female was still ahead. She began the industries and arts through which the race has risen, but beyond that level we find the unique spectacle of a species with highly developed males carrying on all race functions, and hampered by an aborted female living on the male in all degrees of parasitism.

Her early industrial superiority, growing from her maternal activities, was quite naturally taken advantage of by the male. Her services to him proved useful to the tribe's survival; the hunter or fighter who had a competent woman to care for him was obviously more efficient than one who had to take care of himself. This relation has left lasting marks; to this day, and in spite of economic waste, each man thinks himself entitled to one whole woman to wait on him.

It is the fact of that ancient usefulness, and the persistence of its value in the still useful consortium which so complicate the condition of parasitism among women. The working housewife does perform service of a primitive sort, toiling hard and long, but this service is for the family; she does not make a living by it. If the husband dies, or leaves her, she finds that housework will not pay the rent, or the grocer; she must attach herself to another man who will.

Among peasant types the wife who works in the field with her husband certainly performs economic service, but even here she seldom directly profits by it, receiving what he chooses to give her. Children often work in the same way, but the growing son, wishing to be economically independent, soon works for another employer, and draws his own pay.

Personal service, however hallowed by affection and dignified by a sense of duty, is extremely low in industrial evolution. As a developer of faculties it has the same effect on men and women, as shown in the servant class the world over. However competent and devoted the servant, his or her income is an expense to the master, and in the case of slaves or women there is no income, there is only support.

So accustomed are we to admire and enjoy the labours of the working housewife, and so natural is the objection among women to admit the low industrial level of their position, that a recent statistician has calmly classed the housewife among the "employed." In previous censuses the occupation "housewife" was promptly marked "N.G." — not gainful, which was mostly correct.

The level at which it is gainful is that of the solitary farmer who needs every moment of daylight for his productive industry, to which the wife's labour is indispensable. In such case the two should be classed as farmers, and she entitled to half the product. But as man increases in earning power, in skill, in wealth due only to his superior abilities, so that he is able to hire servants to do squaw-labour for him, the wife's economic value decreases in proportion.

With the rich man, who even hires a housekeeper to manage his servants, the wife retains only a species of social value as hostess and entertainer. While this is sometimes of economic service in promoting some business plan, it is not as a rule equal to the large expense of maintaining a wife of this sort.

Leaving any direct or indirect service aside we come to the real basis of woman's parasitism, the sex relation. For this use alone is the pocketed cirriped or pendant devil-fish maintained by the female, for this alone is the "gold digger" of all grades maintained by the male.

However much the female might be left behind in social progress she must be kept abreast in the physical processes which hold the race alive. As man learned, grew and improved, and woman, denied freedom and specialisation, lagging farther and farther behind in economic efficiency, it became essential that he should shoulder the burden he had made, and therefore were constructed marriage laws compelling each man to support his own wife and children.

Our polygamous customs doubtless arose during the pastoral stage when there was milk for many children, meat for the killing, and little work for women. The cattle they lived with being by nature polygamous, the more so by removal of superfluous males, furnished men a visible pattern of conduct, and as the stud animals kept for that use increased in capacity and so in value, their owner quite naturally began to give high esteem to such surplus capacity in himself.

With other animals, living close to the compelling limits of necessity, each appetite and impulse is held in check by others, or by conditions about them. The human animal, with his enlarging consciousness and increasing command of conditions, was able to indulge himself more freely; the keeper of cattle for instance could eat more and oftener than the hunter. With no knowledge to check desire early man naturally indulged in any pleasurable exercise, and from that time to this he has established a record for excesses of every kind.

These excesses, in food and drink, were more promptly checked by natural penalties of disease, than those of sex indulgence,[3] and the practice of polygamy gave the latter wide opportunity in men. With agriculture and the settled home we see a return to the monogamy natural to our species, but marred by the excesses developed in polygamy. In observation of the habits of his cattle man had failed to notice that they were only polygamous once a year, by nature.

Even among peoples where polygamy is sanctioned by law and religion the mass of the population remains monogamous if agriculture is their source of subsistence. This is partly due to economic pressure, but most finally to the simple biological fact that, being a monogamous species, the sexes are born in about equal numbers, with a slight preponderance of males to cover their lower viability. If any man has more than one wife some other man must go without.

It is only the rich and powerful who were able to maintain a group of women, and to get them they must purchase and enslave, a constant cause of warfare. The plural wives without occupation, the slave women with no other use, the harem women, these were fed and protected in return for sex-service, and became sex-parasites.

Bearing in mind the natural equality in numbers between the sexes and the unequal distribution resultant from a partial polygamy, adding to this the excessive desires developed by over-use, we have the basis for that peculiar human sex-relationship we call "vice." The weaker and poorer men, deprived by purchase or force of their complement of women, were driven to misuse what remained.

That vice obtains in proportion to the progress of civilisation is but too evident. That progress has been almost exclusively male. Men have grown through all the stages of industrial development, of reli-

---

[3] *sex indulgence:* Sexual intercourse or activity for its own sake; nonreproductive sexual activity.

gious, artistic, scientific, mechanistic, political, legal, educational development, while women until quite recently have remained at the stage of squaw-labour, lightened by the inventions of men. That there were notable exceptions is well known. The record of women where education and opportunity were allowed them, and the large and increasing number now specialised and economically independent, give clear proof of their possession of race qualities, but the majority of them were and are getting their livings in the consortium as a working housewife, or as parasites, partial or complete.

So accustomed are we to the monopolisation of all race faculties and occupations by men that we believe them to be sex characteristics, and to this day the manifestation of such faculties by women is described as "trying to be like men." If that poor pendant devil-fish could think, he might similarly assume swimming to be a feminine characteristic, quite unbecoming to a male. The processes of inheritance by which certain race qualities become associated with one sex or the other and are so transmitted, are obscure, but they certainly are shown, for instance, in the pathetic limitations of a male without a mouth. A mouth is not a sex characteristic, assuredly.

As before said, one of the confusions attending our female parasitism is in its checking not so much the physical as the psychological faculties. The human female, while somewhat smaller and weaker, remains quite recognisably human, physically. But humanity, in all its high distinction, is not a physical development, it is one of mental and material growth, and wholly dependent upon organisation. Men, had they remained separate individuals, could never have produced one human faculty, not even the power of speech; in related groups they have built the world we know. Women have remained for the most part separate individuals, associated mainly with the family group, which is pre-human in its origin.

The passionate devotion of women to the church, the only form of large association allowed them, and their equally passionate devotion to that mock-organisation called "society," show the urge of this "suppressed desire" — the quite natural desire of a human creature to function as such.

The complete feminine parasite shows no such urge, but seems content to draw as much nourishment as possible from her male or males, living in a luxury and idleness utterly sub-human.

The relation between progress and prostitution is clear. While men, increasing in power, skill and knowledge, added to the world all its accumulated comforts and conveniences, arts and sciences, there appeared new tastes and needs, the standard of living rose. But the women did not rise. They were less and less able to "take care of themselves," more and more dependent on the care of men. By inheritance and association they shared the higher tastes and needs, but not the ability to secure them.

Furthermore there has been bred into them, trained into them, forced into them, an artificial sense of duty to the male, and of the superiority of a well-supported wife over a woman who "had to work." A self-supporting woman was looked down upon by a supported one much as a well cared for slave used to look down on a "free nigger."

The prize for a woman was "a good match," and since this was only to be obtained by sex-attraction[4] the whole pressure of economic necessity was added to a strong natural impulse long overdeveloped. If unable to marry, she must work at low-grade and poorly paid tasks, mainly in house-service, debarred from any hope of achieving wealth for herself, and to this hungry helplessness was always open the payment for sex-service. It is a well-established fact that there is a connection between an increase in the price of bread and in prostitution.

The laws of marriage were made by men, that each might safeguard his own woman and be sure of his own children. Outside of marriage there was scant protection for any woman. The inevitability of civilised vice is patent.

For the man there was the excessive urge of a desire quite strong enough in its natural state, and increased by unbridled indulgence. For the woman the same excessive urge, and no means of subsistence save from men. Employment generally was denied women, but sex-service was always in demand. With civilisation comes greater riches, greater desires, greater indulgence — greater vice.

Mere promiscuity, indulged from mutual desire, is not in itself vice. It is a normal relation in many species, therefore to them right. The essential quality of our human vice is in its abnormality, its utter misuse of function, making sex union an economic process.

In its more obvious form of direct sale we have condemned it. In its almost as obvious form of mercenary marriage we reprobate it. But the general condition wherein women are "supported" in this relation we have assumed to be natural and right. That their industrial service, if any, was of a primitive sort we thought natural to them;

---

[4] *sex-attraction:* The studied enhancement of secondary sex characteristics designed to lure the opposite sex.

and the obvious limitations of women as compared to men were considered sex characteristics.

Vice, in its common definition, we attributed to illegal sex union, not to excesses carried on within recognised bounds; this is not to be wondered at, in view of the common and conspicuous results. These results are so well known, so widespread, so offensively dangerous, that we have called vice "The Social Evil." At the same time we have also called it "a social necessity."

Why anything so absolutely personal as sex indulgence should be called social is hard to see; and still harder is it to account for an acknowledged evil being thought a necessity. This last appears to rest on the assumption that the sex passion of man demands gratification aside from and beyond that offered by matrimony; and that if this spillway were not provided men would assail other men's wives and daughters and society dissolve in private warfare.

Most conspicuous sequelæ of civilised vice are its attendant diseases. Syphilis, with its still-births counted, is asserted to be our most destructive disease, it destroys the mind as well as the body, is peculiarly offensive — a loathsome disorder, and is not only contagious but inheritable. Gonorrhœa, even more common, is not so dangerous to men, but is the cause of more than ninety per cent of the pelvic operations on married women, and of a large share of sterility, both complete and the "ein kind sterilitat"[5] named in Germany; Chancroid is a milder third.

Next we recognise the other vices closely connected with and resultant from the first; as drug habits, and the theft and robbery and sometimes murder committed to secure means of indulgence, to gratify the insatiable demands of greedy women, or in jealousy and revenge.

All this group of evils is patent and well known, so well known as to have given rise to the caustic proverb, applied to any criminal problem, "Cherchez la femme."[6]

But civilised vice covers far wider ground than this. Further results of our sex parasitism are much more general, though less plainly seen. Something wrong in the relation of women to life we have felt but not understood. It is shown in the fierce diatribes against women in ancient literature, and the still older myths in which they are blamed for all evil, as with Eve and Pandora.

---

[5] *"ein kind sterilitat"*: The inability to have children (German).
[6] *"Cherchez la femme"*: "Look for the woman" (French); often used pejoratively.

This bitter contempt is deepest in those Oriental races where sex indulgence has become a fine art and long excess has enfeebled the people and arrested their social evolution; it is not for the mate and mother but for the parasite, and for the effect of parasitism in aborting the human faculties. With that abortion follows the unavoidable consequence of mating such widely dissimilar beings, a difference not of sex but of thousands of years of social progress, between the primitive culture of squaw-labour or harem idleness and the progressive culture carried on by civilised man.

Our development in knowledge, in all arts, sciences, trades and crafts, in the higher feelings which come through widening organisation and interservice, is social progress. It is as natural as the growth of a tree, as the evolution of the horse, but it has been impeded and perverted by various crippling conditions of our own making, among which one of the most universal and continuous is the parasitism of woman. With over-used sex-faculties and no others used at all beyond household labour, she remained at the foot of the ladder, and the higher man ascended the farther down he must reach in marriage.

What kind of progress can be expected in a race of animals where the female makes none? What civilisation can endure which is made and practiced by one sex only? To which rhetorical questions the plain answer is, the kind we have so far produced, the kind which has followed so often the same course, made the same mistakes, produced the same vices, and broken under the assaults of some less developed people where the gulf between male and female was not so wide.

The difference between parents in their degree of social development complicates heredity and education. We know the visible results of "marrying out of one's class" as so recognised, but we do not see that civilised man, marrying a parasitic socially aborted woman, marries out of his class by long ages of social distinction.

He has not minded this. The inferiority he was quite assured of, assuming it to be a feminine characteristic. All that he required was physical beauty, with traits of gentleness and appeal long associated with feminine charm. Modern women in general do not yet understand how limited was the masculine demand even into this century, as shown so clearly by Mr. H. B. Marriot Watson in an article on "The American Woman in the Nineteenth Century and After," about 1903, wherein he says, "Her constitutional restlessness has caused her to abandon those functions which alone explain or excuse her existence."

Possessing those functions, and long habits of house service, she gave all that men asked in marriage. Many men have found satisfaction in marrying women of frankly lower race, and in their company it is not uncommon for the man to "go native." Sharply here is shown the influence of our socially aborted women upon civilisation. They maintain mental attitudes, instincts, capacities and emotions native to the race in its dim beginnings, and modern men, mated with them, continually "go native" in easy reversion.

We have here the clear explanation for many of the peculiar defects in what we call "human nature." Other creatures have worked out a kind of "nature" shared by both sexes, they have no "vices," but all behave in accordance with the interests of their species. Those who did not have not survived.

But we, of such superior intelligence, of such superior organisation, of such immeasurable superiority in all the accumulated products of hand and brain, we show a suicidal irregularity of behaviour which has made us the sickest beast alive, cursed with idiocy, lunacy, a moronic average, vice, crime, poverty, and the never-ending destruction of our foolish wars.

All our discordant irreconcilable conduct we have attributed to "human nature," as we attributed the defects of women to feminine nature; or we have cast about in our shamed and distracted minds and invented fates and devils to account for our amazing misbehaviour.

Our natural growth in social consciousness, in that intelligent coordination which means peace, wealth and progress, has been hampered by the persistence of a primitive egoism, an exaggerated personality, with its lack of perspective, its narrow judgment, its unreasoning emotions; and this essential discord born in us all, comes directly from the gulf dividing the social development of men and women.

It can easily be seen that a civilisation composed of one-half Englishmen and one-half Hottentots[7] would be defective. The only method of continuance in such case would be in the subjection of the Hottentots to their undoubted superiors. This condition has obtained throughout history, civilisation based on slavery, but the social qualities bred in both master and slave have had most damaging results.

Social evolution has brought us on the way to democracy. We have liberated our slaves and even enfranchised our women, but

---

[7] *Hottentots:* The black tribe considered by nineteenth-century racial pseudoscientists to be the lowest example of humankind.

political freedom and equality are but names when there remains wide inequality in human progress.

We are at present moving swiftly into an era of rapid advancement for women, which will lead to as swift development of the capacities and culture proper to their race and time. This is shown irrefutably by the increasing numbers now sustaining themselves by the use of human faculties, given as 23 per cent in our last census, while their possession of these faculties is made clear by the steady rise in the scale of their occupations.

This natural and gratifying progress, so beneficial to the world, is by no means smooth nor unhindered. The main check is in the undeveloped state of the work to which they have been hitherto confined, the primitive status of domestic labour and child care. These professions are, however, perceptibly in motion and rising in efficiency as they escape from the hopelessly low level of the private servant, hired or married.

Another obstacle is that resurgence of phallic worship set before us in the solemn phraseology of psychoanalysis. This pitifully narrow and morbid philosophy presumes to discuss sex from observation of humanity only. It is confronted with our excessive development and assumes it to be normal. It ignores the evidence of the entire living world below us, basing its conclusions on the behaviour and desires of an animal which stands alone in nature for misery and disease in sex relation.

Sex was introduced, not as necessary to life or even to reproduction, which had gone on efficiently for many ages, but as an agent of variation and selection, so tending to the improvement of species. Being valuable it was adopted by all higher forms; in the vegetable as well as the animal world. Surely a process so universal deserves wider study than may be found in one race of animals, especially a race of animals with so poor a record in this field.

Our knowledge of biology, of evolution, of the essential unity of life, is so recent and ill-understood that most people still think of humanity as a separate creation. This is about the level of information of those who believe the earth is flat and the stars something to tell fortunes by.

Counting the other forms of sexual life as a million and man as one; counting the years of evolution as a million and our history as one; — which is far within the facts; observe the incredible presumption which discusses a factor found in all the million forms for all the million years and argues only from the one.

In all the others, for all the ages, sex is unquestionably a process aiding reproduction and improvement. In the one, this morbid philosophy boldly states that sex is "not for procreation but for recreation."

In all the others the sex processes are carried on in health and harmony, from the unconscious methods of vegetable life up to a high degree of activity and pleasure, and, among monogamous animals, even the psychic pleasure of long association.

In the one we find every degree of dis-harmony, all extremes of disease and vice, and such frequent unhappiness in mating that it is the commonest joke. What is there in the sex behaviour of the human race which leads us to believe that it is normal and advantageous?

It is true that we have developed the lasting joy of what is called "romantic love." This is found in other mating creatures, as the paired swans, where if one is killed the other lives alone till death; but with us, as belongs to our farther growth, it has become the highest personal happiness. As a monogamous species we have had this always to some degree, and admired it always in song and story, no matter what might be our marriage customs, but few of us attain to it.

The sex-olatry of to-day sneers at such union, attributes monogamy to artificial restriction, and advocates miscellaneous and continuous "sex experience" as natural, healthy and happy.

For justification they revert to lower cultures, carefully selecting certain sunny islands where food is to be had for the picking and children need no long continued parental care, and where the sexes mingle unashamed. It is to be noted in all such instances that the healthy, happy and promiscuous remain savages.

No progressive culture has risen on that foundation. They are not a primal stock, but a pleasant decadence, deriving from an earlier culture. Even if we wished to, we cannot set back the clock for all the world.

Again for justification these protagonists of sex for recreation point out the sad results of celibacy, the stunted, thwarted lives of "old maids." Some such there are, but why not count the full and vigorous lives of other old maids, of whom there are many. At its worst it can hardly be shown that the nervous diseases credited to repression are more to be dreaded than those due to excessive indulgence, the former being neither contagious nor hereditary.

No authoritative study has been made to prove that in a thousand cases the subject, man or woman, is healthy, happy, and socially valuable in proportion to sex indulgence. Could Leonardo, for instance, compete with Don Juan? Or vice versa?

We do know absolutely that our race alone has separated sex from its universal purpose and used its initial processes for a barren gratification; and that our race alone shows with every rising civilisation a rising tide of vice.

It is not easy for the average "feminist" to admit the parasitism of women, with its accompanying abortion of social faculties. In the new recognition of the initial superiority of the female, and her continued advantage up to the early stages of our human culture, it is hard to reconcile that essential superiority with the inferiority produced by parasitism.

Yet as those who hold the male to be superior must admit the painful fact of his early parasitism with its accompanying defects, so the fact of female superiority ought not to blind us to her similar degradation when ceasing to use the constructive capacities of her race and getting her living through the sex relation, legal or illegal.

The female, as such, is a highly specialised sex, the long and elaborate processes of which, beyond a brief initial contact with the male, are devoted to reproduction. Among plants, after the pollen is set free and reaches the ova there is no further male process, all the slow ripening of seed and nut and fruit is feminine.

In the animal world it is the same, the male contribution is of the briefest, the whole range of activities which bear and nurse and rear the young are feminine, save in cases where the labours of rearing are shared by the male. All these instincts and efforts are those of sex, and mainly of the female sex. How gross is the absurdity of those who attribute sex only to that initial contact, its impulses and pleasures; who are willing to avoid the whole range of life-continuing processes which naturally follow, and who, divorcing sex impulse from its universal purpose, still claim it to be the mainspring of all our activities.

False as is this view it has taken a vigorous hold on the mind of to-day, because we all share to greater or less degree in the excessive sex-development of our race, and find it gratifying to see removed what restraints we have hitherto sought to apply to an overmastering impulse, to find what we had felt to be wrong was more than right.

It is through the woman, so long kept for sex use only, and so used to limitless excess, that our over-development has mainly come. Men, however much they used this faculty, were obliged also to use others. The women of to-day, emerging from long repression, finding themselves overcharged with sex-energy and warmly urged to use it, in the justification of this highly masculine philosophy, seem quite largely to have adopted the theory that the purpose of sex is recreation.

This influence will not last long. Man's old foolish theories of asceticism and celibacy never seriously interfered with the reproduction of species, nor will this new foolish theory that the striking of matches is the main use of fire.

It should not take much study to acquaint our women with the world of facts about sex in all vegetable and animal life, nor to convince them that however uneasily insistent is the present degree of sex impulse it is not a "biological urge" but a pathological one, the demand of a function inflamed and misused for thousands of years. It will take more than one generation to outgrow it, to re-establish the normal use which will give our species the same health and peace in this relation which is enjoyed by other animals, plus the whole range of human joy in love.

This is not to be reached by any legal, religious or "moral" interference, by no talk of sin or shame. It is merely a matter of misuse of function on the one side and disuse of function on the other. As the human female rises in human capacities by the use of them, and recognises her real dignity and power as a female through the full use of her maternal functions, ninety-nine per cent of which are beyond the preliminary act of fertilisation, she will repudiate both the old idea that her sex was for his gratification and the new one that it is for hers.

As a sex she will see to it that the reproduction and improvement of the race is carried on intelligently, with rapid advance in health, beauty and intellectual power. As a human being she will think of her previous parasitism with pity and shame, and find in the free exercise of race faculties more power and pleasure than she knew life held.

With such women and the men they will breed and rear we shall have a civilisation no longer calling for apology, and no longer succumbing to the social disorders we call vice, so largely the product of female parasitism.

4

Movements for Social Change

Not all of the nineteenth-century debates about sexuality were repressive or coercive. Angela Heywood's essays for *The Word* (a periodical published from 1872 until 1893 under the aegis of the free love banner) aimed to discuss sexuality openly and without prudery. Similarly, Gilman edited the *Forerunner* as an organ for social reform. Heywood and her husband, Ezra, claimed that as long as language was restrained, human sexuality would be restrained and efforts to achieve gender equality would be stymied. They argued that linguistic freedom would help to cure their culture's repressiveness and its unhealthy attitude toward the human body. As we can see in "The Yellow Wallpaper," Gilman's narrator cannot confess her desire to write, let alone her desire for pleasure of any sort with her husband John. John's efforts to infantilize his wife suggest that he espouses mainstream conservative attitudes toward sexuality. He offers her only nonstimulating pleasures and tranquil times, such as reading to her. For Gilman, changing language alone would not be enough to change women's status. She wanted to channel the energy of social reform into a collectivism aspiring to improve women's, and hence humanity's, lot.

Gilman's belief in collectivism was kindled by the publication of Edward Bellamy's best-selling utopian novel, *Looking Backward, 2000–1887* (1888). Bellamy introduced and popularized an American version of Christian socialism in late-nineteenth-century culture. Based on the spiritual belief that American morality would only be restored through a rejection of self-interest and greed, Bellamy's proposed utopia was one in which solidarity and mutuality replaced class hierarchy and competition and in which national service led to national unity: "But how could I live without service to the world?" Bellamy's hero, Julian West, asks. "Why should the world have supported in utter idleness one who was able to render service?" (see p. 288). Bellamy's utopian ideals were founded on such ethical and rhetorical stances as these and supported by his followers, "Bellamyites."

The social reformer Jane Addams, writing in her memoir *Twenty Years at Hull-House* (1910), asked herself similar questions: "there was also growing within me an almost passionate devotion to the ideals of democracy, and when in all history had these ideals been so thrillingly expressed as when the faith of the fisherman and the slave had been boldly opposed to the accepted moral belief that the well-being of a privileged few might justly be built upon the ignorance and sacrifice of many?" (see p. 302). Addams's questions concerned the duties to society that she could perform, and she dedicated much of her life to the foundation of settlement houses for the working poor.

Like Bellamy and Gilman, Addams saw one of the goals of philanthropy as that of bringing people from different classes *together*, in social unity, through social welfarism. The settlement house reconstituted the nation as family, with middle-class women coming out of the private home and working alongside the poor in community houses. Challenging the Victorian norms of women's domestic influence, Addams wanted to reorganize society so that women's moral influence would sanitize the culture at large; she moved women out of private homes and into the collectivity. Addams's settlement houses put a modified socialism into practice. She created cooperative communities that operated on the principles of collectivity in order to combat poverty and disease. The family claim was the social claim writ large.

Perhaps the most profound and influential critic of gender relations in American culture was Thorstein Veblen, whose seminal work, *The Theory of the Leisure Class* (1899), complemented Gilman's 1898 *Women and Economics* in its discussion of how women became "conspicuous consumers" — trophies or signs of their husbands' wealth. Both Gilman and Veblen argued that women had been relegated to secondary roles in culture in order to preserve the separation of the spheres (with women in the private domestic realm and men in the public arena). The selection from Veblen reprinted in this chapter represents his major theories about how middle- and upper-class women came — through their consumption of material goods and enjoyment of leisure time — to function as symbols of their husbands' stature while creating or producing nothing themselves. Veblen analyzes the goals and successes of the New Women reformers who hoped that all women would eventually rebel against their subordinate status, choosing to be producers of culture rather than reproducers of the race.

Gilman left behind a careful record of her own intellectual growth in her 1935 autobiography, *The Living of Charlotte Perkins Gilman*. In this work, she contrasts her early determination to exert her will on coming of age with the breakdown that resulted from her postpartum depression and the realization that her marriage was in trouble. Gilman notes that she resented the dependency of her child on her as well as her own dependence on her first husband, Walter Stetson. "The Yellow Wallpaper" can be read as a product of Gilman's terrible need to redeem motherhood for herself and for her culture. Part of Gilman's reformist social vision included a revaluation and redemption of motherhood from the debasement she thought it had suffered in consumer culture. Gilman wanted motherhood to be voluntary and professionalized rather than left to those most unprepared for it — the young, the illiterate, the mentally unfit, and the poor. She believed that motherhood involved an act of will, and she was thus deserving of the highest recognition and supervision. Seeing motherhood as subject for social engineering, Gilman planned to overcome women's subordination in part through a reconception and reformation of the cultural practices of childraising. Thus, Gilman's vision of "social motherhood" was part of the larger cultural revolution of reimagining individualism and channeling it into collective, reformist endeavors. However, Gilman's place within the social reform movement was tenuous: she was ultimately not a settlement or reform worker. She paid Addams a three-month visit at Hull-House in 1895, but despite her belief in collectivism, she did not stay. Addams later praised Gilman's *Women and Economics* as a "masterpiece."

Included in this chapter are several versions of Gilman's feminist and utopian thought, from her earliest and most important work, *Women and Economics* (1898), to her later meditations on the difficulties of achieving social change in a preeminently individualistic society. In "The Yellow Wallpaper," Gilman highlights the narrator's struggle to oppose her individual will — her interpretations and diagnosis of her "case" — to that of her culture, embodied by her doctor-husband, his sister, Jennie, and the medical establishment. What Gilman had fictionalized in her 1892 short story, she theorizes in her 1898 study of how patriarchal culture deforms women's will. Her economic and sociological treatise, *Women and Economics,* documents the social forces that serve to erode women's wills, making them dependent on men for basic human resources. In "Dr. Clair's Place," Gilman imagines a cure that, rather than destroying patients, builds up their internal energy through stimulation and employment. Unlike the doctor-husband in "The Yellow Wallpaper," the female Dr. Clair creates a context in which self-development and expression can flourish instead of being stunted or denied.

ANGELA HEYWOOD

Selections from The Word

Angela Fiducia Tilton Heywood and her husband, Ezra Heywood, were sex reformers — some would even say sex radicals — who published a magazine entitled *The Word* from 1872 until 1893. *The Word* was aligned with the free love movement for sexual reform, which rejected Victorian hypocrisy and the sexual double standard. One of the publication's primary goals was to make the language of sexuality available and public for both men and women. The Heywoods saw governmental restrictions on the use of "obscene" language as the central obstacle to the social change they desired. Angela's frequent contributions to *The Word,* which are excerpted here, defended the use of "obscene" language and anatomically correct expressions (what she called "fleshed realism") if they served the purpose of advancing sexual liberation or equalizing gender relations. She wanted to be able to use such words as *cock, cunt,* and *fuck* to describe more plainly and less clinically the processes of sexual connection and intimacy.

As Linda Gordon argues in *Woman's Body, Woman's Right* (1990), the Heywoods' analysis of sexuality greatly influenced Gilman, for whom restrictive social codes and enforced sexual sublimation only perverted "natural sexual self-regulation" (100). Gilman revised the Heywoods' analysis "two decades later to emphasize its effects on women. The economic dependence of woman on man, in Gilman's analysis, made her sexual attractiveness necessary not only for winning a mate, but as a means of getting a livelihood. . . . Like Heywood [Gilman] believed that the path of progressive social evolution ran toward monogamy and toward reducing the promiscuous sex instinct" (Gordon 100–01).

The text of the following excerpts from *The Word* (Princeton, MA: 1873–1893) are taken from vol. 15, no. 6 (April 1887) and vol. 19, no. 2 (June 1890).

Sex-Nomenclature — Plain English

Truth, the ethical name of fact, serves all in direct statement; objects, actions, ideas, powers must have honest, expressive *names:* responsibility rests not on words but on the Persons using them. Since out of sex-power we all come, since sex issues are so pregnant with cause and consequence begotten by persons, and since well-informed, sincere Integrity in Sex-life bespeaks all other good, Free Lovers are more and more moved to explicit utterance — . . .

The word Penis which is now generally accepted, especially by those resisting further evolution in sex-nomenclature, raised a tumult of revolt amoung "nice" reformers when I first used it, from the platform, ten years ago. For distributing one of my articles on the street containing the printed word penis, Mr. Heywood, after the national Courts had been twice opened as school-rooms for Sex-Ethics, was arrested and held, 16 months, liable to five years in the State Prison; Comstock had said the word penis should not ride in U.S. mails; yet all that is past and penis is now recognized in court, convention, parlors and *the mails*. But, while I feel quite at home with that word, destiny evidently does not intend that English-speaking nations shall be restricted to Latin, a dead language to designate the creative Instrument of Life which Bible Jews reverenced as Jehovah. The idea that words are defiled, or anywise degraded, by their use to denote Sex-Power originates in inferior views of sex, reveals abortive mentality and discredits human nature itself. None object to English words to define other objects: — . . .

What mother can look in the face of her welcome child and not religiously respect the rigid, erect, ready-for-service, persistent male-organ that bred it? Penis is a smooth, musical, almost feminine word;

man's vigor in creative heat is not expressed by it; Latins had character enough to use their own word: our more explicitly pertinent word
honors the English language and ennobles persons having chaste
sense to use it. . . . Hypocricy is no name for that diseased state of
mind which prompts fear and shame in pursuing knowledge or
healthy practice, in words needed to intelligently consider the origin
and processes of human life. . . .

The question is whether girls and boys of the street, who speak
strait to the fact, as sun-light shineth, are truer and purer than
"ladies" in parlors who call man's penis his "teapot," his "thing."
Why not be as truly polite as men in speaking of the object they are
thinking about? Three words challenge Integrity in the human race;[1]
as well rob the Indian of his grunt, or roses of their beauty as try to
take true, Anglo-Saxon words out of the mouths of men and children. In this impulse to be natural I find nothing to be vulgar about;
the trouble is not with children but in the neglect of parents. . . .
Cock is a fowl but not a *foul* word; upright, integral, insisting truth is
the soul of it, sex-wise; welcome the strength of oaks as well as the
sweetness of violets! If man's intuitive genius coins a word of *masculine vigor* he thereby brings to woman the full order of himself; naturally rooted in the use of it, as well tear from him the Instrument of
Life itself, or pull the sun out of sky, as deny him that word. To solve
vexing social problems man must court woman's mind as well as propose to her physical nature; the logic of events seconds the motion of
personal impulse in Wordocratic destiny. As evolutionary action, the
Spirit of Progress, again and again, evolves us into OPEN COURT to
reveal Style and affirm Ethics, thereby accepting rational masculine
Opportunity, the profferd State-schoolroom, beckoning Church femi-
nite intuitive Reciprocity, physical Purpose loyal to mental Enterprise, — Liberty and Analysis will continue to enlighten the world in
electric Salutation, face-to-face attention to central vital imperative
requests of Human Being. Intelligence assures *responsibility,* ever-
serving Inspiration appears in plain words, honest deeds, — Faith
and Practice quickening persons to re-creating, all-animating
Endeavor.

---

[1] *Three words . . . race:* Heywood refers to "fuck" and "cunt" in addition to
"cock"; she maintains that using these three words could improve the sex lives of men
and women because they more accurately describe the "fleshed realism" and urgency
of sexual desire.

The Grace and Use of Sex Life

The truth of the case as I know about it is that man's generative *nature* is NOT "obscene," that his generative *organs* are NOT "obscene," that the generative *act* is NOT "obscene," that the *names* of these organs and acts are NOT "obscene." All this being truth, much thereon depends — mountains of wisdom, billowy oceans of light, a new literature, a new drama, new social harmonies, a new heaven and a new earth, all opening themselves to man and to his complementary, equally well-sexed and beautifully rounded co-partner in Race Re-generation — WOMAN. We ideally assume that both man and woman are, each with equal sense, forcefully and with good intent acting and associating in this sex realm of themselves, using the best mental power they have at the time of such action. The facts of the case are that the two great forces of the universe, Principle and Particle, Mind and Matter, Gravity and Levity, Man and Woman, in deep central phases, are nearing each other for a truer and grander accord, and man is called upon to give his testimony as to the reality and worth of himself. *Is* he well, fully and firmly endowed, or is he the degenerate relic of a rude baboon? Is man a being permanently erect, or is he still half beast, needful to be mentally and physically caged and castrated, harnessed by law and compulsively driven lest of his native self he claw and gore the very life out of his fellow man and present himself to woman as a dissolute and loathsome monster in this nineteenth century?

Men must not emasculate themselves for the sake of "virtue"; they must, they will, recognize manliness and the life element of manliness as the fountain source of good manners. Women and girls demand strong, well-bred generative, vitalizing sex ability. Potency, virility, is the grand basic principle of man, and it holds him, clean, sweet and elegant, to the delicacy of his counterpart. Know it, therefore, ye men, know that we know it, and say to yourselves, each worthy one of you. "I am man, full of the perpetuating power of the race. I am by nature good and healthful, vigorous and wholesome. I am here, well sexed for good purpose, and I will do my work with high-minded recognition of its worth."

Men and women, young and old, deal daily with the physical side of sex, all open to each other. Why not so deal with its mental side and preserve an equilibrium? Think more: Feel less; and so interchange the forces that, better poised, serene and safe, each may gather greater good from the other. The native cleanliness of man must be adhered to. Questioning girlhood looks, as it should, to men and women, expecting and hoping that they will *say* something about this mighty method of creation and the means and instruments by which man, through woman, peoples the world. That they may wisely and safely meet and utilize man's native instinct and specific generative sex peculiarity (what shall I call *it?* — the English and the Latin word, each is "obscene" — this "obscene" *thing* without a name! what *shall* it be called?) when brought face to face with them, as they hope and expect to be, they listen for the voice of experience, hoping that it will speak plainly to their understanding and tell them the truth about man. Shall they be told that he is vile, "nasty," "dirty?" Shall they be answered by a silence that signifies that he is *unmentionable?* Shall they settle down upon a conviction that man is "obscene?"

Conventional religion has frowned, conventional society has sneered and conventional morality has scowled at all these matters these many years. We raise no new shibboleth; we flaunt no personal rags; we simply respond as sympathetic human beings to the cry of misery that goes so far and wide over facts older than history. Men have long waited for this day's coming — for a woman to come and say her say. And I have come. Hear me. I am the product of a sunny and beautiful life, well worthy of examination if ye would know a good woman. I am not ashamed of myself — or of you either. I come at this critical hour unto yourselves as well for your sakes as for the sake of Mr. Heywood, the chosen father of my four children. Don't "criminate" your best blood, your cleanest men and women, because of this passing vertigo of *fear* that man cannot carry himself robust and erect through the slough of intemperance that confronts him here and there — the tangled thicket of ignorance not wrought off by the power of the mind to dissolve misery. I come not to malign, to accuse or upbraid man. My methods are not those of slander or blackmail. I come openly, frankly to *converse* about man, as seriously, as impassionately, as though my subject were the stars above our heads or the rocks beneath our feet. Little girls wish to know, young and middle aged women wish to know, old and experienced women wish to know how to so conduct themselves toward men that man's natural goodness may easiest and best express itself to them and to men, graced with more and more elegance and balanced with more and more personal responsibility within and of himself, in that combination of strength and refinement which makes a man a *gentle*man. About all this they wish to know. . . .

I have gathered material and piled it ready for use in building a new Temple of Peace and Enlightenment, and I am condemned because perchance some of my piles are in the way or unsightly — as if by-standers should rave because in rearing the beautiful new court house in Boston the workmen have temporarily encumbered the sidewalks with uncouth piles of timber, stone and iron, around which dainty pedestrians must pick their steps till Labor and Art have done their work and the nobly designed structure is an accomplished fact. Doth not the legitimacy of my work, the splendid purpose and the crying need of it, justify, or at least excuse, some ruck and litter?

EDWARD BELLAMY

From Looking Backward: 2000–1887

Edward Bellamy (1850–1898) was educated as a lawyer but became a journalist and writer dedicated to social reform and the proletarian movement. In his novel *Looking Backward: 2000–1887* (1888), Bellamy introduced a political movement, Nationalism, and popularized the literary genre of utopianism, which had its origins in the narrative and polemic of Thomas More's *Utopia* (1516). Bellamy's novel was a bestseller, since it touched the nerves of a nation worried about the moral dangers associated with the accumulation of wealth (see Roosevelt in Part Two, Chapter 3 and Veblen in this chapter) and the ever-widening disparity between the working, middle, and leisure classes. *Looking Backward* foresees an end to economic competition, followed by peaceful social evolution. Bellamy's citizens work in a kind of centralized cooperative system, but he pays homage to individualism by sending his citizens home at night, where they consume goods and services according to their private desires. For Bellamy, social progress is achieved by means of rational choices and humane precepts. Bellamy's novel had a multilayered effect on Gilman, who herself wrote several utopias, the most famous of which, *Herland* (1915), concerns an all-women community invaded by three men.

The selections included here — chapters 1 and 6 — detail the before and after of narrator Julian West's time travels. West describes his position in the leisure class of the late nineteenth century in chapter 1, and in chapter 6, Dr. Leete — his host in the year 2000 — describes the overhaul of competitive capitalism for the new state-centered government that equalizes the classes.

The text of the following excerpt is taken from *Looking Backward: 2000–1887* (Cambridge, MA: Riverside, 1889), 7–19; 59–64.

Chapter I

I first saw the light in the city of Boston in the year 1857. "What!" you say, "eighteen fifty-seven? That is an odd slip. He means nineteen fifty-seven, of course." I beg pardon, but there is no mistake. It was about four in the afternoon of December the 26th, one day after Christmas, in the year 1857, not 1957, that I first breathed the east wind of Boston, which, I assure the reader, was at that remote period marked by the same penetrating quality characterizing it in the present year of grace, 2000.

These statements seem so absurd on their face, especially when I add that I am a young man apparently of about thirty years of age, that no person can be blamed for refusing to read another word of what promises to be a mere imposition upon his credulity. Nevertheless I earnestly assure the reader that no imposition is intended, and will undertake, if he shall follow me a few pages, to entirely convince him of this. If I may, then, provisionally assume, with the pledge of justifying the assumption, that I know better than the reader when I was born, I will go on with my narrative. As every schoolboy knows, in the latter part of the nineteenth century the civilization of to-day, or anything like it, did not exist, although the elements which were to develop it were already in ferment. Nothing had, however, occurred to modify the immemorial division of society into the four classes, or nations, as they may be more fitly called, since the differences between them were far greater than those between any nations nowadays, of the rich and the poor, the educated and the ignorant. I myself was rich and also educated, and possessed, therefore, all the elements of happiness enjoyed by the most fortunate in that age. Living in luxury, and occupied only with the pursuit of the pleasures and refinements of life, I derived the means of my support from the labor of others, rendering no sort of service in return. My parents and grandparents had lived in the same way, and I expected that my descendants, if I had any, would enjoy a like existence.

But how could I live without service to the world? you ask. Why should the world have supported in utter idleness one who was able to render service? The answer is that my great-grandfather had accumulated a sum of money on which his descendants had ever since lived. The sum, you will naturally infer, must have been very large not to have been exhausted in supporting three generations in idleness. This, however, was not the fact. The sum had been originally by no means large. It was, in fact, much larger now that three generations had been supported upon it in idleness, than it was at first. This mystery of use without consumption, of warmth without combustion, seems like magic, but was merely an ingenious application of the art now happily lost but carried to great perfection by your ancestors, of shifting the burden of one's support on the shoulders of others. The man who had accomplished this, and it was the end all sought, was said to live on the income of his investments. To explain at this point how the ancient methods of industry made this possible would delay us too much. I shall only stop now to say that interest on investments was a species of tax in perpetuity upon the product of those engaged in industry which a person possessing or inheriting money was able to levy. It must not be supposed that an arrangement which seems so unnatural and preposterous according to modern notions was never criticised by your ancestors. It had been the effort of law-givers and prophets from the earliest ages to abolish interest, or at least to limit it to the smallest possible rate. All these efforts had, however, failed, as they necessarily must so long as the ancient social organizations prevailed. At the time of which I write, the latter part of the nineteenth century, governments had generally given up trying to regulate the subject at all.

By way of attempting to give the reader some general impression of the way people lived together in those days, and especially of the relations of the rich and poor to one another, perhaps I cannot do better than to compare society as it then was to a prodigious coach which the masses of humanity were harnessed to and dragged toilsomely along a very hilly and sandy road. The driver was hunger, and permitted no lagging, though the pace was necessarily very slow. Despite the difficulty of drawing the coach at all along so hard a road, the top was covered with passengers who never got down, even at the steepest ascents. These seats on top were very breezy and comfortable. Well up out of the dust, their occupants could enjoy the scenery at their leisure, or critically discuss the merits of the straining team.

Naturally such places were in great demand and the competition for them was keen, every one seeking as the first end in life to secure a seat on the coach for himself and to leave it to his child after him. By the rule of the coach a man could leave his seat to whom he wished, but on the other hand there were many accidents by which it might at any time be wholly lost. For all that they were so easy, the seats were very insecure, and at every sudden jolt of the coach persons were slipping out of them and falling to the ground, where they were instantly compelled to take hold of the rope and help to drag the coach on which they had before ridden so pleasantly. It was naturally regarded as a terrible misfortune to lose one's seat, and the apprehension that this might happen to them or their friends was a constant cloud upon the happiness of those who rode.

But did they think only of themselves? you ask. Was not their very luxury rendered intolerable to them by comparison with the lot of their brothers and sisters in the harness, and the knowledge that their own weight added to their toil? Had they no compassion for fellow beings from whom fortune only distinguished them? Oh, yes; commiseration was frequently expressed by those who rode for those who had to pull the coach, especially when the vehicle came to a bad place in the road, as it was constantly doing, or to a particularly steep hill. At such times, the desperate straining of the team, their agonized leaping and plunging under the pitiless lashing of hunger, the many who fainted at the rope and were trampled in the mire, made a very distressing spectacle, which often called forth highly creditable displays of feeling on the top of the coach. At such times the passengers would call down encouragingly to the toilers of the rope, exhorting them to patience, and holding out hopes of possible compensation in another world for the hardness of their lot, while others contributed to buy salves and liniments for the crippled and injured. It was agreed that it was a great pity that the coach should be so hard to pull, and there was a sense of general relief when the specially bad piece of road was gotten over. This relief was not, indeed, wholly on account of the team, for there was always some danger at these bad places of a general overturn in which all would lose their seats.

It must in truth be admitted that the main effect of the spectacle of the misery of the toilers at the rope was to enhance the passengers' sense of the value of their seats upon the coach, and to cause them to hold on to them more desperately than before. If the passengers could only have felt assured that neither they nor their friends would ever fall from the top, it is probable that, beyond contributing to the funds for liniments and bandages, they would have troubled themselves extremely little about those who dragged the coach.

I am well aware that this will appear to the men and women of the twentieth century an incredible inhumanity, but there are two facts, both very curious, which partly explain it. In the first place, it was firmly and sincerely believed that there was no other way in which Society could get along, except the many pulled at the rope and the few rode, and not only this, but that no very radical improvement even was possible, either in the harness, the coach, the roadway, or the distribution of the toil. It had always been as it was, and it always would be so. It was a pity, but it could not be helped, and philosophy forbade wasting compassion on what was beyond remedy.

The other fact is yet more curious, consisting in a singular hallucination which those on the top of the coach generally shared, that they were not exactly like their brothers and sisters who pulled at the rope, but of finer clay, in some way belonging to a higher order of beings who might justly expect to be drawn. This seems unaccountable, but, as I once rode on this very coach and shared that very hallucination, I ought to be believed. The strangest thing about the hallucination was that those who had but just climbed up from the ground, before they had outgrown the marks of the rope upon their hands, began to fall under its influence. As for those whose parents and grandparents before them had been so fortunate as to keep their seats on the top, the conviction they cherished of the essential difference between their sort of humanity and the common article was absolute. The effect of such a delusion in moderating fellow feeling for the sufferings of the mass of men into a distant and philosophical compassion is obvious. To it I refer as the only extenuation I can offer for the indifference which, at the period I write of, marked my own attitude toward the misery of my brothers.

In 1887 I came to my thirtieth year. Although still unmarried, I was engaged to wed Edith Bartlett. She, like myself, rode on the top of the coach. That is to say, not to encumber ourselves further with an illustration which has, I hope, served its purpose of giving the reader some general impression of how we lived then, her family was wealthy. In that age, when money alone commanded all that was agreeable and refined in life, it was enough for a woman to be rich to have suitors; but Edith Bartlett was beautiful and graceful also.

My lady readers, I am aware, will protest at this. "Handsome she might have been," I hear them saying, "but graceful never, in the costumes which were the fashion[1] at that period, when the head covering was a dizzy structure a foot tall, and the almost incredible extension of the skirt behind by means of artificial contrivances more thoroughly dehumanized the form than any former device of dressmakers. Fancy any one graceful in such a costume!" The point is certainly well taken, and I can only reply that while the ladies of the twentieth century are lovely demonstrations of the effect of appropriate drapery in accenting feminine graces, my recollection of their great-grandmothers enables me to maintain that no deformity of costume can wholly disguise them.

Our marriage only waited on the completion of the house which I was building for our occupancy in one of the most desirable parts of the city, that is to say, a part chiefly inhabited by the rich. For it must be understood that the comparative desirability of different parts of Boston for residence depended then, not on natural features, but on the character of the neighboring population. Each class or nation lived by itself, in quarters of its own. A rich man living among the poor, an educated man among the uneducated, was like one living in isolation among a jealous and alien race. When the house had been begun, its completion by the winter of 1886 had been expected. The spring of the following year found it, however, yet incomplete, and my marriage still a thing of the future. The cause of a delay calculated to be particularly exasperating to an ardent lover was a series of strikes, that is to say, concerted refusals to work on the part of the brick-layers, masons, carpenters, painters, plumbers, and other trades concerned in house building. What the specific causes of these strikes were I do not remember. Strikes had become so common at that period[2] that people had ceased to inquire into their particular grounds. In one department of industry or another, they had been nearly incessant ever since the great business crisis of 1873. In fact it has come to be the exceptional thing to see any class of laborers pursue their avocation steadily for more than a few months at a time.

The reader who observers the dates alluded to will of course recognize in these disturbances of industry the first and incoherent phase of the great movement which ended in the establishment of the modern industrial system with all its social consequences. This is all so plain

---

[1] *costumes . . . fashion:* Bellamy refers to the debates about dress reform, in which women rejected restrictive garments, such as the corset, for what was considered more mannish clothing.

[2] *Strikes . . . at that period:* The 1880s saw a rise of organized labor protests, many inspired by socialists or foreign "radicals," calling for better working conditions, including eight-hour days and changes in party politics.

in the retrospect that a child can understand it; but not being prophets, we of that day had no clear idea what was happening to us. What we did see was that industrially the country was in a very queer way. The relation between the workingman and the employer, between labor and capital, appeared in some unaccountable manner to have become dislocated. The working classes had quite suddenly and very generally become infected with a profound discontent with their condition, and an idea that it could be greatly bettered if they only knew how to go about it. On every side, with one accord, they preferred demands for higher pay, shorter hours, better dwellings, better educational advantages, and a share in the refinements and luxuries of life, demands which it was impossible to see the way to granting unless the world were to become a great deal richer than it then was. Though they knew something of what they wanted, they knew nothing of how to accomplish it, and the eager enthusiasm with which they thronged about any one who seemed likely to give them any light on the subject lent sudden reputation to many would-be leaders, some of whom had little enough light to give. However chimerical the aspirations of the laboring classes might be deemed, the devotion with which they supported one another in the strikes, which were their chief weapon, and the sacrifices which they underwent to carry them out left no doubt of their dead earnestness.

As to the final outcome of the labor troubles, which was the phrase by which the movement I have described was most commonly referred to, the opinions of the people of my class differed according to individual temperament. The sanguine argued very forcibly that it was in the very nature of things impossible that the new hopes of the workingmen could be satisfied, simply because the world had not the wherewithal to satisfy them. It was only because the masses worked very hard and lived on short commons that the race did not starve outright, and no considerable improvement in their condition was possible while the world, as a whole, remained so poor. It was not the capitalists whom the laboring men were contending with, these maintained, but the iron-bound environment of humanity, and it was merely a question of the thickness of their skulls when they would discover the fact and make up their minds to endure what they could not cure.

The less sanguine admitted all this. Of course the workingmen's aspirations were impossible of fulfillment for natural reasons, but there were grounds to fear that they would not discover this fact until they had made a sad mess of society. They had the votes and the power to do so if they pleased, and their leaders meant they should. Some of these desponding observers went so far as to predict an impending social cataclysm. Humanity, they argued, having climbed to the top round of the ladder of civilization, was about to take a header into chaos, after which it would doubtless pick itself up, turn round, and begin to climb again. Repeated experiences of this sort in historic and prehistoric times possibly accounted for the puzzling bumps on the human cranium. Human history, like all great movements, was cyclical, and returned to the point of beginning. The idea of indefinite progress in a right line was a chimera of the imagination, with no analogue in nature. The parabola of a comet was perhaps a yet better illustration of the career of humanity. Tending upward and sunward from the aphelion[3] of barbarism, the race attained the perihelion[4] of civilization only to plunge downward once more to its nether goal in the regions of chaos.

This, of course, was an extreme opinion, but I remember serious men among my acquaintances who, in discussing the signs of the times, adopted a very similar tone. It was no doubt the common opinion of thoughtful men that society was approaching a critical period which might result in great changes. The labor troubles, their causes, course, and cure, took lead of all other topics in the public prints, and in serious conversation.

The nervous tension of the public mind could not have been more strikingly illustrated than it was by the alarm resulting from the talk of a small band of men who called themselves anarchists, and proposed to terrify the American people into adopting their ideas by threats of violence, as if a mighty nation which had but just put down a rebellion of half its own numbers, in order to maintain its political system, were likely to adopt a new social system out of fear.

As one of the wealthy, with a large stake in the existing order of things, I naturally shared the apprehensions of my class. The particular grievance I had against the working classes at the time of which I write, on account of the effect of their strikes in postponing my wedded bliss, no doubt lent a special animosity to my feeling toward them. . . .

---

[3] *aphelion:* The farthest point from the sun in the path of a celestial body.
[4] *perihelion:* The closest point to the sun in the path of a celestial body.

Chapter VI

Dr. Leete ceased speaking, and I remained silent, endeavoring to form some general conception of the changes in the arrangements of society implied in the tremendous revolution which he had described.

Finally I said, "The idea of such an extension of the functions of government is, to say the least, rather overwhelming."

"Extension!" he repeated, "where is the extension?"

"In my day," I replied, "it was considered that the proper functions of government, strictly speaking, were limited to keeping the peace and defending the people against the public enemy, that is, to the military and police powers."

"And, in heaven's name, who are the public enemies?" exclaimed Dr. Leete. "Are they France, England, Germany, or hunger, cold, and nakedness? In your day governments were accustomed, on the slightest international misunderstanding, to seize upon the bodies of citizens and deliver them over by hundreds of thousands to death and mutilation, wasting their treasures the while like water; and all this oftenest for no imaginable profit to the victims. We have no wars now, and our governments no war powers, but in order to protect every citizen against hunger, cold, and nakedness, and provide for all his physical and mental needs, the function is assumed of directing his industry for a term of years. No, Mr. West, I am sure on reflection you will perceive that it was in your age, not in ours, that the extension of the functions of governments was extraordinary. Not even for the best ends would men now allow their governments such powers as were then used for the most maleficent."

"Leaving comparisons aside," I said, "the demagoguery and corruption of our public men would have been considered, in my day, insuperable objections to any assumption by government of the charge of the national industries. We should have thought that no arrangement could be worse than to entrust the politicians with control of the wealth-producing machinery of the country. Its material interests were quite too much the football of parties as it was."

"No doubt you were right," rejoined Dr. Leete, "but all that is changed now. We have no parties or politicians, and as for demagoguery and corruption, they are words having only an historical significance."

"Human nature itself must have changed very much," I said.

"Not at all," was Dr. Leete's reply, "but the conditions of human life have changed, and with them the motives of human action. The organization of society with you was such that officials were under a constant temptation to misuse their power for the private profit of themselves or others. Under such circumstances it seems almost strange that you dared entrust them with any of your affairs. Nowadays, on the contrary, society is so constituted that there is absolutely no way in which an official, however ill-disposed, could possibly make any profit for himself or any one else by a misuse of his power. Let him be as bad an official as you please, he cannot be a corrupt one. There is no motive to be. The social system no longer offers a premium on dishonesty. But these are matters which you can only understand as you come, with time, to know us better."

"But you have not yet told me how you have settled the labor problem. It is the problem of capital which we have been discussing," I said. "After the nation had assumed conduct of the mills, machinery, railroads, farms, mines, and capital in general of the country, the labor question still remained. In assuming the responsibilities of capital the nation had assumed the difficulties of the capitalist's position."

"The moment the nation assumed the responsibilities of capital those difficulties vanished," replied Dr. Leete. "The national organization of labor under one direction was the complete solution of what was, in your day and under your system, justly regarded as the insoluble labor problem. When the nation became the sole employer, all the citizens, by virtue of their citizenship, became employees, to be distributed according to the needs of industry."

"That is," I suggested, "you have simply applied the principle of universal military service, as it was understood in our day, to the labor question."

"Yes," said Dr. Leete, "that was something which followed as a matter of course as soon as the nation had become the sole capitalist. The people were already accustomed to the idea that the obligation of every citizen, not physically disabled, to contribute his military services to the defense of the nation was equal and absolute. That it was equally the duty of every citizen to contribute his quota of industrial or intellectual services to the maintenance of the nation was equally evident, though it was not until the nation became the employer of labor that citizens were able to render this sort of service with any pretense either of universality or equity. No organization of labor was possible when the employing power was divided among hundreds or thousands of individuals and corporations, between which concert of any kind was neither desired, nor indeed feasible. It constantly happened then that vast numbers who desired to labor could find no opportunity, and on the other hand, those who desired to evade a part or all of their debt could easily do so."

"Service, now, I suppose, is compulsory upon all," I suggested.

"It is rather a matter of course than of compulsion," replied Dr. Leete. "It is regarded as so absolutely natural and reasonable that the idea of its being compulsory has ceased to be thought of. He would be thought to be an incredibly contemptible person who should need compulsion in such a case. Nevertheless, to speak of service being compulsory would be a weak way to state its absolute inevitableness. Our entire social order is so wholly based upon and deduced from it that if it were conceivable that a man could escape it, he would be left with no possible way to provide for his existence. He would have excluded himself from the world, cut himself off from his kind, in a word, committed suicide."

"Is the term of service in this industrial army for life?"

"Oh, no; it both begins later and ends earlier than the average working period in your day. Your workshops were filled with children and old men, but we hold the period of youth sacred to education, and the period of maturity, when the physical forces begin to flag, equally sacred to ease and agreeable relaxation. The period of industrial service is twenty-four years, beginning at the close of the course of education at twenty-one and terminating at forty-five. After forty-five, while discharged from labor, the citizen still remains liable to special calls, in case of emergencies causing a sudden great increase in the demand for labor, till he reaches the age of fifty-five, but such calls are rarely, in fact almost never, made. The fifteenth day of October of every year is what we call Muster Day, because those who have reached the age of twenty-one are then mustered into the industrial service, and at the same time those who, after twenty-four years' service, have reached the age of forty-five, are honorably mustered out. It is the great day of the year with us, whence we reckon all other events our Olympiad, save that it is annual."

JANE ADDAMS

From Twenty Years at Hull-House

Jane Addams (1860–1935) was a social worker and peace advocate, winning (as corecipient) the Nobel Peace Prize in 1931. Brought up to take her place in genteel society as a "sheltered, educated girl," Addams rejected women's place in domesticity and focused her energies on settlement houses, the first of which she founded in Chicago in 1889 with Ellen Gates Starr — her former classmate at the Rockford Female Seminary. Addams believed that women's "moral nature" would give them an edge in the reformation of culture and the amelioration of social ills such as poverty, illiteracy, and public disease. Addams, like Gilman, was a patient of S. Weir Mitchell. She used her convalescence as an excuse to relinquish medical school, deciding instead on social work, especially after having witnessed the suffering of London's "submerged tenth."

As Addams writes in *Twenty Years at Hull-House* (1910), her social experiment was "soberly opened on the theory that the dependence of classes on each other is reciprocal; and that as the social relation is essentially a reciprocal relation, it gives a form of expression that has peculiar value." In the excerpt reprinted below, Addams contends with William Dean Howells's claim that novel reading has affected middle-class Americans' vision of society leading them to romanticize everyday aspects of life. Addams argues that there is in fact a "romance" in cooperative life that leads people to abandon their prejudices and become friends. This was the "romance" of everyday life that motivated Addams to work for such causes as the reform of party politics, the abolishment of child labor, mandatory attendance at school, and the limitation of work hours and establishment of safe working conditions.

The text of the following excerpt is taken from *Twenty Years at Hull-House* (New York: Macmillan, 1910), 65–73; 79–82; 85; 87–91; 94–97; 101–02; 306–09.

The Snare of Preparation

The winter after I left school was spent in the Woman's Medical College of Philadelphia,[1] but the development of the spinal difficulty which had shadowed me from childhood forced me into Dr. Weir

---

[1] *Woman's Medical College of Philadelphia:* One of the first women's medical colleges to be founded in the mid-nineteenth century; this college did not become coed until the 1970s.

Mitchell's hospital for the late spring, and the next winter I was literally bound to a bed in my sister's house for six months. In spite of its tedium, the long winter had its mitigations, for after the first few weeks I was able to read with a luxurious consciousness of leisure, and I remember opening the first volume of Carlyle's "Frederick the Great"[2] with a lively sense of gratitude that it was not Gray's "Anatomy,"[3] having found, like many another, that general culture is a much easier undertaking than professional study. The long illness inevitably put aside the immediate prosecution of a medical course, and although I had passed my examinations creditably enough in the required subjects for the first year, I was very glad to have a physician's sanction for giving up clinics and dissecting rooms and to follow his prescription of spending the next two years in Europe.

Before I returned to America I had discovered that there were other genuine reasons for living among the poor than that of practicing medicine upon them, and my brief foray into the profession was never resumed.

The long illness left me in a state of nervous exhaustion with which I struggled for years, traces of it remaining long after Hull-House was opened in 1889. At the best it allowed me but a limited amount of energy, so that doubtless there was much nervous depression at the foundation of the spiritual struggles which this chapter is forced to record. However, it could not have been all due to my health, for as my wise little notebook sententiously remarked, "In his own way each man must struggle, lest the moral law become a far-off abstraction utterly separated from his active life."

It would, of course, be impossible to remember that some of these struggles ever took place at all, were it not for these selfsame notebooks, in which, however, I no longer wrote in moments of high resolve, but judging from the internal evidence afforded by the books themselves, only in moments of deep depression when overwhelmed by a sense of failure.

One of the most poignant of these experiences, which occurred during the first few months after our landing upon the other side of the Atlantic, was on a Saturday night, when I received an ineradicable impression of the wretchedness of East London, and also saw

---

[2] Carlyle's "Frederick the Great": Thomas Carlyle's (1795–1881) massive study of Frederick II of Prussia.
[3] Gray's "Anatomy": Comprehensive text (1858) on the human body by English anatomist Henry Gray (1825?–1861).

for the first time the overcrowded quarters of a great city at midnight. A small party of tourists were taken to the East End by a city missionary to witness the Saturday night sale of decaying vegetables and fruit, which, owing to the Sunday laws in London, could not be sold until Monday, and, as they were beyond safe keeping, were disposed of at auction as late as possible on Saturday night. On Mile End Road, from the top of an omnibus which paused at the end of a dingy street lighted by only occasional flares of gas, we saw two huge masses of ill-clad people clamoring around two hucksters' carts. They were bidding their farthings and ha'pennies for a vegetable held up by the auctioneer, which he at last scornfully flung, with a gibe for its cheapness, to the successful bidder. In the momentary pause only one man detached himself from the groups. He had bidden in a cabbage, and when it struck his hand, he instantly sat down on the curb, tore it with his teeth, and hastily devoured it, unwashed and uncooked as it was. He and his fellows were types of the "submerged tenth,"[4] as our missionary guide told us, with some little satisfaction in the then new phrase, and he further added that so many of them could scarcely be seen in one spot save at this Saturday night auction, the desire for cheap food being apparently the one thing which could move them simultaneously. They were huddled into ill-fitting, cast-off clothing, the ragged finery which one sees only in East London. Their pale faces were dominated by that most unlovely of human expressions, the cunning and shrewdness of the bargain-hunter who starves if he cannot make a successful trade, and yet the final impression was not of ragged, tawdry clothing nor of pinched and sallow faces, but of myriads of hands, empty, pathetic, nerveless and workworn, showing white in the uncertain light of the street, and clutching forward for food which was already unfit to eat.

Perhaps nothing is so fraught with significance as the human hand, this oldest tool with which man has dug his way from savagery, and with which he is constantly groping forward. I have never since been able to see a number of hands held upward, even when they are moving rhythmically in a calisthenic exercise, or when they belong to a class of chubby children who wave them in eager response to a teacher's query, without a certain revival of this memory, a clutching at the heart reminiscent of the despair and resentment which seized me then.

---

[4] *"submerged tenth"*: A reference to the underclass of London in the 1860s, living in material and spiritual poverty of the worst slums as social outcasts.

For the following weeks I went about London almost furtively, afraid to look down narrow streets and alleys lest they disclose again this hideous human need and suffering. I carried with me for days at a time that curious surprise we experience when we first come back into the streets after days given over to sorrow and death; we are bewildered that the world should be going on as usual and unable to determine which is real, the inner pang or the outward seeming. In time all huge London came to seem unreal save the poverty in its East End. During the following two years on the continent, while I was irresistibly drawn to the poorer quarters of each city, nothing among the beggars of South Italy nor among the saltminers of Austria carried with it the same conviction of human wretchedness which was conveyed by this momentary glimpse of an East London street. It was, of course, a most fragmentary and lurid view of the poverty of East London, and quite unfair. I should have been shown either less or more, for I went away with no notion of the hundreds of men and women who had gallantly identified their fortunes with these empty-handed people, and who, in church and chapel, "relief works," and charities, were at least making an effort towards its mitigation.

Our visit was made in November, 1883, the very year when the *Pall Mall Gazette* exposure started "The Bitter Cry of Outcast London," and the conscience of England was stirred as never before over this joyless city in the East End of its capital. Even then, vigorous and drastic plans were being discussed, and a splendid program of municipal reforms was already dimly outlined. Of all these, however, I had heard nothing but the vaguest rumor.

No comfort came to me then from any source, and the painful impression was increased because at the very moment of looking down the East London street from the top of the omnibus, I had been sharply and painfully reminded of "The Vision of Sudden Death" which had confronted De Quincey[5] one summer's night as he was being driven through rural England on a high mail coach. Two absorbed lovers suddenly appear between the narrow, blossoming hedgerows in the direct path of the huge vehicle which is sure to crush them to their death. De Quincey tries to send them a warning shout, but finds himself unable to make a sound because his mind is hopelessly entangled in an endeavor to recall the exact lines from the "Iliad" which describe the great cry with which Achilles[6] alarmed all

[5] *"The Vision of Sudden Death"* . . . *De Quincey:* In *The English Mail Coach and Other Essays* (1849), by Thomas De Quincey (1785–1859).

[6] *"Iliad"* . . . *Achilles:* The *Iliad*, Homer's epic poem, recounts the story of the Trojan War; Achilles was the greatest Greek warrior against the Trojans.

Asia militant. Only after his memory responds is his will released from its momentary paralysis, and he rides on through the fragrant night with the horror of the escaped calamity thick upon him, but he also bears with him the consciousness that he had given himself over so many years to classic learning — that when suddenly called upon for a quick decision in the world of life and death, he had been able to act only through a literary suggestion.

This is what we were all doing, lumbering our minds with literature that only served to cloud the really vital situation spread before our eyes. It seemed to me too preposterous that in my first view of the horror of East London I should have recalled De Quincey's literary description of the literary suggestion which had once paralyzed him. In my disgust it all appeared a hateful, vicious circle which even the apostles of culture themselves admitted, for had not one of the greatest among the moderns plainly said that "conduct, and not culture is three fourths of human life."

For two years in the midst of my distress over the poverty which, thus suddenly driven into my consciousness, had become to me the "Weltschmerz,"[7] there was mingled a sense of futility, of misdirected energy, the belief that the pursuit of cultivation would not in the end bring either solace or relief. I gradually reached a conviction that the first generation of college women had taken their learning too quickly, had departed too suddenly from the active, emotional life led by their grandmothers and great-grandmothers; that the contemporary education of young women had developed too exclusively the power of acquiring knowledge and of merely receiving impressions; that somewhere in the process of "being educated" they had lost that simple and almost automatic response to the human appeal, that old healthful reaction resulting in activity from the mere presence of suffering or of helplessness; that they are so sheltered and pampered they have no chance even to make "the great refusal."

In the German and French *pensions,* which twenty-five years ago were crowded with American mothers and their daughters who had crossed the seas in search of culture, one often found the mother making real connection with the life about her, using her inadequate German with great fluency, gayly measuring the enormous sheets or exchanging recipes with the German Hausfrau, visiting impartially the nearest kindergarten and market, making an atmosphere of her own, hearty and genuine as far as it went, in the house and on the

---

[7] *"Weltschmerz":* "World pain" (German); sentimental sadness about the state of the world.

street. On the other hand, her daughter was critical and uncertain of her linguistic acquirements, and only at ease when in the familiar receptive attitude afforded by the art gallery and the opera house. In the latter she was swayed and moved, appreciative of the power and charm of the music, intelligent as to the legend and poetry of the plot, finding use for her trained and developed powers as she sat "being cultivated" in the familiar atmosphere of the classroom which had, as it were, become sublimated and romanticized.

I remember a happy busy mother who, complacent with the knowledge that her daughter daily devoted four hours to her music, looked up from her knitting to say, "If I had had your opportunities when I was young, my dear, I should have been a very happy girl. I always had musical talent, but such training as I had, foolish little songs and waltzes and not time for half an hour's practice a day."

The mother did not dream of the sting her words left and that the sensitive girl appreciated only too well that her opportunities were fine and unusual, but she also knew that in spite of some facility and much good teaching she had no genuine talent and never would fulfill the expectations of her friends. She looked back upon her mother's girlhood with positive envy because it was so full of happy industry and extenuating obstacles, with undisturbed opportunity to believe that her talents were unusual. The girl looked wistfully at her mother, but had not the courage to cry out what was in her heart: "I might believe I had unusual talent if I did not know what good music was; I might enjoy half an hour's practice a day if I were busy and happy the rest of the time. You do not know what life means when all the difficulties are removed! I am simply smothered and sickened with advantages. It is like eating a sweet dessert the first thing in the morning."

This, then, was the difficulty, this sweet dessert in the morning and the assumption that the sheltered, educated girl has nothing to do with the bitter poverty and the social maladjustment which is all about her, and which, after all, cannot be concealed, for it breaks through poetry and literature in a burning tide which overwhelms her; it peers at her in the form of heavy-laden market women and underpaid street laborers, gibing her with a sense of her uselessness.

. . . There was also growing within me an almost passionate devotion to the ideals of democracy, and when in all history had these ideals been so thrillingly expressed as when the faith of the fisherman and the slave had been boldly opposed to the accepted moral belief that the well-being of a privileged few might justly be built upon the ignorance and sacrifice of the many? Who was I, with my dreams of universal fellowship, that I did not identify myself with their institutional statement of this belief, as it stood in the little village in which I was born, and without which testimony in each remote hamlet of Christendom it would be so easy for the world to slip back into the doctrines of selection and aristocracy?

In one of the intervening summers between these European journeys I visited a western state where I had formerly invested a sum of money in mortgages. I was much horrified by the wretched conditions among the farmers, which had resulted from a long period of drought, and one forlorn picture was fairly burned into my mind. A number of starved hogs — collateral for a promissory note — were huddled into an open pen. Their backs were humped in a curious, camel-like fashion, and they were devouring one of their own number, the latest victim of absolute starvation or possibly merely the one least able to defend himself against their voracious hunger. The farmer's wife looked on indifferently, a picture of despair as she stood in the door of the bare, crude house, and the two children behind her, whom she vainly tried to keep out of sight, continually thrust forward their faces almost covered by masses of coarse, sunburned hair, and their little bare feet so black, so hard, the great cracks so filled with dust that they looked like flattened hoofs. The children could not be compared to anything so joyous as satyrs, although they appeared but half-human. It seemed to me quite impossible to receive interest from mortgages placed upon farms which might at any season be reduced to such conditions, and with great inconvenience to my agent and doubtless with hardship to the farmers, as speedily as possible I withdrew all my investment. But something had to be done with the money, and in my reaction against unseen horrors I bought a farm near my native village and also a flock of innocent-looking sheep. My partner in the enterprise had not chosen the shepherd's lot as a permanent occupation, but hoped to speedily finish his college course upon half the proceeds of our venture. This pastoral enterprise still seems to me to have been essentially sound, both economically and morally, but perhaps one partner depended too much upon the impeccability of her motives and the other found himself too preoccupied with study to know that it is not a real kindness to bed a sheepfold with straw, for certainly the venture ended in a spectacle scarcely less harrowing than the memory it was designed to obliterate. At least the sight of two hundred sheep with four rotting hoofs each, was not reassuring to one whose conscience craved economic peace. A fortunate series of sales of mutton, wool, and farm enabled the partners to end the enterprise without loss, and they passed on, one to college and the other to Europe, if not wiser, certainly sadder for the experience.

It was during this second journey to Europe that I attended a meeting of the London match girls who were on strike[8] and who met daily under the leadership of well-known labor men of London. The low wages that were reported at the meetings, the phossy jaw[9] which was described and occasionally exhibited, the appearance of the girls themselves I did not, curiously enough, in any wise connect with what was called the labor movement,[10] nor did I understand the efforts of the London trades-unionists,[11] concerning whom I held the vaguest notions. But of course this impression of human misery was added to the others which were already making me so wretched. I think that up to this time I was still filled with the sense which Wells describes in one of his young characters, that somewhere in Church or State are a body of authoritative people who will put things to rights as soon as they really know what is wrong. Such a young person persistently believes that behind all suffering, behind sin and want, must lie redeeming magnanimity. He may imagine the world to be tragic and terrible, but it never for an instant occurs to him that it may be contemptible or squalid or self-seeking. Apparently I looked upon the efforts of the trades-unionists as I did upon those of Frederic Harrison and the Positivists[12] whom I heard the next Sunday in Newton Hall, as a manifestation of "loyalty to humanity" and an attempt to aid in its progress. I was enormously interested in the Positivists during these European years; I imagined that their philosophical conception of man's religious development might include all expressions of that for which so many ages of men have struggled and aspired. . . .

---

[8] *London match girls . . . on strike:* In July 1888, fourteen hundred match girls employed by Bryant and May's London factory struck for better working conditions.

[9] *phossy jaw:* Necrosis, or phosphorous contamination and deterioration of the jaw and teeth.

[10] *labor movement:* Nineteenth-century response to increasing industrialization, including organized strikes and socialist-inspired unions. The Labour Party was founded in 1900 in England.

[11] *trades-unionists:* Trades unions developed from small guilds of craftsmen into larger and more diverse unions, including socialist-inspired unions of unskilled and younger workers.

[12] *Frederic Harrison and the Positivists:* Harrison (1831–1923) was the foremost English advocate and popularizer of positivism, the movement derived from the philosophy of Auguste Comte (1798–1857); Comte argued that human knowledge moved through successive stages to the eventual improvement of the human race.

It is hard to tell just when the very simple plan which afterward developed into the Settlement began to form itself in my mind. It may have been even before I went to Europe for the second time, but I gradually became convinced that it would be a good thing to rent a house in a part of the city where many primitive and actual needs are found, in which young women who had been given over too exclusively to study, might restore a balance of activity along traditional lines and learn of life from life itself; where they might try out some of the things they had been taught and put truth to "the ultimate test of the conduct it dictates or inspires." I do not remember to have mentioned this plan to any one until we reached Madrid in April, 1888.

. . . I can well recall the stumbling and uncertainty with which I finally set it forth to Miss Starr, my old-time school friend, who was one of our party. I even dared to hope that she might join in carrying out the plan, but nevertheless I told it in the fear of that disheartening experience which is so apt to afflict our most cherished plans when they are at last divulged, when we suddenly feel that there is nothing there to talk about, and as the golden dream slips through our fingers we are left to wonder at our own fatuous belief. But gradually the comfort of Miss Starr's companionship, the vigor and enthusiasm which she brought to bear upon it, told both in the growth of the plan and upon the sense of its validity, so that by the time we had reached the enchantment of the Alhambra,[13] the scheme had become convincing and tangible although still most hazy in detail.

A month later we parted in Paris, Miss Starr to go back to Italy, and I to journey on to London to secure as many suggestions as possible from those wonderful places of which we had heard, Toynbee Hall[14] and the People's Palace. So that it finally came about that in June, 1888, five years after my first visit in East London, I found myself at Toynbee Hall equipped not only with a letter of introduction from Canon Fremantle, but with high expectations and a certain belief that whatever perplexities and discouragement concerning the life of the poor were in store for me, I should at least know something at first hand and have the solace of daily activity. I had confidence that although life itself might contain many difficulties, the period of mere passive receptivity had come to an end, and I had at last finished with the everlasting "preparation for life," however ill-prepared I might be.

---

[13] *Alhambra:* The palace of the Moorish kings at Granada, Spain.
[14] *Toynbee Hall:* Erected in 1885 in honor of Arnold Toynbee (1852–1883), social reformer dedicated to the urban poor and pioneer in the social settlement movement.

It was not until years afterward that I came upon Tolstoy's phrase "the snare of preparation," which he insists we spread before the feet of young people, hopelessly entangling them in a curious inactivity at the very period of life when they are longing to construct the world anew and to conform it to their own ideals.

First Days at Hull-House

The next January found Miss Starr and myself in Chicago, searching for a neighborhood in which we might put our plans into execution. In our eagerness to win friends for the new undertaking, we utilized every opportunity to set forth the meaning of the settlement as it had been embodied in Toynbee Hall, although in those days we made no appeal for money, meaning to start with our own slender resources. From the very first the plan received courteous attention, and the discussion, while often skeptical, was always friendly. Professor Swing wrote a commendatory column in the *Evening Journal,* and our early speeches were reported quite out of proportion to their worth. I recall a spirited evening at the home of Mrs. Wilmarth, which was attended by that renowned scholar, Thomas Davidson, and by a young Englishman who was a member of the then new Fabian society[15] and to whom a peculiar glamour was attached because he had scoured knives all summer in a camp of high-minded philosophers in the Adirondacks. Our new little plan met with criticism, not to say disapproval, from Mr. Davidson, who, as nearly as I can remember, called it "one of those unnatural attempts to understand life through coöperative living."

It was in vain we asserted that the collective living was not an essential part of the plan, that we would always scrupulously pay our own expenses, and that at any moment we might decide to scatter through the neighborhood and to live in separate tenements; he still contended that the fascination for most of those volunteering residence would lie in the collective living aspect of the Settlement. His contention was, of course, essentially sound; there is a constant tendency for the residents to "lose themselves in the cave of their own companionship," as the Toynbee Hall phrase goes, but on the other hand, it is doubtless true that the very companionship, the give and take of colleagues, is what tends to keep the Settlement normal and in

[15] *Fabian society:* Society of intellectual socialists committed to reform rather than revolution.

touch with "the world of things as they are." I am happy to say that we never resented this nor any other difference of opinion, and that fifteen years later Professor Davidson handsomely acknowledged that the advantages of a group far outweighed the weaknesses he had early pointed out. He was at that later moment sharing with a group of young men, on the East Side of New York, his ripest conclusions in philosophy and was much touched by their intelligent interest and absorbed devotion. I think that time has also justified our early contention that the mere foothold of a house, easily accessible, ample in space, hospitable and tolerant in spirit, situated in the midst of the large foreign colonies which so easily isolate themselves in American cities, would be in itself a serviceable thing for Chicago. I am not so sure that we succeeded in our endeavors "to make social intercourse express the growing sense of the economic unity of society and to add the social function to democracy." But Hull-House was soberly opened on the theory that the dependence of classes on each other is reciprocal; and that as the social relation is essentially a reciprocal relation, it gives a form of expression that has peculiar value. . . .

On the 18th of September, 1889, Miss Starr and I moved into it, with Miss Mary Keyser, who began by performing the housework, but who quickly developed into a very important factor in the life of the vicinity as well as in that of the household, and whose death five years later was most sincerely mourned by hundreds of our neighbors. In our enthusiasm over "settling," the first night we forgot not only to lock but to close a side door opening on Polk Street, and were much pleased in the morning to find that we possessed a fine illustration of the honesty and kindliness of our new neighbors.

Our first guest was an interesting young woman who lived in a neighboring tenement, whose widowed mother aided her in the support of the family by scrubbing a downtown theater every night. The mother, of English birth, was well bred and carefully educated, but was in the midst of that bitter struggle which awaits so many strangers in American cities who find that their social position tends to be measured solely by the standards of living they are able to maintain. Our guest has long since married the struggling young lawyer to whom she was then engaged, and he is now leading his profession in an eastern city. She recalls that month's experience always with a sense of amusement over the fact that the succession of visitors who came to see the new Settlement invariably questioned her most minutely concerning "these people" without once suspecting that they were talking to one who had been identified with the neighborhood from childhood. I at least was able to draw a lesson from the incident, and I never addressed a Chicago Audience on the subject of the Settlement and its vicinity without inviting a neighbor to go with me, that I might curb any hasty generalization by the consciousness that I had an auditor who knew the conditions more intimately than I could hope to do. . . .

In the very first weeks of our residence Miss Starr started a reading party in George Eliot's "Romola,"[16] which was attended by a group of young women who followed the wonderful tale with unflagging interest. The weekly reading was held in our little upstairs dining room, and two members of the club came to dinner each week, not only that they might be received as guests, but that they might help us wash the dishes afterwards and so make the table ready for the stacks of Florentine photographs.

Our "first resident," as she gayly designated herself, was a charming old lady who gave five consecutive readings from Hawthorne to a most appreciative audience, interspersing the magic tales most delightfully with recollections of the elusive and fascinating author. Years before she had lived at Brook Farm as a pupil of the Ripleys,[17] and she came to us for ten days because she wished to live once more in an atmosphere where "idealism ran high." We thus early found the type of class which through all the years has remained most popular — a combination of a social atmosphere with serious study.

Volunteers to the new undertaking came quickly; a charming young girl conducted a kindergarten in the drawing-room, coming regularly every morning from her home in a distant part of the North Side of the city. Although a tablet to her memory has stood upon a mantel shelf in Hull-House for five years, we still associate her most vividly with the play of little children, first in her kindergarten and then in her own nursery, which furnished "a veritable illustration of Victor Hugo's[18] definition of heaven, — "a place where parents are always young and children always little." Her daily presence for the first two years made it quite impossible for us to become too solemn and self-conscious in our strenuous routine, for her mirth and buoyancy were irresistible and

[16] *George Eliot's "Romola"*: English writer Eliot's (Mary Ann Evans, 1819–1880) 1862–1863 novel set in Florence and detailing political and religious strife.

[17] *Brook Farm . . . the Ripleys*: Brook Farm was a cooperative community (1841–1847) near Roxbury, Massachusetts, run by George Ripley under the aegis of the Transcendental Club; Nathaniel Hawthorne's *The Blithedale Romance* (1852) is based on his experiences as a member of Brook Farm.

[18] *Victor Hugo*: French man of letters (1802–1885) and leader of the romantic movement in France.

her eager desire to share the life of the neighborhood never failed, although it was often put to a severe test. . . .

Public Activities and Investigations

In the earlier years of the American Settlements, the residents were sometimes impatient with the accepted methods of charitable administration and hoped, through residence in an industrial neighborhood, to discover more coöperative and advanced methods of dealing with the problems of poverty which are so dependent upon industrial maladjustment. But during twenty years, the Settlements have seen the charitable people, through their very knowledge of the poor, constantly approach nearer to those methods formerly designated as radical. The residents, so far from holding aloof from organized charity, find testimony, certainly in the National Conferences, that out of the most persistent and intelligent efforts to alleviate poverty, will in all probability arise the most significant suggestions for eradicating poverty. In the hearing before a congressional committee for the establishment of a Children's Bureau, residents in American Settlements joined their fellow philanthropists in urging the need of this indispensable instrument for collecting and disseminating information which would make possible concerted intelligent action on behalf of children.

Mr. Howells has said that we are all so besotted with our novel reading that we have lost the power of seeing certain aspects of life with any sense of reality because we are continually looking for the possible romance. The description might apply to the earlier years of the American Settlement, but certainly the later years are filled with discoveries in actual life as romantic as they are unexpected. If I may illustrate one of these romantic discoveries from my own experience, I would cite the indications of an internationalism as sturdy and virile as it is unprecedented which I have seen in our cosmopolitan neighborhood: when a South Italian Catholic is forced by the very exigencies of the situation to make friends with an Austrian Jew representing another nationality and another religion, both of which cut into all his most cherished prejudices, he finds it harder to utilize them a second time and gradually loses them. He thus modifies his provincialism for if an old enemy working by his side has turned into a friend, almost anything may happen. When, therefore, I became identified with the peace movement[19] both in its International and

---

[19] *peace movement:* Addams helped to create the Woman's Peace Party, which called for negotiation and "mediation" in all conflicts; she advocated pacifism and stressed women's roles in promoting peace and the value of human life.

National Conventions, I hoped that this internationalism engendered in the immigrant quarters of American cities might be recognized as an effective instrument in the cause of peace. I first set it forth with some misgiving before the Convention held in Boston in 1904 and it is always a pleasure to recall the hearty assent given to it by Professor William James.[20]

I have always objected to the phrase "sociological laboratory" applied to us, because Settlements should be something much more human and spontaneous than such a phrase connotes, and yet it is inevitable that the residents should know their own neighborhoods more thoroughly than any other, and that their experiences there should affect their convictions.

Years ago I was much entertained by a story told at the Chicago Woman's Club by one of its ablest members in the discussion following a paper of mine on "The Outgrowths of Toynbee Hall." She said that when she was a little girl playing in her mother's garden, she one day discovered a small toad who seemed to her very forlorn and lonely, although as she did not in the least know how to comfort him, she reluctantly left him to his fate; later in the day, quite at the other end of the garden, she found a large toad, also apparently without family and friends. With a heart full of tender sympathy, she took a stick and by exercising infinite patience and some skill, she finally pushed the little toad through the entire length of the garden into the company of the big toad, when, to her inexpressible horror and surprise, the big toad opened his mouth and swallowed the little one. The moral of the tale was clear applied to people who lived "where they did not naturally belong," although I protested that was exactly what we wanted — to be swallowed and digested, to disappear into the bulk of the people.

Twenty years later I am willing to testify that something of the sort does take place after years of identification with an industrial community.

---

[20] *Professor William James:* Older brother of Henry and Alice (See Part Two, Chapter 5), William James (1842–1910) was a philosopher and Harvard professor.

THORSTEIN VEBLEN

From The Theory of the Leisure Class

The cultural theorist Thorstein Veblen (1857–1929) undertook the massive project of analyzing American culture and its habits. His writings include books and essays on economics, labor, social science, philosophical traditions, and psychology. Veblen argued that Americans had embarked, with the advent of consumer culture, on great waste induced by advertising. He referred to such squandering as "conspicuous consumption," a term that has been associated with his name ever since. Conspicuous consumption and leisure were markers of one's social status; such items as walking canes and household pets, which had no useful function, served as indicators of the wealth and success of their owners. In the selection included here, Veblen analyzes the "ancillary" status of women, arguing that women's secondary status is a vestige of barbaric society. He also assesses the "woman question": the "New-Woman" movement and its goals of "emancipation" and "work" for women. His tone is highly ironic, making his analysis more subversive than many of his readers at first realized.

The text of the following excerpt is taken from *The Theory of the Leisure Class* (1899; New York: Penguin Books, 1981), 354–62.

The several phases of the "woman question" have brought out in intelligible form the extent to which the life of women in modern society, and in the polite circles especially, is regulated by a body of common sense formulated under the economic circumstances of an earlier phase of development. It is still felt that woman's life, in its civil, economic, and social bearing, is essentially and normally a vicarious life, the merit or demerit of which is, in the nature of things, to be imputed to some other individual who stands in some relation of ownership or tutelage to the woman. So, for instance, any action on the part of a woman which traverses an injunction of the accepted schedule of proprieties is felt to reflect immediately upon the honour of the man whose woman she is. There may of course be some sense of incongruity in the mind of any one passing an opinion of this kind on the woman's frailty or perversity; but the common-sense judgment of the community in such matters is, after all, delivered without much hesitation, and few men would question the legitimacy of their sense of an outraged tutelage in any case that might arise. On the other hand, relatively little discredit attaches to a woman through the evil deeds of the man with whom her life is associated.

The good and beautiful scheme of life, then — that is to say the scheme to which we are habituated — assigns to the woman a "sphere" ancillary to the activity of the man; and it is felt that any departure from the traditions of her assigned round of duties is unwomanly. If the question is as to civil rights or the suffrage, our common sense in the matter — that is to say the logical deliverance of our general scheme of life upon the point in question — says that the woman should be represented in the body politic and before the law, not immediately in her own person, but through the mediation of the head of the household to which she belongs. It is unfeminine in her to aspire to a self-directing, self-centred life; and our common sense tells us that her direct participation in the affairs of the community, civil or industrial, is a menace to that social order which expresses our habits of thought as they have been formed under the guidance of the traditions of the pecuniary culture. "All this fume and froth of 'emancipating woman from the slavery of man' and so on, is, to use the chaste and expressive language of Elizabeth Cady Stanton[1] inversely, 'utter rot.' The social relations of the sexes are fixed by nature. Our entire civilisation — that is whatever is good in it — is based on the home." The "home" is the household with a male head. This view, but commonly expressed even more chastely, is the prevailing view of the woman's status, not only among the common run of the men of civilised communities, but among the women as well. Women have a very alert sense of what the scheme of proprieties requires, and while it is true that many of them are ill at ease under the details which the code imposes, there are few who do not recognise that the existing moral order, of necessity and by the divine right of prescription, places the woman in a position ancillary to the man. In the last analysis, according to her own sense of what is good and beautiful, the woman's life is, and in theory must be, an expression of the man's life at the second remove.

But in spite of this pervading sense of what is the good and natural place for the woman, there is also perceptible an incipient development of sentiment to the effect that this whole arrangement of tute-

---

[1] *Elizabeth Cady Stanton:* Stanton (1815–1902) was a suffragist, women's rights advocate, and organizer of the first women's rights convention in Seneca Falls, New York, in 1848; with Susan B. Anthony (1820–1906), Stanton spearheaded the suffrage campaign.

lage and vicarious life and imputation of merit and demerit is somehow a mistake. Or, at least, that even if it may be a natural growth and a good arrangement in its time and place, and in spite of its patent æsthetic value, still it does not adequately serve the more everyday ends of life in a modern industrial community. Even that large and substantial body of well-bred, upper and middle-class women to whose dispassionate, matronly sense of the traditional proprieties this relation of status commends itself as fundamentally and eternally right — even these, whose attitude is conservative, commonly find some slight discrepancy in detail between things as they are and as they should be in this respect. But that less manageable body of modern women who, by force of youth, education, or temperament, are in some degree out of touch with the traditions of status received from the barbarian culture, and in whom there is, perhaps, an undue reversion to the impulse of self-expression and workmanship, — these are touched with a sense of grievance too vivid to leave them at rest.

In this "New-Woman" movement,[2] — as these blind and incoherent efforts to rehabilitate the woman's pre-glacial standing have been named, — there are at least two elements discernible, both of which are of an economic character. These two elements or motives are expressed by the double watchword, "Emancipation" and "Work." Each of these words is recognised to stand for something in the way of a wide-spread sense of grievance. The prevalence of the sentiment is recognised even by people who do not see that there is any real ground for a grievance in the situation as it stands to-day. It is among the women of the well-to-do classes, in the communities which are farthest advanced in industrial development, that this sense of a grievance to be redressed is most alive and finds most frequent expression. That is to say, in other words, there is a demand, more or less serious, for emancipation from all relation of status, tutelage, or vicarious life; and the revulsion asserts itself especially among the class of women upon whom the scheme of life handed down from the régime of status imposes with least mitigation a vicarious life, and in those communities whose economic development has departed farthest from the circumstances to which this traditional scheme is adapted. The demand comes from that portion of womankind which is excluded by the canons of good repute from all

---

[2] *"New-Woman" movement:* A "revolution," occurring roughly from 1890 through 1920, on the part of women who desired social and sexual independence, including dress reform, suffrage, education, and greater work possibilities.

effectual work, and which is closely reserved for a life of leisure and conspicuous consumption.

More than one critic of this new-woman movement has misapprehended its motive. The case of the American "new woman" has lately been summed up with some warmth by a popular observer of social phenomena: "She is petted by her husband, the most devoted and hardworking of husbands in the world. . . . She is the superior of her husband in education, and in almost every respect. She is surrounded by the most numerous and delicate attentions. Yet she is not satisfied. . . . The Anglo-Saxon 'new woman' is the most ridiculous production of modern times, and destined to be the most ghastly failure of the century." Apart from the deprecation — perhaps well placed — which is contained in this presentment, it adds nothing but obscurity to the woman question. The grievance of the new woman is made up of those things which this typical characterisation of the movement urges as reasons why she should be content. She is petted, and is permitted, or even required, to consume largely and conspicuously — vicariously for her husband or other natural guardian. She is exempted, or debarred, from vulgarly useful employment — in order to perform leisure vicariously for the good repute of her natural (pecuniary) guardian. These offices are the conventional marks of the un-free, at the same time that they are incompatible with the human impulse to purposeful activity. But the woman is endowed with her share — which there is reason to believe is more than an even share — of the instinct of workmanship, to which futility of life or of expenditure is obnoxious. She must unfold her life activity in response to the direct, unmediated stimuli of the economic environment with which she is in contact. The impulse is perhaps stronger upon the woman than upon the man to live her own life in her own way and to enter the industrial process of the community at something nearer than the second remove.

So long as the woman's place is consistently that of a drudge, she is, in the average of cases, fairly contented with her lot. She not only has something tangible and purposeful to do, but she has also no time or thought to spare for a rebellious assertion of such human propensity to self-direction as she has inherited. And after the stage of universal female drudgery is passed, and a vicarious leisure without strenuous application becomes the accredited employment of the women of the well-to-do classes, the prescriptive force of the canon of pecuniary decency, which requires the observance of ceremonial futility on their part, will long preserve high-minded women from any sentimental leaning to self-direction and a "sphere of usefulness."

This is especially true during the earlier phases of the pecuniary culture, while the leisure of the leisure class is still in great measure a predatory activity, an active assertion of mastery in which there is enough of tangible purpose of an invidious kind to admit of its being taken seriously as an employment to which one may without shame put one's hand. This condition of things has obviously lasted well down into the present in some communities. It continues to hold to a different extent for different individuals, varying with the vividness of the sense of status and with the feebleness of the impulse to workmanship with which the individual is endowed. But where the economic structure of the community has so far outgrown the scheme of life based on status that the relation of personal subservience is no longer felt to be the sole "natural" human relation; there the ancient habit of purposeful activity will begin to assert itself in the less conformable individuals, against the more recent, relatively superficial, relatively ephemeral habits and views which the predatory and the pecuniary culture have contributed to our scheme of life. These habits and views begin to lose their coercive force for the community or the class in question so soon as the habit of mind and the views of life due to the predatory and the quasi-peaceable discipline cease to be in fairly close accord with the later-developed economic situation. This is evident in the case of the industrious classes of modern communities; for them the leisure-class scheme of life has lost much of its binding force, especially as regards the element of status. But it is also visibly being verified in the case of the upper classes, though not in the same manner.

The habits derived from the predatory and quasi-peaceable culture are relatively ephemeral variants of certain underlying propensities and mental characteristics of the race; which it owes to the protracted discipline of the earlier, proto-anthropoid cultural stage of peaceable, relatively undifferentiated economic life carried on in contact with a relatively simple and invariable material environment. When the habits superinduced by the emulative method of life have ceased to enjoy the sanction of existing economic exigencies, a process of disintegration sets in whereby the habits of thought of more recent growth and of a less generic character to some extent yield the ground before the more ancient and more pervading spiritual characteristics of the race.

In a sense, then, the new-woman movement marks a reversion to a more generic type of human character, or to a less differentiated expression of human nature. It is a type of human nature which is to be characterised as proto-anthropoid, and, as regards the substance if not the form of its dominant traits, it belongs to a cultural stage that may be classed as possibly sub-human. The particular movement or evolutional feature in question of course shares this characterisation with the rest of the later social development, in so far as this social development shows evidence of a reversion to the spiritual attitude that characterises the earlier, undifferentiated stage of economic evolution. Such evidence of a general tendency to reversion from the dominance of the invidious interest[3] is not entirely wanting, although it is neither plentiful nor unquestionably convincing. The general decay of the sense of status in modern industrial communities goes some way as evidence in this direction; and the perceptible return to a disapproval of futility in human life, and a disapproval of such activities as serve only the individual gain at the cost of the collectivity or at the cost of other social groups, is evidence to a like effect. There is a perceptible tendency to deprecate the infliction of pain, as well as to discredit all marauding enterprises, even where these expressions of the invidious interest do not tangibly work to the material detriment of the community or of the individual who passes an opinion on them. It may even be said that in the modern industrial communities the average, dispassionate sense of men says that the ideal human character is a character which makes for peace, good-will, and economic efficiency, rather than for a life of self-seeking, force, fraud, and mastery.

The influence of the leisure class is not consistently for or against the rehabilitation of this proto-anthropoid human nature. So far as concerns the chance of survival of individuals endowed with an exceptionally large share of the primitive traits, the sheltered position of the class favours its members directly by withdrawing them from the pecuniary struggle; but indirectly, through the leisure-class canons of conspicuous waste of goods and effort, the institution of a leisure class lessens the chance of survival of such individuals in the entire body of the population. The decent requirements of waste absorb the surplus energy of the population in an invidious struggle and leave no margin for the non-invidious expression of life. The remoter, less tangible, spiritual effects of the discipline of decency go in the same direction and work perhaps more effectually to the same end. The canons of decent life are an elaboration of the principle of invidious comparison, and they accordingly act consistently to inhibit all non-invidious effort and to inculcate the self-regarding attitude.

---

[3] *invidious interest:* Envy or resentment resulting from competition among the leisure class and the habit of gauging status on the basis of expenditure and leisure.

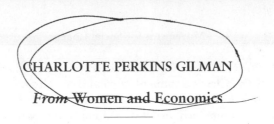

CHARLOTTE PERKINS GILMAN

From Women and Economics

"*Think Husbands Aren't Mainstays*"

"*Dr. Clair's Place*"

From The Living of Charlotte Perkins Gilman

The subtitle of Gilman's famous 1898 economic treatise, *Women and Economics: A Study of the Economic Relation Between Men and Women as a Factor in Social Evolution,* states the premise of Gilman's theory of women's artificial reliance on men for economic security. Decrying women's state of economic development, Gilman argues that racial progress and social evolution cannot continue unless every arbitrary barrier holding women back is struck down. Since housework is not considered employment — (though Gilman would insist that it is and should therefore be professionalized) — women's service to the race as wives and mothers cannot be recognized as productive, as well as reproductive, labor. The text of the first excerpt is from *Women and Economics,* ed. Carl N. Degler (1898; New York: Harper Torchbooks, 1966), 8–22.

In 1909, Gilman was still arguing publicly that women were supported by their husbands. Debating Rev. Anna Shaw at the Carnegie Lyceum, Gilman claimed that women were unpaid servants and parasites on their husbands. Shaw argued the opposite — that women supported men in their household caretaking. The audience voted with Rev. Shaw and against Gilman. The report on the debate, "Think Husbands Aren't Mainstays," that appeared in the *New York Times* on January 7, 1909, gives us insight into the temper of the times and the reaction to Gilman's radical, feminist ideas.

Advocating the "mental hygiene" movement, associated with early psychiatric practice, Gilman wrote the short story "Dr. Clair's Place" in 1915, to testify to the effectiveness of mind cure through psychopathic treatment involving entertainment, productive hobbies, and music and color treatments to stimulate the senses and reawaken bodily pleasures. The story is narrated by one of the fictional Dr. Clair's "graduate patients," who has been afflicted with and cured of neurasthenia, melancholia, and suicidal depression. While the sleep Dr. Clair advocates

317

might be confused with S. Weir Mitchell's rest cure, Gilman takes pains to show that Dr. Clair's treatment is voluntary. The text of the excerpt reprinted here is from the *Forerunner* 6.6 (June 1915): 141–45.

Published posthumously in 1935, Gilman's autobiography, *The Living of Charlotte Perkins Gilman,* details the author's self-construction as an intellectual and a social reformer. It is important to read the following selections from the autobiography not as an account of "the truth" of Gilman's life, but as a narrative she constructs to show how her will and intellect led her to become an acknowledged authority on women's economic status. In the excerpts from *The Living* reprinted here, Gilman describes her self-education through vast reading and narrates her decision to acquire virtues in the style of Ben Franklin. The last two excerpts chronicle her own postpartum depression and her controversial decision to send her daughter to live with her ex-husband and his new wife, her best friend, Grace Ellery Channing. The text is taken from *The Living of Charlotte Perkins Gilman: An Autobiography* (1935; Madison: U of Wisconsin P, 1990), 59–65; 90–98.

From Women and Economics

The economic progress of the race, its maintenance at any period, its continued advance, involve the collective activities of all the trades, crafts, arts, manufactures, inventions, discoveries, and all the civil and military institutions that go to maintain them. The economic status of any race at any time, with its involved effect on all the constituent individuals, depends on their world-wide labors and their free exchange. Economic progress, however, is almost exclusively masculine. Such economic processes as women have been allowed to exercise are of the earliest and most primitive kind. Were men to perform no economic services save such as are still performed by women, our racial status in economics would be reduced to most painful limitations.

To take from any community its male workers would paralyze it economically to a far greater degree than to remove its female workers. The labor now performed by the women could be performed by the men, requiring only the setting back of many advanced workers into earlier forms of industry; but the labor now performed by the men could not be performed by the women without generations of effort and adaptation. Men can cook, clean, and sew as well as women;

but the making and managing of the great engines of modern industry, the threading of earth and sea in our vast systems of transporta-
tion, the handling of our elaborate machinery of trade, commerce,
government, — these things could not be done so well by women in
their present degree of economic development.

This is not owing to lack of the essential human faculties necessary
to such achievements, nor to any inherent disability of sex, but to the
present condition of woman, forbidding the development of this degree of economic ability. The male human being is thousands of years
in advance of the female in economic status. Speaking collectively,
men produce and distribute wealth; and women receive it at their
hands. As men hunt, fish, keep cattle, or raise corn, so do women eat
game, fish, beef, or corn. As men go down to the sea in ships, and
bring coffee and spices and silks and gems from far away, so do
women partake of the coffee and spices and silks and gems the men
bring.

The economic status of the human race in any nation, at any time,
is governed mainly by the activities of the male: the female obtains
her share in the racial advance only through him.

Studied individually, the facts are even more plainly visible, more
open and familiar. From the day laborer to the millionnaire, the
wife's worn dress or flashing jewels, her low roof or her lordly one,
her weary feet or her rich equipage, — these speak of the economic
ability of the husband. The comfort, the luxury, the necessities of life
itself, which the woman receives, are obtained by the husband, and
given her by him. And, when the woman, left alone with no man to
"support" her, tries to meet her own economic necessities, the difficulties which confront her prove conclusively what the general economic status of the woman is. None can deny these patent facts, —
that the economic status of women generally depends upon that of
men generally, and that the economic status of women individually
depends upon that of men individually, those men to whom they are
related. But we are instantly confronted by the commonly received
opinion that, although it must be admitted that men make and distribute the wealth of the world, yet women earn their share of it as
wives. This assumes either that the husband is in the position of employer and the wife as employee, or that marriage is a "partnership,"
and the wife an equal factor with the husband in producing wealth.

Economic independence is a relative condition at best. In the
broadest sense, all living things are economically dependent upon
others, — the animals upon the vegetables, and man upon both. In a

narrower sense, all social life is economically interdependent, man producing collectively what he could by no possibility produce separately. But, in the closest interpretation, individual economic independence among human beings means that the individual pays for what he gets, works for what he gets, gives to the other an equivalent for what the other gives him. I depend on the shoemaker for shoes, and the tailor for coats; but, if I give the shoemaker and the tailor enough of my own labor as a house-builder to pay for the shoes and coats they give me, I retain my personal independence. I have not taken of their product, and given nothing of mine. As long as what I get is obtained by what I give, I am economically independent.

Women consume economic goods. What economic product do they give in exchange for what they consume? The claim that marriage is a partnership, in which the two persons married produce wealth which neither of them, separately, could produce, will not bear examination. A man happy and comfortable can produce more than one unhappy and uncomfortable, but this is as true of a father or son as of a husband. To take from a man any of the conditions which make him happy and strong is to cripple his industry, generally speaking. But those relatives who make him happy are not therefore his business partners, and entitled to share his income.

Grateful return for happiness conferred is not the method of exchange in a partnership. The comfort a man takes with his wife is not in the nature of a business partnership, nor are her frugality and industry. A housekeeper, in her place, might be as frugal, as industrious, but would not therefore be a partner. Man and wife are partners truly in their mutual obligation to their children, — their common love, duty, and service. But a manufacturer who marries, or a doctor, or a lawyer, does not take a partner in his business, when he takes a partner in parenthood, unless his wife is also a manufacturer, a doctor, or a lawyer. In his business, she cannot even advise wisely without training and experience. To love her husband, the composer, does not enable her to compose; and the loss of a man's wife, though it may break his heart, does not cripple his business, unless his mind is affected by grief. She is in no sense a business partner, unless she contributes capital or experience or labor, as a man would in like relation. Most men would hesitate very seriously before entering a business partnership with any woman, wife or not.

If the wife is not, then, truly a business partner, in what way does she earn from her husband the food, clothing, and shelter she receives at his hands? By house service, it will be instantly replied. This is the general misty idea upon the subject, — that women earn all they get, and more, by house service. Here we come to a very practical and definite economic ground. Although not producers of wealth, women serve in the final processes of preparation and distribution. Their labor in the household has a genuine economic value.

For a certain percentage of persons to serve other persons, in order that the ones so served may produce more, is a contribution not to be overlooked. The labor of women in the house, certainly, enables men to produce more wealth than they otherwise could; and in this way women are economic factors in society. But so are horses. The labor of horses enables men to produce more wealth than they otherwise could. The horse is an economic factor in society. But the horse is not economically independent, nor is the woman. If a man plus a valet can perform more useful service than he could minus a valet, then the valet is performing useful service. But, if the valet is the property of the man, is obliged to perform this service, and is not paid for it, he is not economically independent.

The labor which the wife performs in the household is given as part of her functional duty, not as employment. The wife of the poor man, who works hard in a small house, doing all the work for the family, or the wife of the rich man, who wisely and gracefully manages a large house and administers its functions, each is entitled to fair pay for services rendered.

To take this ground and hold it honestly, wives, as earners through domestic service, are entitled to the wages of cooks, housemaids, nursemaids, seamstresses, or housekeepers, and to no more. This would of course reduce the spending money of the wives of the rich, and put it out of the power of the poor man to "support" a wife at all, unless, indeed, the poor man faced the situation fully, paid his wife her wages as house servant, and then she and he combined their funds in the support of their children. He would be keeping a servant: she would be helping keep the family. But nowhere on earth would there be "a rich woman" by these means. Even the highest class of private housekeeper, useful as her services are, does not accumulate a fortune. She does not buy diamonds and sables and keep a carriage. Things like these are not earned by house service.

But the salient fact in this discussion is that, whatever the economic value of the domestic industry of women is, they do not get it. The women who do the most work get the least money, and the women who have the most money do the least work. Their labor is neither given nor taken as a factor in economic exchange. It is held to be their duty as women to do this work; and their economic status bears no relation to their domestic labors, unless an inverse one. Moreover, if they were thus fairly paid, — given what they earned, and no more, — all women working in this way would be reduced to the economic status of the house servant. Few women — or men either — care to face this condition. The ground that women earn their living by domestic labor is instantly forsaken, and we are told that they obtain their livelihood as mothers. This is a peculiar position. We speak of it commonly enough and often with deep feeling, but without due analysis.

In treating of an economic exchange, asking what return in goods or labor women make for the goods and labor given them, — either to the race collectively or to their husbands individually, — what payment women make for their clothes and shoes and furniture and food and shelter, we are told that the duties and services of the mother entitle her to support.

If this is so, if motherhood is an exchangeable commodity given by women in payment for clothes and food, then we must of course find some relation between the quantity or quality of the motherhood and the quantity and quality of the pay. This being true, then the women who are not mothers have no economic status at all; and the economic status of those who are must be shown to be relative to their motherhood. This is obviously absurd. The childless wife has as much money as the mother of many, — more; for the children of the latter consume what would otherwise be hers; and the inefficient mother is no less provided for than the efficient one. Visibly, and upon the face of it, women are not maintained in economic prosperity proportioned to their motherhood. Motherhood bears no relation to their economic status. Among primitive races, it is true, — in the patriarchal period, for instance, — there was some truth in this position. Women being of no value whatever save as bearers of children, their favor and indulgence did bear direct relation to maternity; and they had reason to exult on more grounds than one when they could boast a son. To-day, however, the maintenance of the woman is not conditioned upon this. A man is not allowed to discard his wife because she is barren. The claim of motherhood as a factor in economic exchange is false to-day. But suppose it were true. Are we willing to hold this ground, even in theory? Are we willing to consider motherhood as a business, a form of commercial exchange? Are the cares and duties of the mother, her travail and her love, commodities to be exchanged for bread?

It is revolting so to consider them; and, if we dare face our own thoughts, and force them to their logical conclusion, we shall see that nothing could be more repugnant to human feeling, or more socially and individually injurious, than to make motherhood a trade. Driven off these alleged grounds of women's economic independence; shown that women, as a class, neither produce nor distribute wealth; that women, as individuals, labor mainly as house servants, are not paid as such, and would not be satisfied with such an economic status if they were so paid; that wives are not business partners or co-producers of wealth with their husbands, unless they actually practise the same profession; that they are not salaried as mothers, and that it would be unspeakably degrading if they were, — what remains to those who deny that women are supported by men? This (and a most amusing position it is), — that the function of maternity unfits a woman for economic production, and, therefore, it is right that she should be supported by her husband.

The ground is taken that the human female is not economically independent, that she is fed by the male of her species. In denial of this, it is first alleged that she is economically independent, — that she does support herself by her own industry in the house. It being shown that there is no relation between the economic status of woman and the labor she performs in the home, it is then alleged that not as house servant, but as mother, does woman earn her living. It being shown that the economic status of woman bears no relation to her motherhood, either in quantity or quality, it is then alleged that motherhood renders a woman unfit for economic production, and that, therefore, it is right that she be supported by her husband. Before going farther, let us seize upon this admission, — that she *is* supported by her husband.

Without going into either the ethics or the necessities of the case, we have reached so much common ground: the female of genus homo is supported by the male. Whereas, in other species of animals, male and female alike graze and browse, hunt and kill, climb, swim, dig, run, and fly for their livings, in our species the female does not seek her own living in the specific activities of our race, but is fed by the male.

Now as to the alleged necessity. Because of her maternal duties, the human female is said to be unable to get her own living. As the maternal duties of other females do not unfit them for getting their own living and also the livings of their young, it would seem that the human maternal duties require the segregation of the entire energies of the mother to the service of the child during her entire adult life, or so large a proportion of them that not enough remains to devote to the individual interests of the mother.

Such a condition, did it exist, would of course excuse and justify the pitiful dependence of the human female, and her support by the male. As the queen bee, modified entirely to maternity, is supported, not by the male, to be sure, but by her co-workers, the "old maids," the barren working bees, who labor so patiently and lovingly in their branch of the maternal duties of the hive, so would the human female, modified entirely to maternity, become unfit for any other exertion, and a helpless dependant.

Is this the condition of human motherhood? Does the human mother, by her motherhood, thereby lose control of brain and body, lose power and skill and desire for any other work? Do we see before us the human race, with all its females segregated entirely to the uses of motherhood, consecrated, set apart, specially developed, spending every power of their nature on the service of their children?

We do not. We see the human mother worked far harder than a mare, laboring her life long in the service, not of her children only, but of men; husbands, brothers, fathers, whatever male relatives she has; for mother and sister also; for the church a little, if she is allowed; for society, if she is able; for charity and education and reform, — working in many ways that are not the ways of motherhood.

It is not motherhood that keeps the housewife on her feet from dawn till dark; it is house service, not child service. Women work longer and harder than most men, and not solely in maternal duties. The savage mother carries the burdens, and does all menial service for the tribe. The peasant mother toils in the fields, and the workingman's wife in the home. Many mothers, even now, are wage-earners for the family, as well as bearers and rearers of it. And the women who are not so occupied, the women who belong to rich men, — here perhaps is the exhaustive devotion to maternity which is supposed to justify an admitted economic dependence. But we do not find it even among these. Women of ease and wealth provide for their children better care than the poor woman can; but they do not spend more time upon it themselves, nor more care and effort. They have other occupation.

In spite of her supposed segregation to maternal duties, the human female, the world over, works at extra-maternal duties for hours enough to provide her with an independent living, and then is denied independence on the ground that motherhood prevents her working!

If this ground were tenable, we should find a world full of women who never lifted a finger save in the service of their children, and of men who did *all* the work besides, and waited on the women whom motherhood prevented from waiting on themselves. The ground is not tenable. A human female, healthy, sound, has twenty-five years of life before she is a mother, and should have twenty-five years more after the period of such maternal service as is expected of her has been given. The duties of grandmotherhood are surely not alleged as preventing economic independence.

The working power of the mother has always been a prominent factor in human life. She is the worker *par excellence,* but her work is not such as to affect her economic status. Her living, all that she gets, — food, clothing, ornaments, amusements, luxuries, — these bear no relation to her power to produce wealth, to her services in the house, or to her motherhood. These things bear relation only to the man she marries, the man she depends on, — to how much he has and how much he is willing to give her. The women whose splendid extravagance dazzles the world, whose economic goods are the greatest, are often neither houseworkers nor mothers, but simply the women who hold most power over the men who have the most money. The female of genus homo is economically dependent on the male. He is her food supply.

"Think Husbands Aren't Mainstays"

A good audience of men and women, with the latter predominating, filled the Carnegie Lyceum last evening to listen to a debate on the question, "Is the Wife Supported by Her Husband?" Mrs. Charlotte Perkins Gilman contended that she was and the Rev. Anna Shaw that she was not. Voting a loud and emphatic "No" at the close of the debate the audience decided that the married woman earned her board and clothes. There were a few voices that voted in the affirmative. Lawyer Edmond Kelly summed up.

"There is no other female except that of the human race that is continuously fed by her husband," said Mrs. Gilman in opening the debate. "The only apparent exception is the hornbill, a bird, the female of which is built into its nest, while it is hatching its eggs, only a hole being left for its bill, to which the male bird continually carries food. But even the female hornbill when the young appear proceeds to get its own living like every other self-respecting being."

The woman who not only does not do the work of her own house but keeps a housekeeper to look after her servants is a mere parasite, Mrs. Gilman said, and the working wife is an unpaid servant, merely a comfort and a luxury agreeable to have if a man can afford it.

"I do not say that the human female is fed by the male, but the reverse," said Miss Shaw. "The woman working in the home gives an equivalent in labor to the finances of the man. I should not say that my father supported my mother and the eight children in the family; I should say my mother supported my father and the eight children. When my father sent a barrel of flour to the house my mother did not drive the children to it and say, 'Children, here is the food your father has sent for you.' She made it into bread and her work in doing that was greater than his work in providing the money for it.

"So if a bolt of cloth came to the house my mother did not wind it around the eight children as if it was the American flag: She first made it into clothes. The conditions in the house have now changed, but the economic value of a woman's work is the same.

"Recently I was advising a nephew of mine who was thinking of marrying not to do so because he had only an income sufficient for himself and he had nothing saved.

"'I never expect, and no man does,' he replied, 'to save a dollar until he has a wife to save it for him.'

"There is not only a financial side of domestic life," continued Miss Shaw; "there is the spiritual and ethical, and in the financial a woman gives work for what she gets, and work is the only value in the world. Men and women work together and support each other."

"Mr. Wiley, who is trying to give us pure food, recently refused a large increase to his income," said Mrs. Gilman, to offset the story of Miss Shaw's nephew, "because he said he was a bachelor and did not need it."

She was warmly applauded when she said that women could not have a financial standing in the family because they were not rewarded in proportion to their work.

"The woman who works hardest gets least money, and the one who works least gets the most," she said. "If a young woman typewriter married a delicate man and he stayed at home and did the work of the house, doing it well, as men can, would she be supporting him? What would he say?"

"If I was asked to decide this as a lawyer," said Mr. Kelly, "I should say that even if a man couldn't bear his wife he was obliged to support her. But as a Judge I should say that this was a friendly, not to say collective, suit, each side working for the same end from a different standpoint."

The debate was under the auspices of the Women's Trades Union League, and girls representing different unions, the vest makers', telegraphers', and others, wearing colored sashes, acted as ushers. Mrs. Stanton Blatch and Miss Mary Drier, President of the league, were on the platform.

"Dr. Clair's Place"

"You must count your mercies," said her friendly adviser. "There's no cloud so dark but it has a silver lining, you know, — count your mercies."

She looked at her with dull eyes that had known no hope for many years. "Perhaps you will count them for me: Health — utterly broken and gone since I was twenty-four. Youth gone too — I am thirty-eight. Beauty — I never had it. Happiness — buried in shame and bitterness these fourteen years. Motherhood — had and lost. Usefulness — I am too weak even to support myself. I have no money. I have no friends. I have no home. I have no work. I have no hope in life." Then a dim glow of resolution flickered in those dull eyes. "And what is more I don't propose to bear it much longer."

It is astonishing what people will say to strangers on the cars. These two sat on the seat in front of me, and I had heard every syllable of their acquaintance, from the "Going far?" of the friendly adviser to this confidence as to proposed suicide. The offerer of cheerful commonplaces left before long, and I took her place, or rather the back-turned seat facing it, and studied the Despairing One.

Not a bad looking woman, but so sunk in internal misery that her expression was that of one who had been in prison for a life-time. Her eyes had that burned out look, as hopeless as a cinder heap; her voice a dreary grating sound. The muscles of her face seemed to sag downward. She looked at the other passengers as if they were gray ghosts and she another. She looked at the rushing stretches we sped past as if the window were ground glass. She looked at me as if I were invisible.

"This," said I to myself, "is a case for Dr. Clair."

It was not difficult to make her acquaintance. There was no more protective tissues about her than about a skeleton. I think she would have showed the utter wreck of her life to any who asked to look, and not have realized their scrutiny. In fact it was not so much that she exhibited her misery, as that she was nothing but misery — whoever saw her, saw it.

I was a "graduate patient" of Dr. Clair, as it happened; and had the usual enthusiasms of the class. Also I had learned some rudiments of the method, as one must who has profited by it. By the merest touch of interest and considerate attention I had the "symptoms" — more than were needed; by a few indicated "cases I had known" I touched that spring of special pride in special misery which seems to be co-existent with life; and then I had an account which would have been more than enough for Dr. Clair to work on.

Then I appealed to that queer mingling of this pride and of the deep instinct of social service common to all humanity, which Dr. Clair had pointed out to me, and asked her —

"If you had an obscure and important physical disease you'd be glad to leave your body to be of service to science, wouldn't you?" She would — anyone would, of course.

"You can't leave your mind for an autopsy very well, but there's one thing you can do — if you will; and that is, give this clear and prolonged self-study you have made, to a doctor I know who is profoundly interested in neurasthenia — melancholia — all that kind of thing. I really think you'd be a valuable — what shall I say — exhibit."

She gave a little muscular smile, a mere widening of the lips, the heavy gloom of her eyes unaltered.

"I have only money enough to go where I am going," she said. "I have just one thing to do there — that ought to be done before I — leave."

There was no air of tragedy about her. She was merely dead, or practically so.

"Dr. Clair's is not far from there, as it happens, and I know her well enough to be sure she'd be glad to have you come. You won't mind if I give you the fare up there — purely as a scientific experiment? There are others who may profit by it, you see."

She took the money, looking at it as if she hardly knew what it was, saying dully: "All right — I'll go." And, after a pause, as if she had half forgotten it, "Thank you."

And some time later she added: "My name is Octavia Welch."

Dr. Willy Clair — she was Southern, and really named Willy — was first an eager successful young teacher, very young. Then she spent a year or two working with atypical children. Then, profoundly interested, she plunged into the study of medicine and became as eager and successful a doctor as she had been a teacher. She specialized in psychopathic work, developed methods of her own, and with the initial aid of some of her numerous "G. P.'s" established a sanatorium in Southern California. There are plenty of such for "lungers,"[1] but this was of quite another sort.

She married, in the course of her full and rich career, one of her patients, a young man who was brought to her by his mother — a despairing ruin. It took five years to make him over, but it was done, and then they were married. He worshipped her; and she said he was the real mainstay of the business — and he was, as far as the business part of it went.

Dr. Clair was about forty when I sent Octavia Welch up there. She had been married some six years, and had, among her other assets, two splendid children. But other women have husbands and children, also splendid — no one else had a psycho-sanatorium. She didn't call it that; the name on the stationery was just "The Hills."

On the southern face of the Sierra Madres she had bought a highlying bit of mesa-land and steep-sided arroyo, and gradually added to it both above and below, until it was now quite a large extent of land. Also she had her own water; had built a solid little reservoir in her deepest canyon; had sunk an artesian well far up in the hills behind, ran a windmill to keep the water up, and used the overflow for power as well as for irrigation. That had made the whole place such garden land as only Southern California knows. From year to year, the fame of the place increased, and its income also, she built and improved; and now it was the most wonderful combination of peaceful, silent wilderness and blossoming fertility.

The business end of it was very simply managed. On one of the steep flat-topped mesas, the one nearest the town that lay so pleasantly in the valley below, she had built a comfortable, solid little Center surrounded by small tent-houses. Here she took ordinary patients, and provided them not only with good medical advice but with good beds and good food, and further with both work and play.

"The trouble with Sanatoriums," said Dr. Clair to me — we were friends since the teaching period, and when I broke down at my

---

[1] *sanatorium . . . for "lungers"*: Hospitals designed for the custodial care of tuberculosis patients; Gilman's Dr. Clair plans her psycho-sanatorium as a therapeutic retreat for her psychological cases.

teaching I came to her and was mended — "is that the sick folks have nothing to do but sit about and think of themselves and their 'cases.' Now I let the relatives come too; some well ones are a resource; and I have one or more regularly engaged persons whose business it is to keep them busy — and amused."

She did. She had for the weakest ones just chairs and hammocks; but these were moved from day to day so that the patient had new views. There was an excellent library, and all manner of magazines and papers. There were picture-puzzles too, with little rimmed trays to set them up in — they could be carried here and there, but not easily lost. Then there were all manner of easy things to learn to do; basket-work, spinning, weaving, knitting, embroidery; it cost very little to the patients and kept them occupied. For those who were able there was gardening and building — always some new little place going up, or a walk or something to make. Her people enjoyed life every day. All this was not compulsory, of course, but they mostly liked it.

In the evenings there was music, and dancing too, for those who were up to it; cards and so on, at the Center; while the others went off to their quiet little separate rooms. Everyone of them had a stove in it; they were as dry and warm as need be — which is more than you can say of most California places.

People wanted to come and board — well people, I mean — and from year to year she ran up more cheap comfortable little shacks, each with its plumbing, electric lights and heating — she had water-power, you see — and a sort of caffeteria place where they could eat together or buy food and take to their homes. I tell you it was popular. Mr. Wolsey (that's her husband, but she kept on as Dr. Clair) ran all this part of it, and ran it well. He had been a hotel man.

All this was only a foundation for her real work with the psychopathic cases. But it was a good foundation, and it paid in more ways than one. She not only had the usual string of Grateful Patients, but another group of friends among those boarders. And there's one thing she did which is well worth the notice of other people who are trying to help humanity — or to make money — in the same way.

You know how a hotel will have a string of "rules and regulations" strung up in every room? She had that — and more. She had a "Plain Talk With Boarders" leaflet, which was freely distributed — a most amusing and useful document. I haven't one here to quote directly, but it ran like this:

You come here of your own choice, for your own health and pleasure, freely; and are free to go when dissatisfied. The comfort and happiness of such a place depends not only on the natural resources, on
the quality of the accommodations, food, service and entertainment,
but on the behavior of the guests.

Each visitor is requested to put in a complaint at the office, not only
of fault in the management, but of objectionable conduct on the part of
patrons.

Even without such complaint any visitor who is deemed detrimental
in character or behavior will be requested to leave.

She did it too. She made the place so attractive, so *comfortable,* in
every way so desirable, that there was usually a waiting list; and if
one of these fault-finding old women, or noisy, disagreeable young
men, or desperately flirtatious persons got in, Dr. Clair would have it
out with them.

"I am sorry to announce that you have been black-balled by seven of
your fellow guests. I have investigated the complaints and find them
well founded. We herewith return your board from date (that was
always paid in advance) and shall require your room tomorrow."

People didn't like to own to a thing like that — not and tell the
truth. They did tell all manner of lies about the place, of course; but
she didn't mind — there were far more people to tell the truth. I can
tell you a boarding-place that is as beautiful, as healthful, as exquis-
itely clean and comfortable, and as reasonable as hers in price, is
pretty popular. Then, from year to year, she enlarged and developed
her plan till she had, I believe, the only place in the world where a
sick soul could go and be sure of help.

Here's what Octavia Welch wrote about it. She showed it to me
years later:

I was dead — worse than dead — buried — decayed — gone to
foul dirt. In my body I still walked heavily — but out of accumulated
despair I had slowly gathered about enough courage to drop that burden. Then I met the Friend on the train who sent me to Dr. Clair. . . .

I sent the post-card, and was met at the train, by a motor. We
went up and up — even I could see how lovely the country was — up
into the clear air, close to those shaggy, steep dry mountains.

We passed from ordinary streets with pretty homes through a region of pleasant groups of big and little houses which the driver said
was the "boarding section," through a higher place where he said
there were "lungers and such," on to "Dr. Clair's Place."

The Place was apparently just out of doors. I did not dream then of all the cunningly contrived walks and seats and shelters, the fruits and flowers just where they were wanted, the marvellous mixture of natural beauty and ingenious loving-kindness, which make this place the wonder it is. All I saw was a big beautiful wide house, flower-hung, clean and quiet, and this nice woman, who received me in her office, just like any doctor, and said:

"I'm glad to see you, Mrs. Welch. I have the card announcing your coming, and you can be of very great service to me, if you are willing. Please understand — I do not undertake to cure you; I do not criticize in the least your purpose to leave an unbearable world. That I think is the last human right — to cut short unbearable and useless pain. But if you are willing to let me study you awhile and experiment on you a little — it won't hurt, I assure you — "

Sitting limp and heavy, I looked at her, the old slow tears rolling down as usual. "You can do anything you want to," I said. "Even hurt — what's a little more pain? — if it's any use."

She made a thorough physical examination, blood-test and all. Then she let me tell her all I wanted to about myself, asking occasional questions, making notes, setting it all down on a sort of chart. "That's enough to show me the way for a start," she said. "Tell me — do you dread anaesthetics?"

"No," said I, "so that you give me enough."

"Enough to begin with," she said cheerfully. "May I show you your room?"

It was the prettiest room I had ever seen, as fair and shining as the inside of a shell.

"You are to have the bath treatment first," she said, "then a sleep — then food — I mean to keep you very busy for a while."

So I was put through an elaborate course of bathing, shampoo, and massage, and finally put to bed, in that quiet fragrant rosy room, so physically comfortable that even my corroding grief and shame were forgotten, and I slept.

It was late next day when I woke. Someone had been watching all the time, and at any sign of waking a gentle anaesthetic was given, quite unknown to me. My special attendant, a sweet-faced young giantess from Sweden, brought me a tray of breakfast and flowers, and asked if I liked music.

"It is here by your bed," she said. "Here is the card — you ask for what you like, and just regulate the sound as you please."

There was a light moveable telephone, with a little megaphone attached to the receiver, and a long list of records. I had only to order what I chose, and listen to it as close or as far off as I desired. Between certain hours there was a sort of "table d'hote" to which we could listen or not as we liked, and these other hours wherein we called for favorites. I found it very restful. There were books and magazines, if I chose, and a rose-draped balcony with a hammock where I could sit or lie, taking my music there if I preferred. I was bathed and oiled and rubbed and fed; I slept better than I had for years, and more than I knew at the time, for when the restless misery came up they promptly put me to sleep and kept me there.

Dr. Clair came in twice a day, with notebook and pencil, asking me many careful questions; not as a physician to a patient, but as an inquiring scientific searcher for valuable truths. She told me about other cases, somewhat similar to my own, consulted me in a way, as to this or that bit of analysis she had made; and again and again as to certain points in my own case. Insensibly under her handling this grew more and more objective, more as if it were someone else who was suffering, and not myself.

"I want you to keep a record, if you will," she said, "when the worst paroxysms come, the overwhelming waves of despair, or that slow tidal ebb of misery — here's a little chart by your bed. When you feel the worst will you be so good as to try either of these three things, and note the result. The Music, as you have used it, noting the effect of the different airs. The Color — we have not introduced you to the color treatment yet — see here — "

She put in my hand a little card of buttons, as it were, with wire attachments. I pressed one; the room was darkened, save for the tiny glow by which I saw the color list. Then, playing on the others, I could fill the room with any lovely hue I chose, and see them driving, mingling, changing as I played.

"There," she said, "I would much like to have you make a study of these effects and note it for me. Then — don't laugh! — I want you to try tastes, also. Have you never noticed the close connection between a pleasant flavor and a state of mind?"

For this experiment I had a numbered set of little sweetmeats, each delicious and all beneficial, which I was to deliberately use when my misery was acute or wearing. Still further, she had a list of odors for similar use.

This bedroom and balcony treatment lasted a month, and at the end of that time I was so much stronger physically that Dr. Clair said, if I could stand it, she wanted to use certain physical tests on me. I almost hated to admit how much better I felt, but told her I would do anything she said. Then I was sent out with my attending maiden up the canyon to a certain halfway house. There I spent another month of physical enlargement. Part of it was slowly graduated mountain climbing; part was bathing and swimming in a long narrow pool. I grew gradually to feel the delight of mere ascent, so that every hilltop called me, and the joy of plain physical exhaustion and utter rest. To come down from a day on the mountain, to dip deep in that pure water and be rubbed by my ever careful masseuse; to eat heartily of the plain but delicious food, and sleep — out of doors now, on a pine needle bed — that was new life.

My misery and pain and shame seemed to fade into a remote past, as a wholesome rampart of bodily health grew up between me and it.

Then came the People.

This was her Secret. She had People there who were better than Music and Color and Fragrance and Sweetness, — People who lived up there with work and interests of their own, some teachers, some writers, some makers of various things, but all Associates in her wonderful cures.

It was the People who did it. First she made my body as strong as might be, and rebuilt my worn-out nerves with sleep — sleep — sleep. Then I had the right Contact, Soul to Soul.

And now? Why now I am still under forty; I have a little cottage up here in these heavenly hills; I am a well woman; I earn my living by knitting and teaching it to others. And out of the waste and wreck of my life — which is of small consequence to me, I can myself serve to help new-comers. I am an Associate — even I! And I am Happy!

From The Living of Charlotte Perkins Gilman

Girlhood — If Any

. . . Each year I would lay out one, or perhaps two, desirable traits to acquire, and in a leisurely manner acquire them. We are told to hitch our wagons to a star, but why pick on Betelgeuse?[2] I selected more modestly, more gradually, carefully choosing for imitation

---

[2] *Betelgeuse:* Red giant star in the constellation Orion.

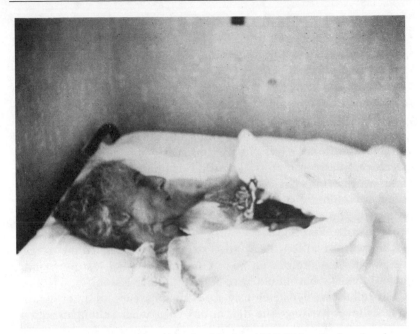

Charlotte Perkins Gilman on her deathbed in 1935. Taken by her daughter, Katharine Stetson Chamberlin. Reproduced by permission of the Schlesinger Library, Radcliffe College.

some admired character in history or fiction, not too far beyond me, and then catching up; followed by the selection of another more difficult. At the time when this long effort calamitously ended I had got as far as Socrates. . . .[3]

One New Year's prayer heard during these years provoked me almost to interrupt. The minister was droning along in the "Thou knowest" style — (if it was plain "you know" how inelegant it would be!) "Thou knowest how a year ago we made good resolutions and have broken them. Thou knowest how we undertook to develop a better character and have failed." . . . I wanted to speak out and tell him that there was one person present who had undertaken to develop better character and succeeded, who had made good resolutions and kept them every one. But I was careful not to make too many at once.

---

[3] *Socrates:* Ancient Greek philosopher (469–399 B.C.); Plato's teacher.

One of the later and more difficult was the establishing a habit of absolute truthfulness. Not that I had ever been a liar, but that now I meant to practise the most meticulous accuracy, to become so reliable that people would declare, "If Charlotte Perkins says so, it's so." There came a day when I was sorely tried in the acquirement of this stern reputation. A young acquaintance, well known for the exact opposite, called on me with solemn purpose.

"Charlotte, I have heard that you said that I lied! You didn't, did you?" This was not easy. We are more carefully trained in not hurting people's feelings than stark truth. But I hung on to my principles, and the arms of my chair. "Yes, I did."

She was thunder-struck, had never dreamed that I would own it, protested, "But you don't believe it do you?" Another effort, harder than the last. "Yes, I do."

That was a real test. Being successfully met it enabled me to meet others with less strain. And as to consequences — I lost a "friend," but she gained what should have been a salutary lesson.

Self-righteous? Tremendously so. For eight years I did not do anything I thought wrong, and did, at any cost, what I thought right — which is not saying that all my decisions were correct.

Power and Glory

Among our immediate associates I heard nothing of the larger movements of the time, but with the Channing family[4] and their friends was a larger outlook, while in my steady reading I lived in the world as a whole. This world seemed to be suffering from many needless evils, evils for which some remedies seemed clear to me even then. I was deeply impressed with the injustices under which women suffered, and still more with the ill effects upon all mankind of this injustice; but was not in close touch with the suffrage movement.[5] Once I went to a meeting of some earnest young temperance workers,[6] but was not at all at home in that atmosphere of orthodox reli-

---

[4] *Channing family:* The Channings were a famous nineteenth-century family of professors, pastors, and writers. Grace Ellery Channing (1862–1937) was Charlotte's friend from girlhood. The family had moved to Pasadena for Grace's health. Grace eventually married Charlotte's first husband, Walter Stetson.

[5] *suffrage movement:* Late-nineteenth- and early-twentieth-century movement to give women the vote.

[6] *temperance workers:* Women and men devoted to banning the consumption of alcohol; the first such ban took place in Maine in 1851.

gion and strong emotion. My method was to approach a difficulty as if it was a problem in physics, trying to invent the best solution.

It was a period of large beginnings in many lines. "Strong-minded" girls were going to college under criticism and ridicule, the usual curriculum in those days was held quite beyond "the feminine mind." Some thirty years later, an editor, sadly impressed by the majority of prize-takers being girls, protested that these same curricula were "evidently too feminine." I recall part of a bit of newspaper wit at the time, about 1880:

> She'd a great and varied knowledge she'd picked up at a woman's
>   college,
> Of quadratics, hydrostatics and pneumatics[7] very vast;
> She'd discuss, the learned charmer, the theology of Brahma,[8]
> All the 'ologies of the colleges and the knowledges of the past.
>
> She knew all the forms and features of the prehistoric creatures,
> Icththyosaurus, megliosaurus, plestosaurus, and many more,
> She could talk about the Tuscans and the Greeks and the
>   Etruscans,
> All the scandals of the Vandals and the sandals that they wore.
>
> But she couldn't get up a dinner for a gaunt and starving sinner,
> Or concoct a simple supper for her poor old hungry Poppa,
> For she never was constructed on the old domestic plan.

The "charmer" before marriage and the cook afterward were the prevailing ideas at the time, as indeed they still are in some places. But things began to change, women appeared in stores and offices — I once met a man from Maine who told me how he was severely criticized for employing saleswomen — so unwomanly! such a public occupation! Doubtless our Civil War, like this last one, drove women to do what men had done before. Clothing changed, there appeared the "tailored suit," even made by men! made for street wear, plain and serviceable. Ideas began to change. Mona Caird in England produced that then much talked of book, *Is Marriage a Failure?*[9]

Education was advancing, the kindergarten making slow but sure impression. Far-seeing mothers were beginning to give their children

[7] *quadratics, hydrostatics, pneumatics:* Branches of physics and mechanics dealing with space, fluids, and gasses.

[8] *Brahma:* The universal creative force in Hindu religious thought; also Brahmins, the name for upper-class New England society.

[9] *Mona Caird . . . Is Marriage a Failure?:* Mona Caird (1858–1932), British feminist journalist and novelist, famous for attacking the institution of marriage as equal to prostitution and slavery. Caird published her collected essays in 1897, *The Morality of Marriage.*

information about sex. There was a start toward an equal standard in chastity, equal *up*, not down as at present. A little paper called *The Alpha* was brought out in Washington to urge this ideal. The first poem I had published was in this tiny paper. It was called "One Girl of Many," a defense of what was then termed the "fallen" woman.

In the present-day lowering of standards of behavior one exhibition of ignorance and meanness of spirit is the charge, "You did the same in your day, only you were secretive about it." Any one whose memory covers fifty years knows better. There were plenty of young men who were "fast," and some girls who were called "pretty gay," but even at that the words had different meanings.

For instance there was just one damsel in all my acquaintance who was certainly "gay." She was so proud of the "wasp-waist" admired at the time, that she tied her corset-laces to the bedpost and pulled, to draw them tight enough. Her behavior with young men was so much discussed that I determined to learn something of her.

"You know I am not 'in society,'" I told her. "I am interested as a student, and I wish you would tell me just what the game is — what it is that you are trying to do." She recognized my honest interest, and was quite willing to explain. Considering thoughtfully she presently replied, "It is to get a fellow so he cannot keep his hands off you — and then not let him touch you."

This was bad enough in all conscience, but she was the only one out of scores. Among the more daring girls there was some discussion of whether, when a fellow came home with you, he might also claim a kiss. But there was also discussion, quite popular, of this question of Emerson's, "Does the soul underlie a condition of infinite remoteness?" I remember coming to the conclusion that it did.

On sleighing-parties and "straw-rides" there was a good deal of holding hands and some kissing, all in cheerful, giggling groups; and I do not doubt that going to ride with what livery-stable men called a "courtin' horse" involved a good deal of hugging. But the standards and general behavior of "nice girls" — and most of them were nice — are shown clearly in the books of Louisa M. Alcott[10] and Mrs. A. D. T. Whitney.[11]

Among the many splendid movements of the late nineteenth century was one dear to my heart, that toward a higher physical culture.

---

[10] *Louisa M. Alcott (1832–1888):* Writer of domestic fiction; most famous for *Little Women* (1868).

[11] *Mrs. A.D.T. Whitney (1824–1906):* Novelist, poet, and writer of nonfiction works for children and adults, including *Faith Gartney's Girlhood* (1863).

In Europe and then here the impulse was felt, building gymnasiums, practice of calisthenics even for girls, and the rapid development of college athletics. In this line of improvement I was highly ambitious. With right early training I could easily have been an acrobat, having good nervous coördination, strength, courage, and excellent balancing power.

High places never daunted me. As a child in Rehoboth[12] I used to parade the ridge-pole of the barn and stand on the very end of it, to alarm people driving by — mischievous wretch! In the simple task of walking rails, railroad rails, I have kept on steadily over a hundred of them. Dancing would have been a passion, but dancing was one of the many forbiddings of my youth.

What I did determine on and largely secure was the development of a fine physique. Blaikie's *How To Get Strong and How To Stay So*[13] was a great help. Early country life gave a good start, and housework kept some muscles in use, the best of it is scrubbing the floor. That is good back and arm work, and not dusty or steamy like sweeping and washing. . . .

Needless to say that I never wore corsets, that my shoes were "common sense" (and more people seemed to have common sense at the time), that all my clothing "hung from the shoulder" — the custom being to drag all those heavy skirts from the waist. I devised a sort of side-garter suspender, to which skirts were buttoned, and, not a flat bandage to make a woman look like a boy, but after many trials evolved a species of brassière which supported the breasts without constriction anywhere. It had elastic over the shoulder and under the arm, allowing perfect freedom for breathing and arm-motion, while snug and efficient as a support. . . .

The Breakdown

In those days a new disease had dawned on the medical horizon. It was called "nervous prostration." No one knew much about it, and there were many who openly scoffed, saying it was only a new name for laziness. To be recognizably ill one must be confined to one's bed, and preferably in pain.

---

[12] *Rehoboth:* Rehoboth, Massachusetts, in Bristol County, where Gilman and her mother and brother lived between 1863 and 1873.

[13] *Blaikie's How To Get Strong and How To Stay So:* William Blaikie (1843–1904) published this physical exercise book in 1879, followed by his *Sound Bodies for Our Boys and Girls* (1883), in which he urged "the need and ease of physical culture" for the public at large.

That a heretofore markedly vigorous young woman, with every comfort about her, should collapse in this lamentable manner was inexplicable. "You should use your will," said earnest friends. I had used it, hard and long, perhaps too hard and too long; at any rate it wouldn't work now.

"Force some happiness into your life," said one sympathizer. "Take an agreeable book to bed with you, occupy your mind with pleasant things." She did not realize that I was unable to read, and that my mind was exclusively occupied with unpleasant things. This disorder involved a growing melancholia, and that, as those know who have tasted it, consists of every painful mental sensation, shame, fear, remorse, a blind oppressive confusion, utter weakness, a steady brainache that fills the conscious mind with crowding images of distress.

The misery is doubtless as physical as a toothache, but a brain, of its own nature, gropes for reasons for its misery. Feeling the sensation fear, the mind suggests every possible calamity; the sensation shame — remorse — and one remembers every mistake and misdeeds of a lifetime, and grovels to the earth in abasement.

"If you would get up and do something you would feel better," said my mother. I rose drearily, and essayed to brush up the floor a little, with a dustpan and small whiskbroom, but soon dropped those implements exhausted, and wept again in helpless shame.

I, the ceaselessly industrious, could do no work of any kind. I was so weak that the knife and fork sank from my hands — too tired to eat. I could not read nor write nor paint nor sew nor talk nor listen to talking, nor anything. I lay on that lounge and wept all day. The tears ran down into my ears on either side. I went to bed crying, woke in the night crying, sat on the edge of the bed in the morning and cried — from sheer continuous pain. Not physical, the doctors examined me and found nothing the matter.

The only physical pain I ever knew, besides dentistry and one sore finger, was having the baby, and I would rather have had a baby every week than suffer as I suffered in my mind. A constant dragging weariness miles below zero. Absolute incapacity. Absolute misery. To the spirit it was as if one were an armless, legless, eyeless, voiceless cripple. Prominent among the tumbling suggestions of a suffering brain was the thought, "You did it yourself! You did it yourself! You had health and strength and hope and glorious work before you — and you threw it all away. You were called to serve humanity, and you cannot serve yourself. No good as a wife, no good as a mother, no good at anything. And you did it yourself!" . . .

The baby? I nursed her for five months. I would hold her close — that lovely child! — and instead of love and happiness, feel only pain. The tears ran down on my breast. . . . Nothing was more utterly bitter than this, that even motherhood brought no joy.

The doctor said I must wean her, and go away, for a change. So she was duly weaned and throve finely on Mellins' Food,[14] drinking eagerly from the cup — no bottle needed. With mother there and the excellent maid I was free to go. . . .

Pasadena was then but little changed from the sheep-ranch it used to be. The Channings had bought a beautiful place by the little reservoir at the corner of Walnut Street and Orange Avenue. Already their year-old trees were shooting up unbelievably, their flowers a glory.

The Arroyo Seco was then wild and clean, its steep banks a tangle of loveliness. About opposite us a point ran out where stood a huge twin live oak, still to be seen, but not to be reached by strangers. There was no house by them then, callas bloomed by the hydrant, and sweet alyssum ran wild in the grass.

Never before had my passion for beauty been satisfied. This place did not seem like earth, it was paradise. Kind and congenial friends, pleasant society, amusement, out-door sports, the blessed mountains, the long, unbroken sweep of the valley, with snow-peaks at the far eastern end — with such surroundings I recovered so fast, to outward appearance at least, that I was taken for a vigorous young girl. Hope came back, love came back, I was eager to get home to husband and child, life was bright again.

The return trip was made a little sooner than I had intended because of a railroad war of unparalleled violence which drove prices down unbelievably. It seemed foolish not to take advantage of it, and I bought my ticket from Los Angeles to Chicago, standard, for $5.00. If I had waited for a few days more it could have been bought for $1. The eastern end was unchanged, twenty dollars from Chicago to Boston, but that cut-throat competition was all over the western roads, the sleepers had every berth filled, often two in each. So many traveled that it was said the roads made quite as much money as usual.

Leaving California in March, in the warm rush of its rich spring, I found snow in Denver, and from then on hardly saw the sun for a

---

[14] *Mellins' Food:* Best known of the prepared infant foods to substitute nutritionally for breast milk; it was diluted with water and milk and was first prepared by English chemist Gustav Mellin (1803–1876) in the 1860s.

fortnight. I reached home with a heavy bronchial cold, which hung on long, the dark fog rose again in my mind, the miserable weakness — within a month I was as low as before leaving. . . .

This was a worse horror than before, for now I saw the stark fact — that I was well while away and sick while at home — a heartening prospect! Soon ensued the same utter prostration, the unbearable inner misery, the ceaseless tears. A new tonic had been invented, Essence of Oats, which was given me, and did some good for a time. I pulled up enough to do a little painting that fall, but soon slipped down again and stayed down. An old friend of my mother's, dear Mrs. Diman, was so grieved at this condition that she gave me a hundred dollars and urged me to go away somewhere and get cured.

At that time the greatest nerve specialist in the country was Dr. S. W. Mitchell of Philadelphia. Through the kindness of a friend of Mr. Stetson's living in that city, I went to him and took "the rest cure"; went with the utmost confidence, prefacing the visit with a long letter giving "the history of the case" in a way a modern psychologist would have appreciated. Dr. Mitchell only thought it proved self-conceit. He had a prejudice against the Beechers. "I've had two women of your blood here already," he told me scornfully. This eminent physician was well versed in two kinds of nervous prostration; that of the business man exhausted from too much work, and the society woman exhausted from too much play. The kind I had was evidently beyond him. But he did reassure me on one point — there was no dementia, he said, only hysteria.

I was put to bed and kept there. I was fed, bathed, rubbed, and responded with the vigorous body of twenty-six. As far as he could see there was nothing the matter with me, so after a month of this agreeable treatment he sent me home, with this prescription:

"Live as domestic a life as possible. Have your child with you all the time." (Be it remarked that if I did but dress the baby it left me shaking and crying — certainly far from a healthy companionship for her, to say nothing of the effect on me.) "Lie down an hour after each meal. Have but two hours' intellectual life a day. And never touch pen, brush or pencil as long as you live."

I went home, followed those directions rigidly for months, and came perilously near to losing my mind. The mental agony grew so unbearable that I would sit blankly moving my head from side to side — to get out from under the pain. Not physical pain, not the least "headache" even, just mental torment, and so heavy in its nightmare gloom that it seemed real enough to dodge.

I made a rag baby, hung it on a doorknob and played with it. I would crawl into remote closets and under beds — to hide from the grinding pressure of that profound distress. . . .

Finally, in the fall of '87, in a moment of clear vision, we agreed to separate, to get a divorce. There was no quarrel, no blame for either one, never an unkind word between us, unbroken mutual affection — but it seemed plain that if I went crazy it would do my husband no good, and be a deadly injury to my child.

What this meant to the young artist, the devoted husband, the loving father, was so bitter a grief and loss that nothing would have justified breaking the marriage save this worse loss which threatened. It was not a choice between going and staying, but between going, sane, and staying, insane. If I had been of the slightest use to him or to the child, I would have "stuck it," as the English say. But this progressive weakening of the mind made a horror unnecessary to face; better for that dear child to have separated parents than a lunatic mother.

We had been married four years and more. This miserable condition of mind, this darkness, feebleness and gloom, had begun in those difficult years of courtship, had grown rapidly worse after marriage, and was now threatening utter loss; whereas I had repeated proof that the moment I left home I began to recover. It seemed right to give up a mistaken marriage.

Our mistake was mutual. If I had been stronger and wiser I should never have been persuaded into it. Our suffering was mutual too, his unbroken devotion, his manifold cares and labors in tending a sick wife, his adoring pride in the best of babies, all coming to naught, ending in utter failure — we sympathized with each other but faced a bitter necessity. The separation must come as soon as possible, the divorce must wait for conditions.[15]

If this decision could have been reached sooner it would have been much better for me, the lasting mental injury would have been less. Such recovery as I have made in forty years, and the work accomplished, seem to show that the fear of insanity was not fulfilled, but the effects of nerve bankruptcy remain to this day. So much of my many failures, of misplay and misunderstanding and "queerness" is due to this lasting weakness, and kind friends so unfailingly refuse to

---

[15] *the divorce must wait for conditions:* Although the number of divorces in America doubled between 1880 and 1900 due to the liberalizing of divorce laws, divorces were only granted if certain situations pertained: desertion, adultery, lunacy, conviction of a felony. Beyond adultery, legally valid grounds for divorce varied greatly from state to state.

allow for it, to believe it, that I am now going to some length in stating the case.

That part of the ruin was due to the conditions of childhood I do not doubt, and part to the rigid stoicism and constant effort in character-building of my youth; I was "over-trained," had wasted my substance in riotous — virtues. But that the immediate and continuing cause was mismarriage is proved by the instant rebound when I left home and as instant relapse on returning.

After I was finally free, in 1890, wreck though I was, there was a surprising output of work, some of my best. I think that if I could have had a period of care and rest then, I might have made full recovery. But the ensuing four years in California were the hardest of my life. The result has been a lasting loss of power, total in some directions, partial in others; the necessity for a laboriously acquired laziness foreign to both temperament and conviction, a crippled life.

But since my public activities do not show weakness, nor my writings, and since brain and nerve disorder is not visible, short of lunacy or literal "prostration," this lifetime of limitation and wretchedness, when I mention it, is flatly disbelieved. When I am forced to refuse invitations, to back out of work that seems easy, to own that I cannot read a heavy book, apologetically alleging this weakness of mind, friends gibber amiably, "I wish I had your mind!" I wish they had, for a while, as a punishment for doubting my word. What confuses them is the visible work I have been able to accomplish. They see activity, achievement, they do not see blank months of idleness; nor can they see what the work would have been if the powerful mind I had to begin with had not broken at twenty-four.

5

Literary Responses
and Literary Culture

How did the issues of sex-expression and self-expression enter into the literary culture Gilman was part of? Although Gilman claims in her autobiography that she never thought of "The Yellow Wallpaper" as "literary," she wrote her 1892 short story in the context of literary battles over what American national culture should become — a debate that took place largely in the magazines that were an integral part of that culture. Editors of prestigious periodicals, such as William Dean Howells and Horace Scudder at the *Atlantic Monthly,* attempted to influence the ways in which American culture would develop. Howells suggested, in *Criticism and Fiction* (1891), that the American short story was "nearer perfection in an all-round sense" (see p. 353) than the products of almost any other literary culture, a success he attributed to the development of American belletristic journals, such as the *Atlantic*.

Gilman argued that all writing should have a "purpose" — that it should help to promote political and social reform. In her autobiography, she chastised the writer Grant Allen for deviating from his purposeful sociological criticism to write frivolous New Women novels. Gilman chose the short story as one form for conveying her message, but not necessarily because of its "American" or aesthetic perfection. Gilman also wrote hundreds of poems, many novels, and several book-length treatises. The short story fitted her literary purposes insofar as it freed her to illustrate her frustration with the medical profession's prescriptions for the nervous conditions that to her were a product of the restrictions that middle-class notions of ideal womanhood placed on women in her culture. "The Yellow Wallpaper" is distinct from Gilman's other work in the level of sustained critical attention it has received and the literary prestige it has been accorded.

The "American girl" was a subject that preoccupied many American realist writers. In *Criticism and Fiction,* Howells worries about what sort of fiction is appropriate for young audiences, and James frequently made the "American girl," in all of her complacencies and contradictions, the subject of his fiction. The negative review that Gilman's short story received from one of her contemporaries, "M.D." (initials which do not necessarily suggest that the response was from a doctor), displays concern for the influence Gilman's story might have on young mothers. As Henry James observes in his April 8, 1883, notebook entries about his 1886 novel, *The Bostonians,* writing an "*American* tale" means addressing "the situation of women, the decline of the sentiment of sex, the agitation on their behalf" (see p. 363). James made the status of women and the battle between the sexes the subject of his own fictions, especially *The Bostonians.*

Gilman was not the only American woman author to attempt to justify herself through her writing or to explore the conflicts that many women internalized. Alice James's diary throws into relief the status of the female invalid in both British and American culture. Like many nineteenth-century women, Alice James — Henry and William James's invalid sister — kept a diary, in which she recorded her frustrations when her illness kept her from pursuing a profession. Some critics have argued that James's illness *was* her profession. Her brothers were obsessed with their own and others' disabilities, although both had famous careers: Henry as a writer and William as one of the best-known psychologists and philosophers of his day. Like Gilman's narrator, Alice James attests to the loneliness of being marked as an "invalid" and writes in order to explore her self and express the frustration of being confined. The very first sentence of her *Diary* might have been written by Gilman's heroine: "I think that if I get into the habit of writing a bit about what happens, or rather doesn't happen, I may lose a little of the sense of loneliness and desolation which abides with me" (see p. 365). James claims that writing is a way to express, even to cure, herself.

It is illuminating to consider Gilman's explorations of conflicted femininity in connection with Kate Chopin's fiction, which also explores the limitations and cultural restrictions women face in acting out their desires. Kate Chopin's now famous (and once banned) 1899 novel, *The Awakening,* chronicles its heroine's coming to terms with the monolithic social ideal of the "mother-woman," an ideal defined solely in terms of women's reproductivity. Whereas Chopin's heroine in *The Awakening* commits suicide, Gilman's in "The Yellow Wallpaper" does not die; she goes mad, which may — for Gilman — represent a far worse fate.

The growing social sciences of human behavior and psychology influenced Chopin's writing as well as Gilman's. By the turn of the century, the short story written in the style of a "case study" had become a recognizable literary form. Chopin's "Story of an Hour" (1894) is a "case history" of a woman who dies of shock after learning that the husband she is told has died in an accident is still alive. Chopin's story is included here to illustrate the ironic voice she and Gilman shared in writing about the limitations of domesticity.

CHARLOTTE PERKINS GILMAN

"Why I Wrote The Yellow Wallpaper?"

On the Reception of "The Yellow Wallpaper"

Appearing in the *Forerunner* (the monthly magazine that Gilman wrote and published from 1909 to 1916), this one-page justification of her famous short story is a forceful statement of Gilman's own literary defense. Whether or not her portrayal of S. Weir Mitchell's treatment — or of his reaction to her story — is accurate, this response does suggest how Gilman came to see "work" as the one redeeming and definite cure for personal ailments, as well as public limitations on women's roles. As Gilman wrote in her autobiography, one must always write "with a purpose" if one's writing is to find an audience (see p. 351). In "Why I Wrote The Yellow Wallpaper?" Gilman claims that the story "worked," thereby giving double emphasis to her admonishment to all humans that productive labor is crucial to social progress. The story stresses Gilman's primary commitment to social reform and to changing the world in concrete ways rather than to the production of lasting artistic works. The text of the first excerpt is taken from the *Forerunner* 4.10 (October 1913): 271.

The second selection here is from Gilman's autobiography, and it constitutes her recollection of the reception of "The Yellow Wallpaper" by contemporaneous men of letters such as William Dean Howells and Horace Scudder, the editor of the *Atlantic*, who rejected the story when Howells sent it to him in 1890. Gilman interprets the subsequent interest in her short story as a vindication of her efforts to write "with a purpose" — to effect social change through her writing. Her version of the story's publication history has been challenged by recent critics who hold that Howells recommended the story's publication and that S. Weir Mitchell never recanted his position on the rest cure (Dock 57, 62). Nevertheless, Gilman's backward glance on the story provides another vivid context for reading her interpretation of the cultural scene she entered and engaged.

The text of the second excerpt is taken from *The Living of Charlotte Perkins Gilman: An Autobiography* (1935; Madison: U of Wisconsin P, 1990), 118–21.

"Why I Wrote The Yellow Wallpaper?"

Many and many a reader has asked that. When the story first came out, in the *New England Magazine* about 1891, a Boston physician made protest in *The Transcript*. Such a story ought not to be written, he said; it was enough to drive anyone mad to read it.

Another physician, in Kansas I think, wrote to say that it was the best description of incipient insanity he had ever seen, and — begging my pardon — had I been there?

Now the story of the story is this:

For many years I suffered from a severe and continuous nervous breakdown tending to melancholia — and beyond. During about the third year of this trouble I went, in devout faith and some faint stir of hope, to a noted specialist in nervous diseases,[1] the best known in the country. This wise man put me to bed and applied the rest cure, to which a still good physique responded so promptly that he concluded there was nothing much the matter with me, and sent me home with solemn advice to "live as domestic a life as far as possible," to "have but two hours' intellectual life a day," and "never to touch pen, brush or pencil again as long as I lived." This was in 1887.

---

[1] *a noted specialist in nervous diseases:* Dr. S. Weir Mitchell.

I went home and obeyed those directions for some three months, and came so near the border line of utter mental ruin that I could see over. Then, using the remnants of intelligence that remained, and helped by a wise friend, I cast the noted specialist's advice to the winds and went to work again — work, the normal life of every human being; work, in which is joy and growth and service, without which one is a pauper and a parasite; ultimately recovering some measure of power.

Being naturally moved to rejoicing by this narrow escape, I wrote *The Yellow Wallpaper,* with its embellishments and additions to carry out the ideal (I never had hallucinations or objections to my mural decorations) and sent a copy to the physician who so nearly drove me mad. He never acknowledged it.

The little book is valued by alienists[2] and as a good specimen of one kind of literature. It has to my knowledge saved one woman from a similar fate — so terrifying her family that they let her out into normal activity and she recovered.

But the best result is this. Many years later I was told that the great specialist had admitted to friends of his that he had altered his treatment of neurasthenia since reading *The Yellow Wallpaper.*

It was not intended to drive people crazy, but to save people from being driven crazy, and it worked.

On the Reception of "The Yellow Wallpaper"

Besides "Similar Cases" the most outstanding piece of work of 1890 was "The Yellow Wallpaper." It is a description of a case of nervous breakdown beginning something as mine did, and treated as Dr. S. Weir Mitchell treated me with what I considered the inevitable result, progressive insanity.

This I sent to Mr. Howells, and he tried to have the *Atlantic Monthly* print it, but Mr. Scudder, then the editor, sent it back with this brief card:

DEAR MADAM,
    Mr. Howells has handed me this story.
    I could not forgive myself if I made others as miserable as I have made myself!
                    Sincerely yours,
                        H. E. SCUDDER.

[2] *alienists:* Nineteenth-century term for psychiatrists.

This was funny. The story was meant to be dreadful, and succeeded. I suppose he would have sent back one of Poe's on the same ground. Later I put it in the hands of an agent who had written me, one Henry Austin, and he placed it with the *New England Magazine*. Time passed, much time, and at length I wrote to the editor of that periodical to this effect:

> DEAR SIR,
>   A story of mine, "The Yellow Wallpaper," was printed in your issue of May, 1891.[3] Since you do not pay on receipt of ms. nor on publication, nor within six months of publication, may I ask if you pay at all, and if so at what rates?

They replied with some heat that they had paid the agent, Mr. Austin. He, being taxed with it, denied having got the money. It was only forty dollars anyway! As a matter of fact I never got a cent for it till later publishers brought it out in book form, and very little then. But it made a tremendous impression. A protest was sent to the Boston *Transcript*, headed "Perilous Stuff" —

> TO THE EDITOR OF THE TRANSCRIPT:
>   In a well-known magazine has recently appeared a story entitled "The Yellow Wallpaper." It is a sad story of a young wife passing the gradations from slight mental derangement to raving lunacy. It is graphically told, in a somewhat sensational style, which makes it difficult to lay aside, after the first glance, til it is finished, holding the reader in morbid fascination to the end. It certainly seems open to serious question if such literature should be permitted in print.
>   The story can hardly, it would seem, give pleasure to any reader, and to many whose lives have been touched through the dearest ties by this dread disease, it must bring the keenest pain. To others, whose lives have become a struggle against an heredity of mental derangement, such literature contains deadly peril. Should such stories be allowed to pass without severest censure?
>
>   M.D.

Another doctor, one Brummel Jones, of Kansas City, Missouri, wrote me in 1892 concerning this story, saying: "When I read 'The Yellow Wallpaper' I was very much pleased with it; when I read it again I was delighted with it, and now that I have read it again I am

---

[3] *May, 1891:* Gilman is wrong here about the date for the publication of "The Yellow Wallpaper" in *New England Magazine;* the story appeared in January 1892 (her story "The Giant Wisteria" appeared in June 1891).

overwhelmed with the delicacy of your touch and the correctness of portrayal. From a doctor's standpoint, and I am a doctor, you have made a success. So far as I know, and I am fairly well up in literature, there has been no detailed account of incipient insanity." Then he tells of an opium addict who refused to be treated on the ground that physicians had no real knowledge of the disease, but who returned to Dr. Jones, bringing a paper of his on the opium habit, shook it in his face and said, "Doctor, you've been there!" To which my correspondent added, "Have you ever been — er ——; but of course you haven't." I replied that I had been as far as one could go and get back.

One of the *New England Magazine*'s editors wrote to me asking if the story was founded on fact, and I gave him all I decently could of my case as a foundation for the tale. Later he explained that he had a friend who was in similar trouble, even to hallucinations about her wallpaper, and whose family were treating her as in the tale, that he had not dared show them my story till he knew that it was true, in part at least, and that when he did they were so frightened by it, so impressed by the clear implication of what ought to have been done, that they changed her wallpaper and the treatment of the case — and she recovered! This was triumph indeed.

But the real purpose of the story was to reach Dr. S. Weir Mitchell, and convince him of the error of his ways. I sent him a copy as soon as it came out, but got no response. However, many years later, I met some one who knew close friends of Dr. Mitchell's who said he had told them that he had changed his treatment of nervous prostration since reading "The Yellow Wallpaper." If that is a fact, I have not lived in vain.

A few years ago Mr. Howells asked leave to include this story in a collection he was arranging — *Masterpieces of American Fiction*. I was more than willing, but assured him that it was no more "literature" than my other stuff, being definitely written "with a purpose." In my judgment it is a pretty poor thing to write, to talk, without a purpose.

WILLIAM DEAN HOWELLS

From Criticism and Fiction

William Dean Howells (1837–1920) was one of the most influential nineteenth-century American writers. In his career as a novelist, playwright, editor, and critic, he was at the forefront of cultural debates for some fifty years. He is perhaps best known as the author of several novels of critical realism (fictions that address and attempt to correct social ills): *A Modern Instance* (1882), *The Rise of Silas Lapham* (1885), and *A Hazard of New Fortunes* (1890), which treat divorce, materialism, and radicalism respectively. Howells also wrote novels devoted to miscegenation (*An Imperative Duty* [1891]) and corrupt evangelicism (*The Leatherwood God* [1916]). During his career, he wrote thirty-five novels, thirty-five plays, and four books of poetry, as well as works of criticism and cultural analysis. The centrality of Howells's career is suggested by the curious fact that he was the longtime friend of two writers who are seen as embodying opposite trends in American fiction: Henry James and Samuel Clemens (Mark Twain). Howells and James engaged in a lifelong correspondence about American culture and literature, debating what would constitute a truly American fiction.

In *Criticism and Fiction* (1891), Howells discusses the achievements of a particularly American literary genre, the short story. He praises women short story writers, along with their "Americanisms," as being true and faithful to the American scene. He also advises authors not to write "things for young girls to read which you would be put out-of-doors for saying to them." Sensational novels and the emotions they incite are cheap, according to Howells, who wants American literature to concern itself with a balanced view of sex rather than greater sexual freedom. While Howells acknowledges the passion of love, he also believes in the power and passion of grief, avarice, pity, ambition, hate, envy, devotion, and friendship. These, too, are essential to the great range of the American story.

It is important to note that Howells's daughter, Winifred (1863–1889), died while under S. Weir Mitchell's care. She was twenty-six years old, and the cause of her death was not completely clear. However, Mitchell's autopsy revealed that she had an organic disease, not just a "psychic" one. Several other doctors had treated her for "nervous prostration" before Howells brought her to Mitchell. After her death, Howells suffered tremendous guilt, in large part because he and Mitchell had assumed she had "hypochondriacal" fancies.

The text of the following excerpt is taken from *Criticism and Fiction and Other Essays*, ed. Clara Marburg Kirk and Rudolf Kirk (New York: New York UP, 1959), 63–64; 65–71; 72–76.

I am not sure that the Americans have not brought the short story nearer perfection in the all-round sense than almost any other people, and for reasons very simple and near at hand. It might be argued from the national hurry and impatience that it was a literary form peculiarly adapted to the American temperament, but I suspect that its extraordinary development among us is owing much more to more tangible facts. The success of American magazines, which is nothing less than prodigious, is only commensurate with their excellence. Their sort of success is not only from the courage to decide what ought to please, but from the knowledge of what does please; and it is probable that, aside from the pictures, it is the short stories which please the readers of our best magazines. The serial novels they must have, of course; but rather more of course they must have short stories, and by operation of the law of supply and demand, the short stories, abundant in quantity and excellent in quality, are forthcoming because they are wanted. By another operation of the same law, which political economists have more recently taken account of, the demand follows the supply, and short stories are sought for because there is a proven ability to furnish them, and people read them willingly because they are usually very good. The art of writing them is now so disciplined and diffused with us that there is no lack either for the magazines or for the newspaper "syndicates" which deal in them almost to the exclusion of the serials. In other countries the feuilleton[1] of the journals is a novel continued from day to day, but with us the papers, whether daily or weekly, now more rarely print novels, whether they get them at first hand from the writers, as a great many do, or through the syndicates, which purvey a vast variety of literary wares, chiefly for the Sunday editions of the city journals. In the country papers the short story takes the place of the chapters of a serial which used to be given.

---

[1] *feuilleton:* A novel printed in installments, or a work appealing to popular or familiar tastes.

An interesting fact in regard to the different varieties of the short story among us is that the sketches and studies by the women seem faithfuler and more realistic than those of the men, in proportion to their number. Their tendency is more distinctly in that direction, and there is a solidity, an honest observation, in the work of such women as Mrs. Cooke, Miss Murfree, Miss Wilkins and Miss Jewett,[2] which often leaves little to be desired. I should, upon the whole, be disposed to rank American short stories only below those of such Russian writers as I have read, and I should praise rather than blame their free use of our different local parlances, or "dialects," as people call them. I like this because I hope that our inherited English may be constantly freshened and revived from the native sources which our literary decentralization will help to keep open, and I will own that as I turn over novels coming from Philadelphia, from New Mexico, from Boston, from Tennessee, from rural New England, from New York, every local flavor of diction gives me courage and pleasure.

. . . For our novelists to try to write Americanly, from any motive, would be a dismal error, but being born Americans, I would have them use "Americanisms" whenever these serve their turn; and when their characters speak, I should like to hear them speak true American, with all the varying Tennesseean, Philadelphian, Bostonian, and New York accents. If we bother ourselves to write what the critics imagine to be "English," we shall be priggish and artificial, and still more so if we make our Americans talk "English." There is also this serious disadvantage about "English," that if we wrote the best "English" in the world, probably the English themselves would not know it, or, if they did, certainly would not own it. It has always been supposed by grammarians and purists that a language can be kept as they find it; but languages, while they live, are perpetually changing. God apparently meant them for the common people — whom Lincoln believed God liked because he had made so many of them; and the common people will use them freely as they use other gifts of God. On their lips our continental English will differ more and more from the insular English, and I believe that this is not deplorable, but desirable.

---

[2] *Mrs. Cooke, Miss Murfree, Miss Wilkins and Miss Jewett:* Rose Terry Cooke (1827–1892) wrote regional short stories about women's experience; Mary Murfree (1850–1922) wrote regional short fiction and novels about Tennessee; Mary Wilkins Freeman (1852–1930) was a New England regionalist and was popular for her short stories; Sarah Orne Jewett (1849–1909) wrote stories about Maine, among them her famous novel *The Country of the Pointed Firs* (1896).

In fine, I would have our American novelists be as American as they unconsciously can. Matthew Arnold[3] complained that he found no "distinction" in our life, and I would gladly persuade all artists intending greatness in any kind among us that the recognition of the fact pointed out by Mr. Arnold ought to be a source of inspiration to them, and not discouragement. We have been now some hundred years building up a state on the affirmation of the essential equality of men in their rights and duties, and whether we have been right or wrong the gods have taken us at our word, and have responded to us with a civilization in which there is no "distinction" perceptible to the eye that loves and values it. Such beauty and such grandeur as we have is common beauty, common grandeur, or the beauty and grandeur in which the quality of solidarity so prevails that neither distinguishes itself to the disadvantage of anything else. It seems to me that these conditions invite the artist to the study and the appreciation of the common, and to the portrayal in every art of those finer and higher aspects which unite rather than sever humanity, if he would thrive in our new order of things. The talent that is robust enough to front the every-day world and catch the charm of its work-worn, care-worn, brave, kindly face, need not fear the encounter, though it seems terrible to the sort nurtured in the superstition of the romantic, the bizarre, the heroic, the distinguished, as the things alone worthy of painting or carving or writing. The arts must become democratic, and then we shall have the expression of America in art; and the reproach which Mr. Arnold was half right in making us shall have no justice in it any longer; we shall be "distinguished."

In the mean time it has been said with a superficial justice that our fiction is narrow; though in the same sense I suppose the present English fiction is as narrow as our own; and most modern fiction is narrow in a certain sense. In Italy the best men are writing novels as brief and restricted in range as ours; in Spain the novels are intense and deep, and not spacious; the French school, with the exception of Zola, is narrow; the Norwegians are narrow; the Russians, except Tolstoi, are narrow, and the next greatest after him, Tourguéneff,[4] is

[3] *Matthew Arnold:* Arnold (1822–1888) was one of the greatest Victorian poets and prose writers; he argued for the value of humanistic study and "sweetness and light."

[4] *Zola . . . Tolstoi . . . Tourguéneff:* Emile Zola (1840–1902), French author of realist novels; Count Leo Tolstoy (1828–1910), famous Russian writer, best known for his novel *War and Peace* (1865–1869); Ivan Turgenev (1818–1883), Russian novelist and social critic.

the narrowest great novelist, as to mere dimensions, that ever lived, dealing nearly always with small groups, isolated and analyzed in the most American fashion. In fact, the charge of narrowness accuses the whole tendency of modern fiction as much as the American school. But I do not by any means allow that this narrowness is a defect, while denying that it is a universal characteristic of our fiction; it is rather, for the present, a virtue. Indeed, I should call the present American work, North and South, thorough rather than narrow. In one sense it is as broad as life, for each man is a microcosm, and the writer who is able to acquaint us intimately with half a dozen people, or the conditions of a neighborhood or a class, has done something which cannot in any bad sense be called narrow; his breadth is vertical instead of lateral, that is all; and this depth is more desirable than horizontal expansion in a civilization like ours, where the differences are not of classes, but of types, and not of types either so much as of characters. A new method was necessary in dealing with the new conditions, and the new method is world-wide, because the whole world is more or less Americanized. Tolstoi is exceptionally voluminous among modern writers, even Russian writers; and it might be said that the forte of Tolstoi himself is not in his breadth sidewise, but in his breadth upward and downward. The Death of Ivan Illitch leaves as vast an impression on the reader's soul as any episode of War and Peace, which, indeed, can be recalled only in episodes, and not as a whole. I think that our writers may be safely counselled to continue their work in the modern way, because it is the best way yet known. If they make it true, it will be large, no matter what its superficies are; and it would be the greatest mistake to try to make it big. A big book is necessarily a group of episodes more or less loosely connected by a thread of narrative, and there seems no reason why this thread must always be supplied. Each episode may be quite distinct, or it may be one of a connected group; the final effect will be from the truth of each episode, not from the size of the group.

The whole field of human experience was never so nearly covered by imaginative literature in any age as in this; and American life especially is getting represented with unexampled fulness. It is true that no one writer, no one book, represents it, for that is not possible; our social and political decentralization forbids this, and may forever forbid it. But a great number of very good writers are instinctively striving to make each part of the country and each phase of our civilization known to all the other parts; and their work is not narrow in any feeble or vicious sense. The world was once very little, and it is now very large. Formerly, all science could be grasped by a single mind; but now the man who hopes to become great or useful in science must devote himself to a single department. It is so in everything — all arts, all trades; and the novelist is not superior to the universal rule against universality. He contributes his share to a thorough knowledge of groups of the human race under conditions which are full of inspiring novelty and interest. He works more fearlessly, frankly, and faithfully than the novelist ever worked before; his work, or much of it, may be destined never to be reprinted from the monthly magazines; but if he turns to his book-shelf and regards the array of the British or other classics, he knows that they too are for the most part dead; he knows that the planet itself is destined to freeze up and drop into the sun at last, with all its surviving literature upon it. The question is merely one of time. He consoles himself, therefore, if he is wise, and works on; and we may all take some comfort from the thought that most things cannot be helped. Especially a movement in literature like that which the world is now witnessing cannot be helped; and we could no more turn back and be of the literary fashions of any age before this than we could turn back and be of its social, economical, or political conditions.

If I were authorized to address any word directly to our novelists I should say, Do not trouble yourselves about standards or ideals; but try to be faithful and natural: remember that there is no greatness, no beauty, which does not come from truth to your own knowledge of things; and keep on working, even if your work is not long remembered.

At least three-fifths of the literature called classic, in all languages, no more lives than the poems and stories that perish monthly in our magazines. It is all printed and reprinted, generation after generation, century after century; but it is not alive; it is as dead as the people who wrote it and read it, and to whom it meant something, perhaps; with whom it was a fashion, a caprice, a passing taste. A superstitious piety preserves it, and pretends that it has aesthetic qualities which can delight or edify; but nobody really enjoys it, except as a reflection of the past moods and humors of the race, or a revelation of the author's character; otherwise it is trash, and often very filthy trash, which the present trash generally is not.

One of the great newspapers the other day invited the prominent American authors to speak their minds upon a point in the theory and practice of fiction which had already vexed some of them. It was the question of how much or how little the American novel ought to deal with certain facts of life which are not usually talked of before young people, and especially young ladies. Of course the question was not decided, and I forget just how far the balance inclined in favor of a larger freedom in the matter. But it certainly inclined that way; one or two writers of the sex which is somehow supposed to have purity in its keeping (as if purity were a thing that did not practically concern the other sex, preoccupied with serious affairs) gave it a rather vigorous tilt to that side. In view of this fact it would not be the part of prudence to make an effort to dress the balance; and indeed I do not know that I was going to make any such effort. But there are some things to say, around and about the subject, which I should like to have some one else say, and which I may myself possibly be safe in suggesting.

One of the first of these is the fact, generally lost sight of by those who censure the Anglo-Saxon novel for its prudishness, that it is really not such a prude after all; and that if it is sometimes apparently anxious to avoid those experiences of life not spoken of before young people, this may be an appearance only. Sometimes a novel which has this shuffling air, this effect of truckling to propriety, might defend itself, if it could speak for itself, by saying that such experiences happened not to come within its scheme, and that, so far from maiming or mutilating itself in ignoring them, it was all the more faithfully representative of the tone of modern life in dealing with love that was chaste, and with passion so honest that it could be openly spoken of before the tenderest society bud at dinner. It might say that the guilty intrigue, the betrayal, the extreme flirtation even, was the exceptional thing in life, and unless the scheme of the story necessarily involved it, that it would be bad art to lug it in, and as bad taste as to introduce such topics in a mixed company. It could say very justly that the novel in our civilization now always addresses a mixed company, and that the vast majority of the company are ladies, and that very many, if not most, of these ladies are young girls. If the novel were written for men and for married women alone, as in continental Europe, it might be altogether different. But the simple fact is that it is not written for them alone among us, and it is a question of writing, under cover of our universal acceptance, things for young girls to read which you would be put out-of-doors for saying to them, or of frankly giving notice of your intention, and so cutting yourself off from the pleasure — and it is a very high and sweet one — of appealing to these vivid, responsive intelligences, which are none the less brilliant and admirable because they are innocent. . . .

But I do not mean to imply that their case covers the whole ground. So far as it goes, though, it ought to stop the mouths of those who complain that fiction is enslaved to propriety among us. It appears that of a certain kind of impropriety it is free to give us all it will, and more. But this is not what serious men and women writing fiction mean when they rebel against the limitations of their art in our civilization. They have no desire to deal with nakedness, as painters and sculptors freely do in the worship of beauty; or with certain facts of life, as the stage does, in the service of sensation. But they ask why, when the conventions of the plastic and histrionic arts liberate their followers to the portrayal of almost any phase of the physical or of the emotional nature, an American novelist may not write a story on the lines of Anna Karenina or Madame Bovary.[5] Sappho[6] they put aside, and from Zola's work they avert their eyes. They do not condemn him or Daudet,[7] necessarily, or accuse their motives; they leave them out of the question; they do not want to do that kind of thing. But they do sometimes wish to do another kind, to touch one of the most serious and sorrowful problems of life in the spirit of Tolstoi and Flaubert,[8] and they ask why they may not. At one time, they remind us, the Anglo-Saxon novelist did deal with such problems — De Foe in his spirit, Richardson in his, Goldsmith in his.[9] At what moment did our fiction lose this privilege? In what fatal hour did the Young Girl arise and seal the lips of Fiction, with a touch of her finger, to some of the most vital interests of life?

Whether I wished to oppose them in their aspiration for greater freedom, or whether I wished to encourage them, I should begin to answer them by saying that the Young Girl had never done anything of the kind. The manners of the novel have been improving with

---

[5] *Anna Karenina or Madame Bovary:* Nineteenth-century novels by Leo Tolstoy and Gustave Flaubert (1821–1880), respectively, in which the heroine's adultery leads to her suicide.

[6] *Sappho:* Ancient Greek (sixth century B.C.) female lyric poet, who wrote love poems to women; the term *lesbian* derives from the isle of Lesbos, where Sappho lived.

[7] *Daudet:* Alphonse Daudet (1840–1897), successful French novelist.

[8] *Flaubert:* Gustave Flaubert, French novelist most famous for *Madame Bovary* (1856).

[9] *De Foe . . . Richardson . . . Goldsmith:* Daniel Defoe (1660–1731), Samuel Richardson (1689–1761), and Oliver Goldsmith (1730?–1774), eighteenth-century novelists and men of letters.

those of its readers; that is all. Gentlemen no longer swear or fall drunk under the table, or abduct young ladies and shut them up in lonely country-houses, or so habitually set about the ruin of their neighbors' wives, as they once did. Generally, people now call a spade an agricultural implement; they have not grown decent without having also grown a little squeamish, but they have grown comparatively decent; there is no doubt about that. They require of a novelist whom they respect unquestionable proof of his seriousness, if he proposes to deal with certain phases of life; they require a sort of scientific decorum. He can no longer expect to be received on the ground of entertainment only; he assumes a higher function, something like that of a physician or a priest, and they expect him to be bound by laws as sacred as those of such professions; they hold him solemnly pledged not to betray them or abuse their confidence. If he will accept the conditions, they give him their confidence, and he may then treat to his greater honor, and not at all to his disadvantage, of such experiences, such relations of men and women as George Eliot treats in Adam Bede, in Daniel Deronda, in Romola,[10] in almost all her books; such as Hawthorne treats in the Scarlet Letter;[11] such as Dickens treats in David Copperfield;[12] such as Thackeray treats in Pendennis,[13] and glances at in every one of his fictions; such as most of the masters of English fiction have at some time treated more or less openly. It is quite false or quite mistaken to suppose that our novels have left untouched these most important realities of life. They have only not made them their stock in trade; they have kept a true perspective in regard to them; they have relegated them in their pictures of life to the space and place they occupy in life itself, as we know it in England and America. They have kept a correct proportion, knowing perfectly well that unless the novel is to be a map, with everything scrupulously laid down in it, a faithful record of life in far the greater extent could be made to the exclusion of guilty love and all its circumstances and consequences.

[10] George Eliot . . . Adam Bede, in Daniel Deronda, in Romola: Three of novelist George Eliot's (Mary Ann Evans, 1819–1880) novels, published in 1859, 1876, and 1863 respectively.

[11] Scarlet Letter: Nathaniel Hawthorne's (1804–1864) 1850 novel set in Puritan Boston during the mid-seventeenth century.

[12] Dickens . . . David Copperfield: Charles Dickens (1837–1896), prolific novelist whose David Copperfield (1850) is very loosely autobiographical and includes a scathing portrayal of the use of child labor in Britain.

[13] Thackeray . . . Pendennis: William Makepeace Thackeray (1811–1863), novelist and satirist; his bildungsroman, Pendennis (1850), is often compared to Dickens's David Copperfield.

I justify them in this view not only because I hate what is cheap and meretricious, and hold in peculiar loathing the cant of the critics who require "passion" as something in itself admirable and desirable in a novel, but because I prize fidelity in the historian of feeling and character. Most of these critics who demand "passion" would seem to have no conception of any passion but one. Yet there are several other passions: the passion of grief, the passion of avarice, the passion of pity, the passion of ambition, the passion of hate, the passion of envy, the passion of devotion, the passion of friendship; and all these have a greater part in the drama of life than the passion of love, and infinitely greater than the passion of guilty love. Wittingly or unwittingly, English fiction and American fiction have recognized this truth, not fully, not in the measure it merits, but in greater degree than most other fiction.

Who can deny that fiction would be incomparably stronger, incomparably truer, if once it could tear off the habit which enslaves it to the celebration chiefly of a single passion, in one phase or another, and could frankly dedicate itself to the service of all the passions, and all the interests, all the facts? Every novelist who has thought about his art knows that it would, and I think that upon reflection he must doubt whether his sphere would be greatly enlarged if he were allowed to treat freely the darker aspects of the favorite passion. But, as I have shown, the privilege, the right to do this, is already perfectly recognized. This is proved again by the fact that serious criticism recognizes as master-works (I will not push the question of supremacy) the two great novels which above all others have moved the world by their study of guilty love. If by any chance, if by some prodigious miracle, any American should now arise to treat it on the level of Anna Karenina and Madame Bovary, he would be absolutely sure of success, and of fame and gratitude as great as those books have won for their authors.

But what editor of what American magazine would print such a story? . . .

It does not avail to say that the daily papers teem with facts far fouler and deadlier than any which fiction could imagine. That is true, but it is true also that the sex which reads the most novels reads the fewest newspapers; and, besides, the reporter does not command the novelist's skill to fix impressions in a young girl's mind or to suggest conjecture. The magazine is a little despotic, a little arbitrary; but unquestionably its favor is essential to success, and its conditions are not such narrow ones. You cannot deal with Tolstoi's and Flaubert's subjects in the absolute artistic freedom of Tolstoi and Flaubert; since De Foe, that is unknown among us; but if you deal with them in the manner of George Eliot, of Thackeray, of Dickens, of society, you may deal with them even in the magazines. There is no other restriction upon you. All the horrors and miseries and tortures are open to you; your pages may drop blood; sometimes it may happen that the editor will even exact such strong material from you. But probably he will require nothing but the observance of the convention in question; and if you do not yourself prefer bloodshed he will leave you free to use all sweet and peaceable means of interesting his readers.

Believe me, it is no narrow field he throws open to you, with that little sign to keep off the grass up at one point only. Its vastness is still almost unexplored, and whole regions in it are unknown to the fictionist. Dig anywhere, and do but dig deep enough, and you strike riches; or, if you are of the mind to range, the gentler climes, the softer temperatures, the serener skies, are all free to you, and are so little visited that the chance of novelty is greater among them.

HENRY JAMES

From The Notebooks

Henry James (1843–1916) was arguably the most significant American writer of the nineteenth century. An expatriate who lived in England for much of his career, he wrote some 30 novels and 112 stories and novellas, as well as reviews, plays, travel sketches and impressions, several books of criticism, a biography, and thousands of letters. James's writing career spanned the half century between the Civil War and World War I, enabling him to observe the changes in American as well as English society and the struggle with modernity. Once seen primarily as the classical architect of the novel and a subtle witness of changes in manners and morals, James has more lately been understood as a writer concerned with power relations and ideology — with politics in the largest sense. His close observations of culture connect him with some of the most profound modern philosophers of his day, including his brother, the philosopher-psychologist William James.

James will always be best known for his novels, which include *The Portrait of a Lady* (1881), *The Bostonians* (1886), and the great triad of his later career, *The Ambassadors* (1903), *The Wings of the Dove*

(1902), and *The Golden Bowl* (1904). One of his most important recurring figures is the trapped, sometimes bedridden, female spectators, to
be found in such varied works as "The Modern Warning" (1888), "The
Marriages" (1891), "The Patagonia" (1888), *The Turn of the Screw*
(1898), *What Maisie Knew* (1897), and "In the Cage" (1898).

The text of the following excerpts is taken from *The Complete Notebooks of Henry James,* ed. Leon Edel and Lyall H. Powers (New York:
Oxford UP, 1987), 19–20; 73–74.

April 8, 1883

. . . The subject [of *The Bostonians*] is strong and good, with a
large rich interest. The relation of the two girls should be a study of
one of those friendships between women which are so common in
New England. The whole thing as local, as American, as possible,
and as full of Boston: an attempt to show that I *can* write an American story. There must, indispensably, be a type of newspaper man —
the man whose ideal is the energetic reporter. I should like to
bafouer[1] the vulgarity and hideousness of this — the impudent inva-
sion of privacy — the extinction of all conception of privacy, etc.
Daudet's *Évangéliste*[2] has given me the idea of this thing. If I could
only do something with that *pictorial* quality! At any rate, the subject
is very national, very typical. I wished to write a very *American* tale,
a tale very characteristic of our social conditions, and I asked myself
what was the most salient and peculiar point in our social life. The
answer was: the situation of women, the decline of the sentiment of
sex, the agitation on their behalf.

November 26th, 1892

Curiously persistent and comically numerous appear to be the suggestions and situations attached to this endless spectacle — the queer
crudity of which is a theme for the philosopher — of the Anglo-
American marriage. The singular — the intensely significant circumstance of its being all on one side — or rather in one form; always the
union of the male Briton to the female American — *never* the other
way round. Plenty of opportunity for satiric fiction in the facts

---

[1] *bafouer:* To hold up to ridicule (French).
[2] *Daudet's Évangéliste:* Published serially in *Le Figaro* (1882), this novel depicts
the morbid psychological effects of a "religious hypnotist" (the evangelist) on a de-
luded young woman.

involved in all this — plenty of subjects and situations. It seems to me all made on purpose — *on n'a qu' à puiser*. One has only to dip it out. The contrast between the man the American girl marries and the man who marries the American girl. This opens up — or *se rattache* to — the whole subject, or question, about which Godkin,[3] as I remember, one day last summer talked to me very emphatically and interestingly — the growing divorce between the American woman (with her comparative leisure, culture, grace, social instincts, artistic ambitions) and the male American immersed in the ferocity of business, with no time for any but the most sordid interests, purely commercial, professional, democratic and political. This divorce is rapidly becoming a gulf — an abyss of inequality, the like of which has never before been seen under the sun. One might represent it, picture it, in a series of illustrations, of episodes — one might project a lot of light upon it. It would abound in developments, in ramifications.

ALICE JAMES

From The Diary of Alice James

The younger sister of Henry and William, Alice James (1848–1892) made a "career" out of being an invalid, documenting her life in her posthumously published (1934) diary and in her letters. In 1884, Alice moved from America to Europe, where she spent the last years of her life. That life was marked by her gender as much as by her famous family; as Henry once said, "in our family group girls seem scarcely to have had a chance" (8). Beginning her diary in 1889, Alice James claims that she writes to "lose a little of the sense of loneliness and desolation which abides with me," much like the narrator of Gilman's "The Yellow Wallpaper." Indeed, many women in the nineteenth century — separated from their parents and relatives — took to writing journals as a form of relief. Although Alice James had earlier consulted doctors for "hysteria" who treated her with massage, electrotherapy, and sulphuric ether, she developed breast cancer that went untreated and she died in 1892. Her diary insists, however, that she will not be taken as another "hysterical"

---

[3] *Godkin:* Edwin Lawrence Godkin (1831–1902), Irish-born American journalist and editor of *The Nation* from 1865 to 1881.

woman or passive patient: "If the aim of life is the accretion of fat, the consumption of food unattended by digestive disorganization, and a succession of pleasurable sensations, there is no doubt that I am a failure, for as an animal form my insatiable vanity must allow that my existence doesn't justify itself, but every fibre protests against being taken simply as a sick carcass, as foolish friends so flatteringly insist, for what power has dissolving flesh and aching bones to undermine a satisfaction made of imperishable things" (183). James argues that it is her mind rather than her wasting female body that defines her.

The text of the following excerpts is taken from *The Diary of Alice James*, ed. Leon Edel (New York: Penguin, 1987), 25; 31; 206–07.

May 31st, 1889

I think that if I get into the habit of writing a bit about what happens, or rather doesn't happen, I may lose a little of the sense of loneliness and desolation which abides with me. My circumstances allowing of nothing but the ejaculation of one-syllabled reflections, a written monologue by that most interesting being, *myself*, may have its yet to be discovered consolations. I shall at least have it all my own way and it may bring relief as an outlet to that geyser of emotions, sensations, speculations and reflections which ferments perpetually within my poor old carcass for its sins; so here goes, my first Journal!

June 13th, 1889

I went out again today, and behaved like a lunatic, "sobbed," *à la* Kingsley,[1] over a farmhouse, a meadow, some trees and cawing rooks. Nurse says that there are some people downstairs who drive everywhere and admire nothing. How grateful I am that I actually do *see*, to my own consciousness, the quarter of an inch that my eyes fall upon; truly, the subject is all that counts!

Nurse asked me whether I should like to be an artist — imagine the joy and despair of it! the joy of seeing with the trained eye and the despair of *doing* it. Among the beings who are made up of chords which vibrate at every zephyr, of the two orders, which know the least misery, those who are always dumb and never loose the stifled sense, or the others who ever find expression impotent to express! . . .

---

[1] *Kingsley:* Charles Kingsley (1819–1875), British Victorian clergyman and writer whose novels include *Westward Ho!* (1855) and the "social-problem" novel *Alton Locke* (1850).

May 31st, 1891

To him who waits, all things come! My aspirations may have been eccentric, but I cannot complain now, that they have not been brilliantly fulfilled. Ever since I have been ill, I have longed and longed for some palpable disease, no matter how conventionally dreadful a label it might have, but I was always driven back to stagger alone under the monstrous mass of subjective sensations, which that sympathetic being "the medical man" had no higher inspiration than to assure me I was personally responsible for, washing his hands of me with a graceful complacency under my very nose. Dr. Torry was the only man who ever treated me like a rational being, who did not assume, because I was victim to many pains, that I was, of necessity, an arrested mental development too.

Notwithstanding all the happiness and comfort here, I have been going downhill at a steady trot; so they sent for Sir Andrew Clark four days ago, and the blessed being has endowed me not only with cardiac complications, but says that a lump that I have had in one of my breasts for three months, which has given me a great deal of pain, is a tumour, that nothing can be done for me but to alleviate pain, that it is only a question of time, etc. This with a delicate embroidery of "the most distressing case of nervous hyperæsthesia"[2] added to a spinal neurosis that has taken me off my legs for seven years; with attacks of rheumatic gout in my stomach for the last twenty, ought to satisfy the most inflated pathologic vanity. It is decidedly indecent to catalogue oneself in this way; but I put it down in a scientific spirit, to show that though I have no productive worth, I have a certain value as an indestructible quantity.

KATE CHOPIN

"The Story of an Hour"

Kate Chopin (1851–1904), born in St. Louis, is perhaps best known for *The Awakening* (1899), a novel about a married woman's increasing sense of her sexuality and desire for freedom. Chopin's short stories explore similar themes of repressed or suppressed desire. Many of them are

---

[2] *hyperæsthesia:* Increased or pathological sensitivity of the skin or a particular sense. (See also definition in Bloch, p. 230.)

set in New Orleans or other parts of Louisiana, where Chopin lived for many years during her marriage. "The Story of an Hour" (1894) is a case study in dramatic irony, as Mrs. Mallard's "case" is misread by the doctors and family around her. Like Gilman in "The Yellow Wallpaper," Chopin depicts the misreading of a woman's health and state of mind by a medical establishment that imposes its misconceived theories onto the patient.

The text is taken from *The Complete Works of Kate Chopin*, vol. 1, ed. and introd. Per Seyersted (Baton Rouge: Louisiana State UP, 1969), 352–54.

Knowing that Mrs. Mallard was afflicted with a heart trouble, great care was taken to break to her as gently as possible the news of her husband's death.

It was her sister Josephine who told her, in broken sentences; veiled hints that revealed in half concealing. Her husband's friend Richards was there, too, near her. It was he who had been in the newspaper office when intelligence of the railroad disaster was received, with Brently Mallard's name leading the list of "killed." He had only taken the time to assure himself of its truth by a second telegram, and had hastened to forestall any less careful, less tender friend in bearing the sad message.

She did not hear the story as many women have heard the same, with a paralyzed inability to accept its significance. She wept at once, with sudden, wild abandonment, in her sister's arms. When the storm of grief had spent itself she went away to her room alone. She would have no one follow her.

There stood, facing the open window, a comfortable, roomy armchair. Into this she sank, pressed down by a physical exhaustion that haunted her body and seemed to reach into her soul.

She could see in the open square before her house the tops of trees that were all aquiver with the new spring life. The delicious breath of rain was in the air. In the street below a peddler was crying his wares. The notes of a distant song which some one was singing reached her faintly, and countless sparrows were twittering in the eaves.

There were patches of blue sky showing here and there through the clouds that had met and piled one above the other in the west facing her window.

She sat with her head thrown back upon the cushion of the chair, quite motionless, except when a sob came up into her throat and shook her, as a child who has cried itself to sleep continues to sob in its dreams.

She was young, with a fair, calm face, whose lines bespoke repression and even a certain strength. But now there was a dull stare in her eyes, whose gaze was fixed away off yonder on one of those patches of blue sky. It was not a glance of reflection, but rather indicated a suspension of intelligent thought.

There was something coming to her and she was waiting for it, fearfully. What was it? She did not know; it was too subtle and elusive to name. But she felt it, creeping out of the sky, reaching toward her through the sounds, the scents, the color that filled the air.

Now her bosom rose and fell tumultuously. She was beginning to recognize this thing that was approaching to possess her, and she was striving to beat it back with her will — as powerless as her two white slender hands would have been.

When she abandoned herself a little whispered word escaped her slightly parted lips. She said it over and over under her breath: "free, free, free!" The vacant stare and the look of terror that had followed it went from her eyes. They stayed keen and bright. Her pulses beat fast, and the coursing blood warmed and relaxed every inch of her body.

She did not stop to ask if it were or were not a monstrous joy that held her. A clear and exalted perception enabled her to dismiss the suggestion as trivial.

She knew that she would weep again when she saw the kind, tender hands folded in death; the face that had never looked save with love upon her, fixed and gray and dead. But she saw beyond that bitter moment a long procession of years to come that would belong to her absolutely. And she opened and spread her arms out to them in welcome.

There would be no one to live for her during those coming years; she would live for herself. There would be no powerful will bending hers in that blind persistence with which men and women believe they have a right to impose a private will upon a fellow-creature. A kind intention or a cruel intention made the act seem no less a crime as she looked upon it in that brief moment of illumination.

And yet she had loved him — sometimes. Often she had not. What did it matter! What could love, the unsolved mystery, count for in face of this possession of self-assertion which she suddenly recognized as the strongest impulse of her being!

"Free! Body and soul free!" she kept whispering.

Josephine was kneeling before the closed door with her lips to the keyhole, imploring for admission. "Louise, open the door! I beg; open the door — you will make yourself ill. What are you doing, Louise? For heaven's sake open the door."

"Go away. I am not making myself ill." No; she was drinking in a very elixir of life through that open window.

Her fancy was running riot along those days ahead of her. Spring days, and summer days, and all sorts of days that would be her own. She breathed a quick prayer that life might be long. It was only yesterday she had thought with a shudder that life might be long.

She arose at length and opened the door to her sister's importunities. There was a feverish triumph in her eyes, and she carried herself unwittingly like a goddess of Victory. She clasped her sister's waist, and together they descended the stairs. Richards stood waiting for them at the bottom.

Some one was opening the front door with a latchkey. It was Brently Mallard who entered, a little travel-stained, composedly carrying his grip-sack and umbrella. He had been far from the scene of accident, and did not even know there had been one. He stood amazed at Josephine's piercing cry; at Richards' quick motion to screen him from the view of his wife.

But Richards was too late.

When the doctors came they said she had died of heart disease — of joy that kills.

yeah please!

Selected Bibliography

This bibliography is divided into two parts, "Works Cited" and "Suggestions for Further Reading." The first part contains all primary and secondary works quoted or discussed in the general or chapter introductions. The second part is a selective list of materials that will be useful to students who want to know more about Charlotte Perkins Gilman's life and culture or who are interested in reading some of the major critical studies of her work. In addition to biographical and critical works, this list includes suggestions for further reading in the areas covered by the historical documents in Part Two. A book or article that appears in "Works Cited" is not recorded again under "Suggestions for Further Reading." Thus, both lists should be consulted.

WORKS CITED

Battan, Jesse F. "'The Word Made Flesh': Language, Authority, and Sexual Desire in Late Nineteenth-Century America." *American Sexual Politics*. Ed. John C. Fout and Maura Shaw Tantillo. Chicago: U of Chicago P, 1990. 101–22.

Birken, Lawrence. *Consuming Desire: Sexual Science and the Emergence of a Culture of Abundance, 1871–1914*. Ithaca: Cornell UP, 1988.

Blumin, Stuart. *The Emergence of the Middle Class: Social Experience in the American City, 1760–1900*. Cambridge: Cambridge UP, 1989.

Calverton, V.F. *Sex Expression in Literature*. New York: Boni & Liveright, 1926.

Crewe, Jonathan. "Queering 'The Yellow Wallpaper'?: Charlotte Perkins Gilman and the Politics of Form." *Tulsa Studies in Women's Literature* 14.2 (Fall 1995): 273–94.

DeKoven, Marianne. *Rich and Strange: Gender, History, Modernism*. Princeton: Princeton UP, 1991.

Dimock, Wai-Chee. "Feminism, New Historicism, and the Reader." *Readers in History: Nineteenth-Century American Literature and the Contexts of Response*. Baltimore: Johns Hopkins UP, 1993. 85–106.

Dock, Julie Bates, Daphne Ryan Allen, Jennifer Palais, and Kristen Tracy. "'But One Expects That': Charlotte Perkins Gilman's 'The Yellow Wallpaper' and the Shifting Light of Scholarship." *PMLA* 111.1 (January 1996): 52–65.

Engels, Frederick. *The Origin of the Family, Private Property and the State: In Light of the Researches of Lewis H. Morgan*. Trans. Alec West. New York: International, 1972.

Fishkin, Shelley Fisher. "'Making a Change': Strategies of Subversion in Gilman's Journalism and Short Fiction." *Critical Essays on Charlotte Perkins Gilman*. Ed. Joanne B. Karpinski. New York: Hall, 1992. 234–48.

Gilman, Charlotte Perkins. "Birth Control, Religion, and the Unfit." *The Nation* 134.3473 (January 27, 1932): 108–09.

———. *The Home: Its Work and Influence*. Urbana: U of Illinois P, 1972.

———. *The Living of Charlotte Perkins Gilman: An Autobiography*. 1935. Introd. Ann Lane. Madison: U of Wisconsin P, 1990.

———. *The Man-Made World or, Our Androcentric Culture*. New York: Charlton Co., 1911.

———. *Women and Economics: The Economic Factor Between Men and Women as a Factor in Social Evolution*. 1898. Ed. Carl N. Degler. New York: Harper, 1966.

Gordon, Linda. *Woman's Body, Woman's Right: Birth Control in America*. New York: Penguin Books, 1990.

Haller, John S., Jr., and Robin M. Haller. *The Physician and Sexuality in Victorian America*. Urbana: U of Illinois P, 1974.

Hedges, Elaine R. Afterword. *The Yellow Wallpaper*. Old Westbury, NY: Feminist, 1973.

———. "'Out at Last'?: 'The Yellow Wallpaper' after Two Decades of Feminist Criticism." *The Captive Imagination*. Ed. Catherine Golden. New York: Feminist, 1992.

Kellogg, John Harvey. Preface. *The Ladies' Guide in Health and Disease: Girlhood, Maidenhood, Wifehood, and Motherhood.* Des Moines: W.D. Condit, 1884.

Kerber, Linda K. *Women of the Republic: Intellect and Ideology in Revolutionary America.* Chapel Hill: U of North Carolina P, 1980.

Kessler, Carol Farley. *Charlotte Perkins Gilman: Her Progress Toward Utopia with Selected Writings.* Syracuse: Syracuse UP, 1995.

Lane, Ann J. *To Herland and Beyond: The Life and Work of Charlotte Perkins Gilman.* New York: Pantheon, 1990.

Lanser, Susan S. "Feminist Criticism, 'The Yellow Wallpaper,' and the Politics of Color in America." *Feminist Studies* 15.3 (Fall 1989): 415–41.

Lutz, Tom. *American Nervousness, 1903: An Anecdotal History.* Ithaca: Cornell UP, 1991.

Michaels, Walter Benn. *The Gold Standard and the Logic of Naturalism.* Berkeley: U California P, 1987.

Mill, John Stuart. *The Subjection of Women.* 1869. Cambridge, MA: MIT P, 1970.

Newton, Richard Heber. *Womanhood: Lectures on Woman's Work in the World.* New York: Putnam, 1881.

Newton, Sarah E. *Learning to Behave: A Guide to American Conduct Books Before 1900.* Westport, CT: Greenwood, 1994.

Ohmann, Richard. *Selling Culture.* London and New York: Verso, 1996.

Pittenger, Mark. *American Socialists and Evolutionary Thought, 1870–1920.* Madison: U of Wisconsin P, 1993.

Pond Bureau. "Charlotte Perkins Gilman: Under the Exclusive Management of James B. Pond, 'The Pond Bureau.'" New York: Pond Bureau, ca. 1925.

Ross, Edward Alsworth. *Changing America: Studies in Contemporary Society.* New York: Century, 1914.

———. "The Future Human Race." Edward A. Ross Papers, Wisconsin State Historical Society. Reel 32, frame 341–44.

———. "Positions and Attitudes." Edward A. Ross Papers, Wisconsin State Historical Society. Reel 32, frame 816.

Rotundo, Anthony. "Boy Culture: Middle-Class Boyhood in Nineteenth-Century America." *Meanings for Manhood.* Ed. Mark C. Carnes and Clyde Griffen. Chicago: U of Chicago P, 1990. 15–36.

Seidman, Steven. *Romantic Longings: Love in America, 1830–1980.* New York: Routledge, 1991.

Smith-Rosenberg, Carroll. *Disorderly Conduct: Visions of Gender in Victorian America.* New York: Oxford UP, 1985.

Veeder, William. "Who Is Jane? The Intricate Feminism of Charlotte
Perkins Gilman." *Arizona Quarterly* 44.3 (Autumn 1988):
40–70.

SUGGESTIONS FOR FURTHER READING

Selected Works by Gilman

The Charlotte Perkins Gilman Collection at the Schlesinger Library on the History of Women in America, Radcliffe College, Cambridge, Massachusetts, houses the largest collection of primary materials.

Concerning Children. Boston: Small, Maynard, 1900.
Forerunner. New York: C.P. Gilman. Volumes 1.1 (November 1909)
to 7.12 (December 1916).
Herland. 1915. Introd. Ann J. Lane. New York: Pantheon, 1979.
*His Religion and Hers: A Study of the Faith of Our Fathers and the
Work of Our Mothers.* 1923. Westport, Conn.: Hyperion, 1976.
Human Work. New York: Phillips, 1904.
Unpunished. Ed. Catherine J. Golden and Denise D. Knight. New
York: Feminist, 1997.

Bibliographic and Biographical Works

Ceplair, Larry, ed. *Charlotte Perkins Gilman: A Nonfiction Reader.*
New York: Columbia UP, 1991.
Hill, Mary A. *Charlotte Perkins Gilman: The Making of a Radical
Feminist, 1869–1896.* Philadelphia: Temple UP, 1980.
————, ed. *A Journey from Within: The Love Letters of Charlotte
Perkins Gilman, 1897–1900.* Lewisburg, PA: Bucknell UP, 1995.
Howells, William Dean. "A Reminiscent Introduction." *The Captive
Imagination: A Casebook on The Yellow Wallpaper.* New York:
Feminist, 1992. 54–56.
Knight, Denise D., ed. *The Diaries of Charlotte Perkins Gilman.*
Charlottesville: UP of Virginia, 1994.
————. *The Later Poetry of Charlotte Perkins Gilman.* Newark: U of
Delaware P, 1996.
Lancaster, Jane. "'I could easily have been an acrobat': Charlotte
Perkins Gilman and the Providence Ladies' Sanitary Gymnasium
1881–1884." *ATQ* 8.1 (March 1994): 33–52.
Magner, Lois N. "Darwinism and the Woman Question: The Evolving Views of Charlotte Perkins Gilman." *Critical Essays on*

Charlotte Perkins Gilman. Ed. Joanne B. Karpinski. New York: Hall, 1992. 115–28.

Makowsky, Veronica. "Fear of Feeling and the Turn-of-the-Century Woman of Letters." *ALH* 5.2 (Summer 1993): 326–34.

Scharnhorst, Gary. *Charlotte Perkins Gilman: A Bibliography*. Scarecrow Author's Bibliographies, No. 71. Metuchen, N.J., 1985.

———. *Charlotte Perkins Gilman*. Twayne's United States Author's Series. Boston: Twayne, 1985.

Critical Studies of "The Yellow Wallpaper"

Crewe, Jonathan. "Queering 'The Yellow Wallpaper'?: Charlotte Perkins Gilman and the Politics of Form." *Tulsa Studies in Women's Literature* 14.2 (Fall 1995): 273–94.

Fetterley, Judith. "Reading about Reading: 'A Jury of Her Peers,' 'The Murders in the Rue Morgue,' and 'The Yellow Wallpaper.'" *Gender and Reading*. Ed. Elizabeth Flynn and Patrocinio Schweickart. Baltimore: Johns Hopkins UP, 1986. 147–65.

Golden, Catherine, ed. *The Captive Imagination: A Casebook on The Yellow Wallpaper*. New York: Feminist, 1992.

Herndl, Diane Price. *Invalid Women: Figuring Feminine Illness in American Fiction and Culture, 1840–1940*. Chapel Hill: U of North Carolina P, 1993.

Kennard, Jean. "Convention Coverage or How to Read Your Own Life." *New Literary History* 13.1 (1981): 69–88.

Kolodny, Annette. "A Map for Rereading: Or, Gender and the Interpretation of Literary Texts." *New Literary History* 11.3 (Spring 1980): 451–67.

Shumaker, Conrad. "Realism, Reform, and the Audience: Charlotte Perkins Gilman's Unreadable Wallpaper." *Arizona Quarterly* 47.1 (Spring 1991): 81–93.

Treichler, Paula. "Escaping the Sentence: Diagnosis and Discourse in 'The Yellow Wallpaper.'" *Feminist Issues in Literary Scholarship*. Ed. Shari Benstock. Bloomington: Indiana UP, 1987.

Literary and Social History

Ammons, Elizabeth. *Conflicting Stories: American Women Writers at the Turn into the Twentieth Century*. New York: Oxford UP, 1992.

Baker, Paula. "The Domestication of Politics: Women and American Political Society, 1780–1920." *Unequal Sisters: A Multicultural Reader in U.S. Women's History*. Ed. Ellen Carol DuBois and Vicki L. Ruiz. New York: Routledge, 1990. 66–91.

Banta, Martha. *Imaging American Women: Idea and Ideals in Cultural History.* New York: Columbia UP, 1987.

Barker-Benfield, G.J. *The Horrors of the Half-Known Life: Male Attitudes Toward Women and Sexuality in Nineteenth-Century America.* New York: Harper, 1986.

Bassuk, Ellen. "The Rest Cure: Repetition or Resolution of Victorian Women's Conflicts?". *The Female Body in Western Culture.* Ed. Susan Rubin Suleiman. Cambridge, MA: Harvard UP, 1985. 139–51.

Bederman, Gail. *Manliness & Civilization: A Cultural History of Gender & Race in the United States, 1880–1917.* Chicago: U of Chicago P, 1995.

Berlant, Lauren. "The Female Complaint." *Social Text* 19.20 (Fall 1988): 237–59.

Brodhead, Richard. *Cultures of Letters.* Chicago: U of Chicago P, 1993.

Brodie, Janet Farrell. *Contraception and Abortion in Nineteenth-Century America.* Ithaca: Cornell UP, 1994.

Burr, Anna Robeson, ed. *S. Weir Mitchell: His Life and Letters.* New York: Duffield, 1929.

Cott, Nancy F., Jeanne Boydston, Ann Braude, Lori Ginzburg, Molly Ladd-Taylor, eds. *Root of Bitterness: Documents of the Social History of American Women.* 2nd ed. Boston: Northeastern UP, 1996.

Crowley, John W. "Winifred Howells and the Economy of Pain." *The Old Northwest* 10.1 (Spring 1984): 41–75.

Degler, Carl. *In Search of Human Nature: The Decline and Revival of Darwinism in American Social Thought.* New York: Oxford UP, 1991.

D'Emilio, John and Estelle B. Freedman. *Intimate Matters: A History of Sexuality in America.* New York: Harper, 1988.

Fellman, Anita Clair and Michael Fellman. *Making Sense of Self: Medical Advice Literature in Late-Nineteenth-Century America.* Philadelphia: U of Pennsylvania P, 1981.

Gilman, Sander. *Difference and Pathology: Stereotypes of Sexuality, Race, and Madness.* Ithaca: Cornell UP, 1985.

Groneman, Carol. "Nymphomania: The Historical Construction of Female Sexuality." *SIGNS* 19.2 (Winter 1994): 337–67.

Halttunen, Karen. *Confidence Men and Painted Women.* New Haven and London: Yale UP, 1982.

Hayden, Delores. *The Grand Domestic Revolution: A History of Feminist Designs for American Homes, Neighborhoods, and Cities.* Cambridge, MA: MIT P, 1981.

Hewitt, Nancy. "Beyond the Search for Sisterhood: American Women's History in the 1980s." *Unequal Sisters: A Multicul-*

tural Reader in U.S. Women's History. Ed. Ellen Carol DuBois and Vicki L. Ruiz. New York: Routledge, 1990. 1–14.

Jones, Maldwyn Allen. *American Immigration.* Chicago: U of Chicago P, 1960.

Kaplan, Carla. *The Erotics of Talk.* New York: Oxford UP, 1996.

Lears, Jackson. *No Place of Grace: Antimodernism and the Transformation of American Culture, 1880–1920.* New York: Pantheon, 1981.

Leavitt, Judith Walzer, ed. *Women and Health in America.* Madison: U of Wisconsin P, 1984.

Lewes, Darby. *Dream Revisionaries: Gender and Genre in Women's Utopian Fiction, 1870–1920.* Tuscaloosa: U of Alabama P, 1995.

Lunbeck, Elizabeth. *The Psychiatric Persuasion: Knowledge, Gender, and Power in Modern America.* Princeton, N.J.: Princeton UP, 1994.

Miller, Nina. "The Bonds of Free Love: Constructing the Female Bohemian Self." *Genders* 11 (Fall 1991): 37–57.

———. "Making Love Modern: Dorothy Parker and Her Public." *American Literature* 64.4 (December 1992): 763–84.

Mott, Frank Luther. *A History of American Magazines, 1885–1905.* Cambridge, MA: Belknap, 1957.

Pfister, Joel and Nancy Schnog, eds. *Inventing the Psychological: Toward a Cultural History of Emotional Life in America.* New Haven: Yale UP, 1997.

Ross, Dorothy. *The Origins of American Social Science.* New York: Cambridge UP, 1991.

Russett, Cynthia Eagle. *Sexual Science: The Victorian Construction of Womanhood.* Cambridge, MA: Harvard UP, 1989.

Somerville, Siobhan. "Scientific Racism and the Emergence of the Homosexual Body." *Journal of the History of Sexuality* 5.2 (October 1994): 243–66.

Weeks, Jeffrey. *Sexuality and Its Discontents: Meanings, Myths & Modern Sexualities.* London: Routledge, 1985.

Parts of the general introduction to this volume were previously published in "Charlotte Perkins Gilman" by Dale M. Bauer and Mary V. Marchand in *Women Public Speakers in the United States, 1925–1993: A Bio-Critical Sourcebook,* edited by Karlyn Kohrs Campbell. Copyright © 1994 by Greenwood Press, an imprint of Greenwood Publishing Group, Inc., Westport, CT. Reprinted by permission of Greenwood Publishing Group, Inc.

Jane Addams, excerpts from *Twenty Years at Hull-House.* Copyright © 1910 by Macmillan Publishing Company, renewed 1938 by James W. Linn. Reprinted by permission of Simon & Schuster.

Kate Chopin, "The Story of an Hour," from *The Complete Works of Kate Chopin,* edited by Per Seyersted (1969). Reprinted by permission of the Louisiana State University Press.

Charlotte Perkins Gilman, excerpts from *The Living of Charlotte Perkins Gilman: An Autobiography.* Copyright © 1991 by the University of Wisconsin Press. Reprinted by permission of the University of Wisconsin Press.

Charlotte Perkins Gilman, "Parasitism and Civilised Vice," from *Woman's Coming of Age: A Symposium,* edited by S. D. Schmalhausen and V. F. Calverton. Copyright © 1931 by Horace Liveright, Inc., renewed 1958 by Liveright Publishing Corporation. Reprinted by permission of Liveright Publishing Corporation.

Henry James, excerpts from *The Complete Notebooks of Henry James,* edited by Leon Edel and Lyall H. Powers. Copyright © 1988 by Leon Edel and Lyall H. Powers. Used by permission of Oxford University Press, Inc.